# Alice™

## FROM DREAM TO DREAM

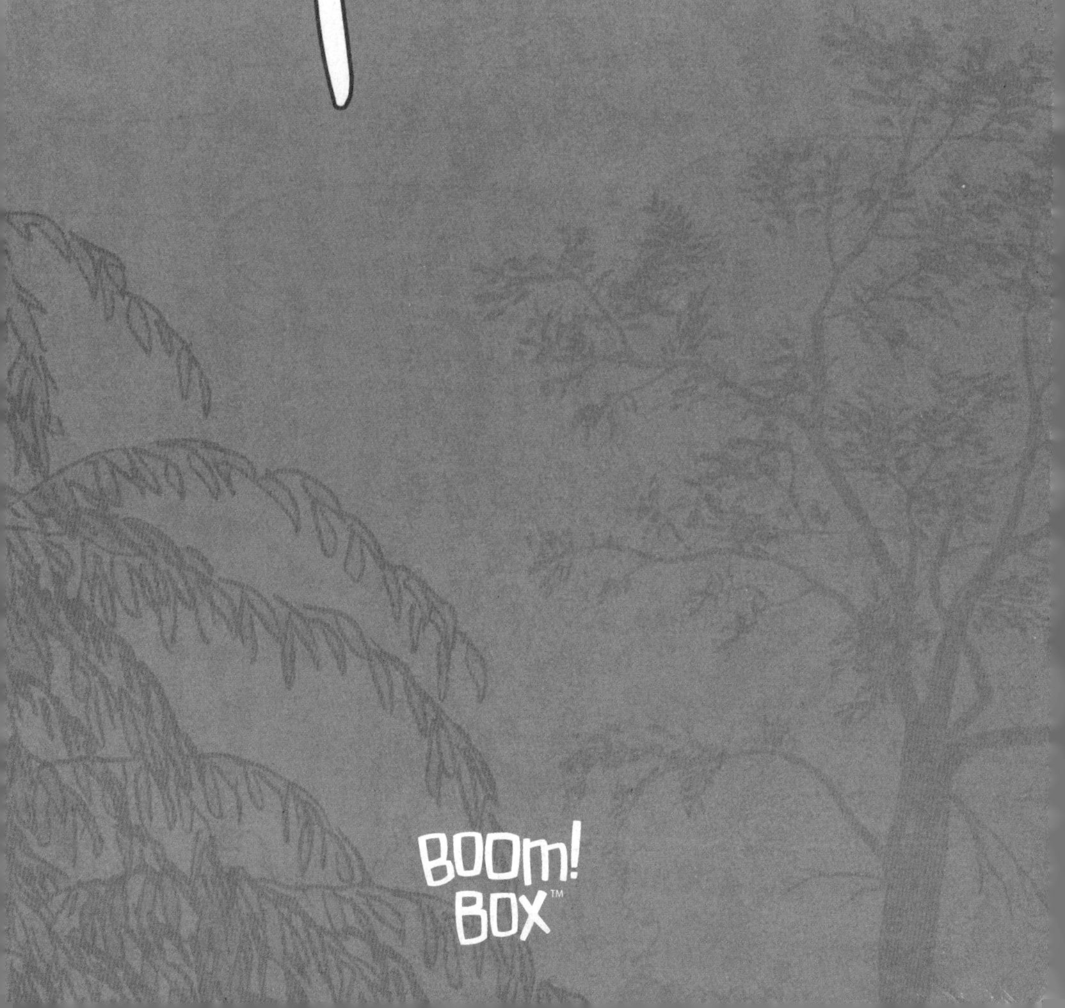

BOOM! BOX™

DESIGNED BY
**KARA LEOPARD**

ASSISTANT EDITOR
**SOPHIE PHILIPS-ROBERTS**

EDITOR
**SHANNON WATTERS**

**ROSS RICHIE** CEO & Founder
**MATT GAGNON** Editor-in-Chief
**FILIP SABLIK** President, Publishing & Marketing
**STEPHEN CHRISTY** President, Development
**LANCE KREITER** Vice President, Licensing & Merchandising
**PHIL BARBARO** Vice President, Finance & Human Resources
**ARUNE SINGH** Vice President, Marketing
**BRYCE CARLSON** Vice President, Editorial & Creative Strategy
**SCOTT NEWMAN** Manager, Production Design
**KATE HENNING** Manager, Operations
**SPENCER SIMPSON** Manager, Sales
**SIERRA HAHN** Executive Editor
**JEANINE SCHAEFER** Executive Editor
**DAFNA PLEBAN** Senior Editor
**SHANNON WATTERS** Senior Editor
**ERIC HARBURN** Senior Editor
**WHITNEY LEOPARD** Editor
**CAMERON CHITTOCK** Editor
**CHRIS ROSA** Editor
**MATTHEW LEVINE** Editor

**SOPHIE PHILIPS-ROBERTS** Assistant Editor
**GAVIN GRONENTHAL** Assistant Editor
**MICHAEL MOCCIO** Assistant Editor
**AMANDA LAFRANCO** Executive Assistant
**JILLIAN CRAB** Design Coordinator
**MICHELLE ANKLEY** Design Coordinator
**KARA LEOPARD** Production Designer
**MARIE KRUPINA** Production Designer
**GRACE PARK** Production Design Assistant
**CHELSEA ROBERTS** Production Design Assistant
**ELIZABETH LOUGHRIDGE** Accounting Coordinator
**STEPHANIE HOCUTT** Social Media Coordinator
**JOSÉ MEZA** Event Coordinator
**HOLLY AITCHISON** Operations Coordinator
**MEGAN CHRISTOPHER** Operations Assistant
**RODRIGO HERNANDEZ** Mailroom Assistant
**MORGAN PERRY** Direct Market Representative
**CAT O'GRADY** Marketing Assistant
**CORNELIA TZANA** Publicity Assistant
**BREANNA SARPY** Executive Assistant

# BOOM! BOX™

**ALICE: FROM DREAM TO DREAM, September 2018.** Published by BOOM! Box, a division of Boom Entertainment, Inc. Alice: From Dream to Dream is ™ & © 2018 Giulio Macaione. All rights reserved. BOOM! Box™ and the BOOM! Box logo are trademarks of Boom Entertainment, Inc., registered in various countries and categories. All characters, events, and institutions depicted herein are fictional. Any similarity between any of the names, characters, persons, events, and/or institutions in this publication to actual names, characters, and persons, whether living or dead, events, and/or institutions is unintended and purely coincidental. BOOM! Box does not read or accept unsolicited submissions of ideas, stories, or artwork.

For information regarding the CSPIA on this printed material, call: (203) 595-3636 and provide reference #RICH - 807192.

BOOM! Studios, 5670 Wilshire Boulevard, Suite 400, Los Angeles, CA 90036-5679. Printed in USA. First Printing.

ISBN: 978-1-68415-180-6, eISBN: 978-1-61398-995-1

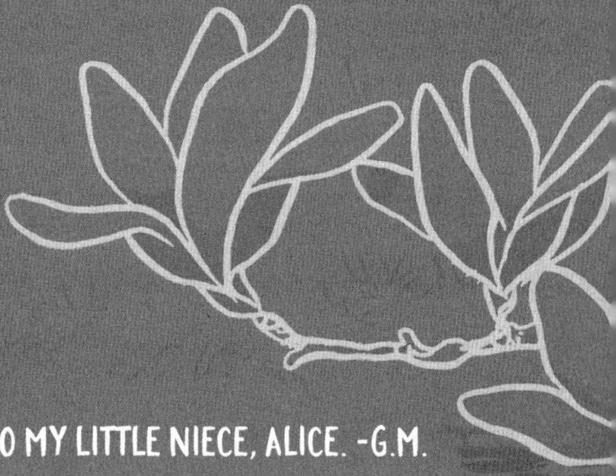

THIS BOOK IS DEDICATED TO MY LITTLE NIECE, ALICE. -G.M.

TO MY DAYDREAMS. -G.A.

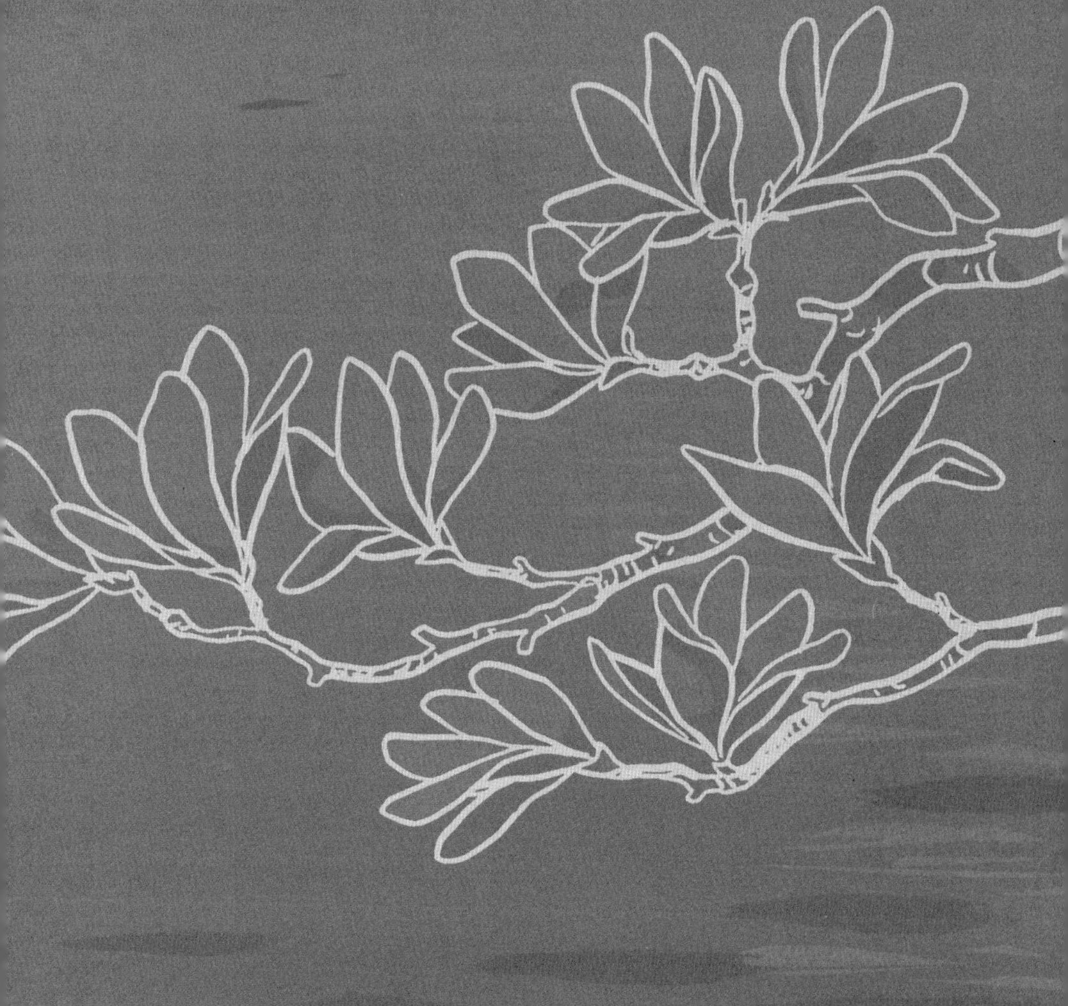

WRITTEN & ILLUSTRATED BY
# GIULIO MACAIONE

ENGLISH ADAPTATION BY
# JACKIE BALL

COLORED BY
# GIULIA ADRAGNA

LETTERED BY
# JIM CAMPBELL

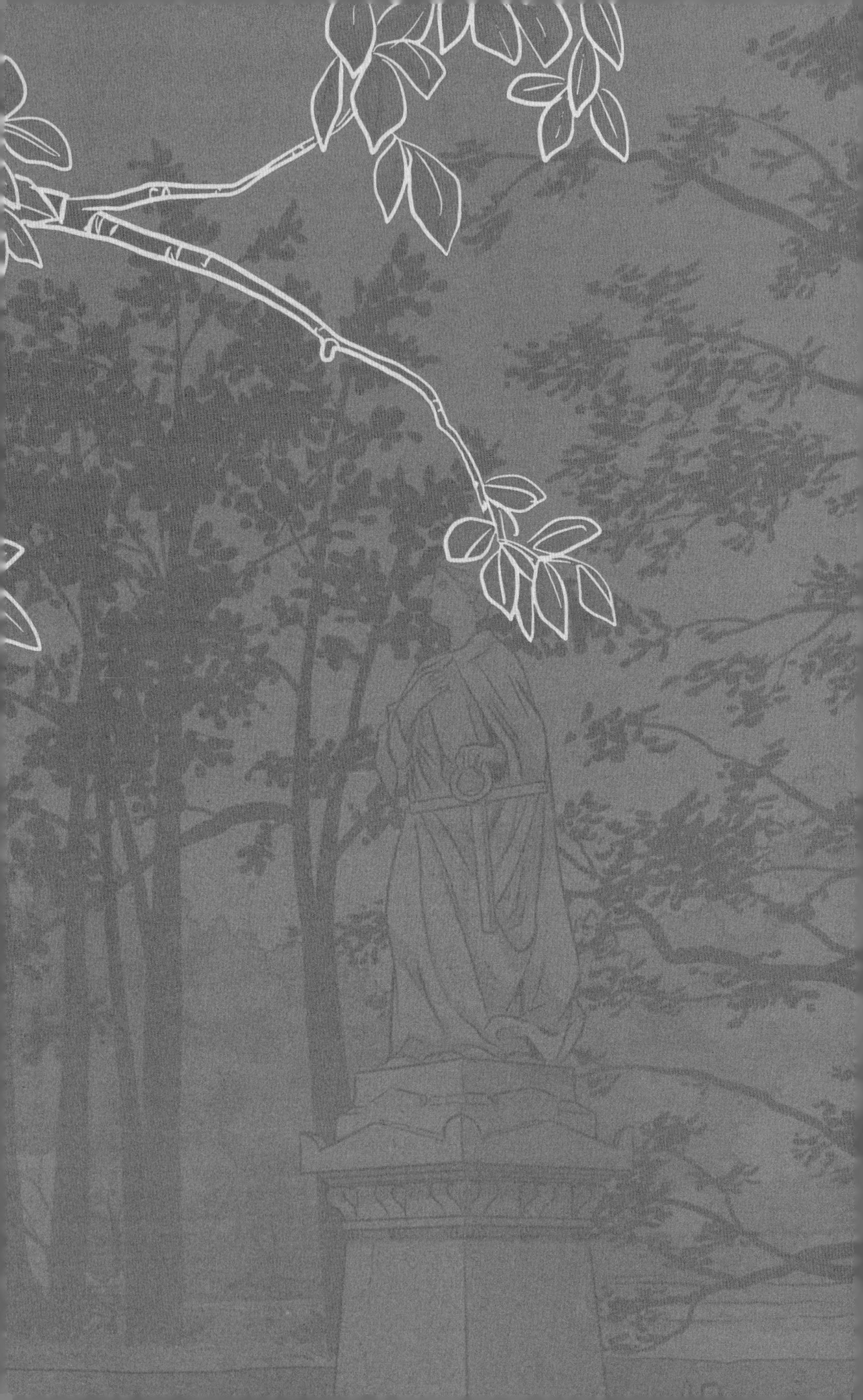

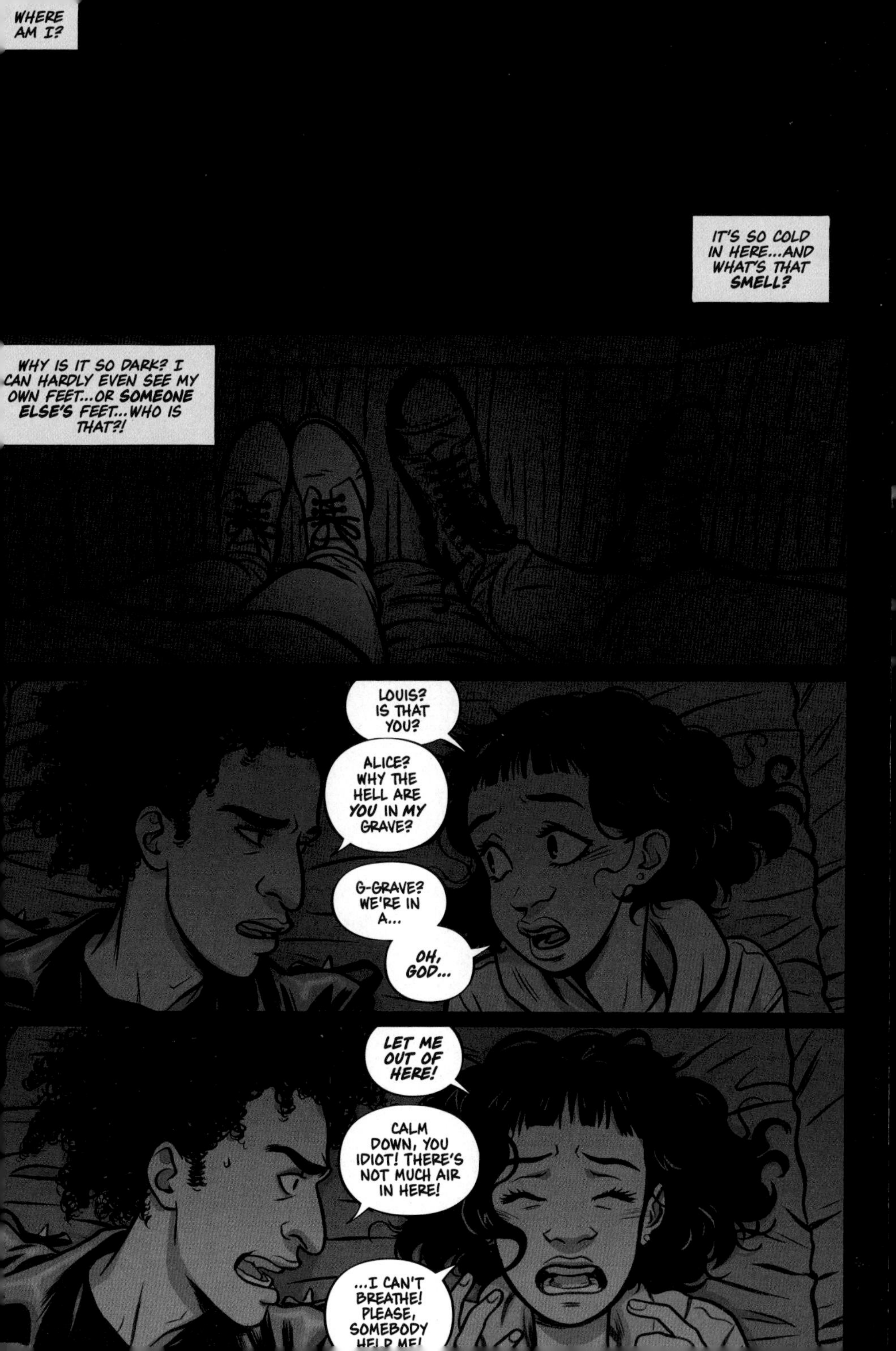
WHERE AM I?
IT'S SO COLD IN HERE...AND WHAT'S THAT SMELL?
WHY IS IT SO DARK? I CAN HARDLY EVEN SEE MY OWN FEET...OR SOMEONE ELSE'S FEET...WHO IS THAT?!
LOUIS? IS THAT YOU?
ALICE? WHY THE HELL ARE YOU IN MY GRAVE?
G-GRAVE? WE'RE IN A...
OH, GOD...
LET ME OUT OF HERE!
CALM DOWN, YOU IDIOT! THERE'S NOT MUCH AIR IN HERE!
...I CAN'T BREATHE! PLEASE, SOMEBODY

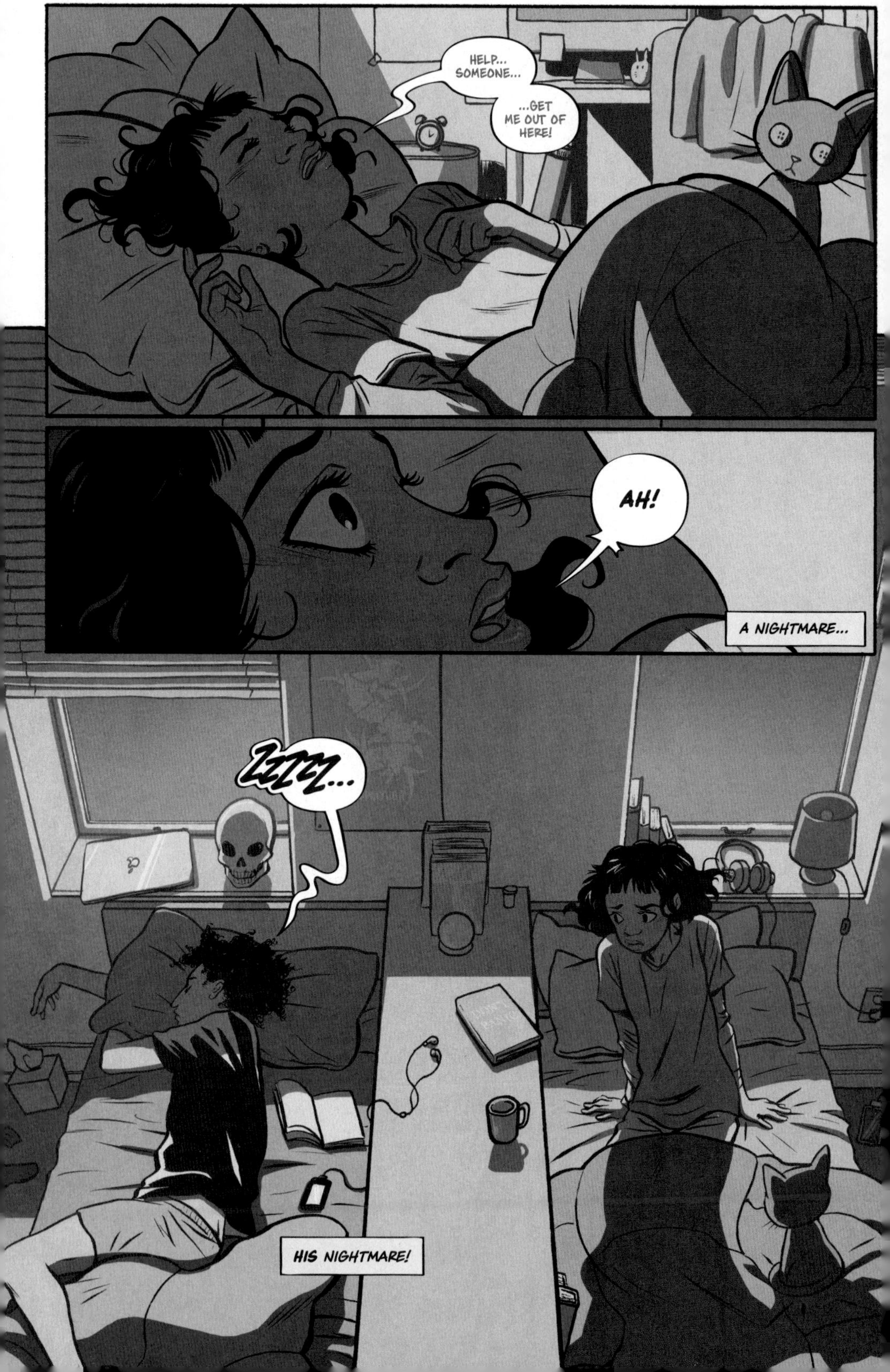
HELP... SOMEONE...
...GET ME OUT OF HERE!
AH!
A NIGHTMARE...
ZZZZ...
HIS NIGHTMARE!

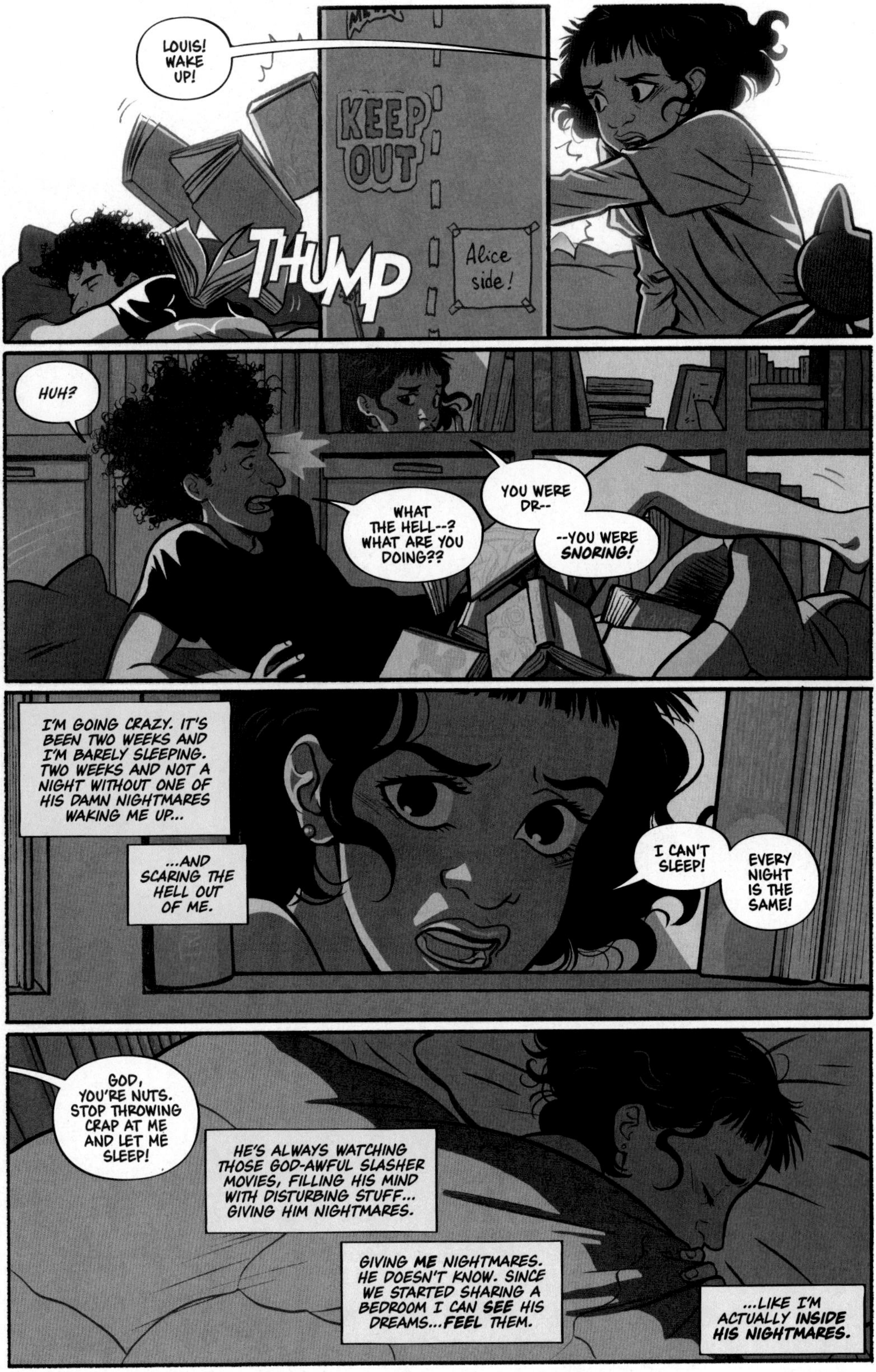

LOUIS! WAKE UP!
KEEP OUT
Alice side!
THUMP
HUH?
WHAT THE HELL--? WHAT ARE YOU DOING??
YOU WERE DR--
--YOU WERE SNORING!
I'M GOING CRAZY. IT'S BEEN TWO WEEKS AND I'M BARELY SLEEPING. TWO WEEKS AND NOT A NIGHT WITHOUT ONE OF HIS DAMN NIGHTMARES WAKING ME UP...
...AND SCARING THE HELL OUT OF ME.
I CAN'T SLEEP!
EVERY NIGHT IS THE SAME!
GOD, YOU'RE NUTS. STOP THROWING CRAP AT ME AND LET ME SLEEP!
HE'S ALWAYS WATCHING THOSE GOD-AWFUL SLASHER MOVIES, FILLING HIS MIND WITH DISTURBING STUFF... GIVING HIM NIGHTMARES.
GIVING ME NIGHTMARES. HE DOESN'T KNOW. SINCE WE STARTED SHARING A BEDROOM I CAN SEE HIS DREAMS...FEEL THEM.
...LIKE I'M ACTUALLY INSIDE HIS NIGHTMARES.

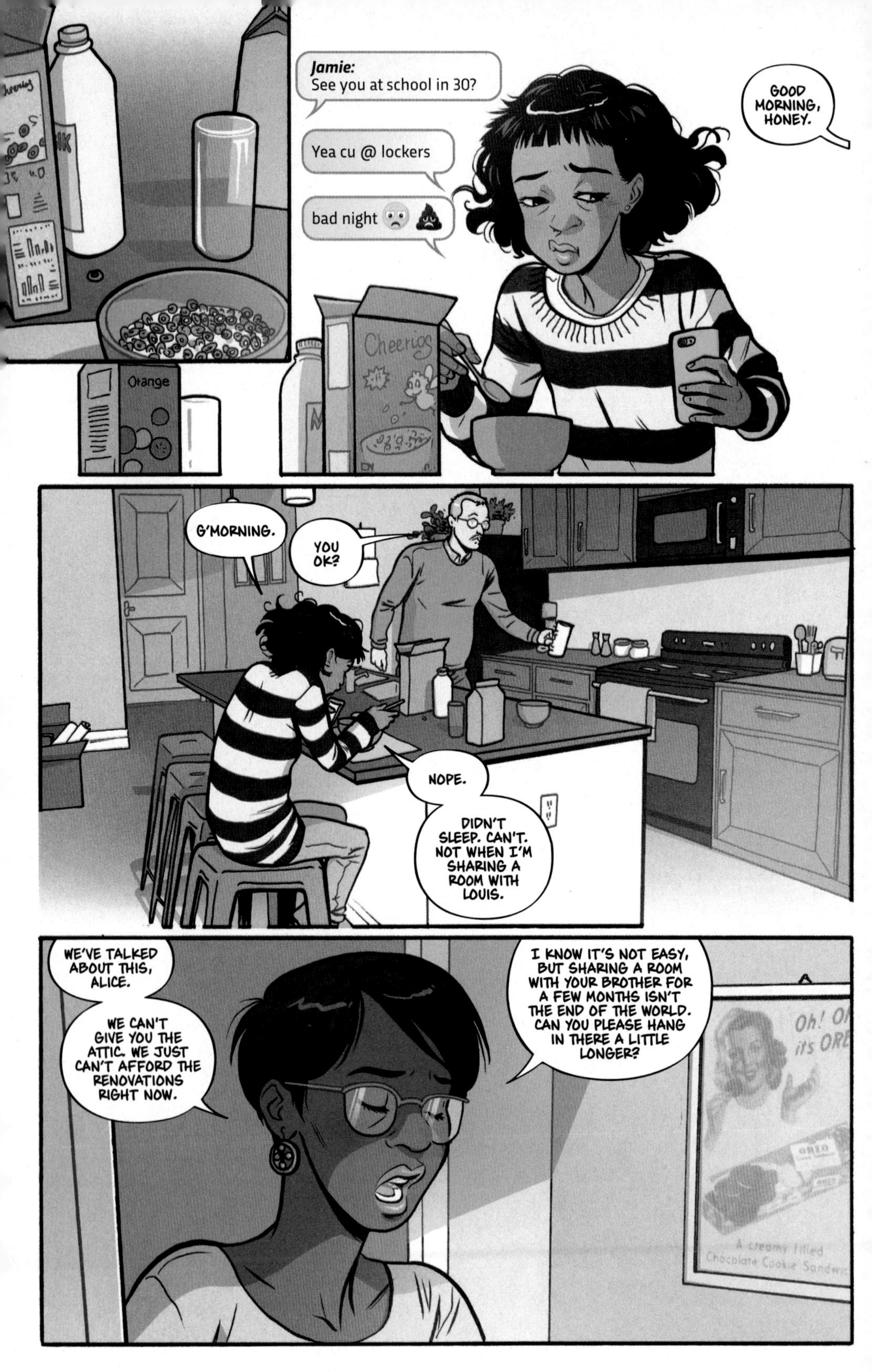
Jamie:
See you at school in 30?
Yea cu @ lockers
bad night
GOOD MORNING, HONEY.
G'MORNING.
YOU OK?
NOPE.
DIDN'T SLEEP. CAN'T. NOT WHEN I'M SHARING A ROOM WITH LOUIS.
WE'VE TALKED ABOUT THIS, ALICE.
WE CAN'T GIVE YOU THE ATTIC. WE JUST CAN'T AFFORD THE RENOVATIONS RIGHT NOW.
I KNOW IT'S NOT EASY, BUT SHARING A ROOM WITH YOUR BROTHER FOR A FEW MONTHS ISN'T THE END OF THE WORLD. CAN YOU PLEASE HANG IN THERE A LITTLE LONGER?

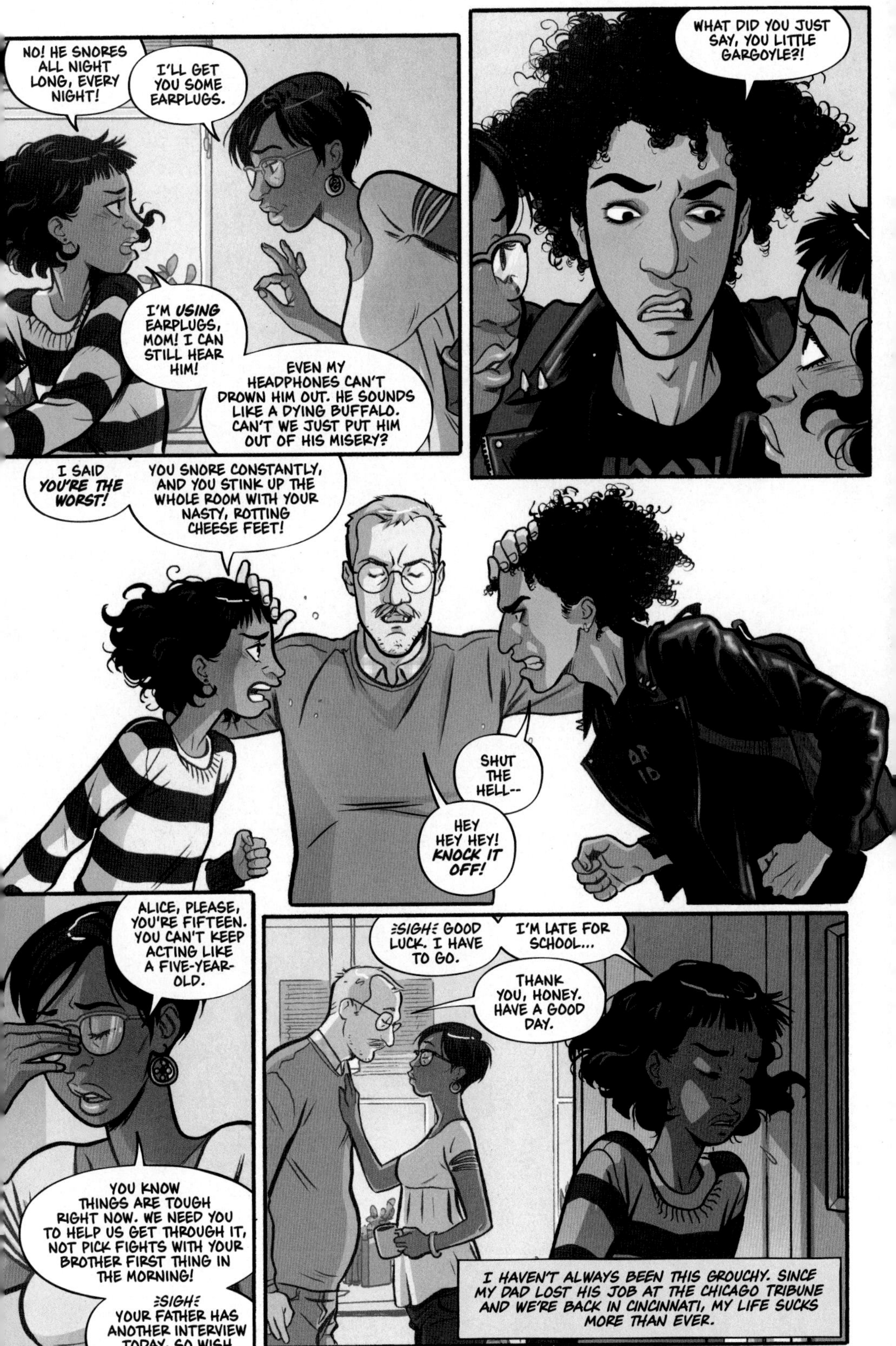
NO! HE SNORES ALL NIGHT LONG, EVERY NIGHT!
I'LL GET YOU SOME EARPLUGS.
I'M USING EARPLUGS, MOM! I CAN STILL HEAR HIM!
EVEN MY HEADPHONES CAN'T DROWN HIM OUT. HE SOUNDS LIKE A DYING BUFFALO. CAN'T WE JUST PUT HIM OUT OF HIS MISERY?
WHAT DID YOU JUST SAY, YOU LITTLE GARGOYLE?!
I SAID YOU'RE THE WORST!
YOU SNORE CONSTANTLY, AND YOU STINK UP THE WHOLE ROOM WITH YOUR NASTY, ROTTING CHEESE FEET!
SHUT THE HELL--
HEY HEY HEY! KNOCK IT OFF!
ALICE, PLEASE, YOU'RE FIFTEEN. YOU CAN'T KEEP ACTING LIKE A FIVE-YEAR-OLD.
YOU KNOW THINGS ARE TOUGH RIGHT NOW. WE NEED YOU TO HELP US GET THROUGH IT, NOT PICK FIGHTS WITH YOUR BROTHER FIRST THING IN THE MORNING!
SIGH
YOUR FATHER HAS ANOTHER INTERVIEW TODAY, SO WISH HIM LUCK.
SIGH GOOD LUCK. I HAVE TO GO.
I'M LATE FOR SCHOOL...
THANK YOU, HONEY. HAVE A GOOD DAY.
I HAVEN'T ALWAYS BEEN THIS GROUCHY. SINCE MY DAD LOST HIS JOB AT THE CHICAGO TRIBUNE AND WE'RE BACK IN CINCINNATI, MY LIFE SUCKS MORE THAN EVER.

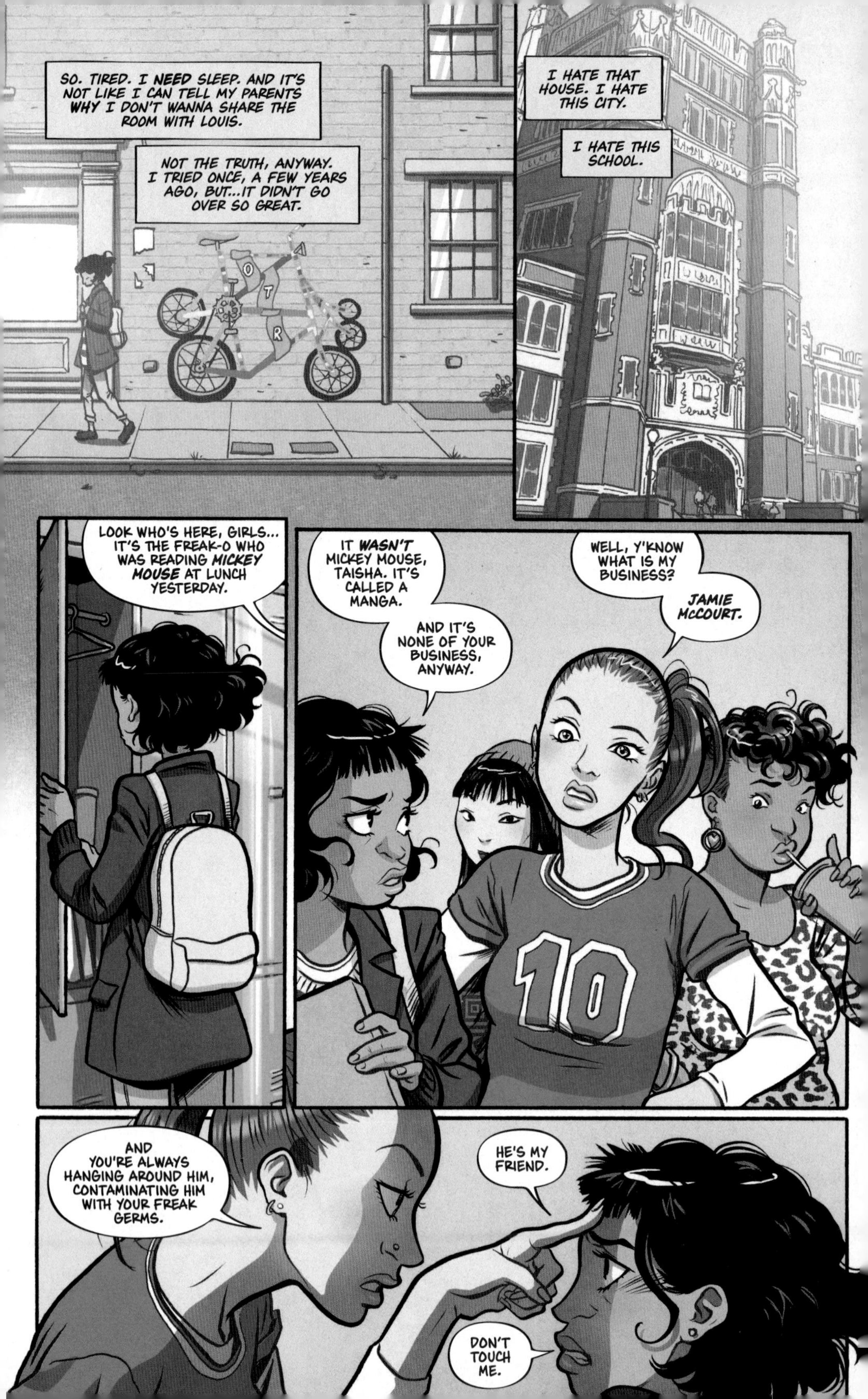
SO. TIRED. I NEED SLEEP. AND IT'S NOT LIKE I CAN TELL MY PARENTS WHY I DON'T WANNA SHARE THE ROOM WITH LOUIS.
NOT THE TRUTH, ANYWAY. I TRIED ONCE, A FEW YEARS AGO, BUT...IT DIDN'T GO OVER SO GREAT.
I HATE THAT HOUSE. I HATE THIS CITY.
I HATE THIS SCHOOL.
LOOK WHO'S HERE, GIRLS... IT'S THE FREAK-O WHO WAS READING MICKEY MOUSE AT LUNCH YESTERDAY.
IT WASN'T MICKEY MOUSE, TAISHA. IT'S CALLED A MANGA.
AND IT'S NONE OF YOUR BUSINESS, ANYWAY.
WELL, Y'KNOW WHAT IS MY BUSINESS?
JAMIE McCOURT.
AND YOU'RE ALWAYS HANGING AROUND HIM, CONTAMINATING HIM WITH YOUR FREAK GERMS.
HE'S MY FRIEND.
DON'T TOUCH ME.

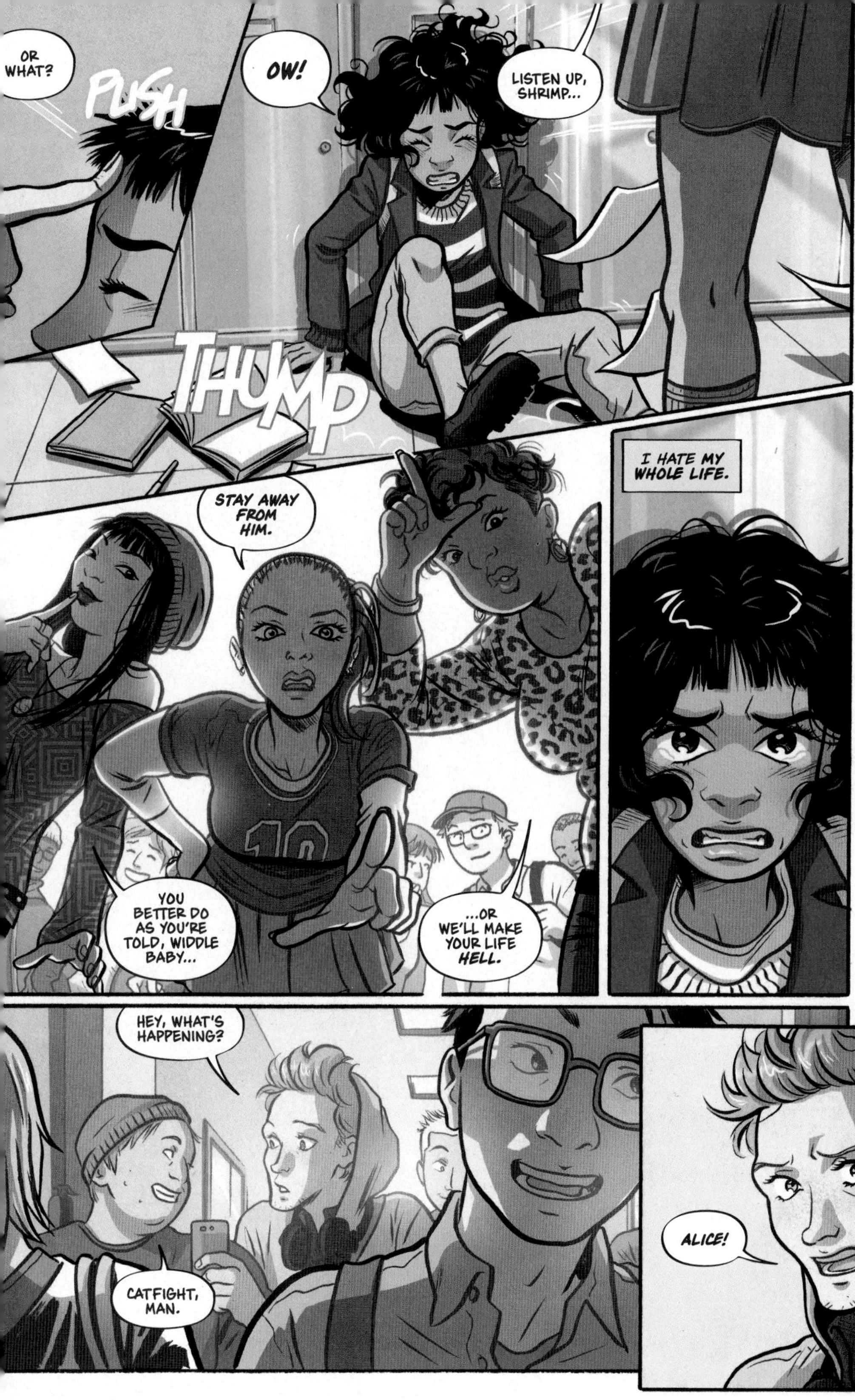
OR WHAT?
PUSH
OW!
LISTEN UP, SHRIMP...
THUMP
STAY AWAY FROM HIM.
YOU BETTER DO AS YOU'RE TOLD, WIDDLE BABY...
...OR WE'LL MAKE YOUR LIFE HELL.
I HATE MY WHOLE LIFE.
HEY, WHAT'S HAPPENING?
CATFIGHT, MAN.
ALICE!

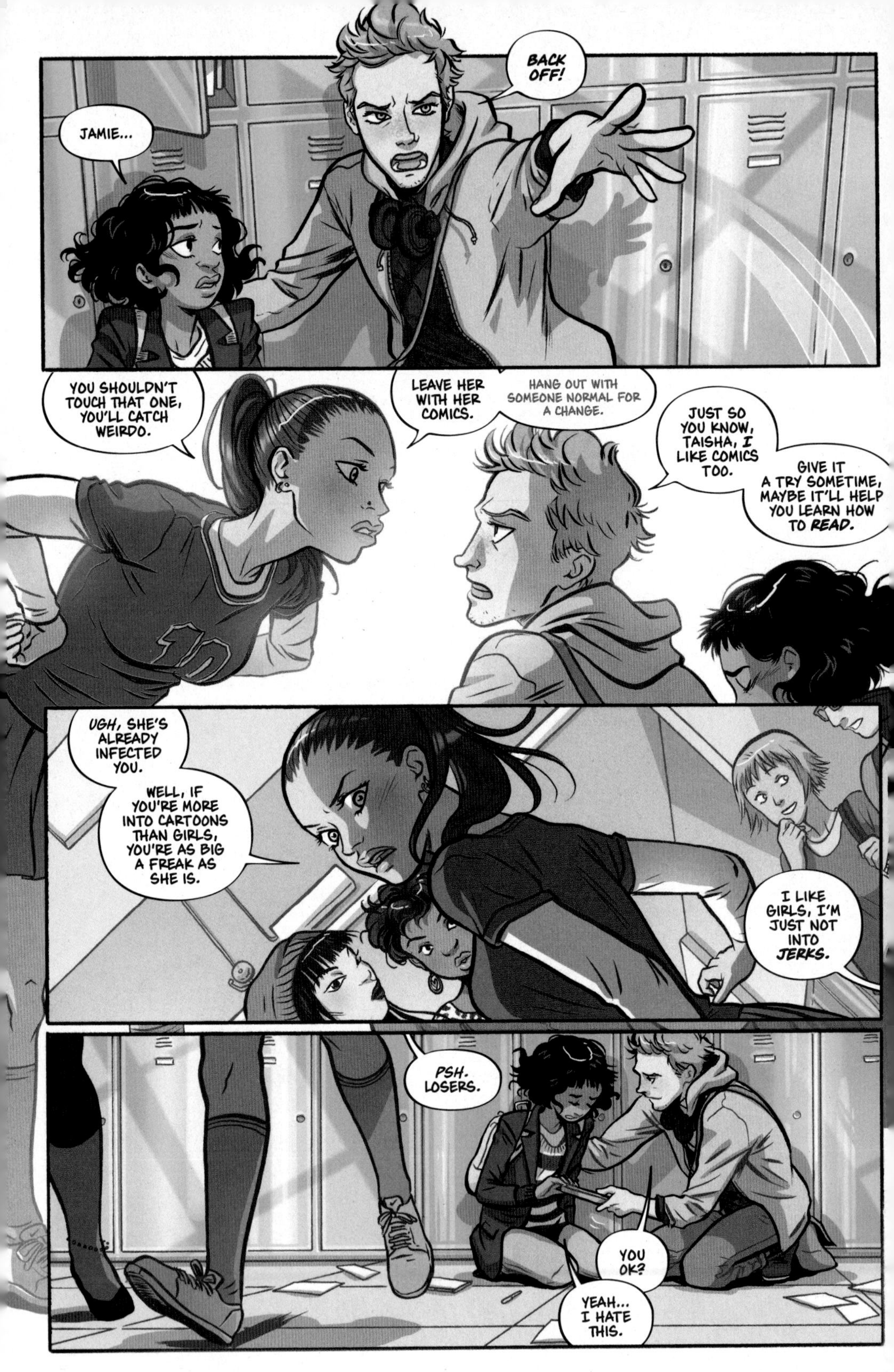
JAMIE...
BACK OFF!
YOU SHOULDN'T TOUCH THAT ONE, YOU'LL CATCH WEIRDO.
LEAVE HER WITH HER COMICS.
HANG OUT WITH SOMEONE NORMAL FOR A CHANGE.
JUST SO YOU KNOW, TAISHA, I LIKE COMICS TOO.
GIVE IT A TRY SOMETIME, MAYBE IT'LL HELP YOU LEARN HOW TO READ.
UGH, SHE'S ALREADY INFECTED YOU.
WELL, IF YOU'RE MORE INTO CARTOONS THAN GIRLS, YOU'RE AS BIG A FREAK AS SHE IS.
I LIKE GIRLS, I'M JUST NOT INTO JERKS.
PSH. LOSERS.
YOU OK?
YEAH... I HATE THIS.

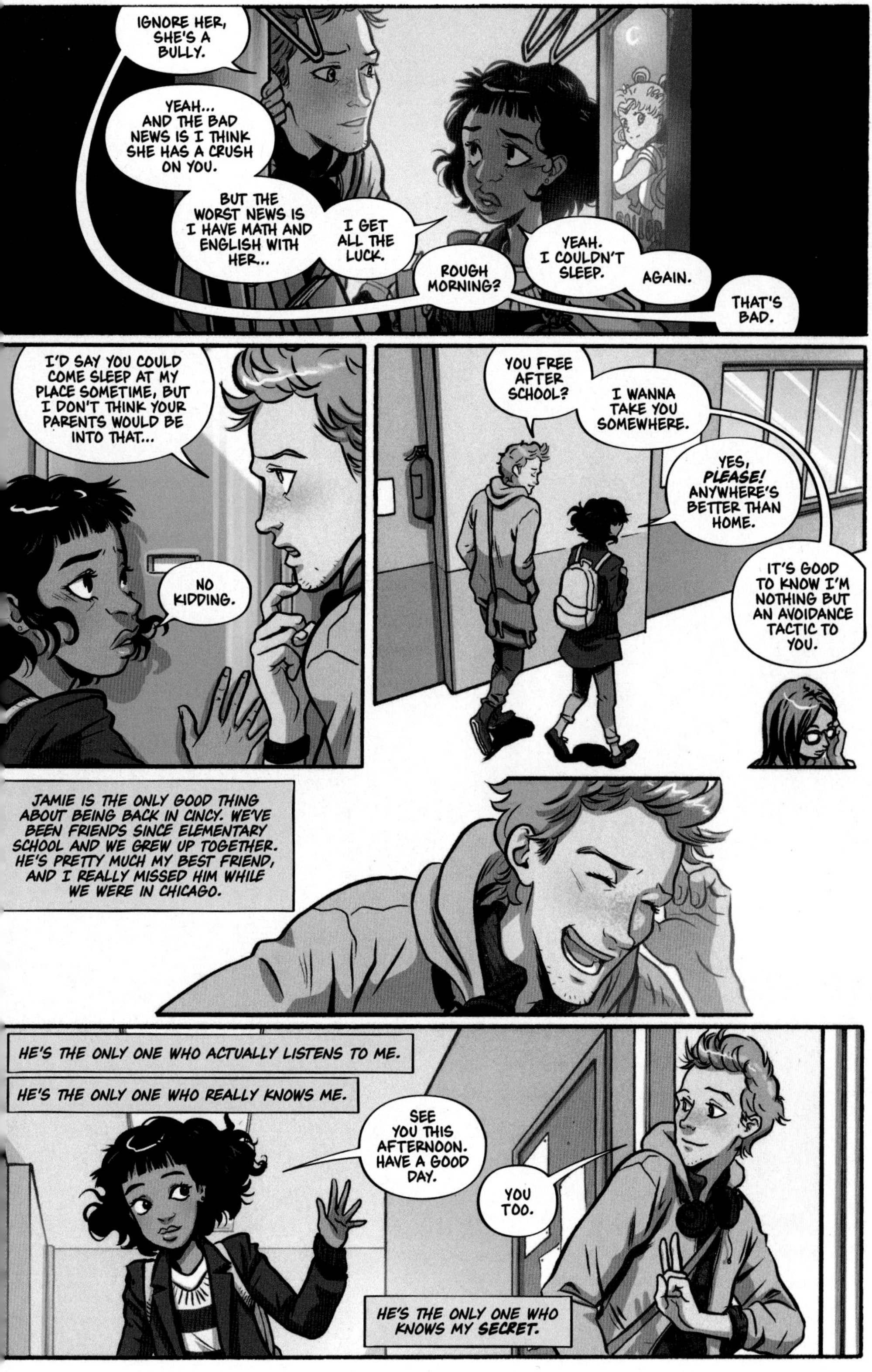

IGNORE HER, SHE'S A BULLY.
YEAH... AND THE BAD NEWS IS I THINK SHE HAS A CRUSH ON YOU.
BUT THE WORST NEWS IS I HAVE MATH AND ENGLISH WITH HER...
I GET ALL THE LUCK.
ROUGH MORNING?
YEAH. I COULDN'T SLEEP.
AGAIN.
THAT'S BAD.
I'D SAY YOU COULD COME SLEEP AT MY PLACE SOMETIME, BUT I DON'T THINK YOUR PARENTS WOULD BE INTO THAT...
NO KIDDING.
YOU FREE AFTER SCHOOL?
I WANNA TAKE YOU SOMEWHERE.
YES, *PLEASE!* ANYWHERE'S BETTER THAN HOME.
IT'S GOOD TO KNOW I'M NOTHING BUT AN AVOIDANCE TACTIC TO YOU.
JAMIE IS THE ONLY GOOD THING ABOUT BEING BACK IN CINCY. WE'VE BEEN FRIENDS SINCE ELEMENTARY SCHOOL AND WE GREW UP TOGETHER. HE'S PRETTY MUCH MY BEST FRIEND, AND I REALLY MISSED HIM WHILE WE WERE IN CHICAGO.
HE'S THE ONLY ONE WHO ACTUALLY LISTENS TO ME.
HE'S THE ONLY ONE WHO REALLY KNOWS ME.
SEE YOU THIS AFTERNOON. HAVE A GOOD DAY.
YOU TOO.
HE'S THE ONLY ONE WHO KNOWS MY *SECRET.*

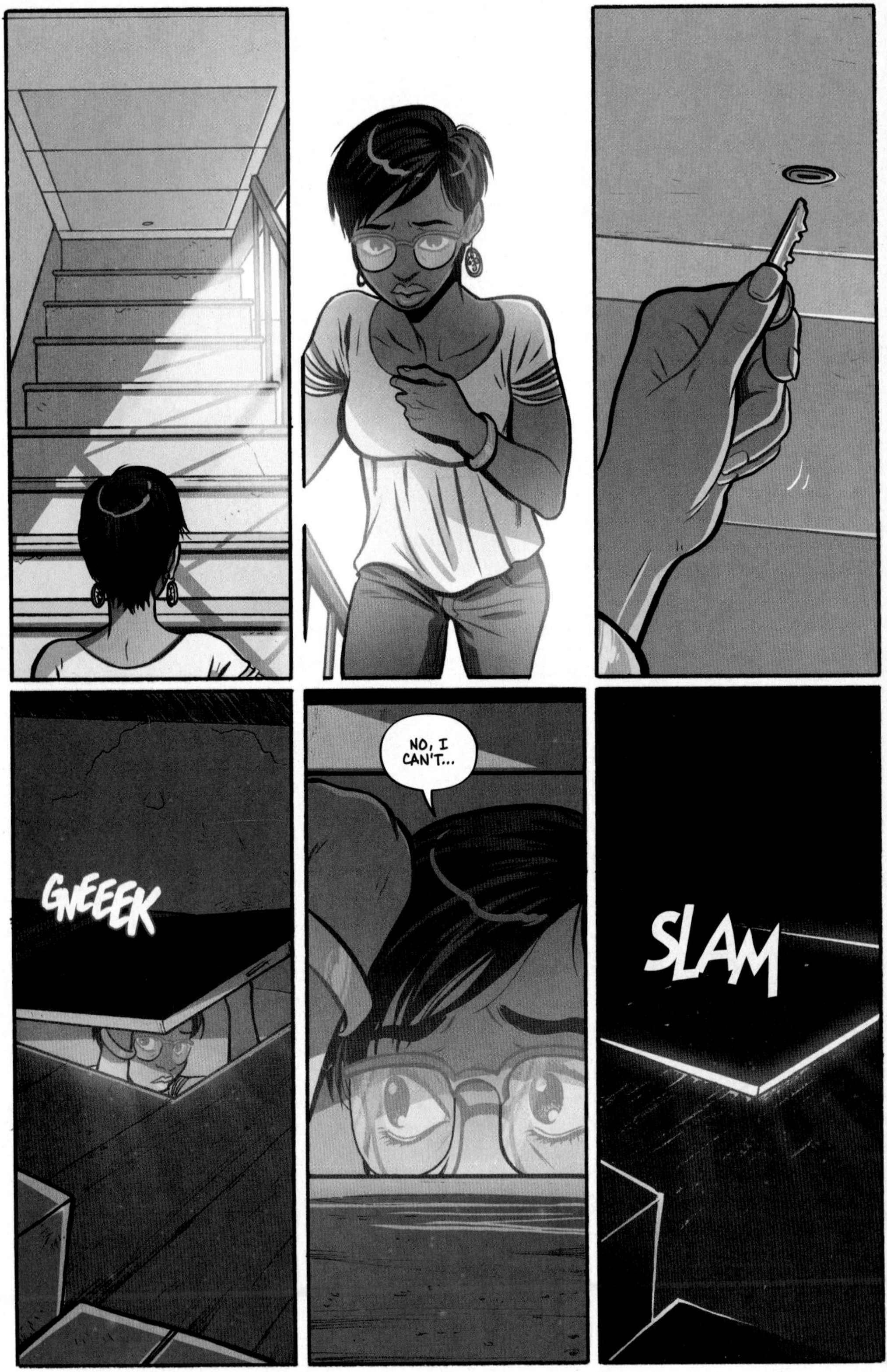
GNEEEK
NO, I CAN'T...
SLAM

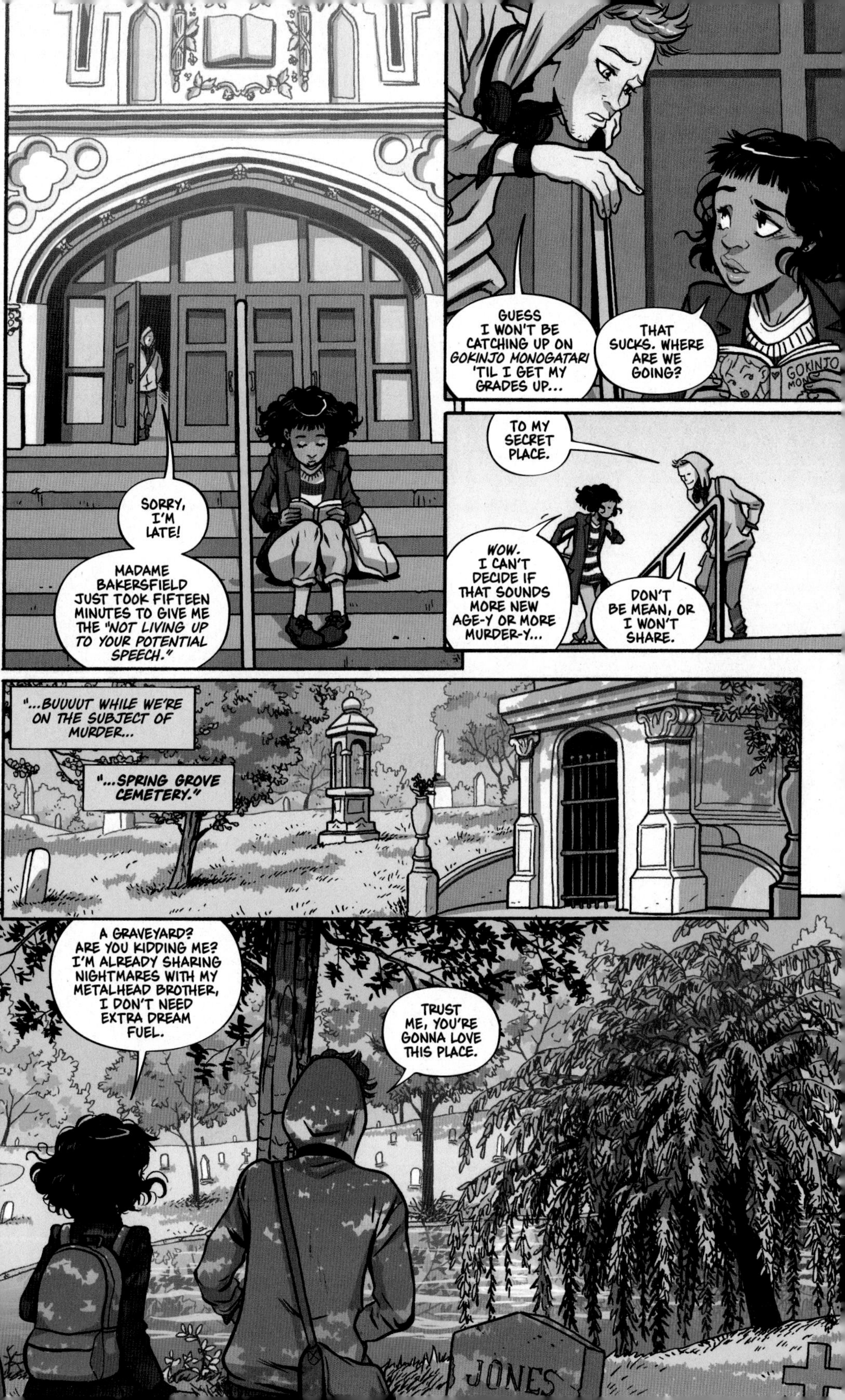
SORRY, I'M LATE!
MADAME BAKERSFIELD JUST TOOK FIFTEEN MINUTES TO GIVE ME THE "NOT LIVING UP TO YOUR POTENTIAL SPEECH."
GUESS I WON'T BE CATCHING UP ON GOKINJO MONOGATARI 'TIL I GET MY GRADES UP...
THAT SUCKS. WHERE ARE WE GOING?
GOKINJO MON
TO MY SECRET PLACE.
WOW. I CAN'T DECIDE IF THAT SOUNDS MORE NEW AGE-Y OR MORE MURDER-Y...
DON'T BE MEAN, OR I WON'T SHARE.
"...BUUUUT WHILE WE'RE ON THE SUBJECT OF MURDER...
"...SPRING GROVE CEMETERY."
A GRAVEYARD? ARE YOU KIDDING ME? I'M ALREADY SHARING NIGHTMARES WITH MY METALHEAD BROTHER, I DON'T NEED EXTRA DREAM FUEL.
TRUST ME, YOU'RE GONNA LOVE THIS PLACE.
JONES

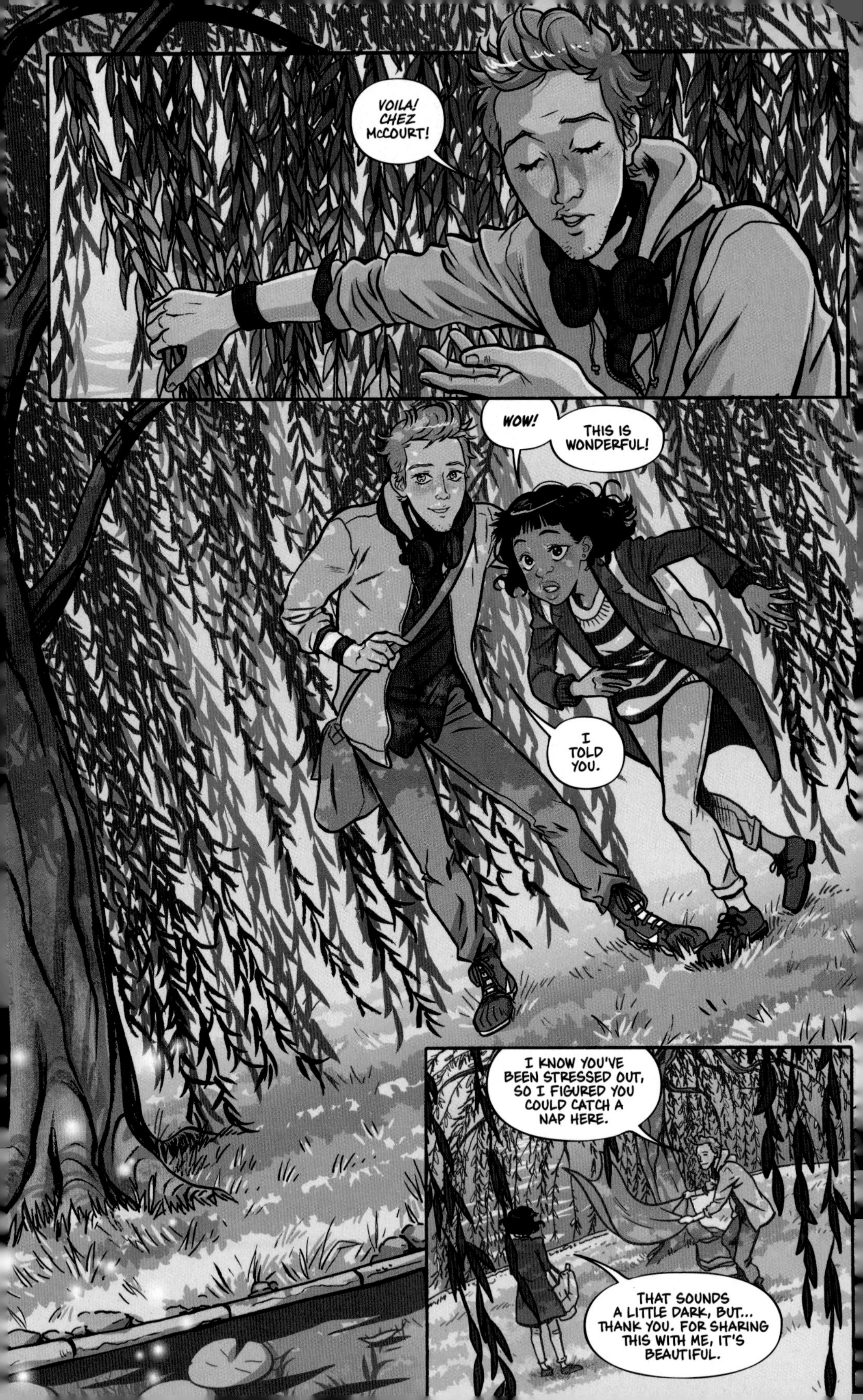
VOILA! CHEZ McCOURT!
WOW!
THIS IS WONDERFUL!
I TOLD YOU.
I KNOW YOU'VE BEEN STRESSED OUT, SO I FIGURED YOU COULD CATCH A NAP HERE.
THAT SOUNDS A LITTLE DARK, BUT... THANK YOU. FOR SHARING THIS WITH ME, IT'S BEAUTIFUL.

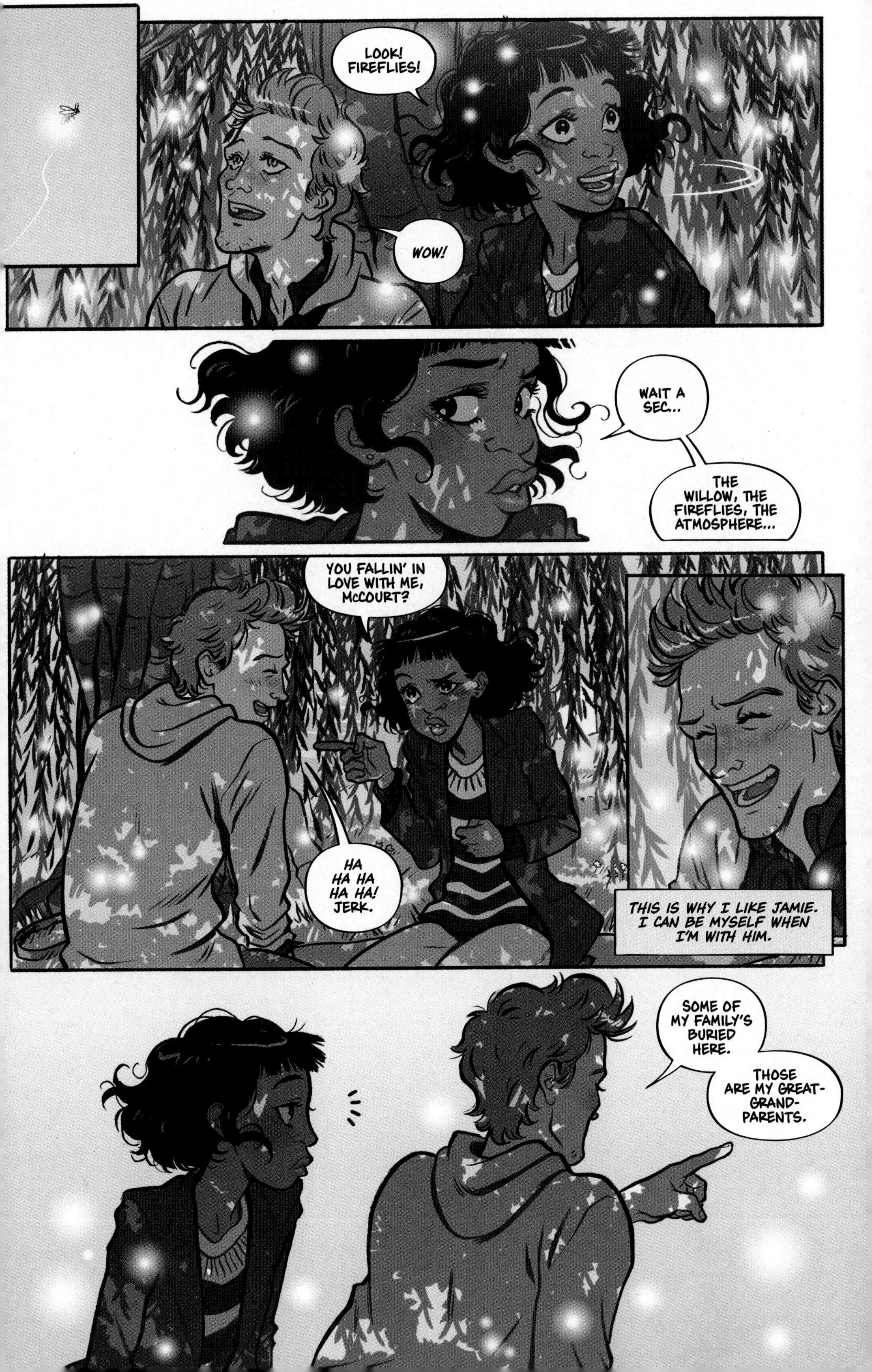
LOOK! FIREFLIES!
WOW!
WAIT A SEC...
THE WILLOW, THE FIREFLIES, THE ATMOSPHERE...
YOU FALLIN' IN LOVE WITH ME, McCOURT?
HA HA HA HA HA! JERK.
THIS IS WHY I LIKE JAMIE. I CAN BE MYSELF WHEN I'M WITH HIM.
SOME OF MY FAMILY'S BURIED HERE.
THOSE ARE MY GREAT-GRAND-PARENTS.

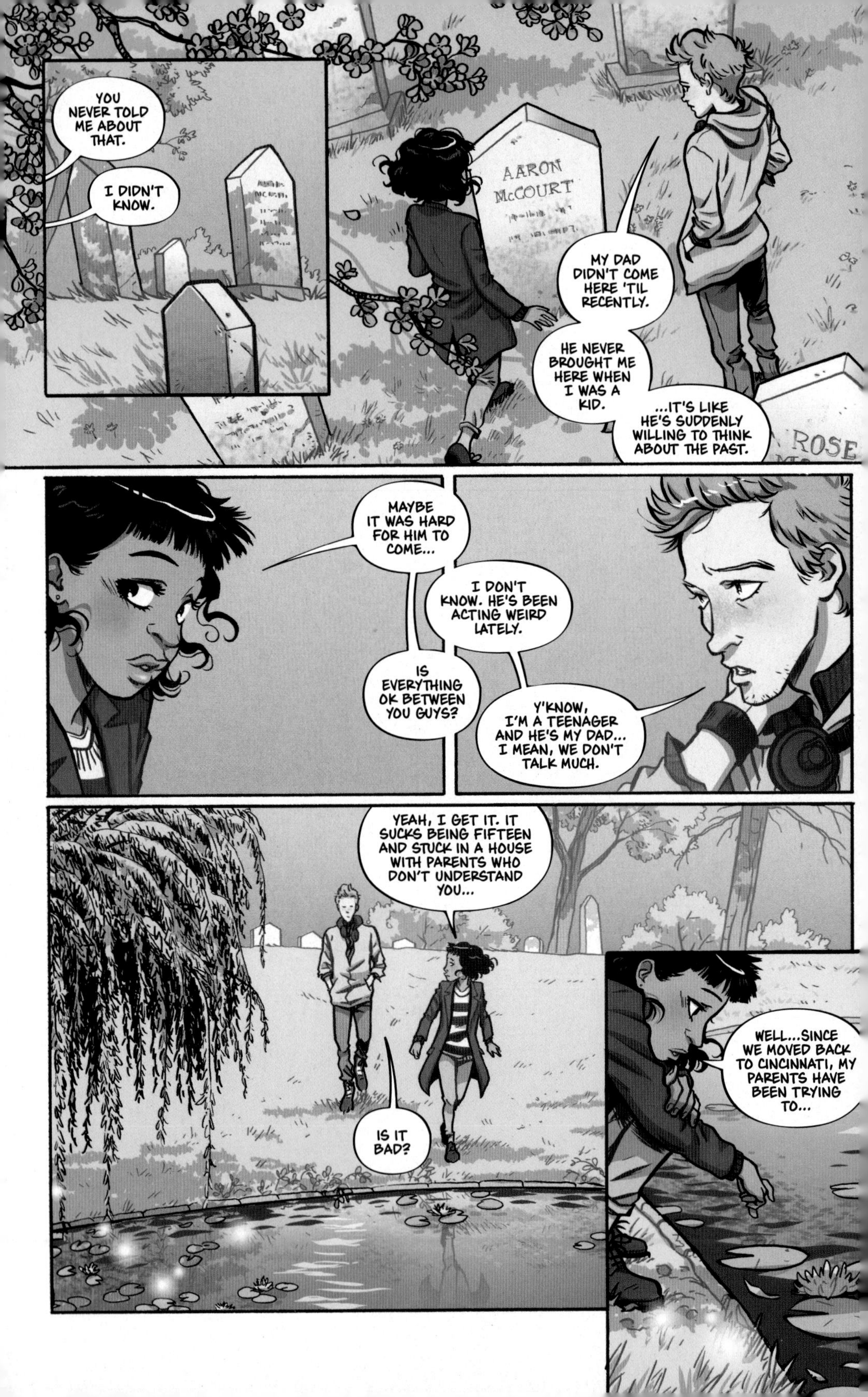
YOU NEVER TOLD ME ABOUT THAT.
I DIDN'T KNOW.
AARON McCOURT
MY DAD DIDN'T COME HERE 'TIL RECENTLY.
HE NEVER BROUGHT ME HERE WHEN I WAS A KID.
...IT'S LIKE HE'S SUDDENLY WILLING TO THINK ABOUT THE PAST.
ROSE
MAYBE IT WAS HARD FOR HIM TO COME...
I DON'T KNOW. HE'S BEEN ACTING WEIRD LATELY.
IS EVERYTHING OK BETWEEN YOU GUYS?
Y'KNOW, I'M A TEENAGER AND HE'S MY DAD... I MEAN, WE DON'T TALK MUCH.
YEAH, I GET IT. IT SUCKS BEING FIFTEEN AND STUCK IN A HOUSE WITH PARENTS WHO DON'T UNDERSTAND YOU...
IS IT BAD?
WELL...SINCE WE MOVED BACK TO CINCINNATI, MY PARENTS HAVE BEEN TRYING TO...

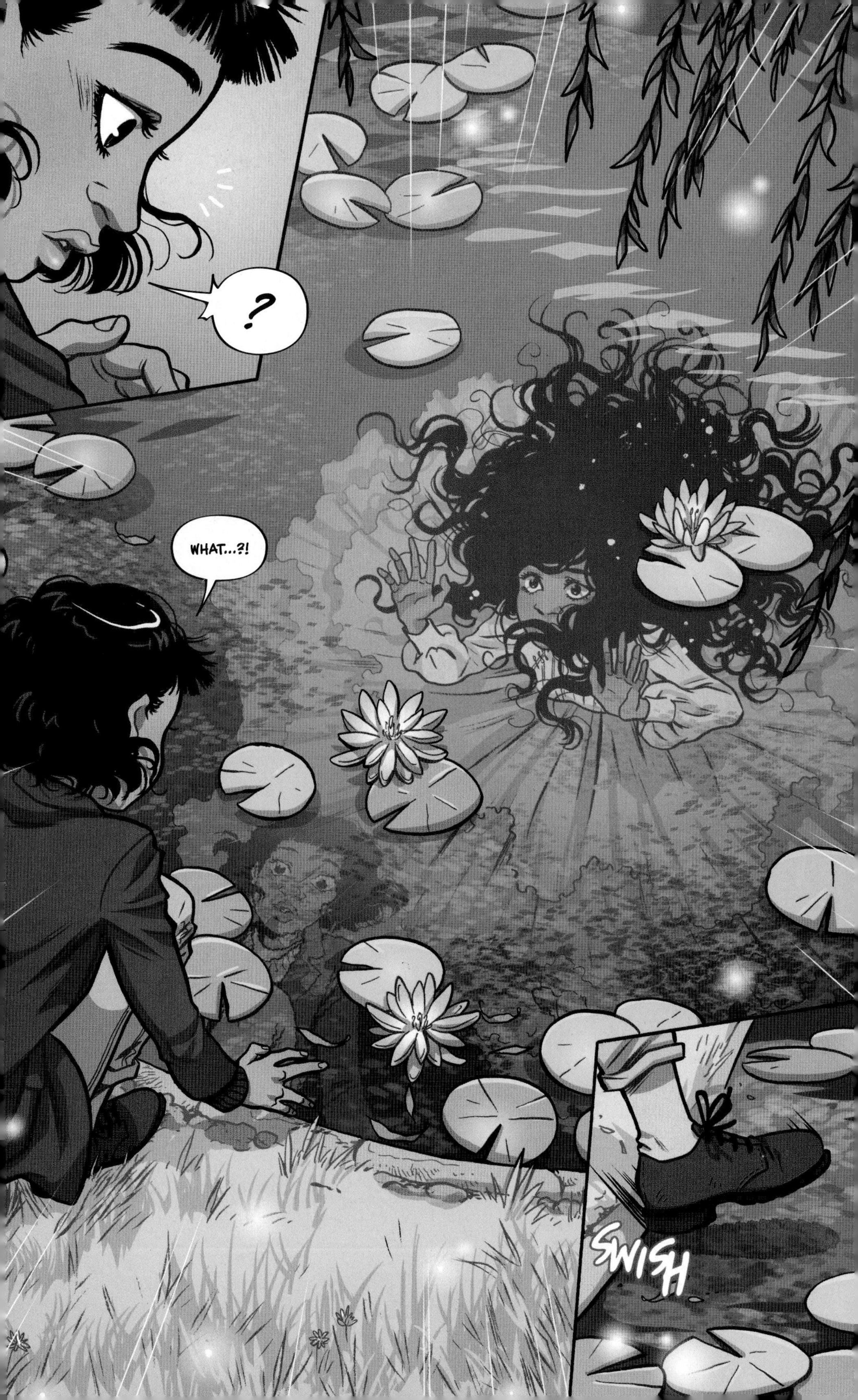
?
WHAT...?!
SWISH

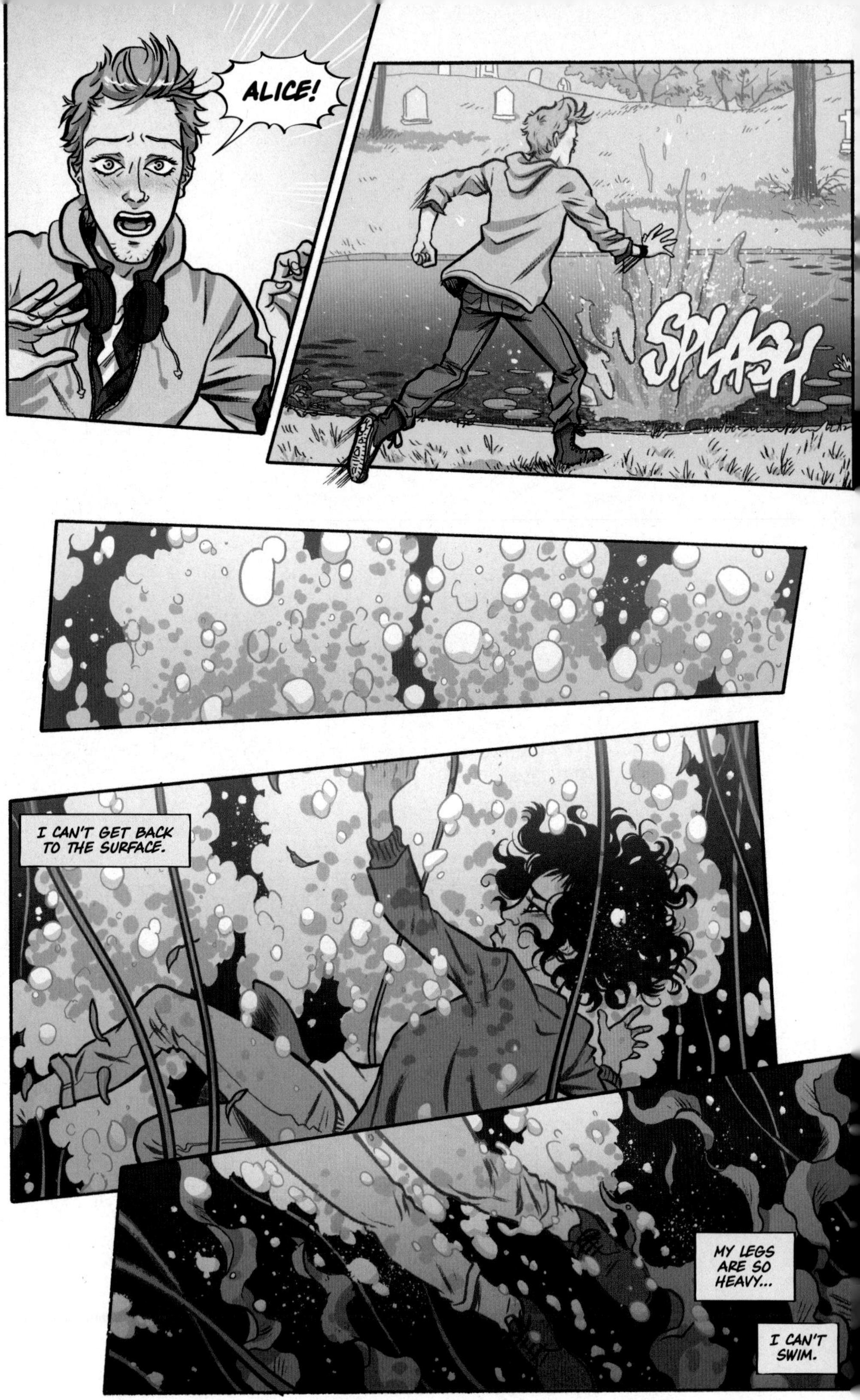
ALICE!
SPLASH
I CAN'T GET BACK TO THE SURFACE.
MY LEGS ARE SO HEAVY...
I CAN'T SWIM.

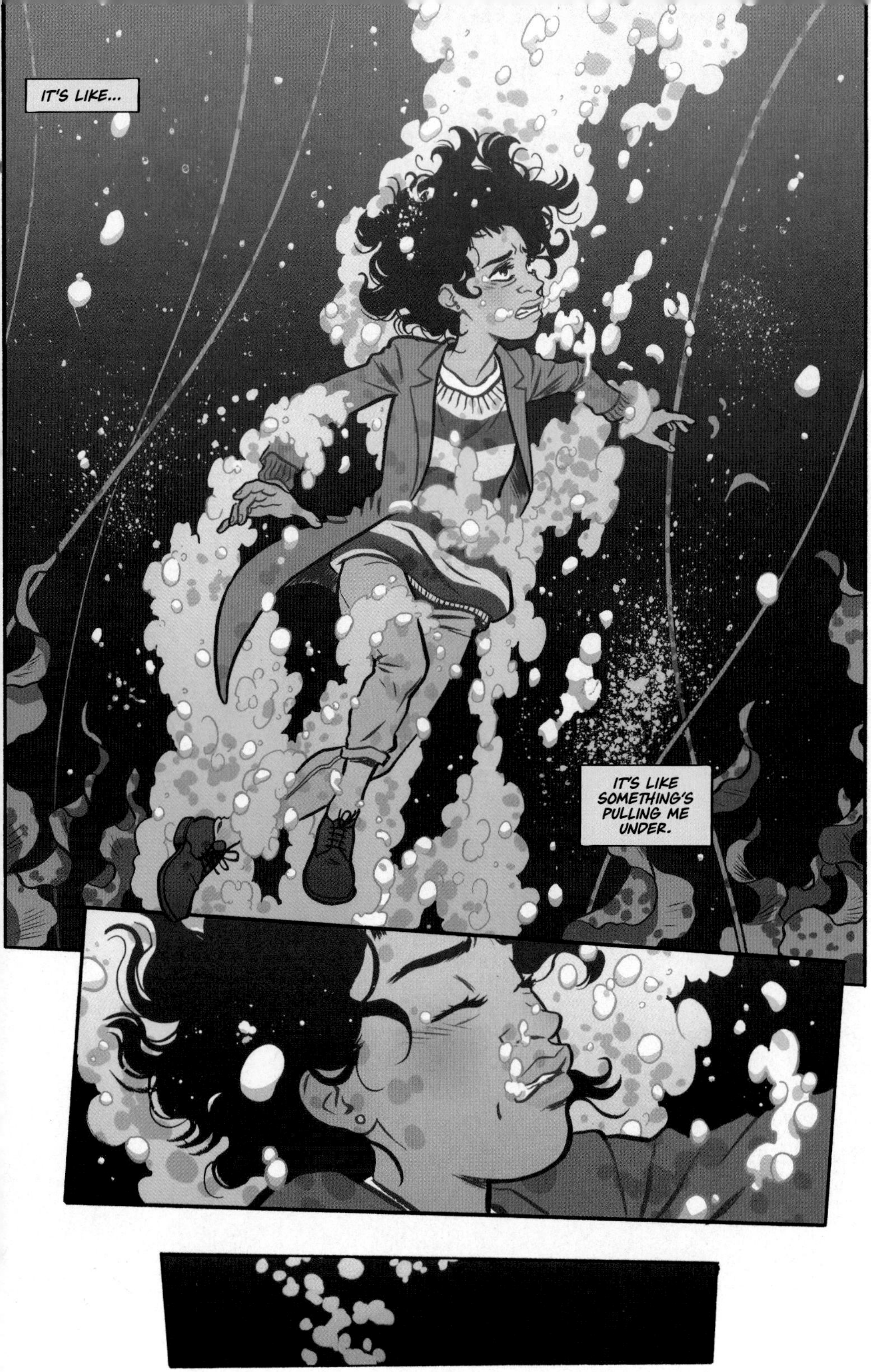
IT'S LIKE...
IT'S LIKE SOMETHING'S PULLING ME UNDER.

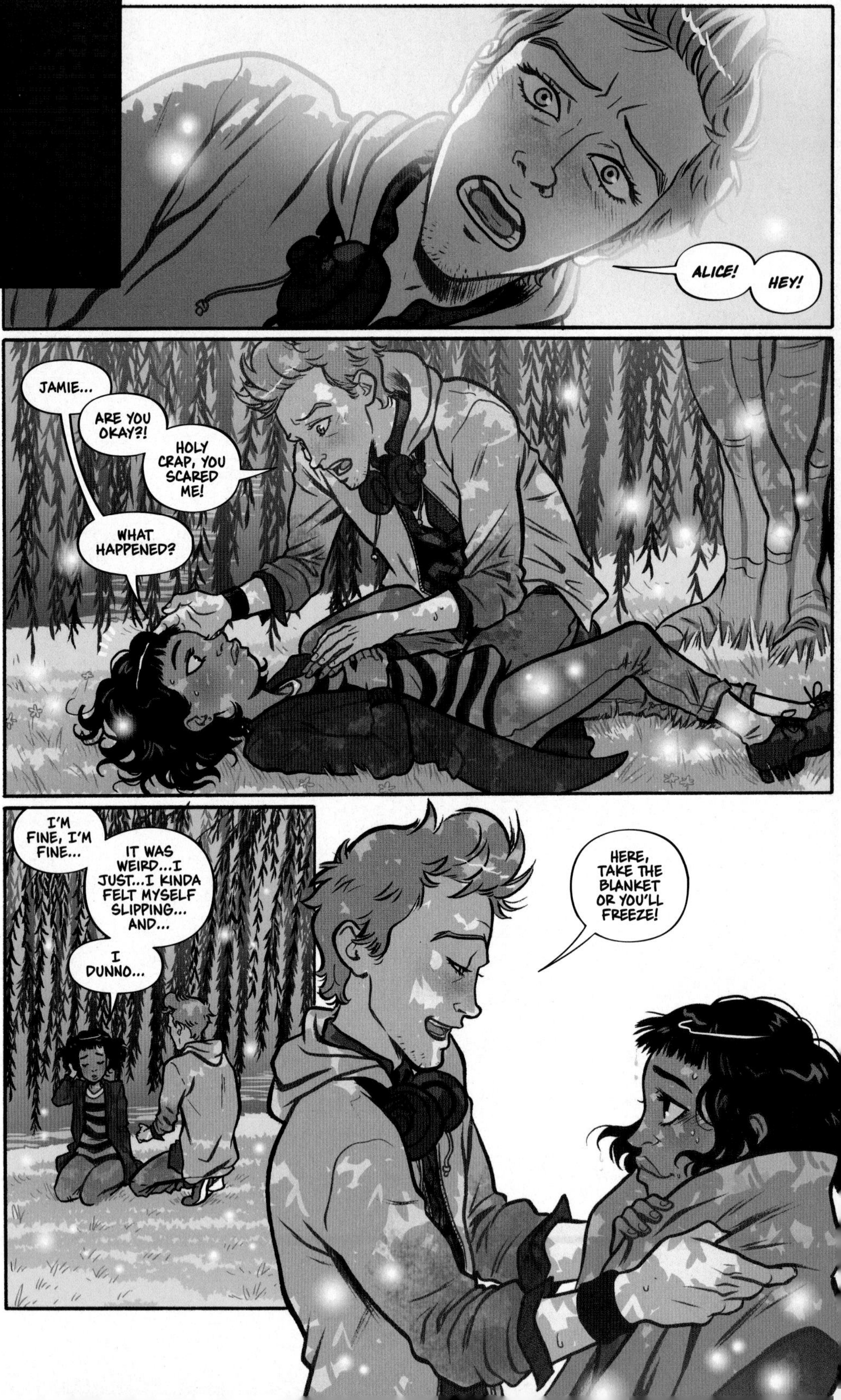
ALICE!
HEY!
JAMIE...
ARE YOU OKAY?!
HOLY CRAP, YOU SCARED ME!
WHAT HAPPENED?
I'M FINE, I'M FINE...
IT WAS WEIRD...I JUST...I KINDA FELT MYSELF SLIPPING... AND...
I DUNNO...
HERE, TAKE THE BLANKET OR YOU'LL FREEZE!

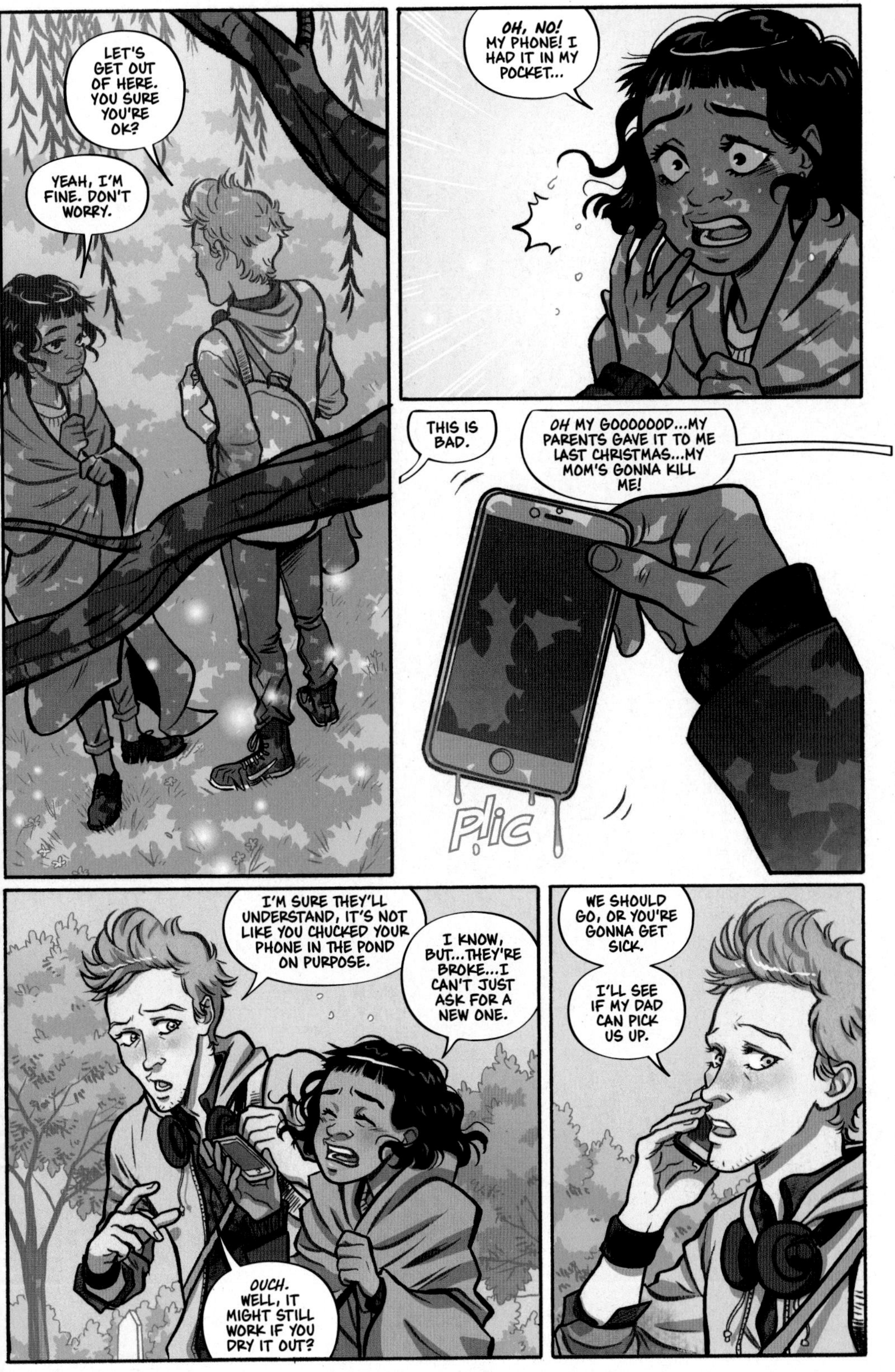
LET'S GET OUT OF HERE. YOU SURE YOU'RE OK?
YEAH, I'M FINE. DON'T WORRY.
OH, NO! MY PHONE! I HAD IT IN MY POCKET...
THIS IS BAD.
OH MY GOOOOOOD...MY PARENTS GAVE IT TO ME LAST CHRISTMAS...MY MOM'S GONNA KILL ME!
PLIC
I'M SURE THEY'LL UNDERSTAND, IT'S NOT LIKE YOU CHUCKED YOUR PHONE IN THE POND ON PURPOSE.
I KNOW, BUT...THEY'RE BROKE...I CAN'T JUST ASK FOR A NEW ONE.
OUCH. WELL, IT MIGHT STILL WORK IF YOU DRY IT OUT?
WE SHOULD GO, OR YOU'RE GONNA GET SICK.
I'LL SEE IF MY DAD CAN PICK US UP.

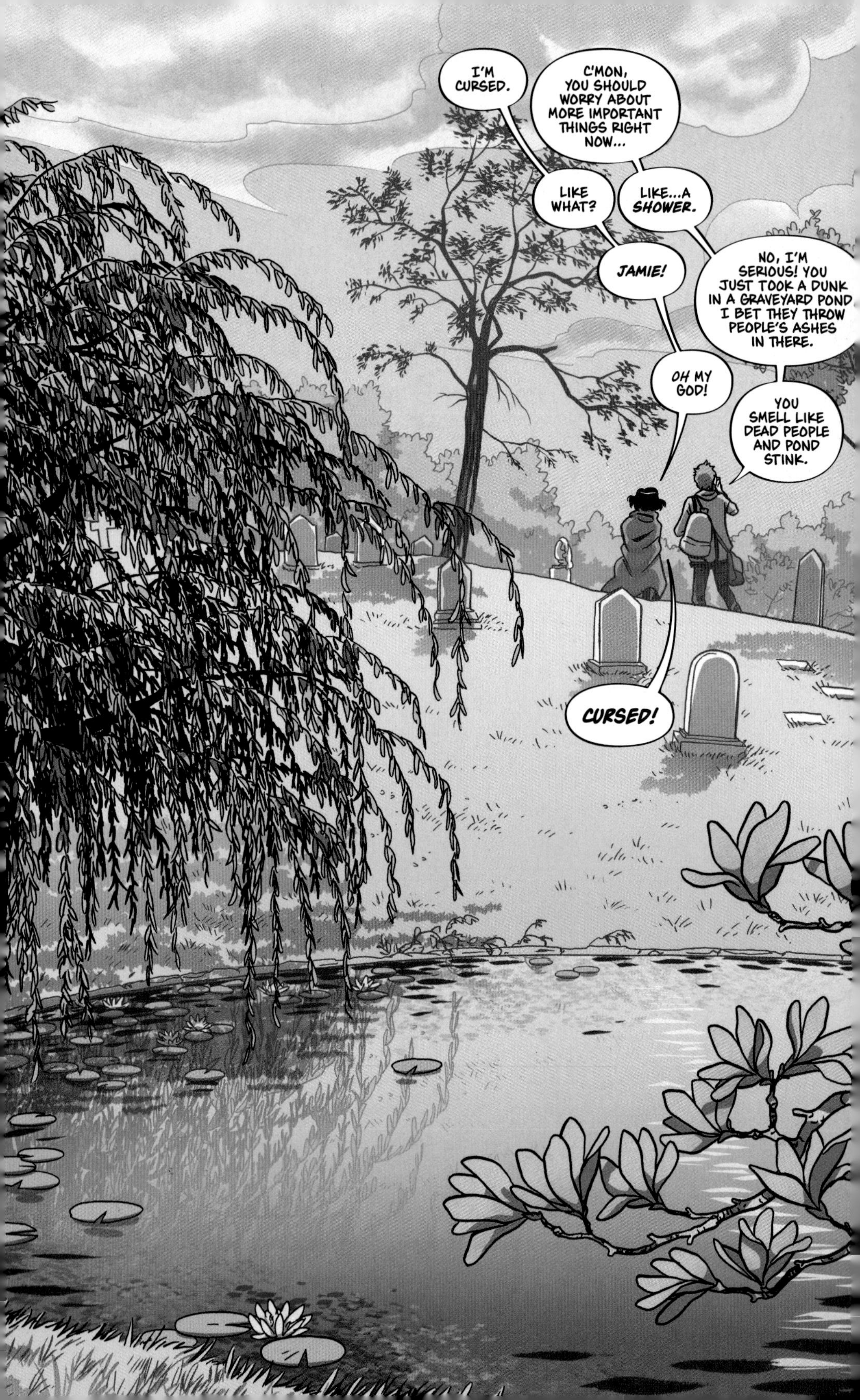
I'M CURSED.
C'MON, YOU SHOULD WORRY ABOUT MORE IMPORTANT THINGS RIGHT NOW...
LIKE WHAT?
LIKE...A *SHOWER.*
*JAMIE!*
NO, I'M SERIOUS! YOU JUST TOOK A DUNK IN A GRAVEYARD POND I BET THEY THROW PEOPLE'S ASHES IN THERE.
*OH MY GOD!*
YOU SMELL LIKE DEAD PEOPLE AND POND STINK.
**CURSED!**

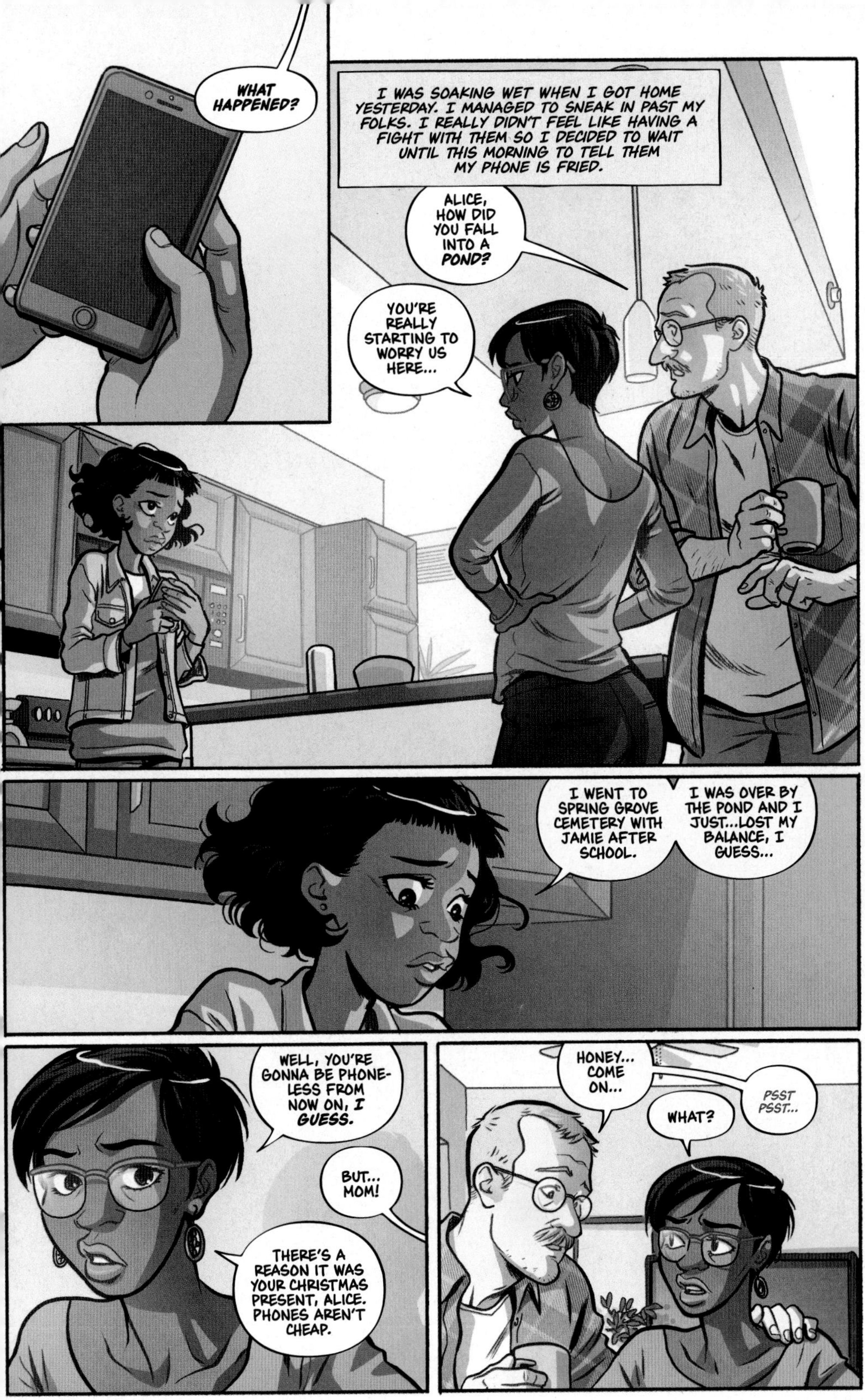
WHAT HAPPENED?
I WAS SOAKING WET WHEN I GOT HOME YESTERDAY. I MANAGED TO SNEAK IN PAST MY FOLKS. I REALLY DIDN'T FEEL LIKE HAVING A FIGHT WITH THEM SO I DECIDED TO WAIT UNTIL THIS MORNING TO TELL THEM MY PHONE IS FRIED.
ALICE, HOW DID YOU FALL INTO A POND?
YOU'RE REALLY STARTING TO WORRY US HERE...
I WENT TO SPRING GROVE CEMETERY WITH JAMIE AFTER SCHOOL.
I WAS OVER BY THE POND AND I JUST...LOST MY BALANCE, I GUESS...
WELL, YOU'RE GONNA BE PHONE-LESS FROM NOW ON, I GUESS.
BUT... MOM!
THERE'S A REASON IT WAS YOUR CHRISTMAS PRESENT, ALICE. PHONES AREN'T CHEAP.
HONEY... COME ON...
PSST PSST...
WHAT?

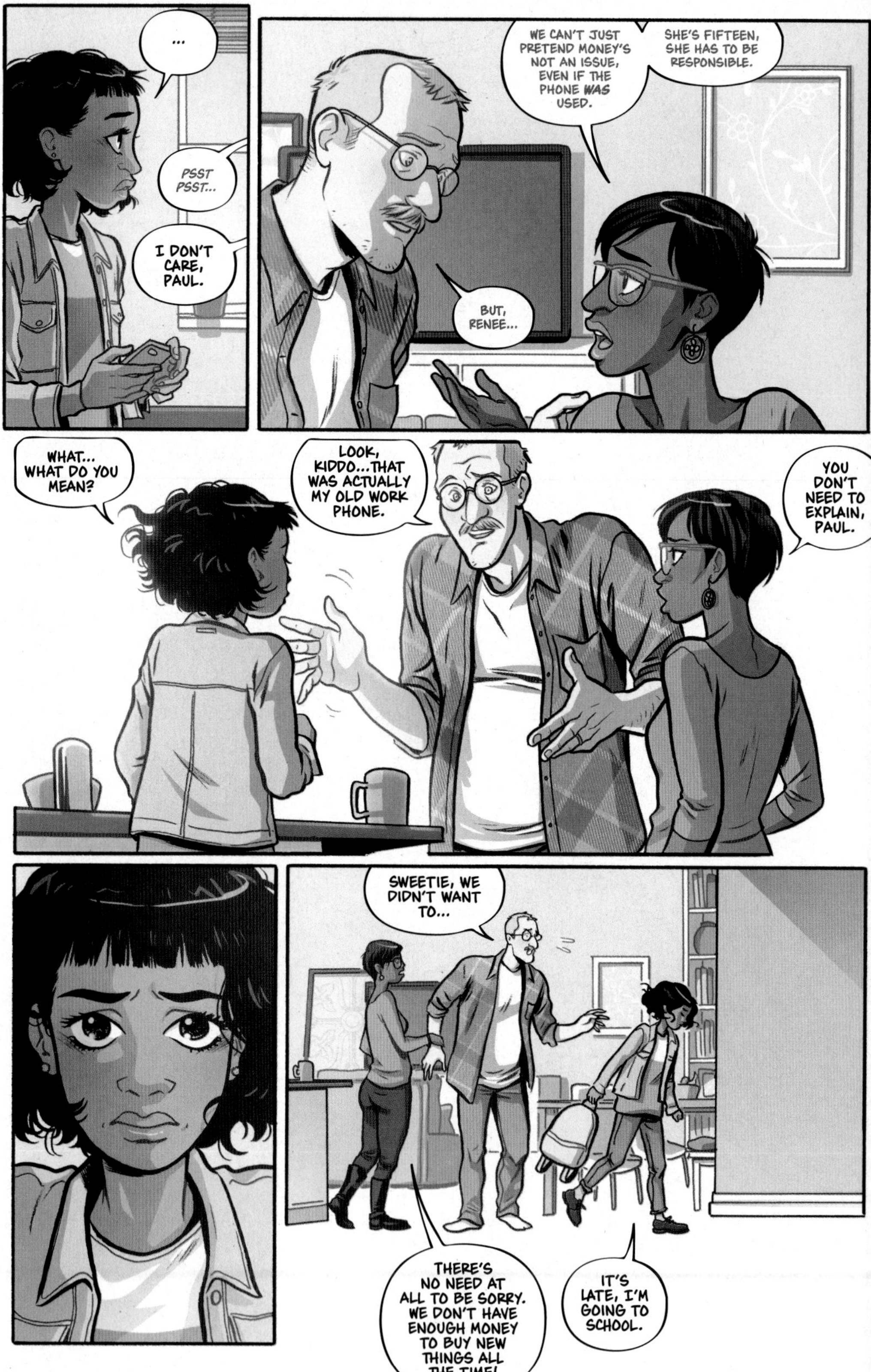
...
PSST PSST...
I DON'T CARE, PAUL.
WE CAN'T JUST PRETEND MONEY'S NOT AN ISSUE, EVEN IF THE PHONE *WAS* USED.
SHE'S FIFTEEN, SHE HAS TO BE RESPONSIBLE.
BUT, RENEE...
WHAT... WHAT DO YOU MEAN?
LOOK, KIDDO...THAT WAS ACTUALLY MY OLD WORK PHONE.
YOU DON'T NEED TO EXPLAIN, PAUL.
SWEETIE, WE DIDN'T WANT TO...
THERE'S NO NEED AT ALL TO BE SORRY. WE DON'T HAVE ENOUGH MONEY TO BUY NEW THINGS ALL THE TIME!
IT'S LATE, I'M GOING TO SCHOOL.

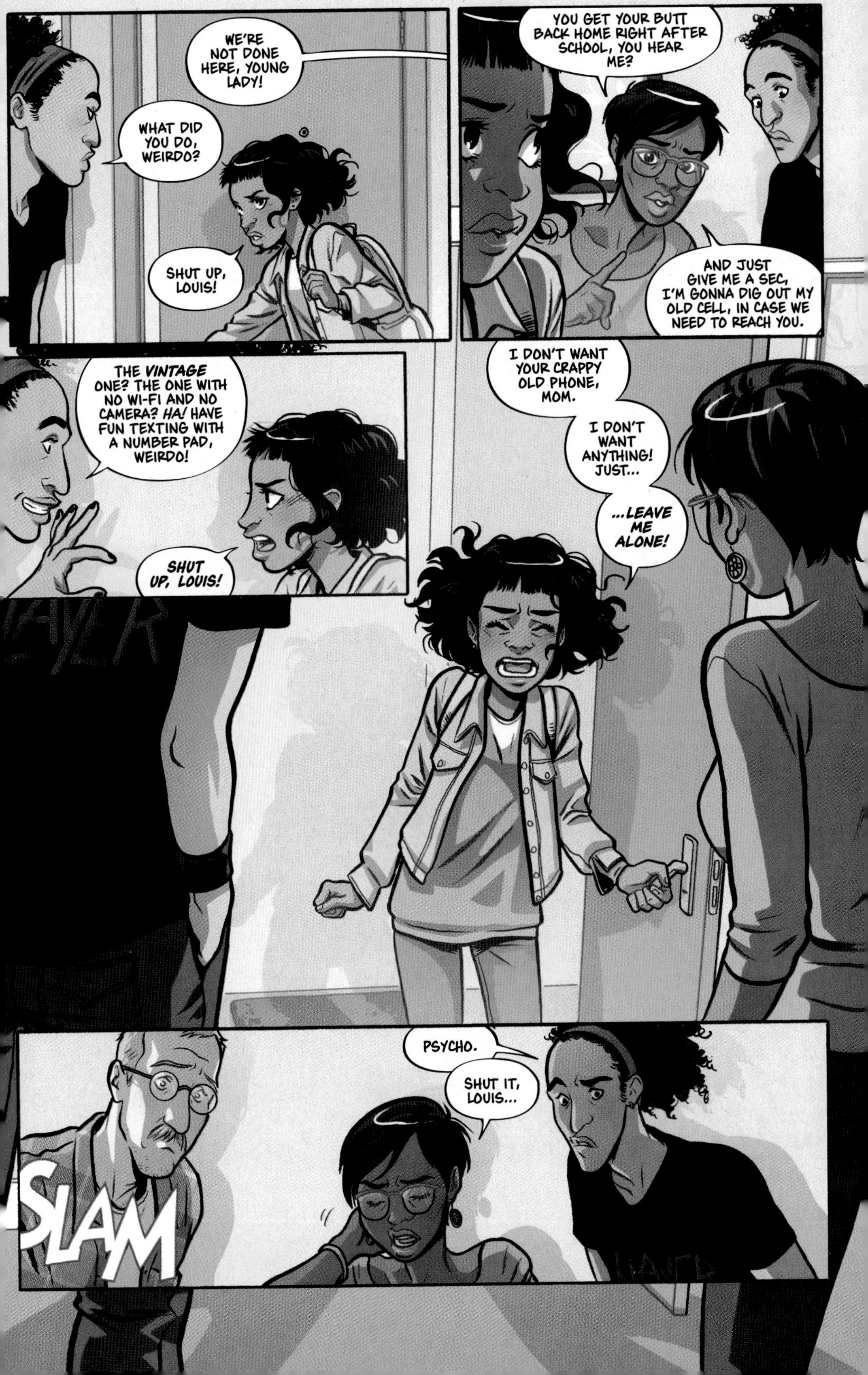
WE'RE NOT DONE HERE, YOUNG LADY!
WHAT DID YOU DO, WEIRDO?
SHUT UP, LOUIS!
YOU GET YOUR BUTT BACK HOME RIGHT AFTER SCHOOL, YOU HEAR ME?
AND JUST GIVE ME A SEC, I'M GONNA DIG OUT MY OLD CELL, IN CASE WE NEED TO REACH YOU.
THE *VINTAGE* ONE? THE ONE WITH NO WI-FI AND NO CAMERA? *HA!* HAVE FUN TEXTING WITH A NUMBER PAD, WEIRDO!
SHUT UP, LOUIS!
I DON'T WANT YOUR CRAPPY OLD PHONE, MOM.
I DON'T WANT ANYTHING! JUST...
...LEAVE ME ALONE!
PSYCHO.
SHUT IT, LOUIS...
SLAM

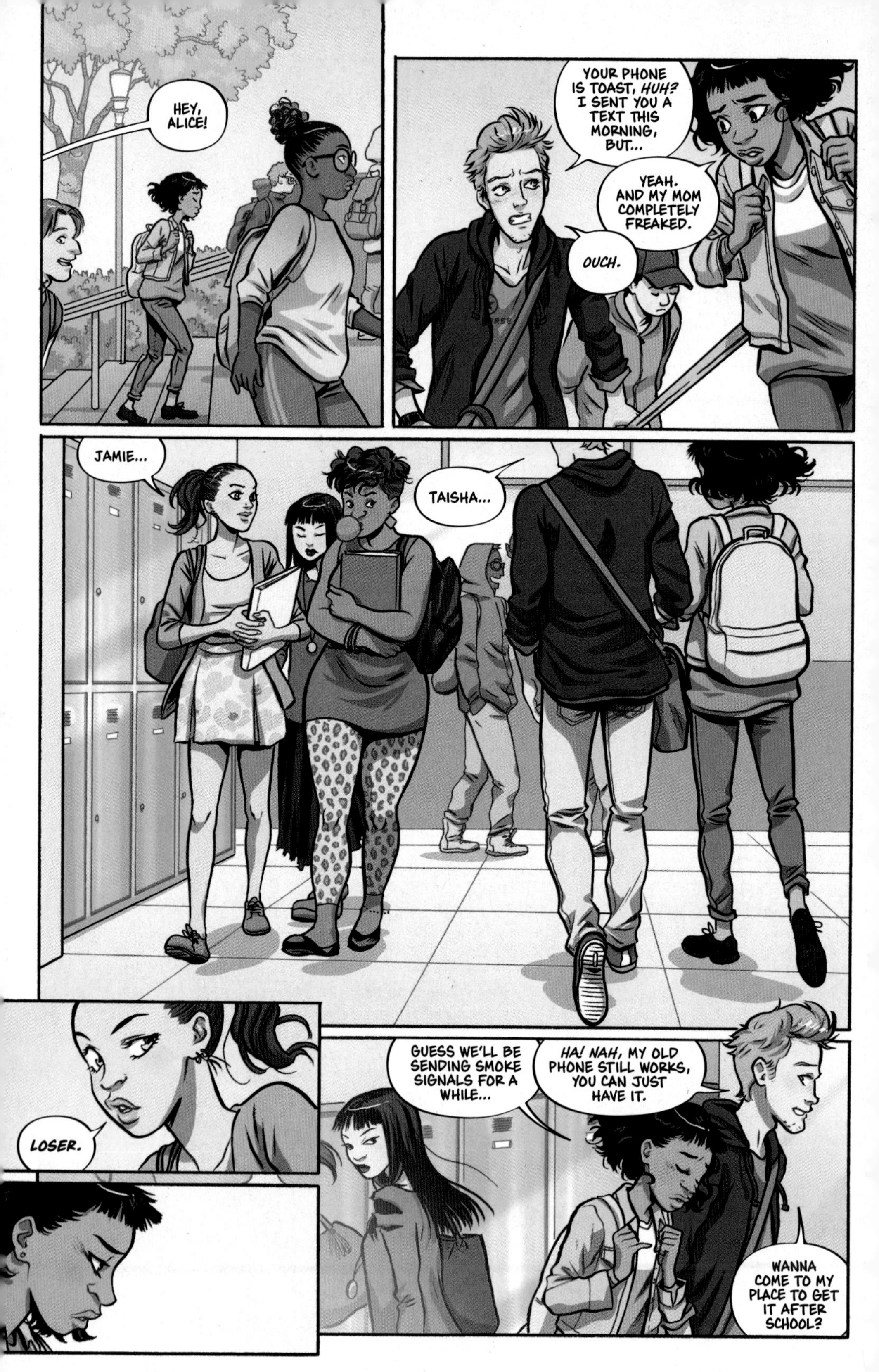

HEY, ALICE!
YOUR PHONE IS TOAST, HUH? I SENT YOU A TEXT THIS MORNING, BUT...
YEAH. AND MY MOM COMPLETELY FREAKED.
OUCH.
JAMIE...
TAISHA...
LOSER.
GUESS WE'LL BE SENDING SMOKE SIGNALS FOR A WHILE...
HA! NAH, MY OLD PHONE STILL WORKS, YOU CAN JUST HAVE IT.
WANNA COME TO MY PLACE TO GET IT AFTER SCHOOL?

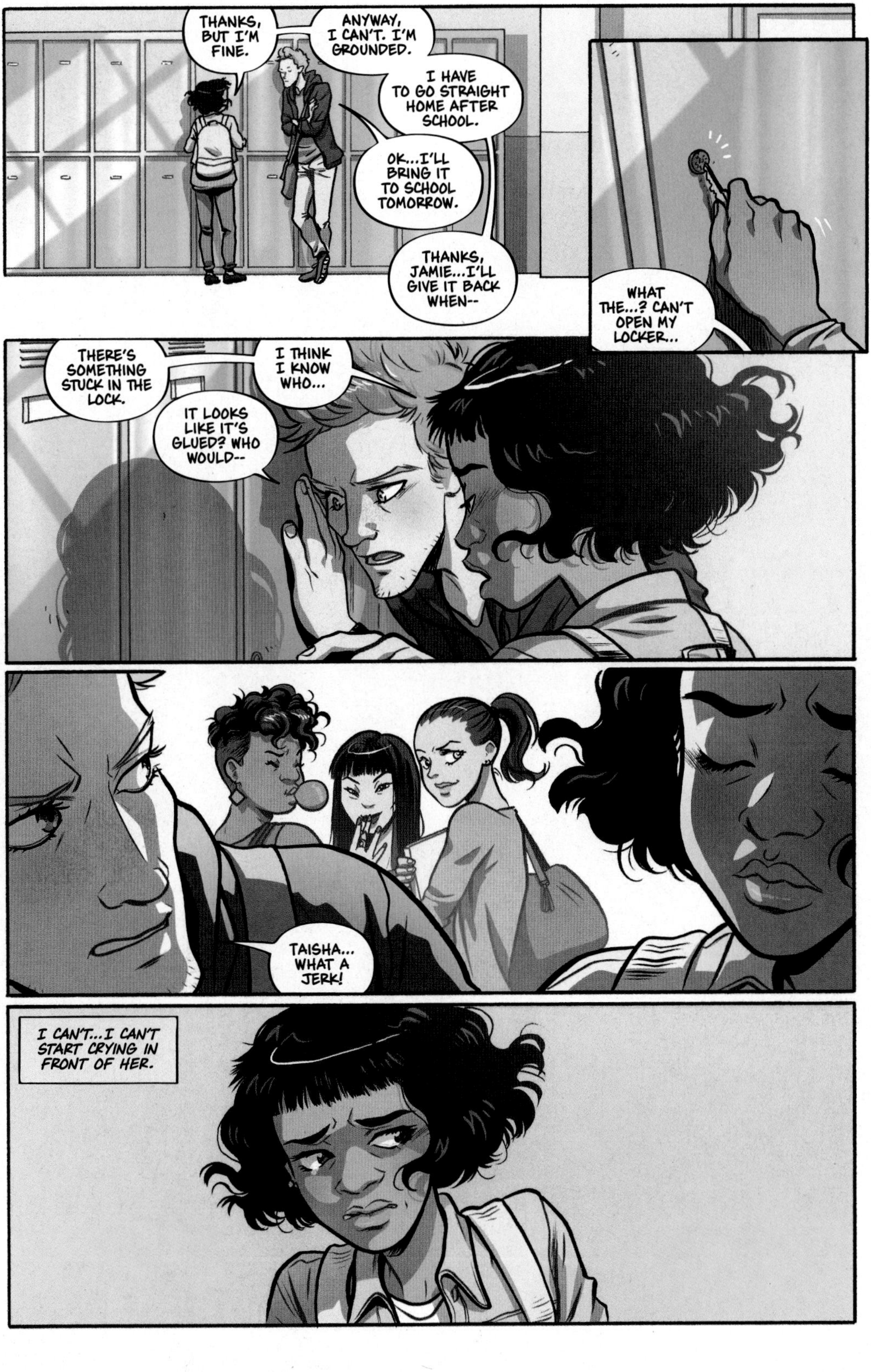
THANKS, BUT I'M FINE.
ANYWAY, I CAN'T. I'M GROUNDED.
I HAVE TO GO STRAIGHT HOME AFTER SCHOOL.
OK...I'LL BRING IT TO SCHOOL TOMORROW.
THANKS, JAMIE...I'LL GIVE IT BACK WHEN--
WHAT THE...? CAN'T OPEN MY LOCKER...
THERE'S SOMETHING STUCK IN THE LOCK.
IT LOOKS LIKE IT'S GLUED? WHO WOULD--
I THINK I KNOW WHO...
TAISHA... WHAT A JERK!
I CAN'T...I CAN'T START CRYING IN FRONT OF HER.

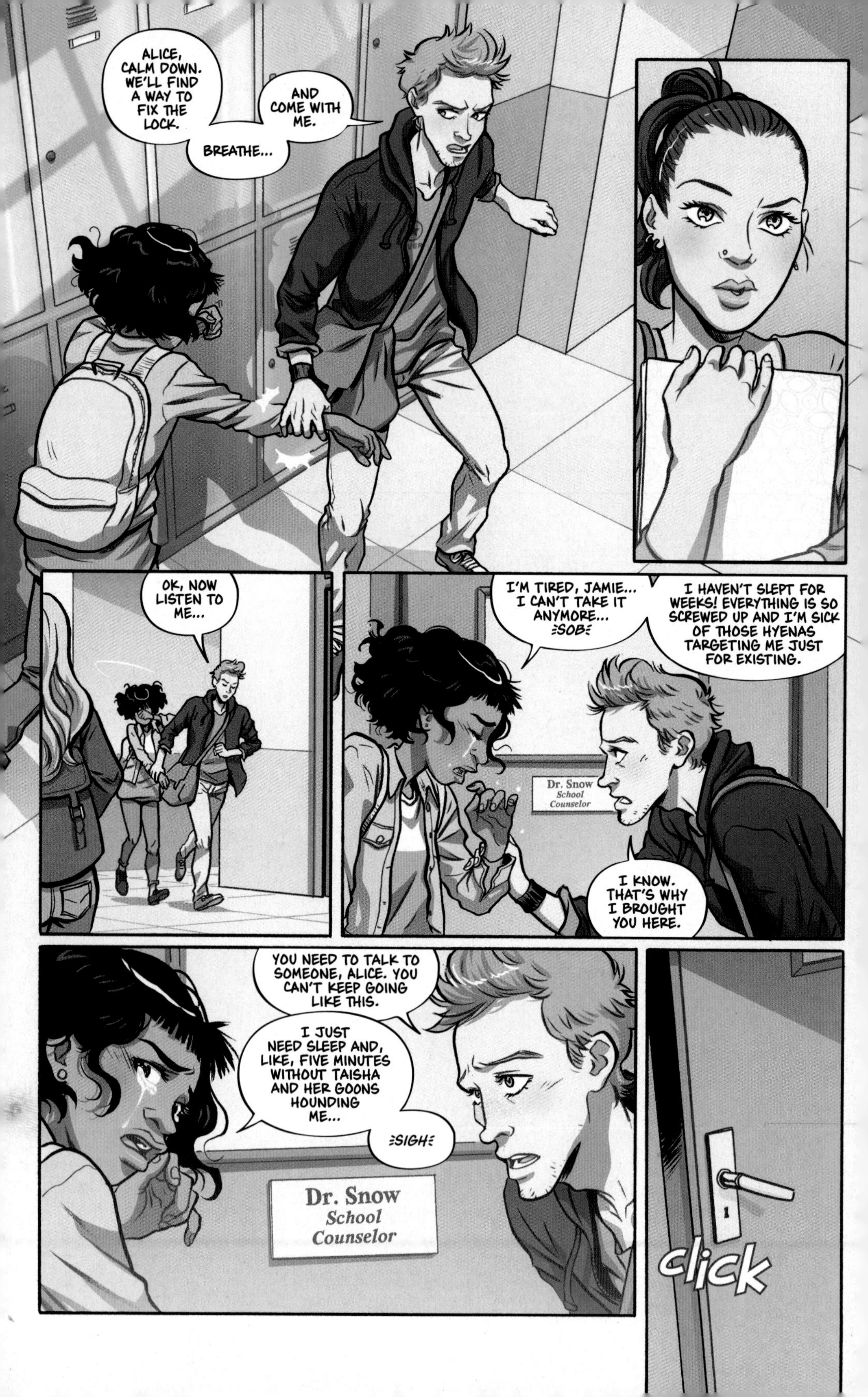
ALICE, CALM DOWN. WE'LL FIND A WAY TO FIX THE LOCK.
BREATHE...
AND COME WITH ME.
OK, NOW LISTEN TO ME...
I'M TIRED, JAMIE... I CAN'T TAKE IT ANYMORE... SOB
I HAVEN'T SLEPT FOR WEEKS! EVERYTHING IS SO SCREWED UP AND I'M SICK OF THOSE HYENAS TARGETING ME JUST FOR EXISTING.
Dr. Snow School Counselor
I KNOW. THAT'S WHY I BROUGHT YOU HERE.
YOU NEED TO TALK TO SOMEONE, ALICE. YOU CAN'T KEEP GOING LIKE THIS.
I JUST NEED SLEEP AND, LIKE, FIVE MINUTES WITHOUT TAISHA AND HER GOONS HOUNDING ME...
SIGH
Dr. Snow School Counselor
Click

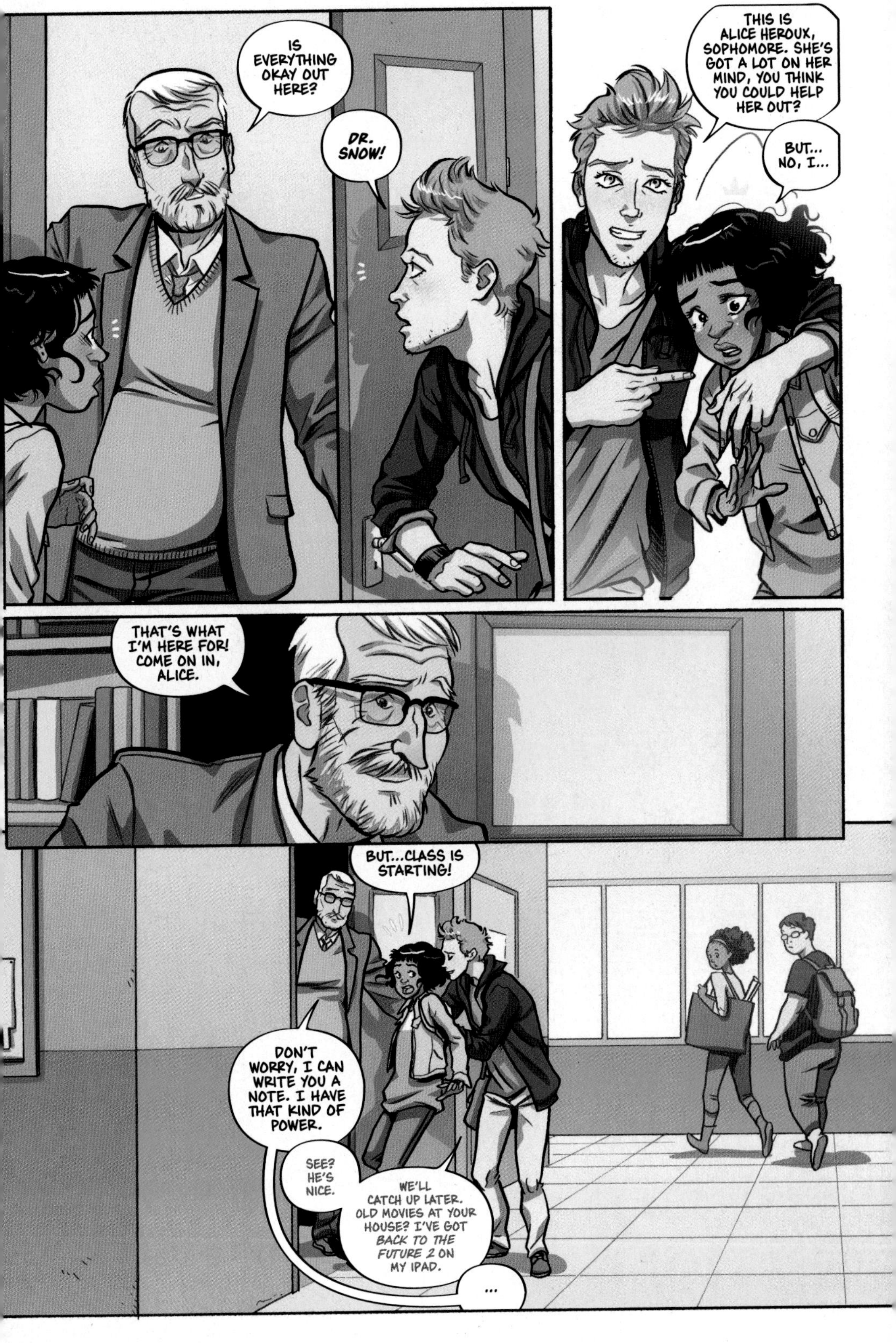
IS EVERYTHING OKAY OUT HERE?
DR. SNOW!
THIS IS ALICE HEROUX, SOPHOMORE. SHE'S GOT A LOT ON HER MIND, YOU THINK YOU COULD HELP HER OUT?
BUT... NO, I...
THAT'S WHAT I'M HERE FOR! COME ON IN, ALICE.
BUT...CLASS IS STARTING!
DON'T WORRY, I CAN WRITE YOU A NOTE. I HAVE THAT KIND OF POWER.
SEE? HE'S NICE.
WE'LL CATCH UP LATER. OLD MOVIES AT YOUR HOUSE? I'VE GOT *BACK TO THE FUTURE 2* ON MY IPAD.
...

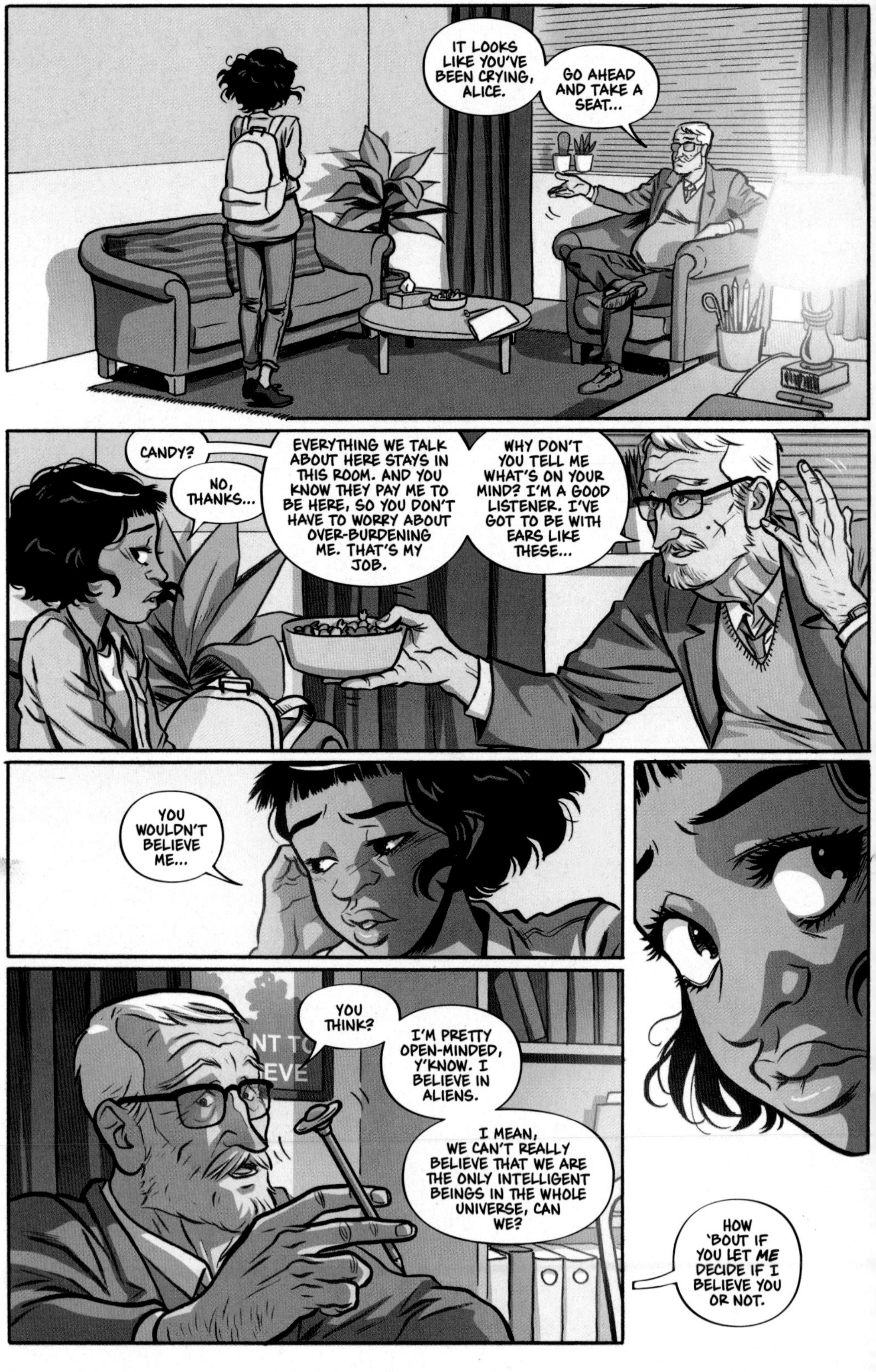
IT LOOKS LIKE YOU'VE BEEN CRYING, ALICE.
GO AHEAD AND TAKE A SEAT...
CANDY?
NO, THANKS...
EVERYTHING WE TALK ABOUT HERE STAYS IN THIS ROOM. AND YOU KNOW THEY PAY ME TO BE HERE, SO YOU DON'T HAVE TO WORRY ABOUT OVER-BURDENING ME. THAT'S MY JOB.
WHY DON'T YOU TELL ME WHAT'S ON YOUR MIND? I'M A GOOD LISTENER. I'VE GOT TO BE WITH EARS LIKE THESE...
YOU WOULDN'T BELIEVE ME...
YOU THINK?
I'M PRETTY OPEN-MINDED, Y'KNOW. I BELIEVE IN ALIENS.
I MEAN, WE CAN'T REALLY BELIEVE THAT WE ARE THE ONLY INTELLIGENT BEINGS IN THE WHOLE UNIVERSE, CAN WE?
HOW 'BOUT IF YOU LET ME DECIDE IF I BELIEVE YOU OR NOT.

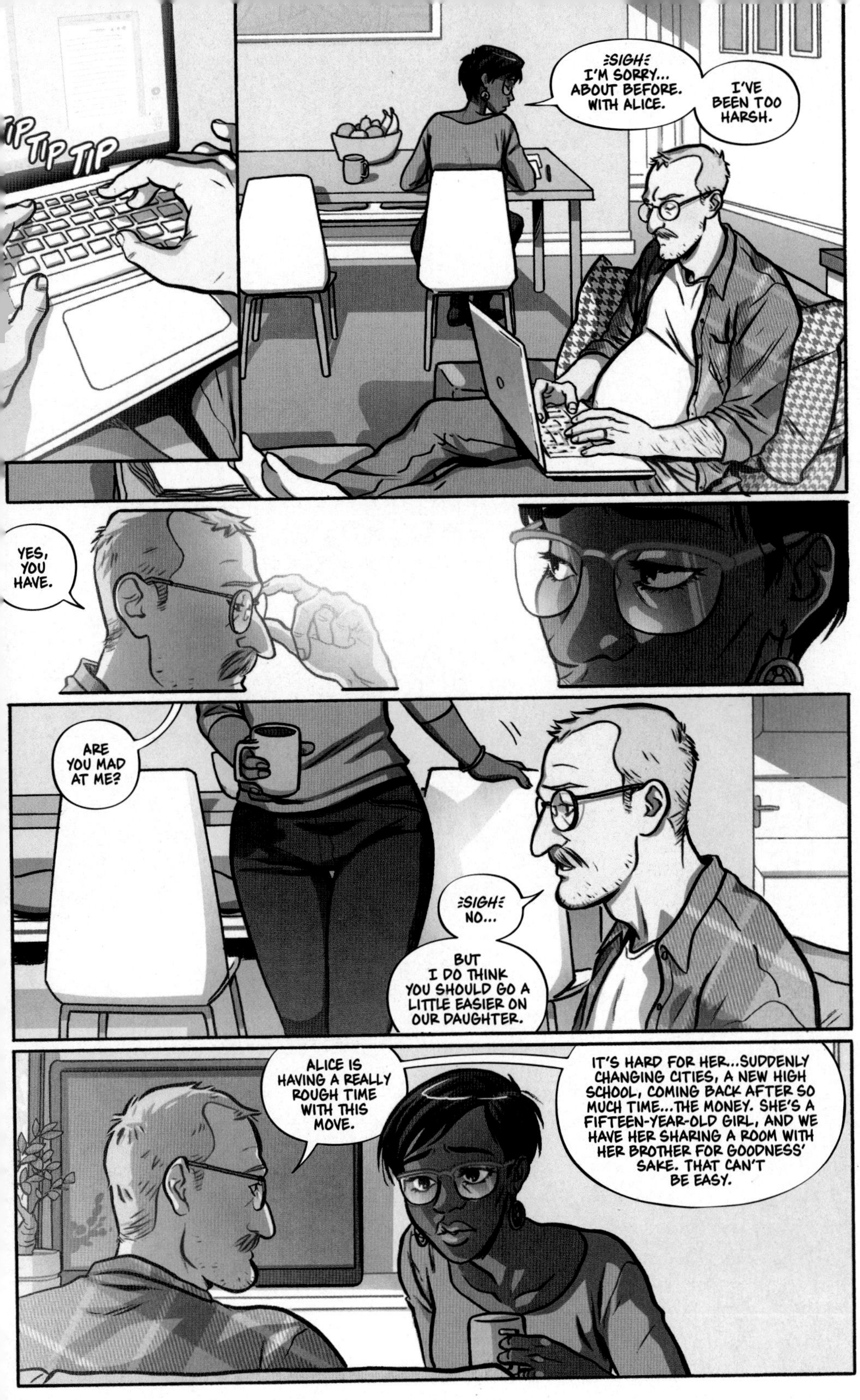
TIP TIP TIP
≡SIGH≡ I'M SORRY... ABOUT BEFORE. WITH ALICE.
I'VE BEEN TOO HARSH.
YES, YOU HAVE.
ARE YOU MAD AT ME?
≡SIGH≡ NO...
BUT I DO THINK YOU SHOULD GO A LITTLE EASIER ON OUR DAUGHTER.
ALICE IS HAVING A REALLY ROUGH TIME WITH THIS MOVE.
IT'S HARD FOR HER...SUDDENLY CHANGING CITIES, A NEW HIGH SCHOOL, COMING BACK AFTER SO MUCH TIME...THE MONEY. SHE'S A FIFTEEN-YEAR-OLD GIRL, AND WE HAVE HER SHARING A ROOM WITH HER BROTHER FOR GOODNESS' SAKE. THAT CAN'T BE EASY.

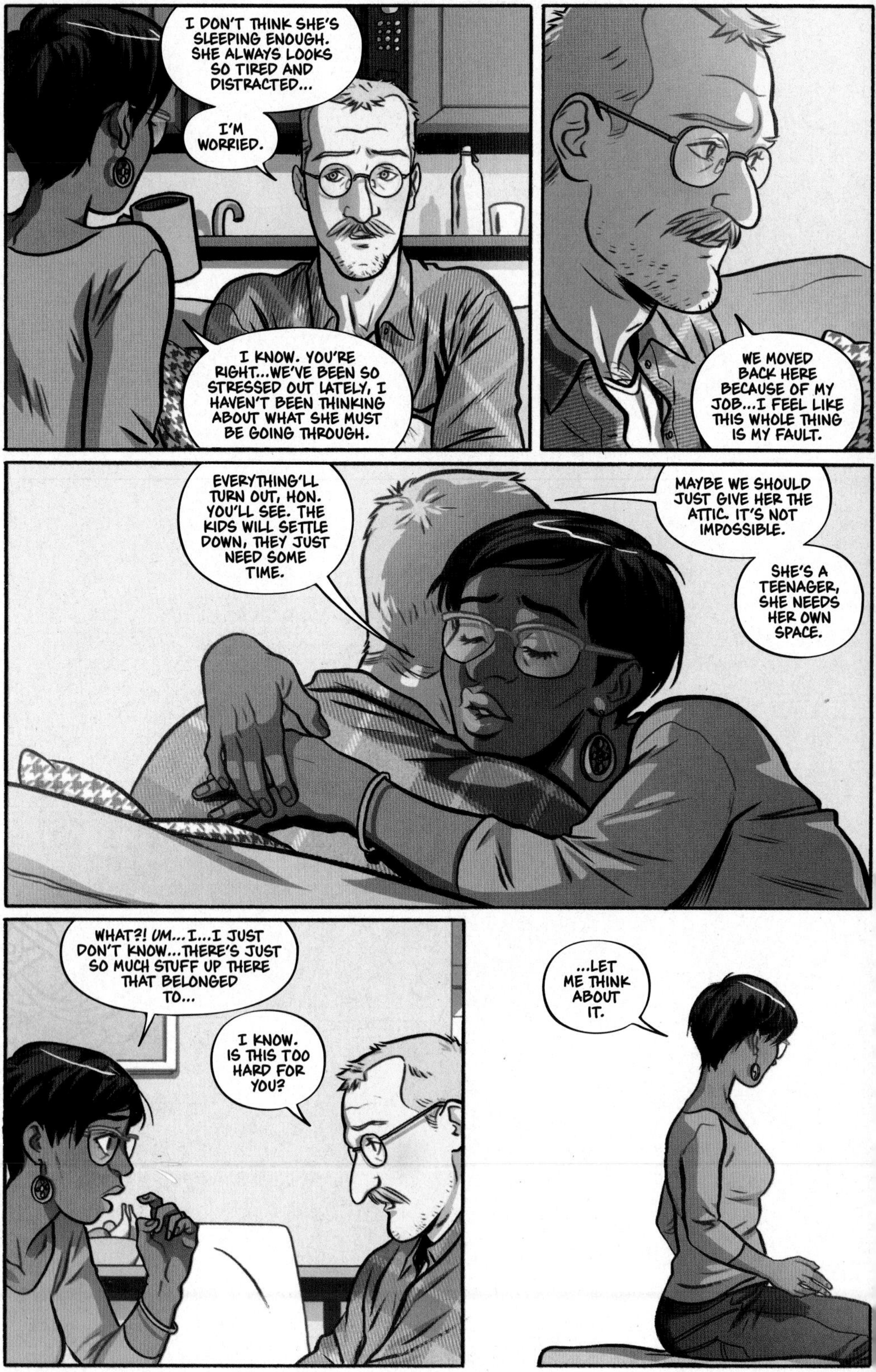
I DON'T THINK SHE'S SLEEPING ENOUGH. SHE ALWAYS LOOKS SO TIRED AND DISTRACTED...
I'M WORRIED.
I KNOW. YOU'RE RIGHT...WE'VE BEEN SO STRESSED OUT LATELY, I HAVEN'T BEEN THINKING ABOUT WHAT SHE MUST BE GOING THROUGH.
WE MOVED BACK HERE BECAUSE OF MY JOB...I FEEL LIKE THIS WHOLE THING IS MY FAULT.
EVERYTHING'LL TURN OUT, HON. YOU'LL SEE. THE KIDS WILL SETTLE DOWN, THEY JUST NEED SOME TIME.
MAYBE WE SHOULD JUST GIVE HER THE ATTIC. IT'S NOT IMPOSSIBLE.
SHE'S A TEENAGER, SHE NEEDS HER OWN SPACE.
WHAT?! UM...I...I JUST DON'T KNOW...THERE'S JUST SO MUCH STUFF UP THERE THAT BELONGED TO...
I KNOW. IS THIS TOO HARD FOR YOU?
...LET ME THINK ABOUT IT.

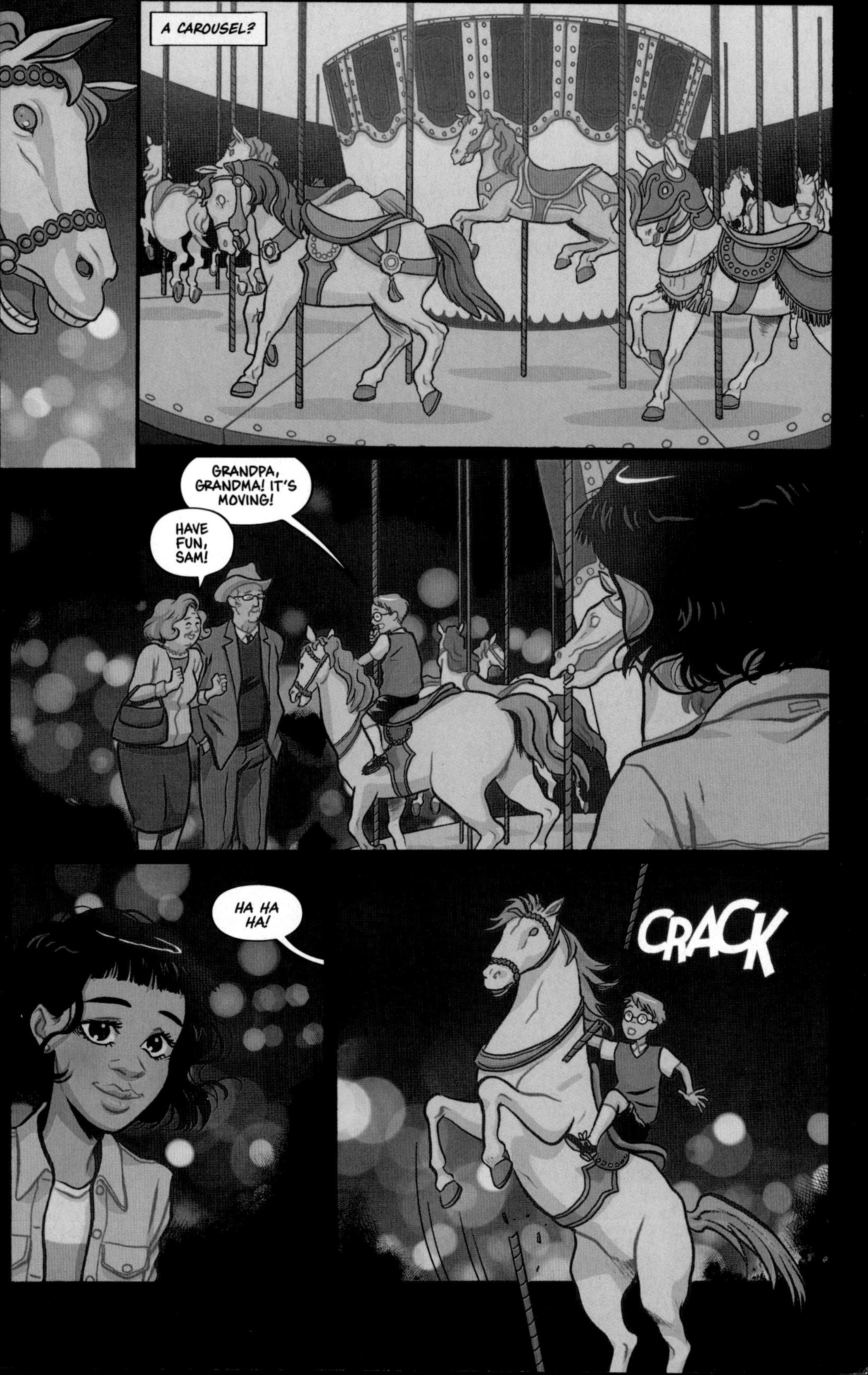
A CAROUSEL?
GRANDPA, GRANDMA! IT'S MOVING!
HAVE FUN, SAM!
HA HA HA!
CRACK

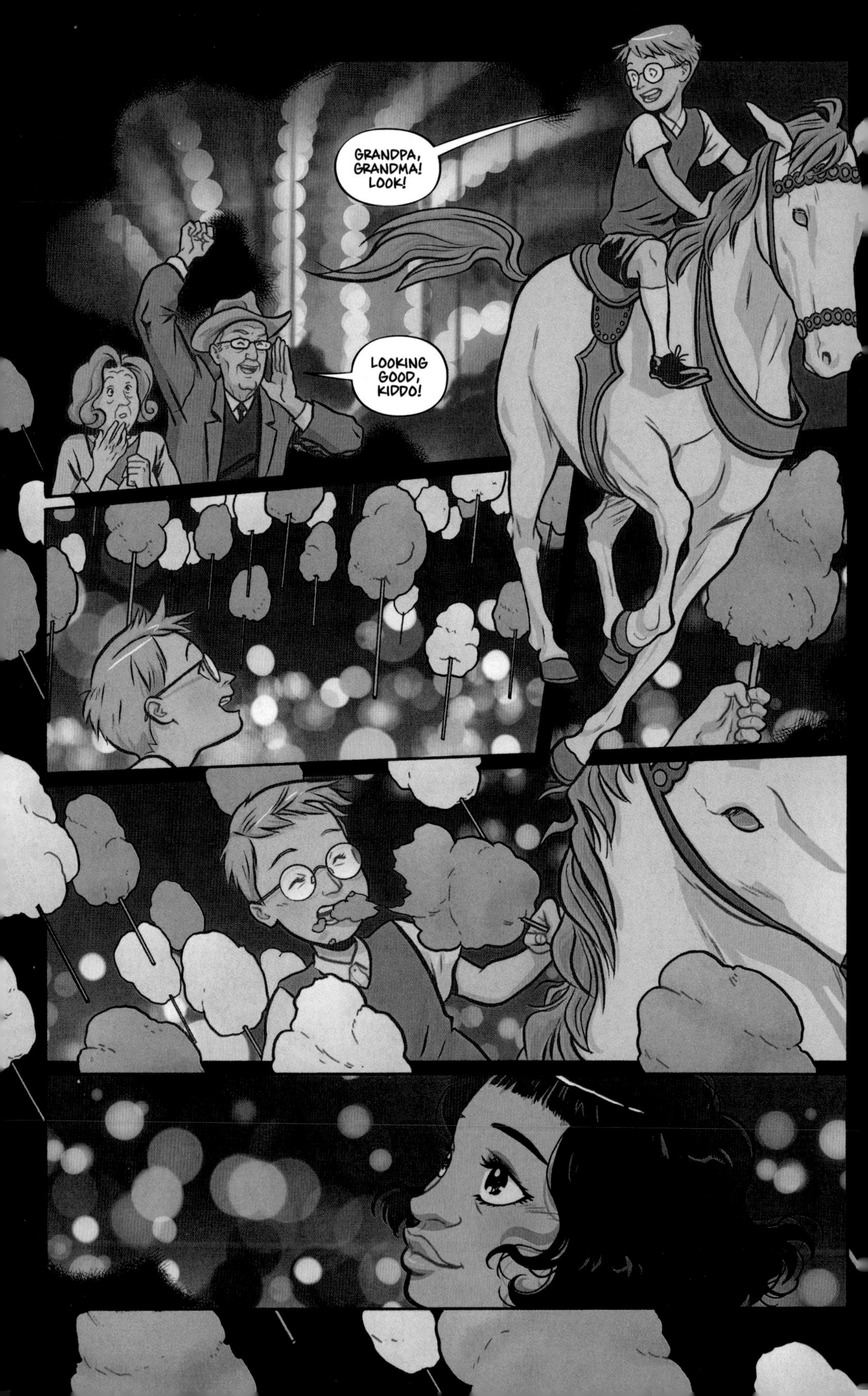
GRANDPA, GRANDMA! LOOK!
LOOKING GOOD, KIDDO!

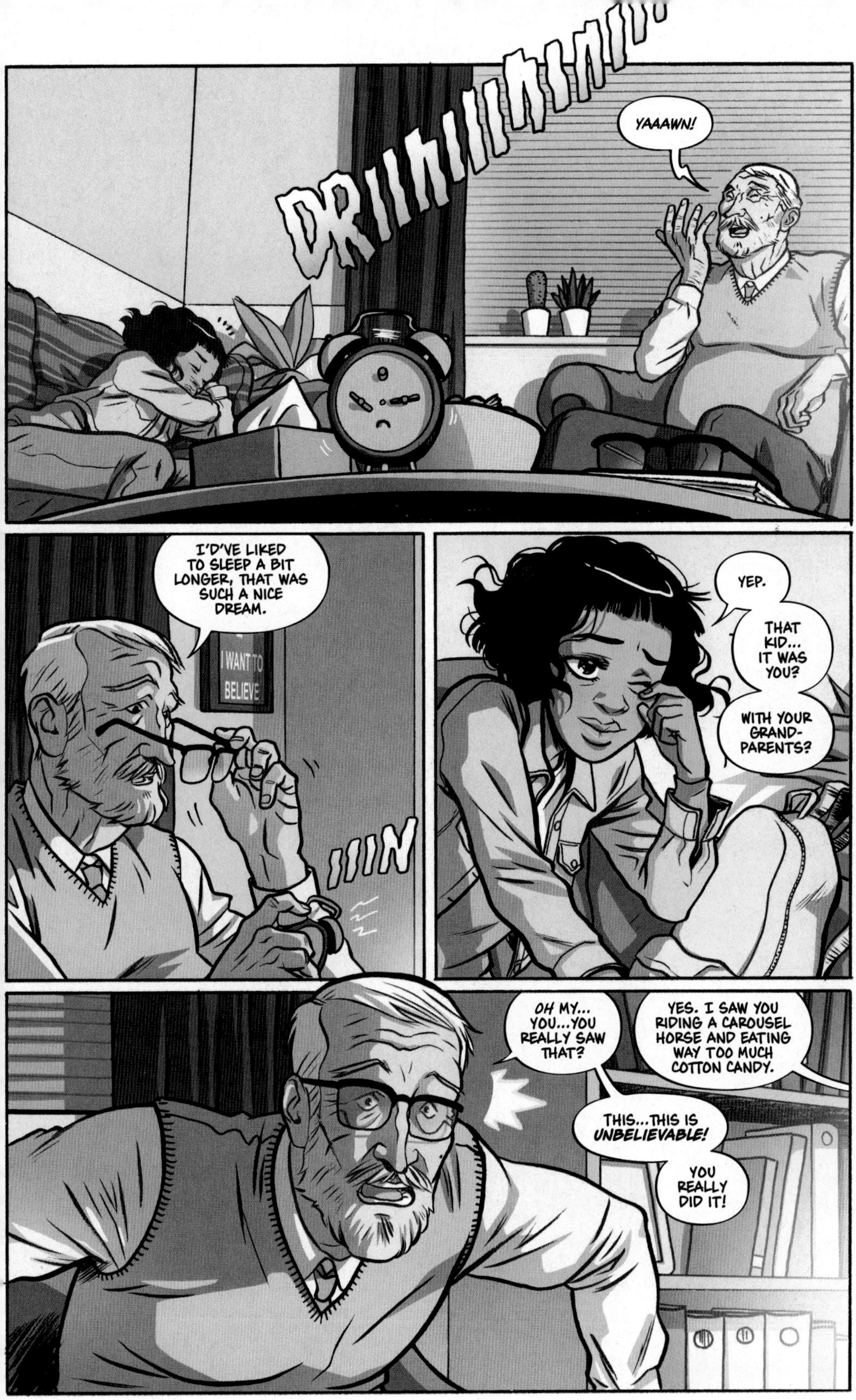
DRIIIIIIIIIIN
YAAAWN!
I'D'VE LIKED TO SLEEP A BIT LONGER, THAT WAS SUCH A NICE DREAM.
I WANT TO BELIEVE
IIIN
YEP.
THAT KID... IT WAS YOU?
WITH YOUR GRAND-PARENTS?
OH MY... YOU...YOU REALLY SAW THAT?
YES. I SAW YOU RIDING A CAROUSEL HORSE AND EATING WAY TOO MUCH COTTON CANDY.
THIS...THIS IS *UNBELIEVABLE!*
YOU REALLY DID IT!

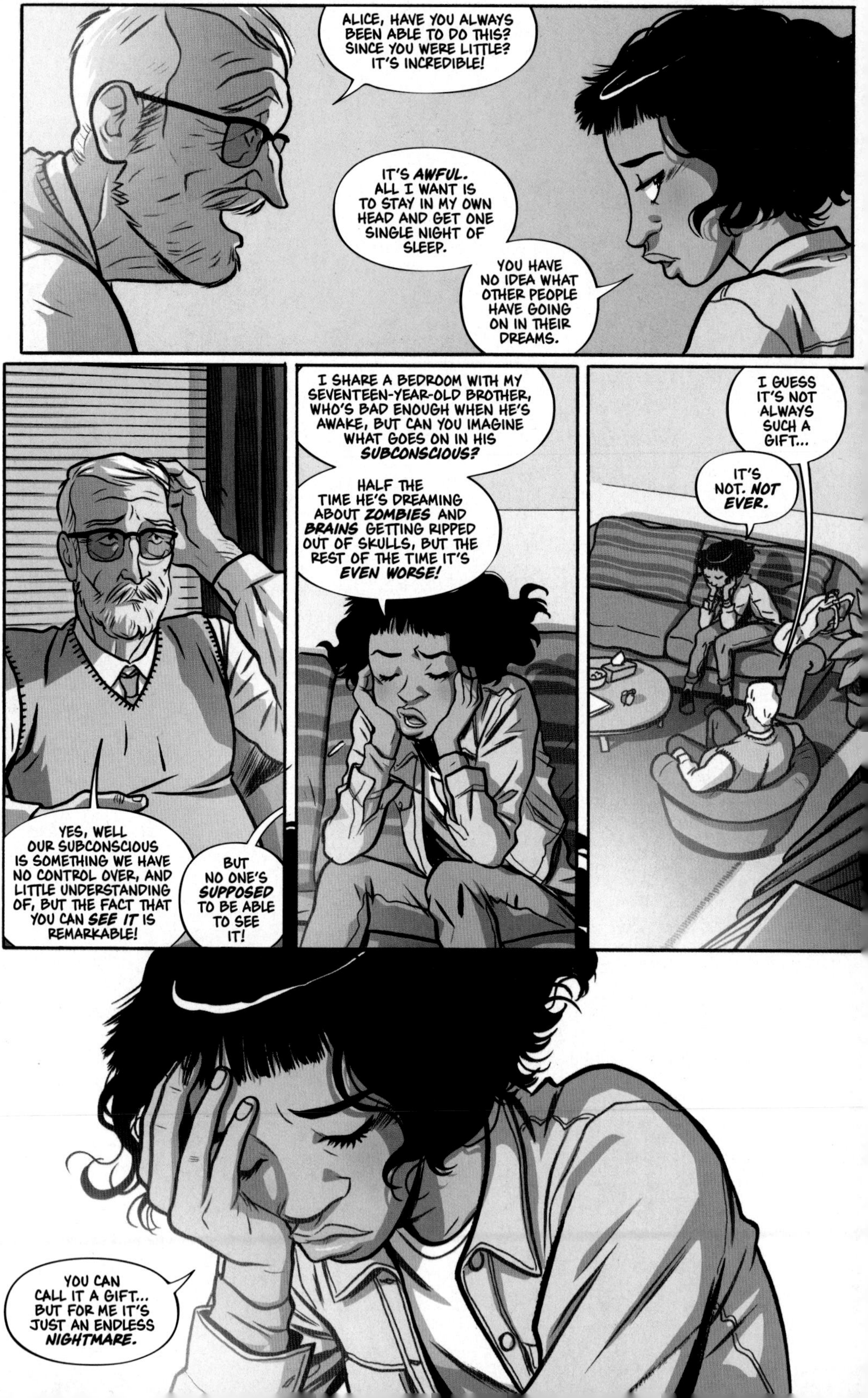
ALICE, HAVE YOU ALWAYS BEEN ABLE TO DO THIS? SINCE YOU WERE LITTLE? IT'S INCREDIBLE!
IT'S AWFUL. ALL I WANT IS TO STAY IN MY OWN HEAD AND GET ONE SINGLE NIGHT OF SLEEP.
YOU HAVE NO IDEA WHAT OTHER PEOPLE HAVE GOING ON IN THEIR DREAMS.
YES, WELL OUR SUBCONSCIOUS IS SOMETHING WE HAVE NO CONTROL OVER, AND LITTLE UNDERSTANDING OF, BUT THE FACT THAT YOU CAN SEE IT IS REMARKABLE!
BUT NO ONE'S SUPPOSED TO BE ABLE TO SEE IT!
I SHARE A BEDROOM WITH MY SEVENTEEN-YEAR-OLD BROTHER, WHO'S BAD ENOUGH WHEN HE'S AWAKE, BUT CAN YOU IMAGINE WHAT GOES ON IN HIS SUBCONSCIOUS?
HALF THE TIME HE'S DREAMING ABOUT ZOMBIES AND BRAINS GETTING RIPPED OUT OF SKULLS, BUT THE REST OF THE TIME IT'S EVEN WORSE!
I GUESS IT'S NOT ALWAYS SUCH A GIFT...
IT'S NOT. NOT EVER.
YOU CAN CALL IT A GIFT... BUT FOR ME IT'S JUST AN ENDLESS NIGHTMARE.

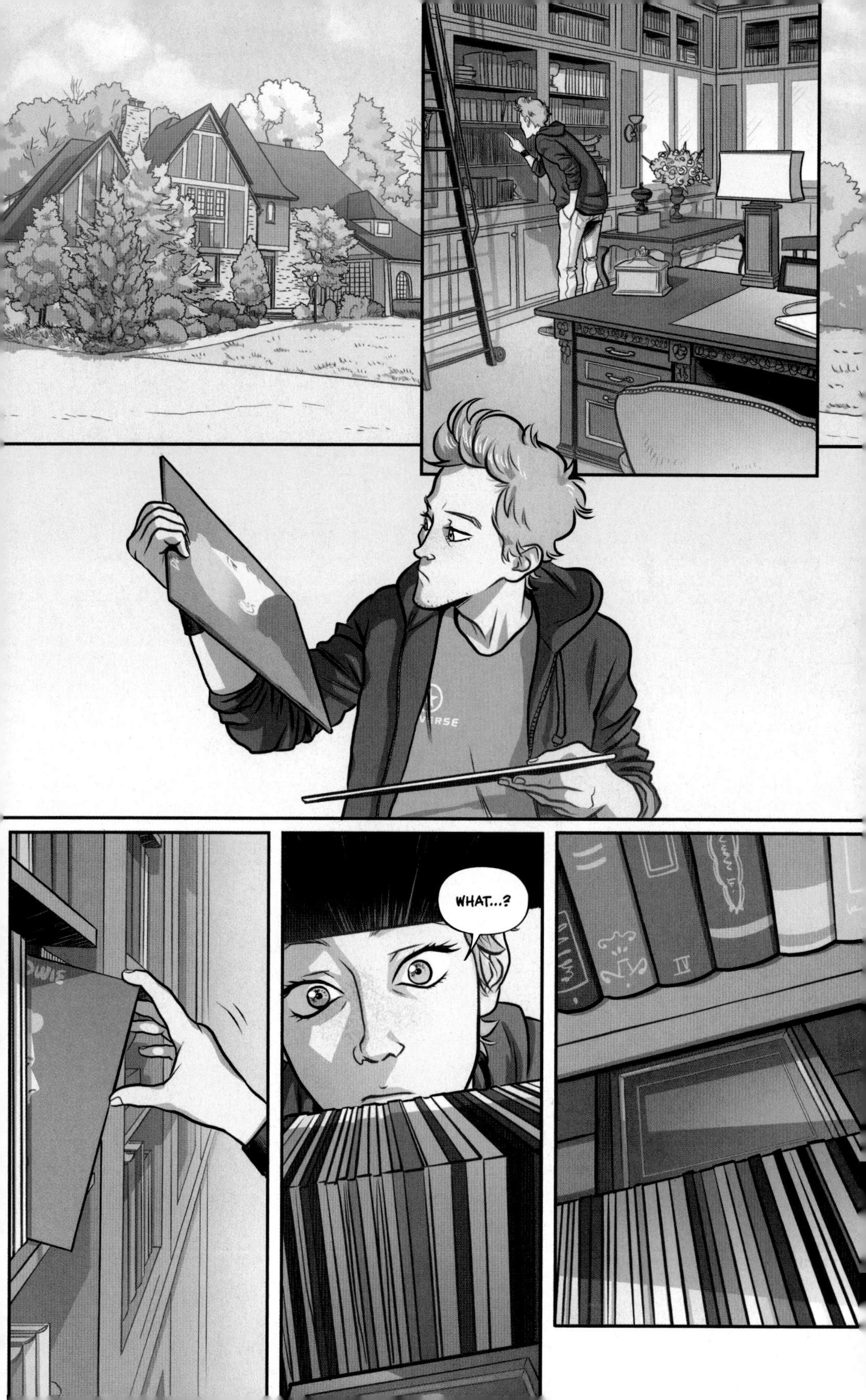
WHAT...?

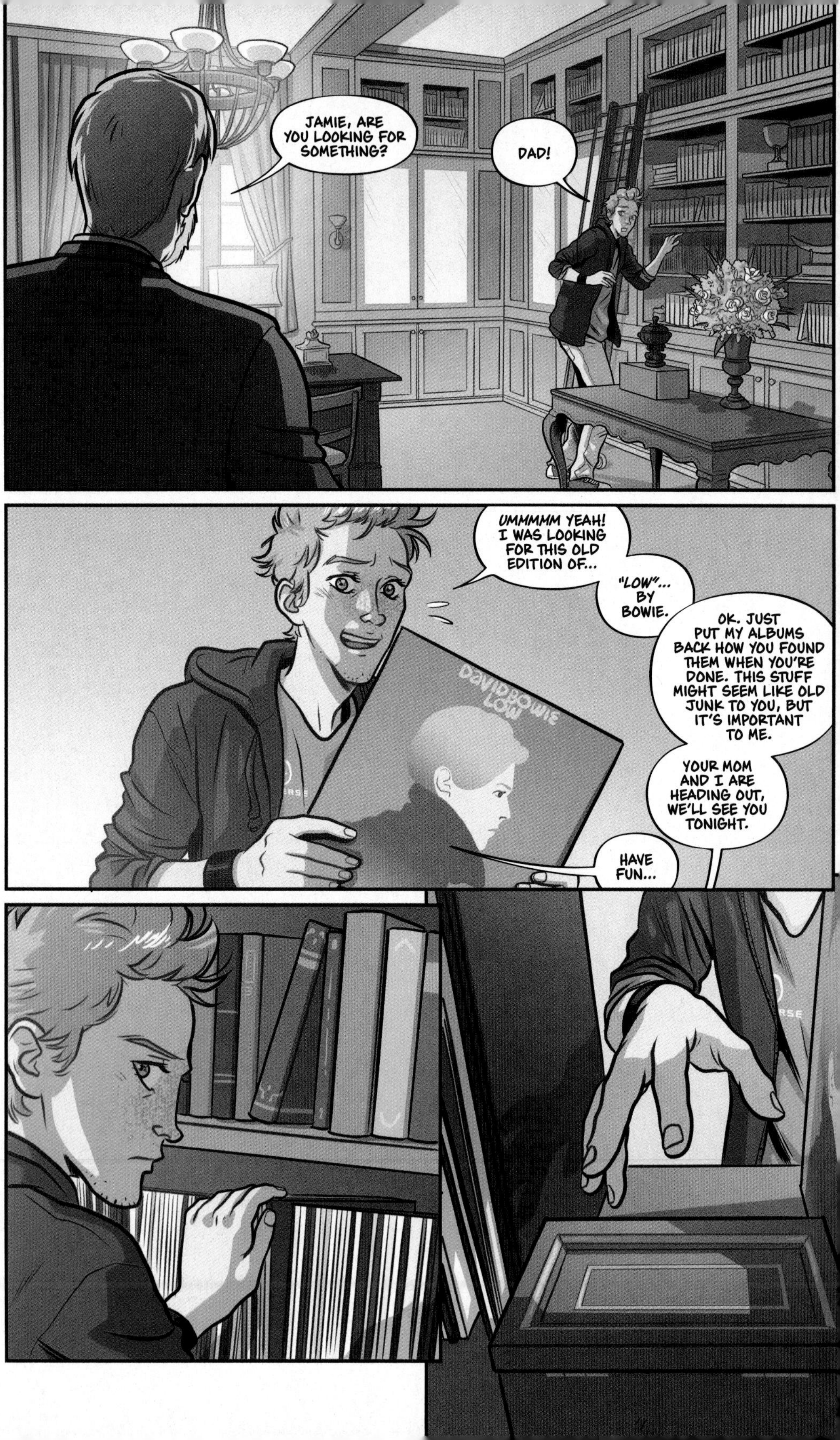
JAMIE, ARE YOU LOOKING FOR SOMETHING?
DAD!
UMMMMM YEAH! I WAS LOOKING FOR THIS OLD EDITION OF...
"LOW"... BY BOWIE.
OK. JUST PUT MY ALBUMS BACK HOW YOU FOUND THEM WHEN YOU'RE DONE. THIS STUFF MIGHT SEEM LIKE OLD JUNK TO YOU, BUT IT'S IMPORTANT TO ME.
YOUR MOM AND I ARE HEADING OUT, WE'LL SEE YOU TONIGHT.
HAVE FUN...

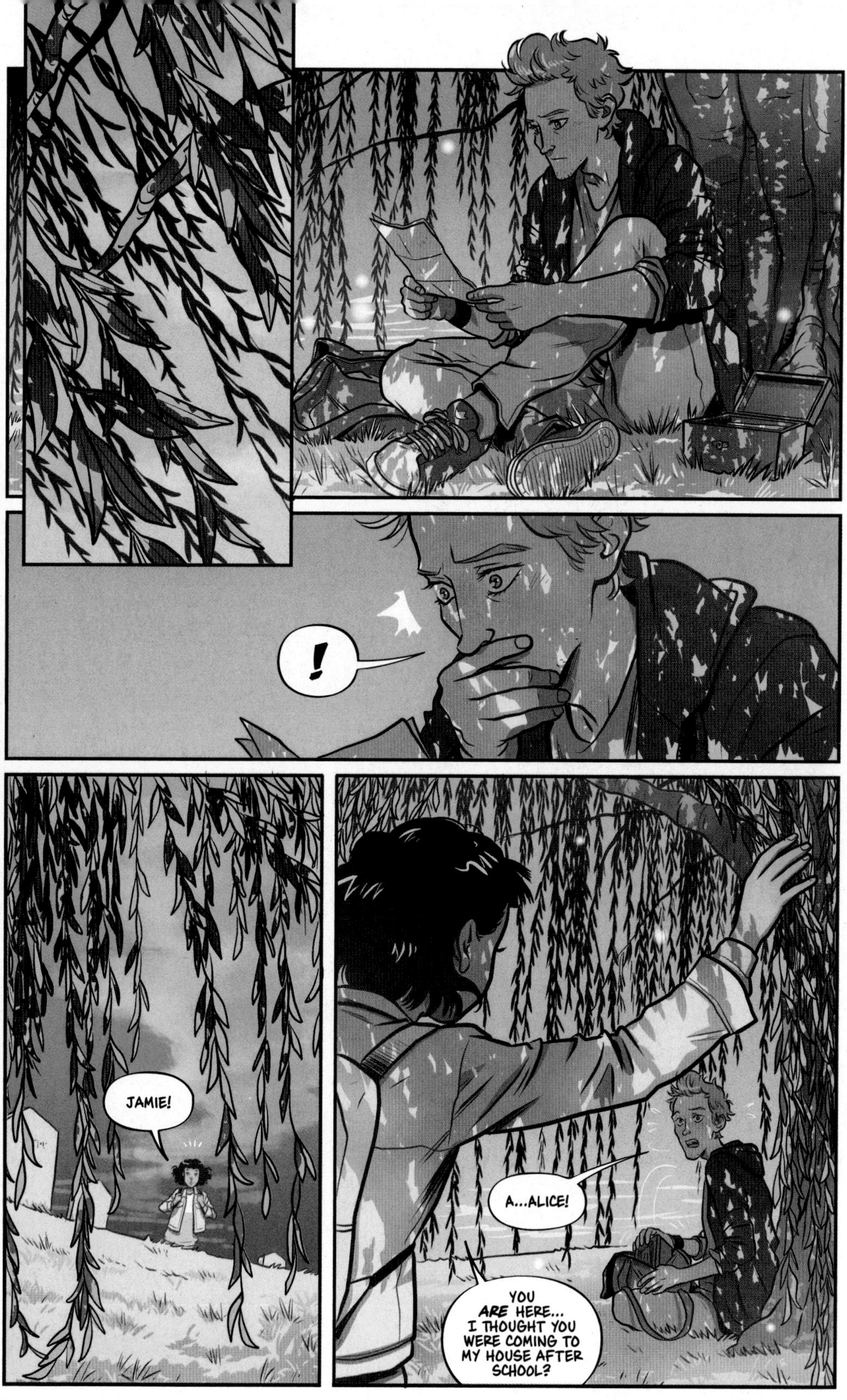
!
JAMIE!
A...ALICE!
YOU ARE HERE... I THOUGHT YOU WERE COMING TO MY HOUSE AFTER SCHOOL?

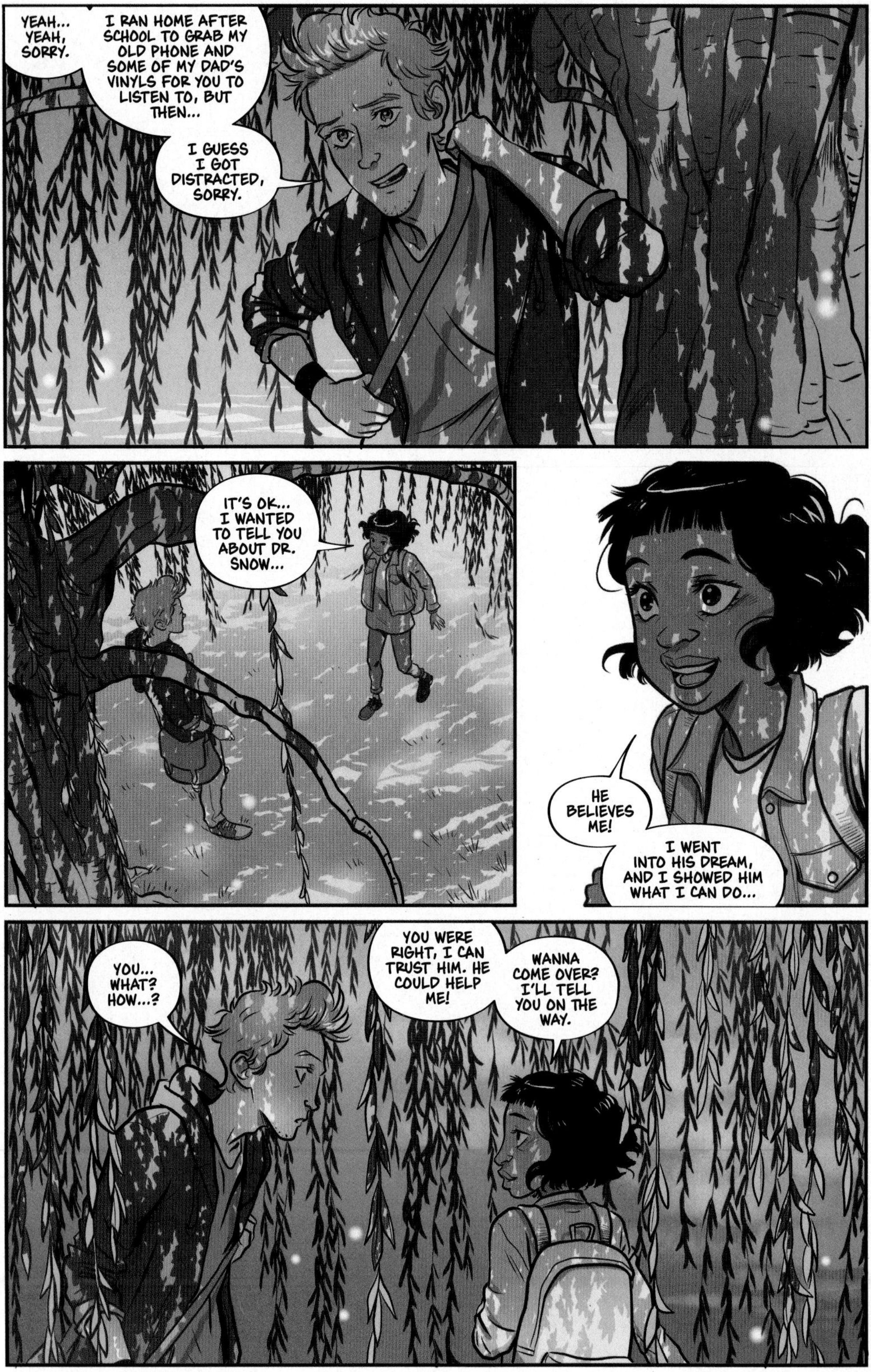
YEAH... YEAH, SORRY.
I RAN HOME AFTER SCHOOL TO GRAB MY OLD PHONE AND SOME OF MY DAD'S VINYLS FOR YOU TO LISTEN TO, BUT THEN...
I GUESS I GOT DISTRACTED, SORRY.
IT'S OK... I WANTED TO TELL YOU ABOUT DR. SNOW...
HE BELIEVES ME!
I WENT INTO HIS DREAM, AND I SHOWED HIM WHAT I CAN DO...
YOU... WHAT? HOW...?
YOU WERE RIGHT, I CAN TRUST HIM. HE COULD HELP ME!
WANNA COME OVER? I'LL TELL YOU ON THE WAY.

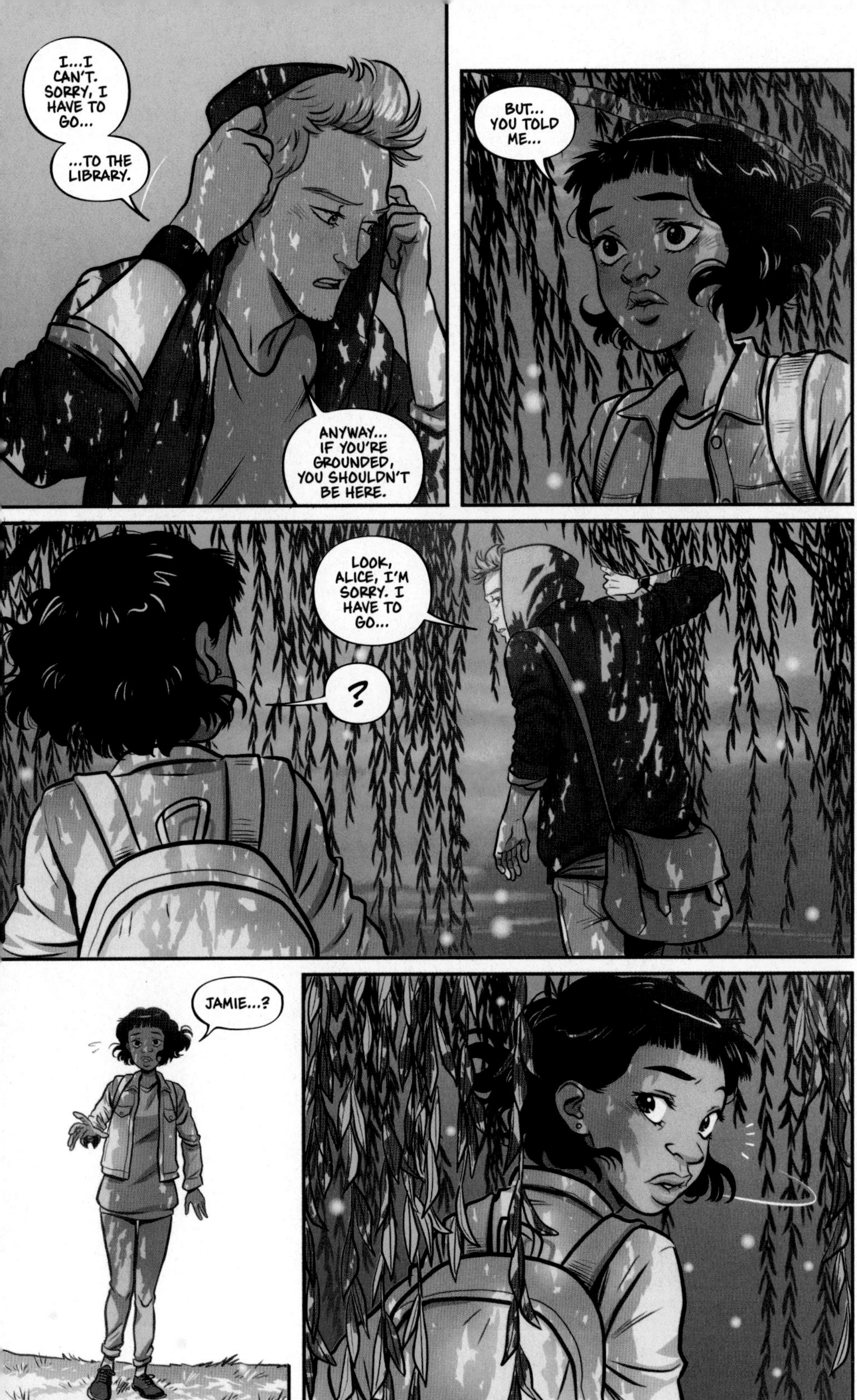
I...I CAN'T. SORRY, I HAVE TO GO...
...TO THE LIBRARY.
ANYWAY... IF YOU'RE GROUNDED, YOU SHOULDN'T BE HERE.
BUT... YOU TOLD ME...
LOOK, ALICE, I'M SORRY. I HAVE TO GO...
?
JAMIE...?

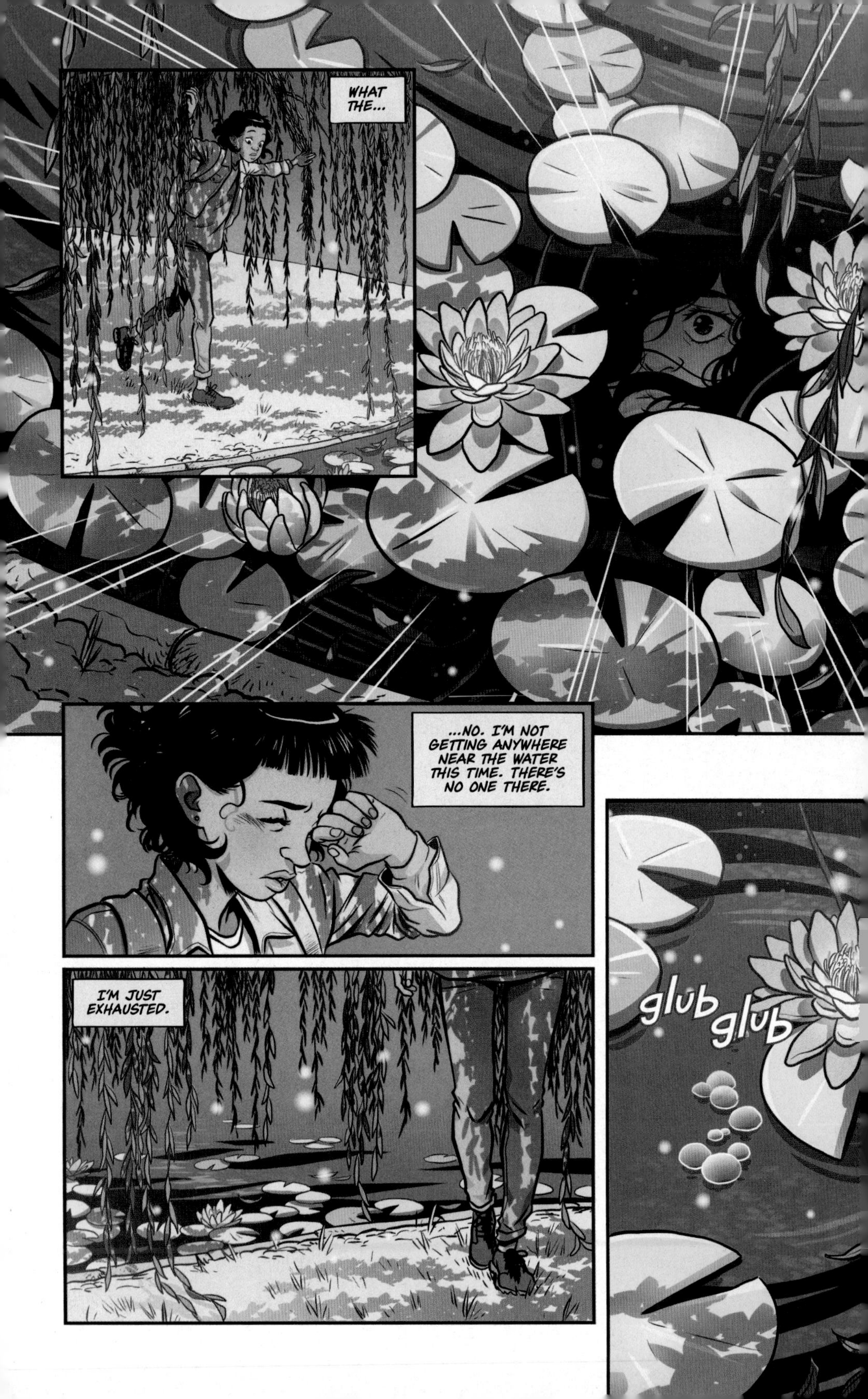
WHAT THE...
...NO. I'M NOT GETTING ANYWHERE NEAR THE WATER THIS TIME. THERE'S NO ONE THERE.
I'M JUST EXHAUSTED.
glub glub

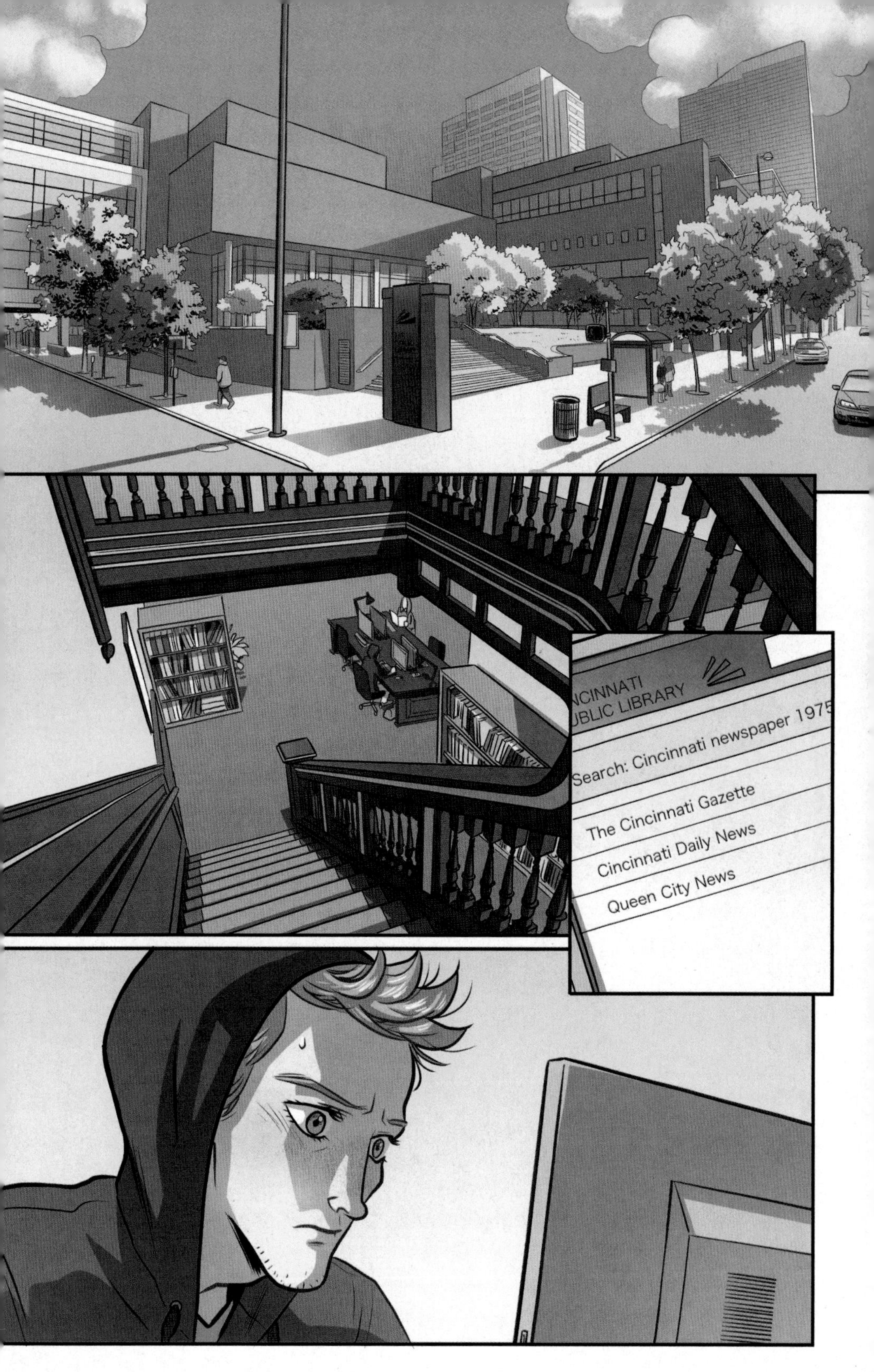
NCINNATI
UBLIC LIBRARY
Search: Cincinnati newspaper 1975
The Cincinnati Gazette
Cincinnati Daily News
Queen City News

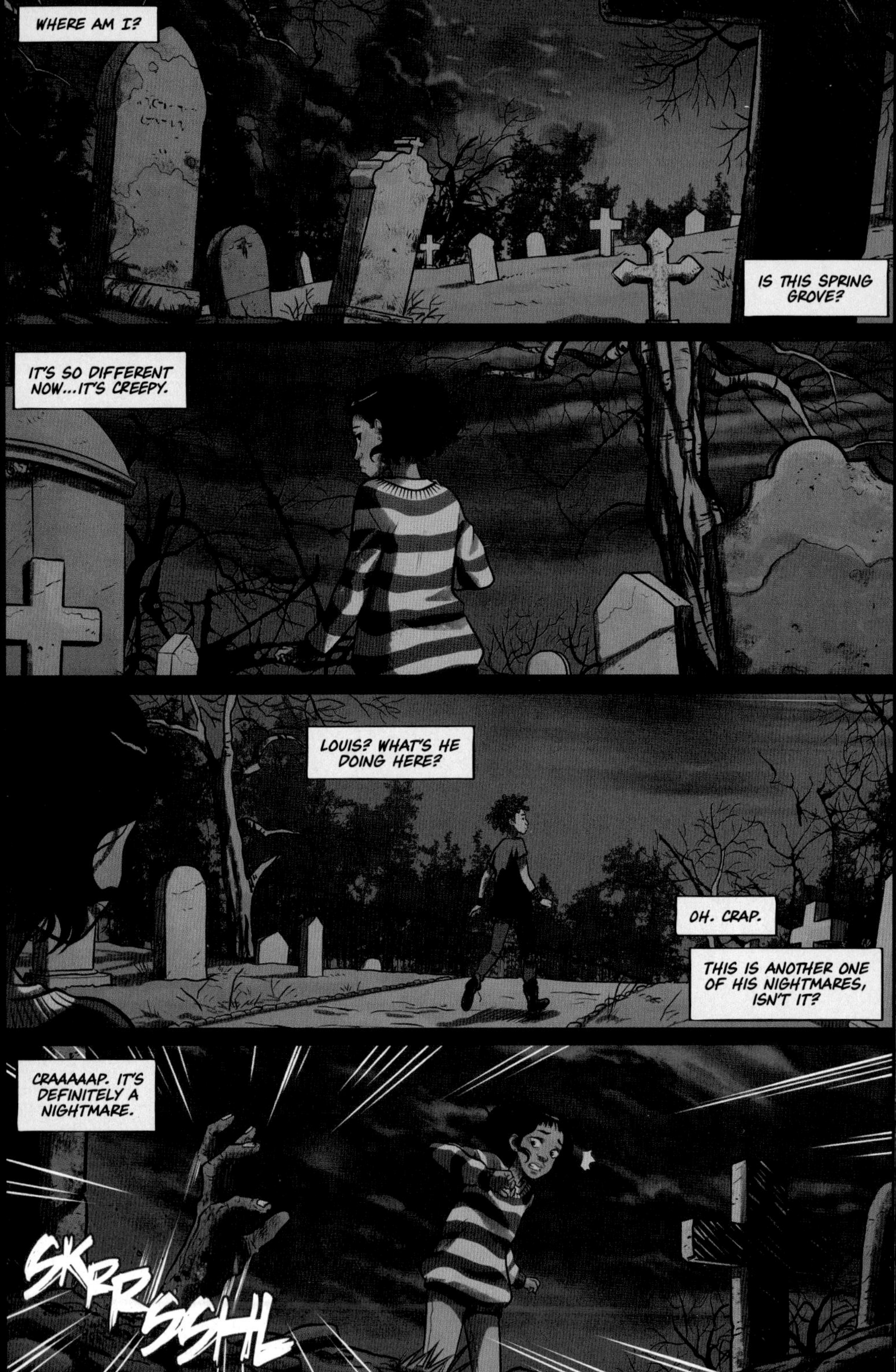
WHERE AM I?
IS THIS SPRING GROVE?
IT'S SO DIFFERENT NOW...IT'S CREEPY.
LOUIS? WHAT'S HE DOING HERE?
OH. CRAP.
THIS IS ANOTHER ONE OF HIS NIGHTMARES, ISN'T IT?
CRAAAAAP. IT'S DEFINITELY A NIGHTMARE.
SKRRSSHL

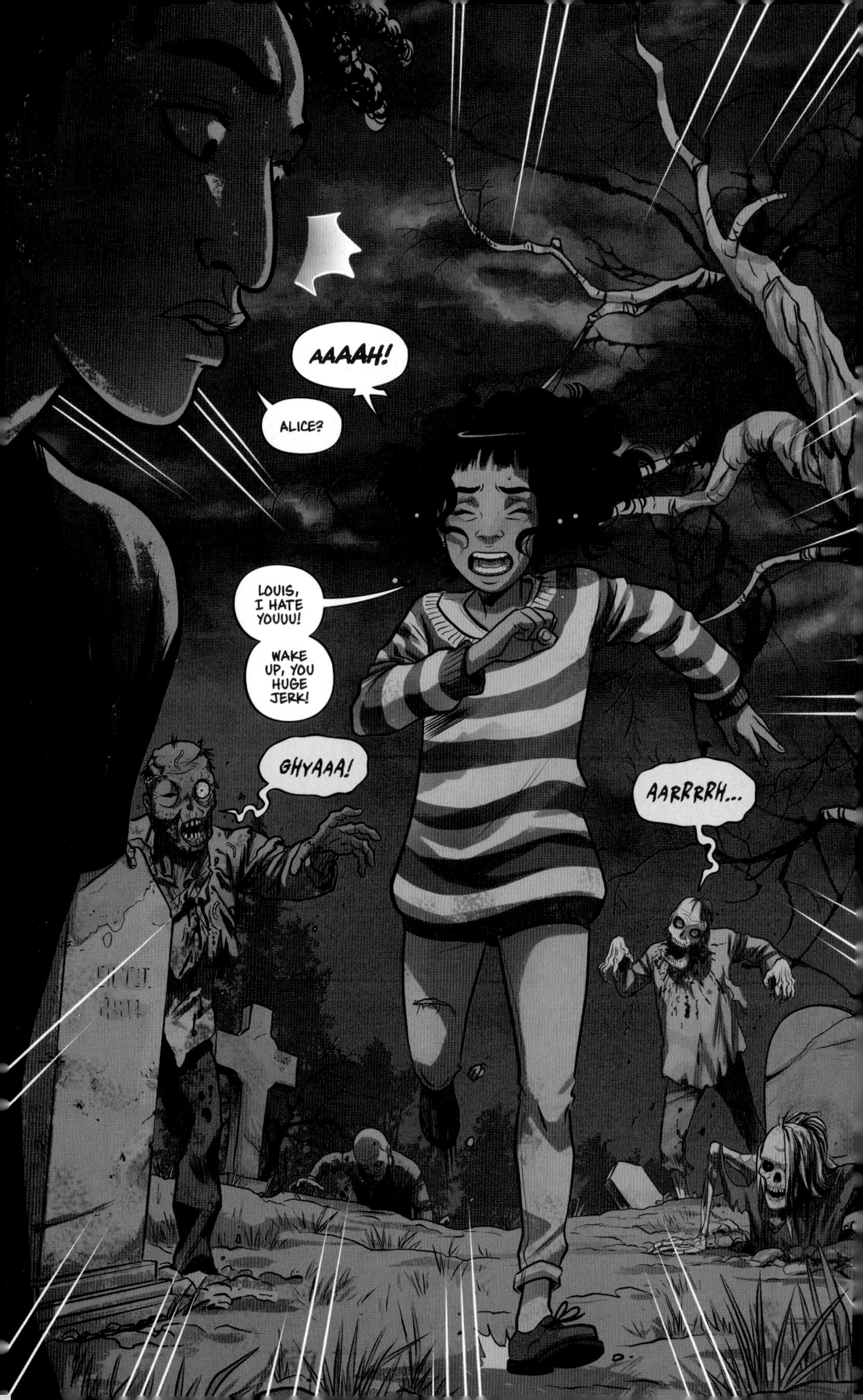
AAAAH!
ALICE?
LOUIS, I HATE YOUUU!
WAKE UP, YOU HUGE JERK!
GHYAAA!
AARRRRH...

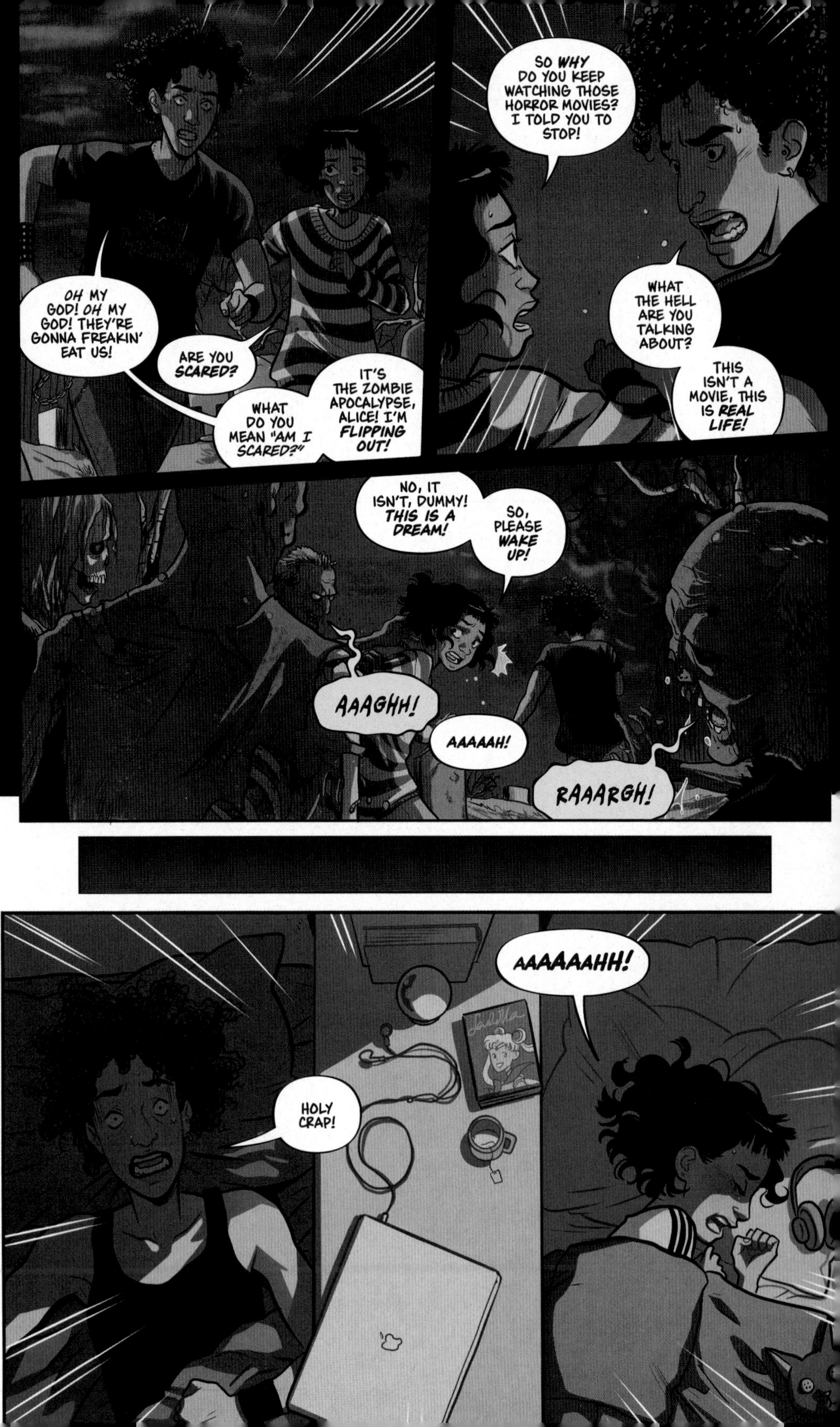

OH MY GOD! OH MY GOD! THEY'RE GONNA FREAKIN' EAT US!
ARE YOU SCARED?
WHAT DO YOU MEAN "AM I SCARED?"
IT'S THE ZOMBIE APOCALYPSE, ALICE! I'M FLIPPING OUT!
SO WHY DO YOU KEEP WATCHING THOSE HORROR MOVIES? I TOLD YOU TO STOP!
WHAT THE HELL ARE YOU TALKING ABOUT?
THIS ISN'T A MOVIE, THIS IS REAL LIFE!
NO, IT ISN'T, DUMMY! THIS IS A DREAM!
SO, PLEASE WAKE UP!
AAAGHH!
AAAAAH!
RAAARGH!
AAAAAAHH!
HOLY CRAP!

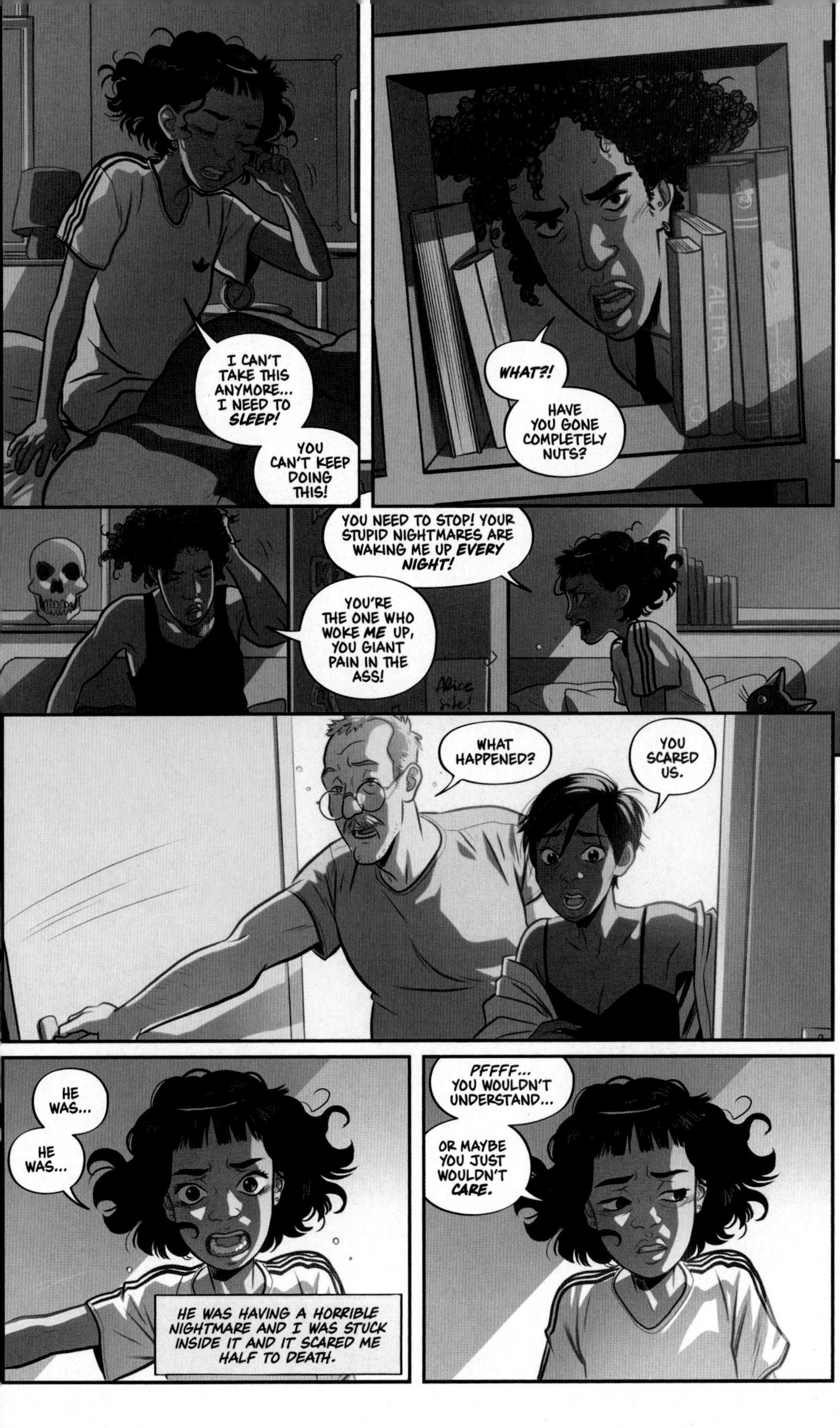
I CAN'T TAKE THIS ANYMORE... I NEED TO *SLEEP!*
YOU CAN'T KEEP DOING THIS!
*WHAT?!*
HAVE YOU GONE COMPLETELY NUTS?
YOU NEED TO STOP! YOUR STUPID NIGHTMARES ARE WAKING ME UP *EVERY NIGHT!*
YOU'RE THE ONE WHO WOKE *ME* UP, YOU GIANT PAIN IN THE ASS!
Alice side!
WHAT HAPPENED?
YOU SCARED US.
HE WAS...
HE WAS...
HE WAS HAVING A HORRIBLE NIGHTMARE AND I WAS STUCK INSIDE IT AND IT SCARED ME HALF TO DEATH.
PFFFF... YOU WOULDN'T UNDERSTAND...
OR MAYBE YOU JUST WOULDN'T *CARE.*

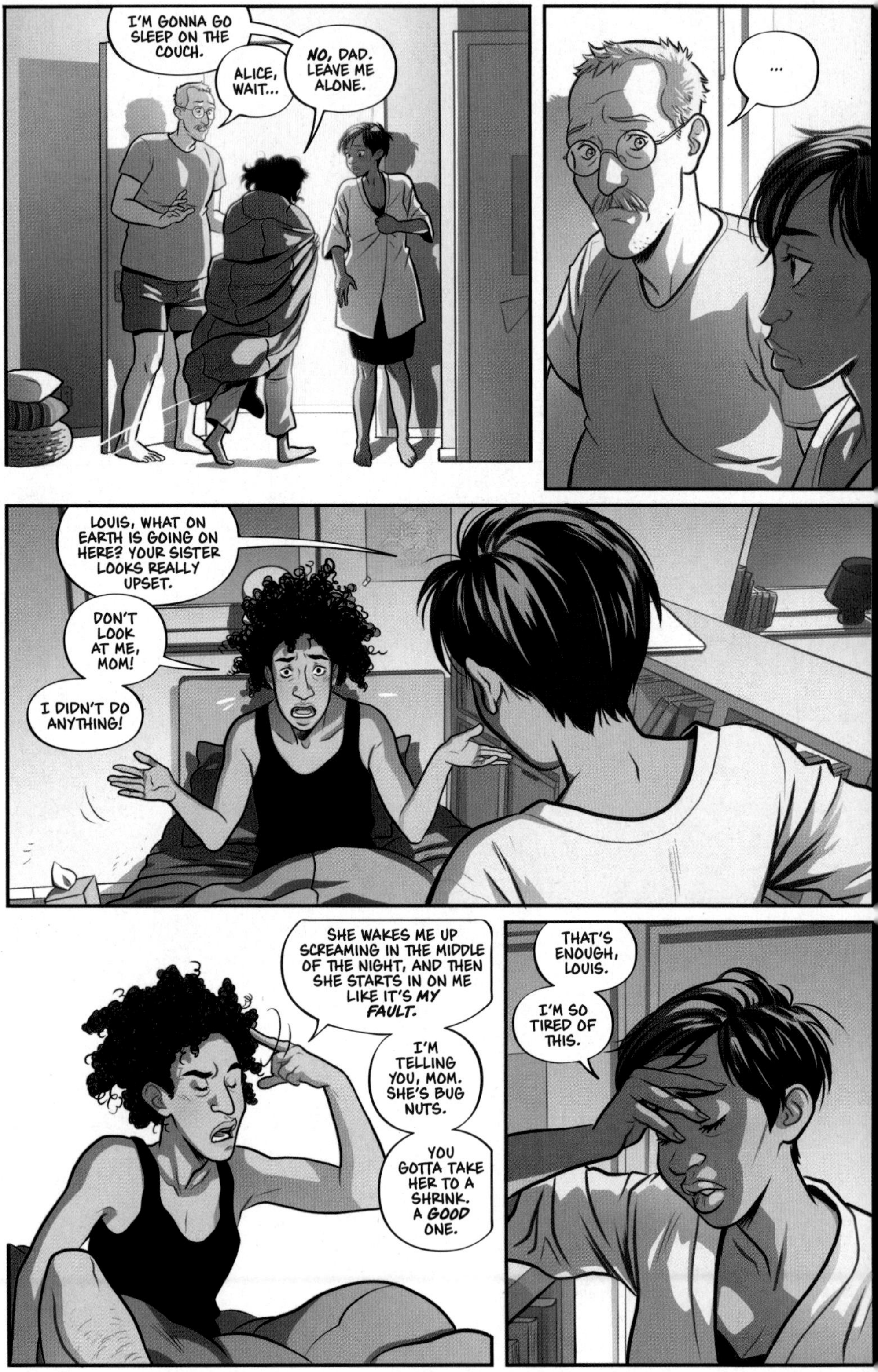
I'M GONNA GO SLEEP ON THE COUCH.
ALICE, WAIT...
NO, DAD. LEAVE ME ALONE.
...
LOUIS, WHAT ON EARTH IS GOING ON HERE? YOUR SISTER LOOKS REALLY UPSET.
DON'T LOOK AT ME, MOM!
I DIDN'T DO ANYTHING!
SHE WAKES ME UP SCREAMING IN THE MIDDLE OF THE NIGHT, AND THEN SHE STARTS IN ON ME LIKE IT'S MY FAULT.
I'M TELLING YOU, MOM. SHE'S BUG NUTS.
YOU GOTTA TAKE HER TO A SHRINK. A GOOD ONE.
THAT'S ENOUGH, LOUIS.
I'M SO TIRED OF THIS.

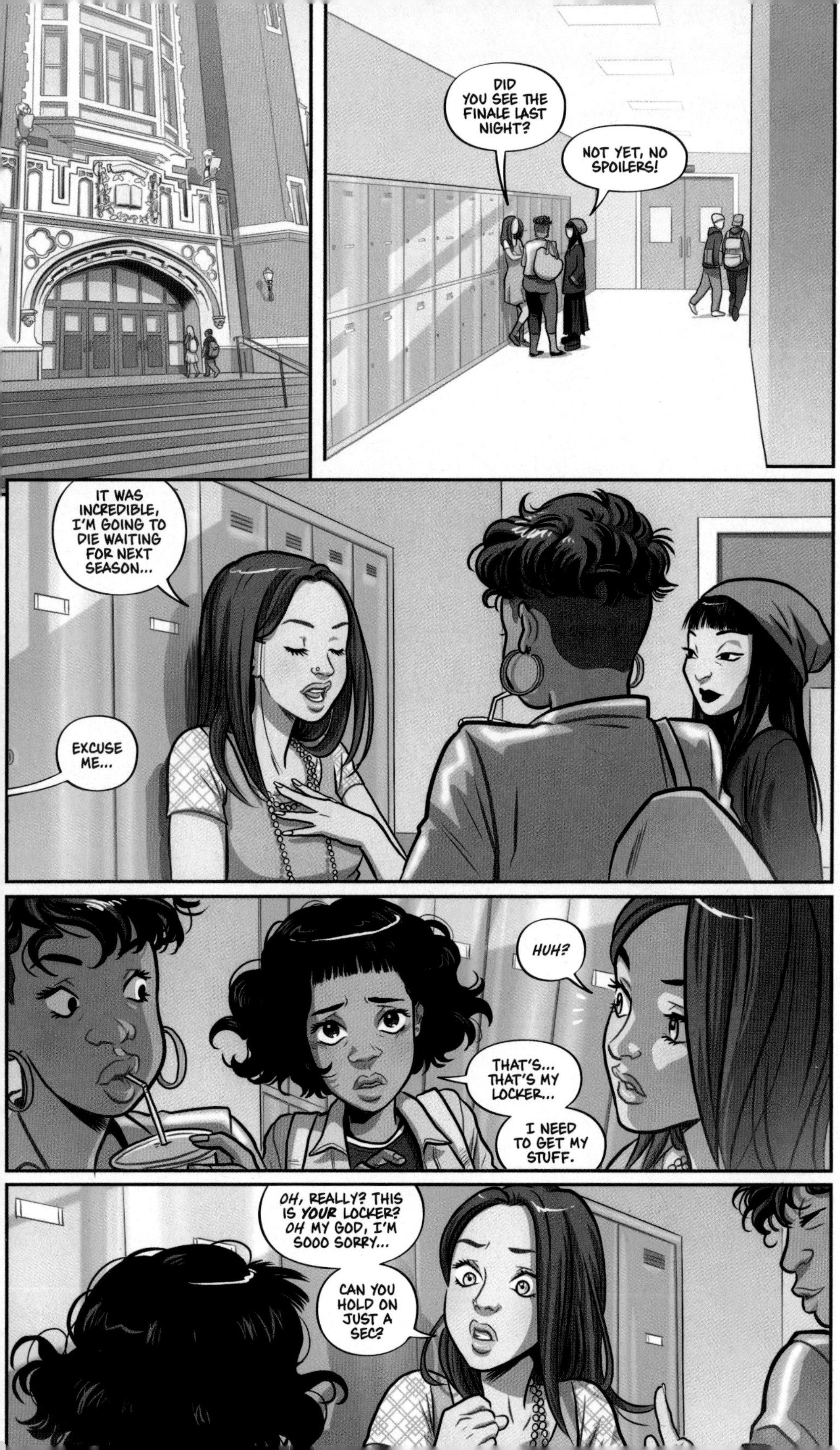

DID YOU SEE THE FINALE LAST NIGHT?
NOT YET, NO SPOILERS!
IT WAS INCREDIBLE, I'M GOING TO DIE WAITING FOR NEXT SEASON...
EXCUSE ME...
HUH?
THAT'S... THAT'S MY LOCKER...
I NEED TO GET MY STUFF.
OH, REALLY? THIS IS YOUR LOCKER? OH MY GOD, I'M SOOO SORRY...
CAN YOU HOLD ON JUST A SEC?

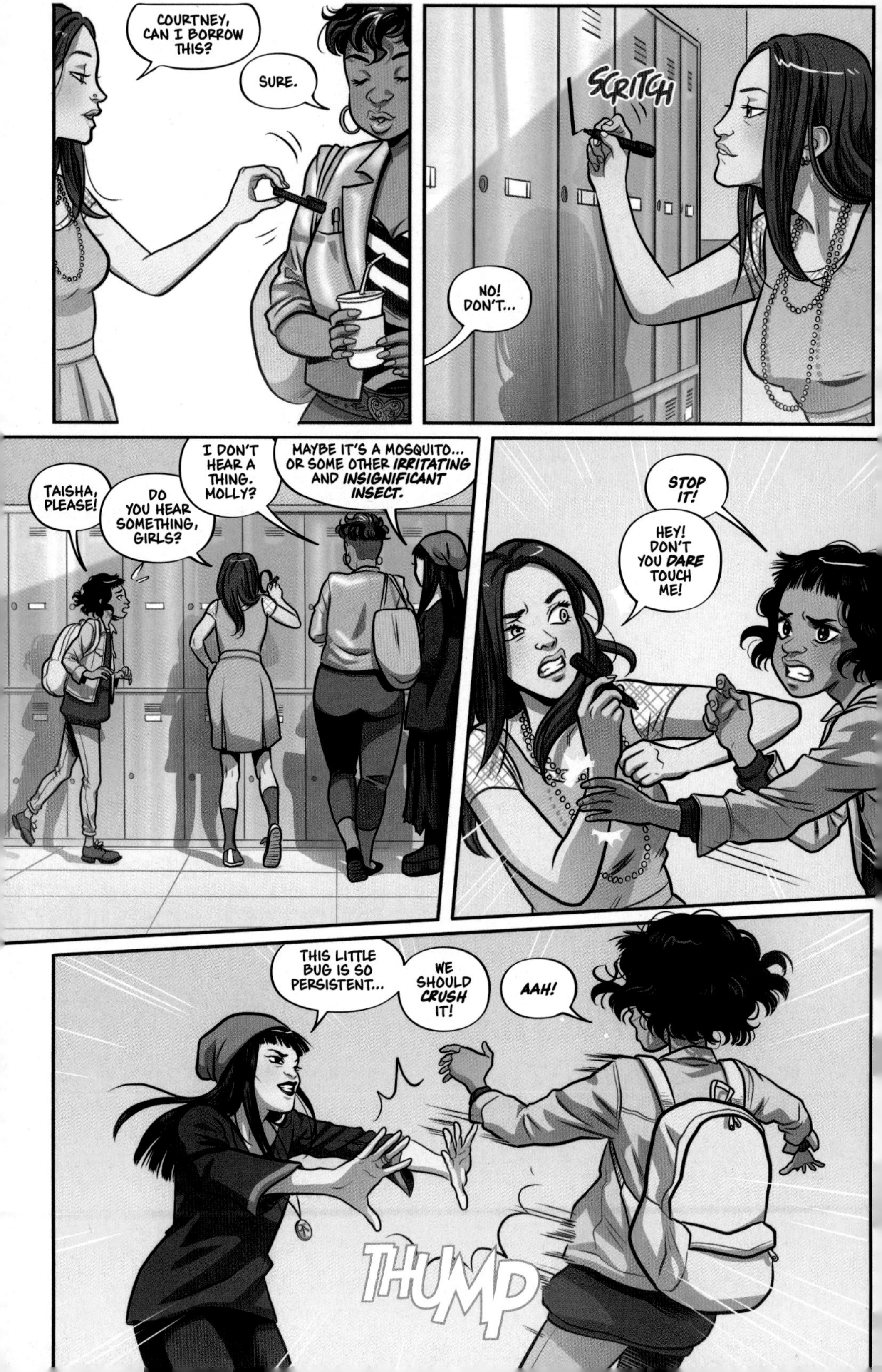
COURTNEY, CAN I BORROW THIS?
SURE.
SCRITCH
NO! DON'T...
TAISHA, PLEASE!
DO YOU HEAR SOMETHING, GIRLS?
I DON'T HEAR A THING. MOLLY?
MAYBE IT'S A MOSQUITO... OR SOME OTHER IRRITATING AND INSIGNIFICANT INSECT.
STOP IT!
HEY! DON'T YOU DARE TOUCH ME!
THIS LITTLE BUG IS SO PERSISTENT...
WE SHOULD CRUSH IT!
AAH!
THUMP

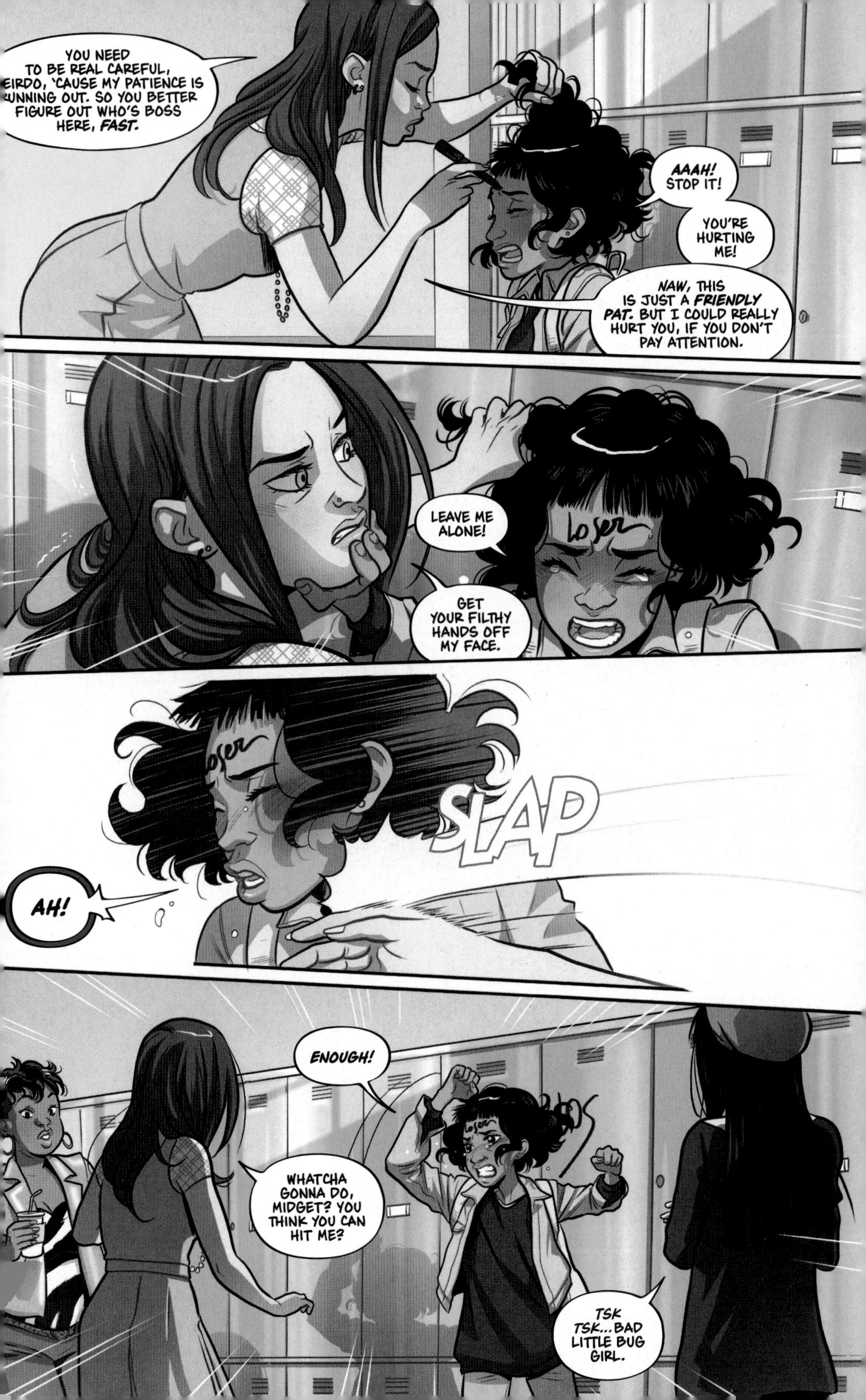
YOU NEED TO BE REAL CAREFUL, EIRDO, 'CAUSE MY PATIENCE IS UNNING OUT. SO YOU BETTER FIGURE OUT WHO'S BOSS HERE, FAST.
AAAH! STOP IT!
YOU'RE HURTING ME!
NAW, THIS IS JUST A FRIENDLY PAT. BUT I COULD REALLY HURT YOU, IF YOU DON'T PAY ATTENTION.
LEAVE ME ALONE!
loser
GET YOUR FILTHY HANDS OFF MY FACE.
loser
SLAP
AH!
ENOUGH!
WHATCHA GONNA DO, MIDGET? YOU THINK YOU CAN HIT ME?
TSK TSK...BAD LITTLE BUG GIRL.

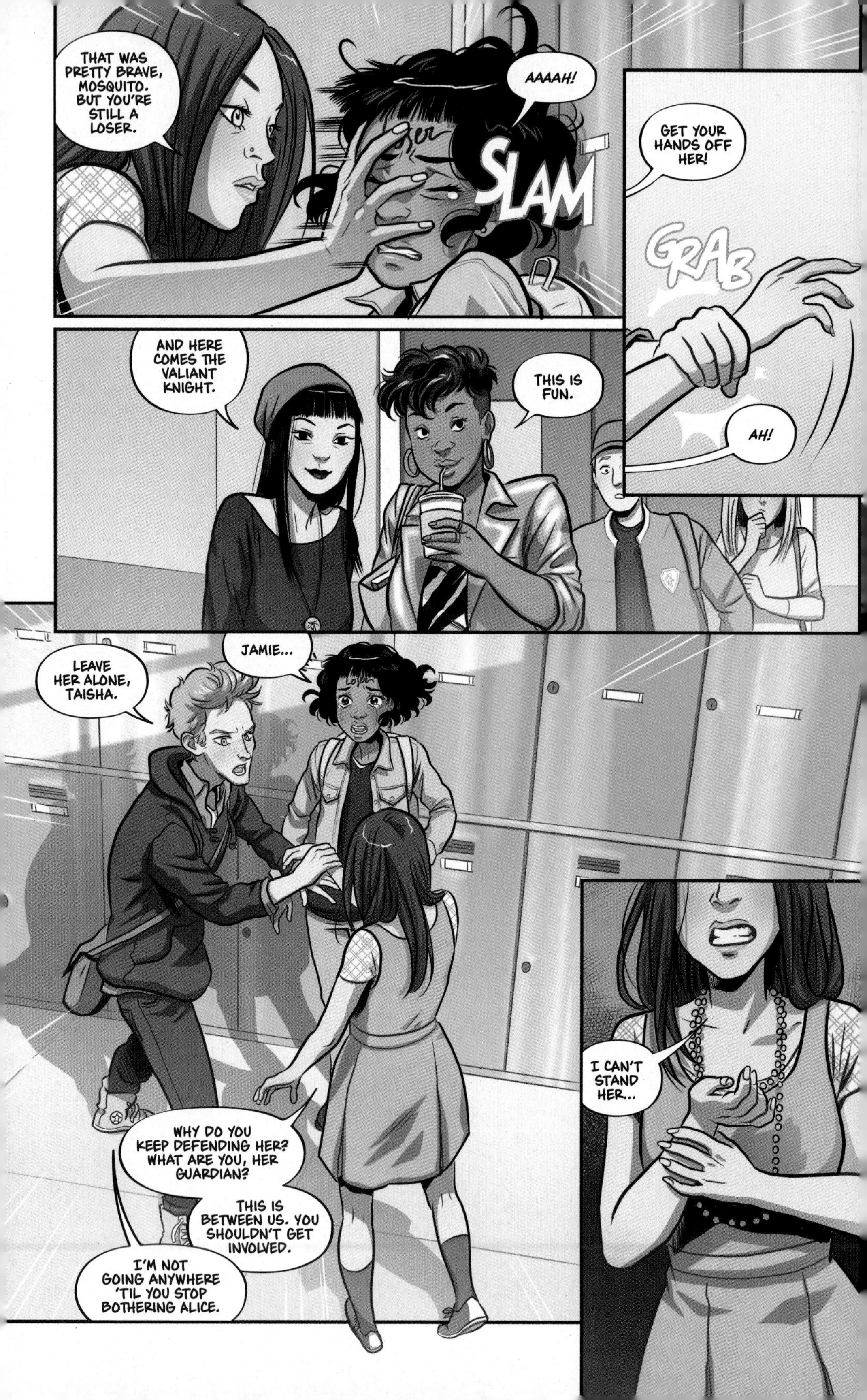
THAT WAS PRETTY BRAVE, MOSQUITO. BUT YOU'RE STILL A LOSER.
AAAAH!
SLAM
GET YOUR HANDS OFF HER!
GRAB
AH!
AND HERE COMES THE VALIANT KNIGHT.
THIS IS FUN.
LEAVE HER ALONE, TAISHA.
JAMIE...
WHY DO YOU KEEP DEFENDING HER? WHAT ARE YOU, HER GUARDIAN?
THIS IS BETWEEN US. YOU SHOULDN'T GET INVOLVED.
I'M NOT GOING ANYWHERE 'TIL YOU STOP BOTHERING ALICE.
I CAN'T STAND HER...

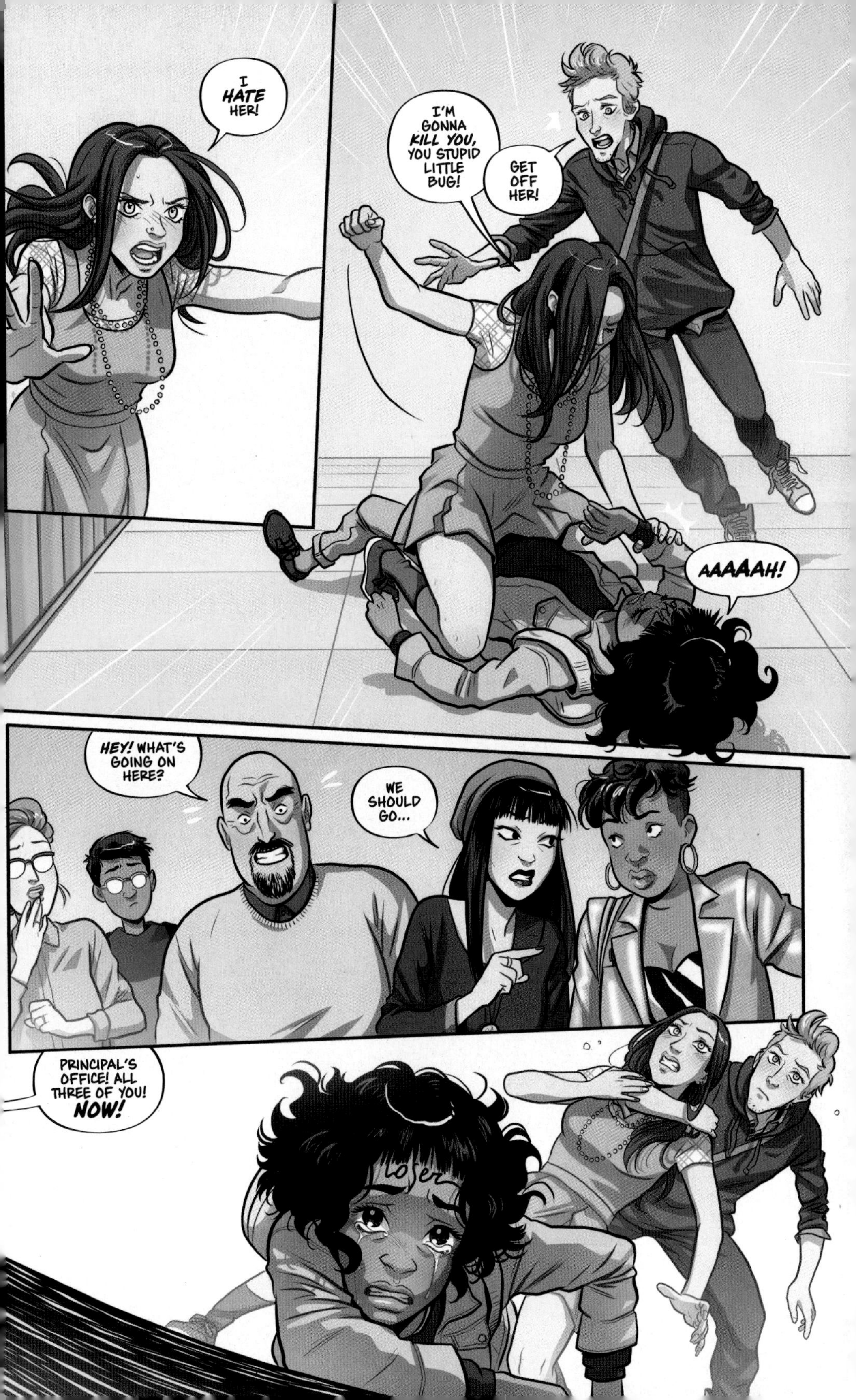
I HATE HER!
I'M GONNA KILL YOU, YOU STUPID LITTLE BUG!
GET OFF HER!
AAAAAH!
HEY! WHAT'S GOING ON HERE?
WE SHOULD GO...
PRINCIPAL'S OFFICE! ALL THREE OF YOU! NOW!
loser

TODAY SUCKS. THEY CALLED OUR PARENTS. JAMIE AND HIS DAD ARE INSIDE TALKING WITH THE PRINCIPAL. I HOPE HE DOESN'T GET IN TROUBLE BECAUSE OF ME.

MOM'S PISSED.

TAISHA!

WHAT HAPPENED? THEY CALLED ME AT WORK...

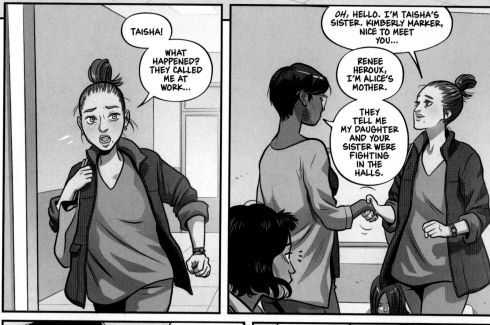

OH, HELLO. I'M TAISHA'S SISTER. KIMBERLY MARKER, NICE TO MEET YOU...

RENEE HEROUX, I'M ALICE'S MOTHER.

THEY TELL ME MY DAUGHTER AND YOUR SISTER WERE FIGHTING IN THE HALLS.

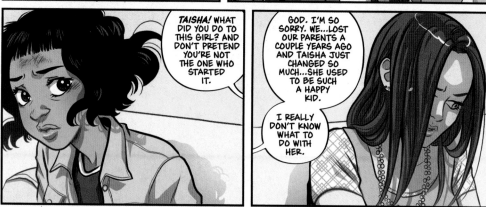

TAISHA! WHAT DID YOU DO TO THIS GIRL? AND DON'T PRETEND YOU'RE NOT THE ONE WHO STARTED IT.

GOD. I'M SO SORRY. WE...LOST OUR PARENTS A COUPLE YEARS AGO AND TAISHA JUST CHANGED SO MUCH...SHE USED TO BE SUCH A HAPPY KID.

I REALLY DON'T KNOW WHAT TO DO WITH HER.

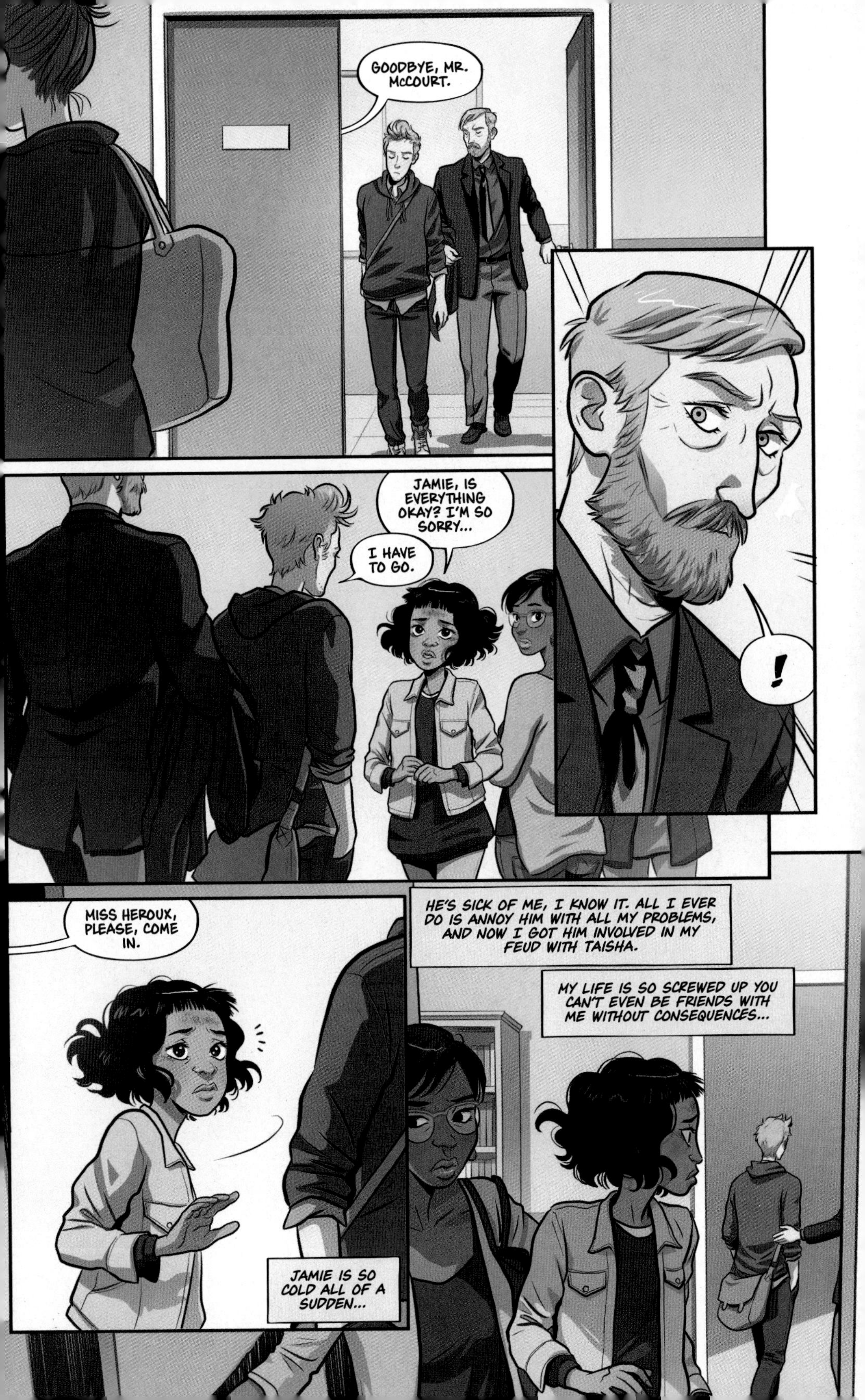
GOODBYE, MR. McCOURT.
!
JAMIE, IS EVERYTHING OKAY? I'M SO SORRY...
I HAVE TO GO.
MISS HEROUX, PLEASE, COME IN.
HE'S SICK OF ME, I KNOW IT. ALL I EVER DO IS ANNOY HIM WITH ALL MY PROBLEMS, AND NOW I GOT HIM INVOLVED IN MY FEUD WITH TAISHA.
MY LIFE IS SO SCREWED UP YOU CAN'T EVEN BE FRIENDS WITH ME WITHOUT CONSEQUENCES...
JAMIE IS SO COLD ALL OF A SUDDEN...

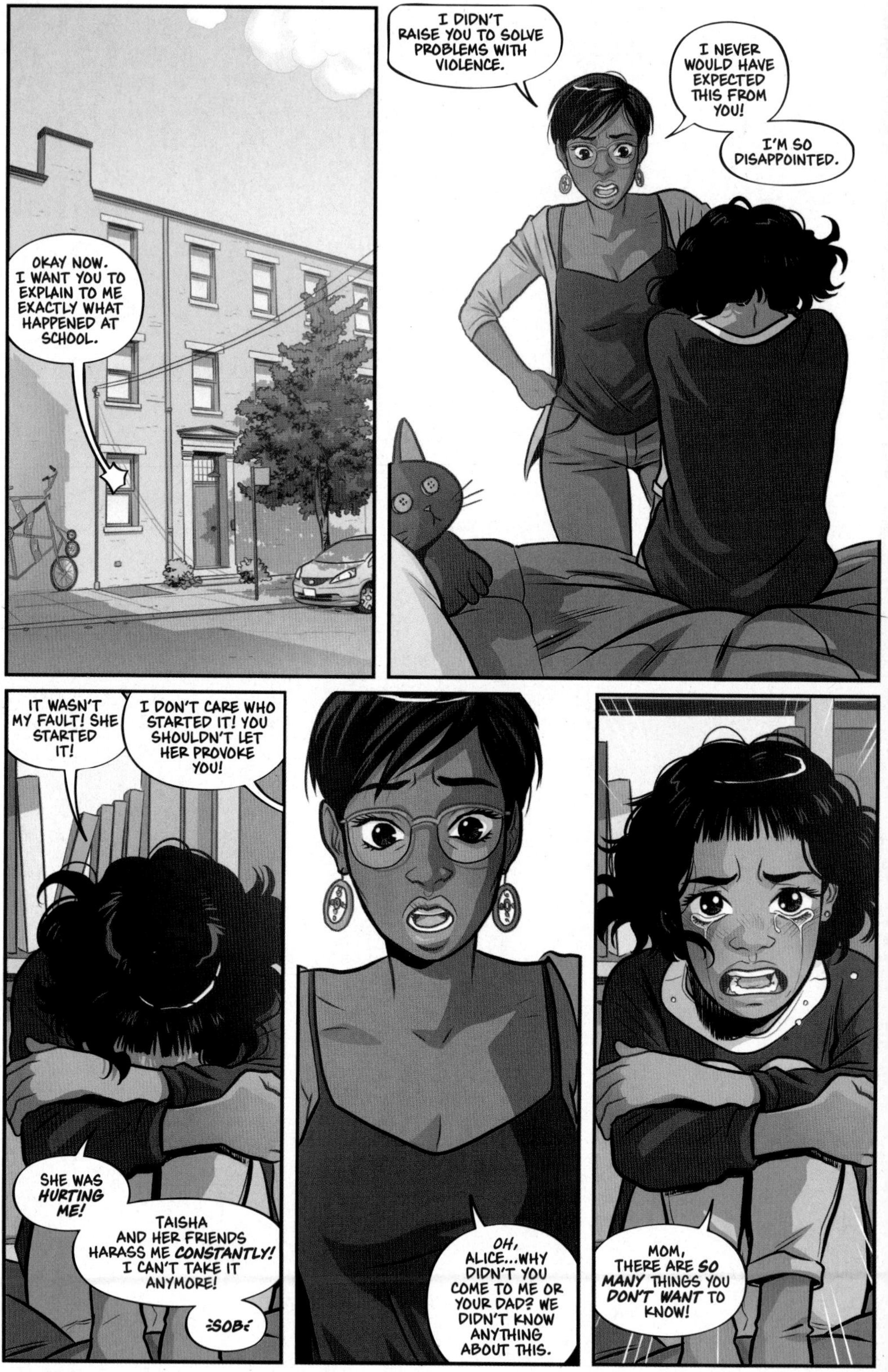
OKAY NOW. I WANT YOU TO EXPLAIN TO ME EXACTLY WHAT HAPPENED AT SCHOOL.
I DIDN'T RAISE YOU TO SOLVE PROBLEMS WITH VIOLENCE.
I NEVER WOULD HAVE EXPECTED THIS FROM YOU!
I'M SO DISAPPOINTED.
IT WASN'T MY FAULT! SHE STARTED IT!
I DON'T CARE WHO STARTED IT! YOU SHOULDN'T LET HER PROVOKE YOU!
SHE WAS *HURTING* *ME!*
TAISHA AND HER FRIENDS HARASS ME **CONSTANTLY!** I CAN'T TAKE IT ANYMORE!
SOB
*OH,* ALICE...WHY DIDN'T YOU COME TO ME OR YOUR DAD? WE DIDN'T KNOW ANYTHING ABOUT THIS.
MOM, THERE ARE ***SO MANY*** THINGS YOU ***DON'T WANT*** TO KNOW!

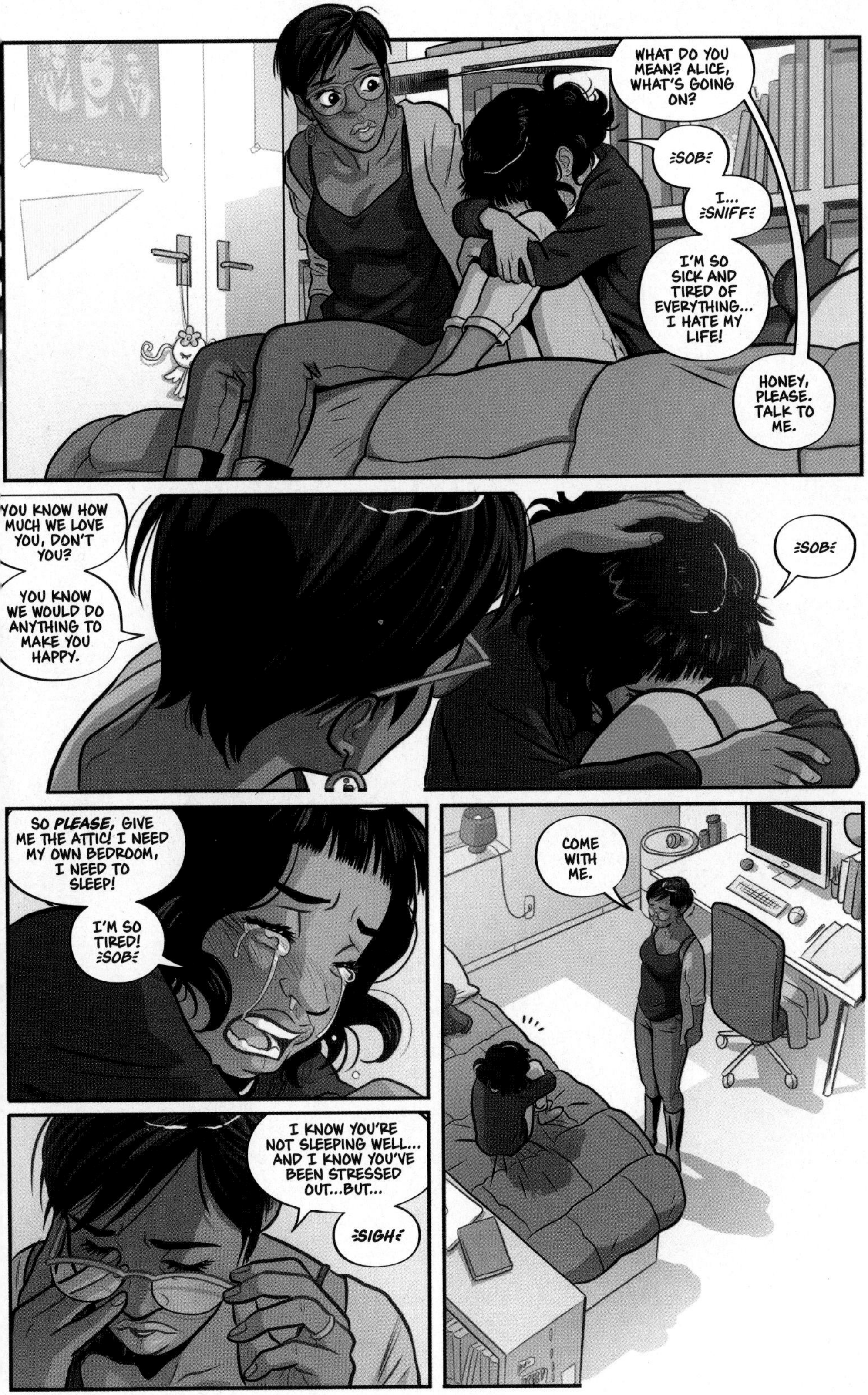
WHAT DO YOU MEAN? ALICE, WHAT'S GOING ON?
SOB
I... SNIFF
I'M SO SICK AND TIRED OF EVERYTHING... I HATE MY LIFE!
HONEY, PLEASE. TALK TO ME.
YOU KNOW HOW MUCH WE LOVE YOU, DON'T YOU?
YOU KNOW WE WOULD DO ANYTHING TO MAKE YOU HAPPY.
SOB
SO PLEASE, GIVE ME THE ATTIC! I NEED MY OWN BEDROOM, I NEED TO SLEEP!
I'M SO TIRED! SOB
I KNOW YOU'RE NOT SLEEPING WELL... AND I KNOW YOU'VE BEEN STRESSED OUT...BUT...
SIGH
COME WITH ME.

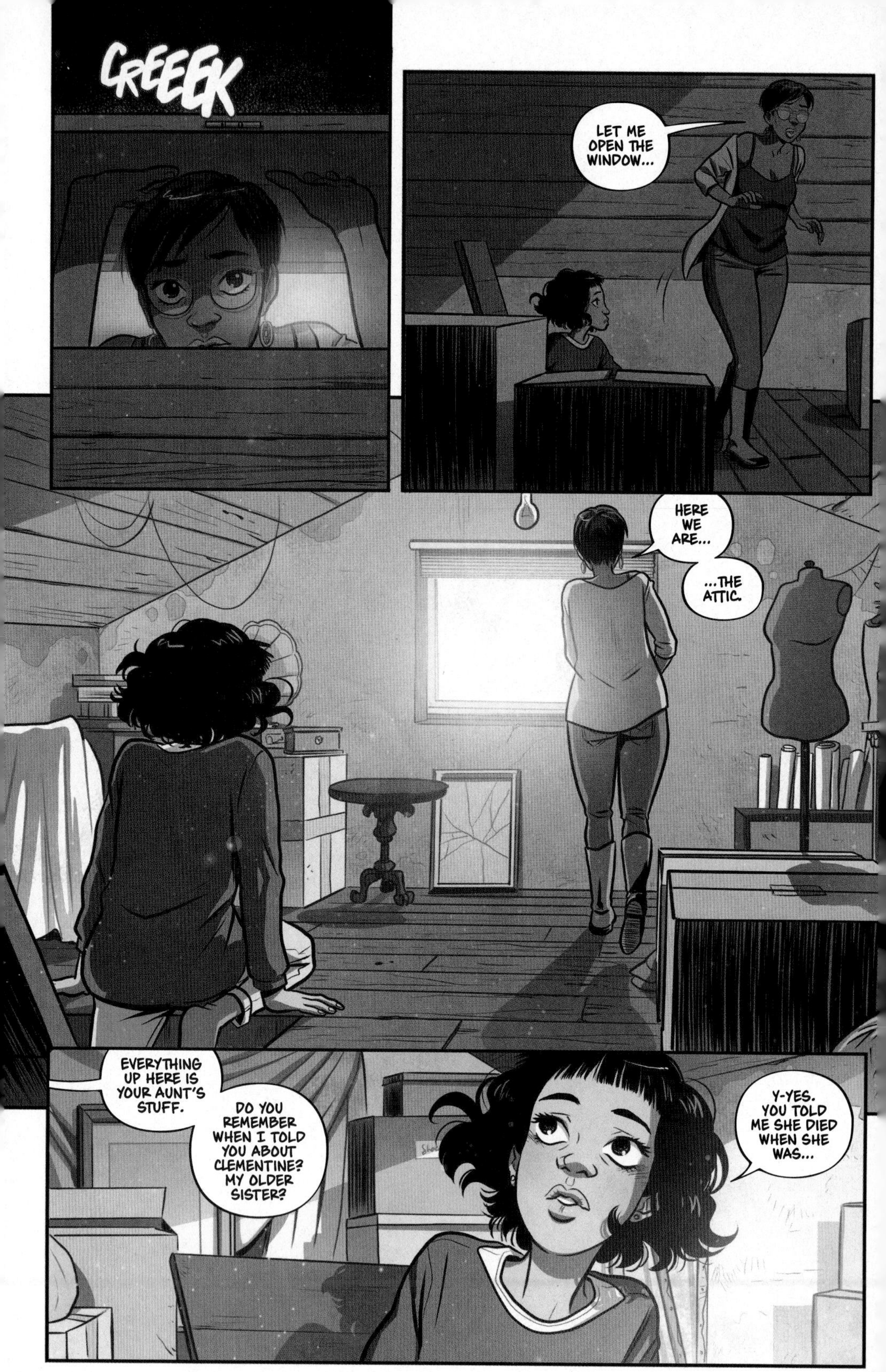
CREEEK
LET ME OPEN THE WINDOW...
HERE WE ARE...
...THE ATTIC.
EVERYTHING UP HERE IS YOUR AUNT'S STUFF.
DO YOU REMEMBER WHEN I TOLD YOU ABOUT CLEMENTINE? MY OLDER SISTER?
Y-YES. YOU TOLD ME SHE DIED WHEN SHE WAS...

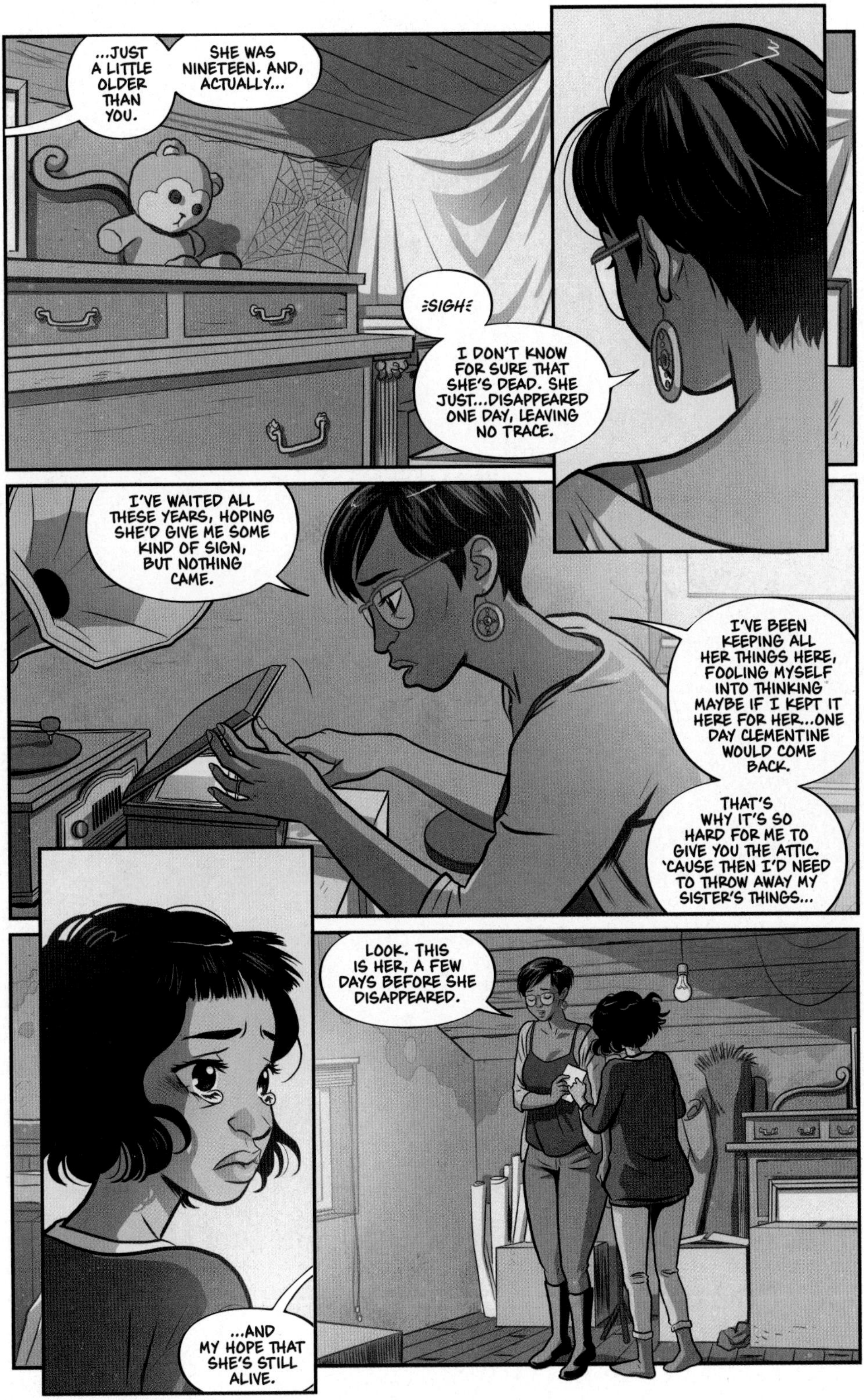
...JUST A LITTLE OLDER THAN YOU.
SHE WAS NINETEEN. AND, ACTUALLY...
SIGH
I DON'T KNOW FOR SURE THAT SHE'S DEAD. SHE JUST...DISAPPEARED ONE DAY, LEAVING NO TRACE.
I'VE WAITED ALL THESE YEARS, HOPING SHE'D GIVE ME SOME KIND OF SIGN, BUT NOTHING CAME.
I'VE BEEN KEEPING ALL HER THINGS HERE, FOOLING MYSELF INTO THINKING MAYBE IF I KEPT IT HERE FOR HER...ONE DAY CLEMENTINE WOULD COME BACK.
THAT'S WHY IT'S SO HARD FOR ME TO GIVE YOU THE ATTIC. 'CAUSE THEN I'D NEED TO THROW AWAY MY SISTER'S THINGS...
...AND MY HOPE THAT SHE'S STILL ALIVE.
LOOK. THIS IS HER, A FEW DAYS BEFORE SHE DISAPPEARED.

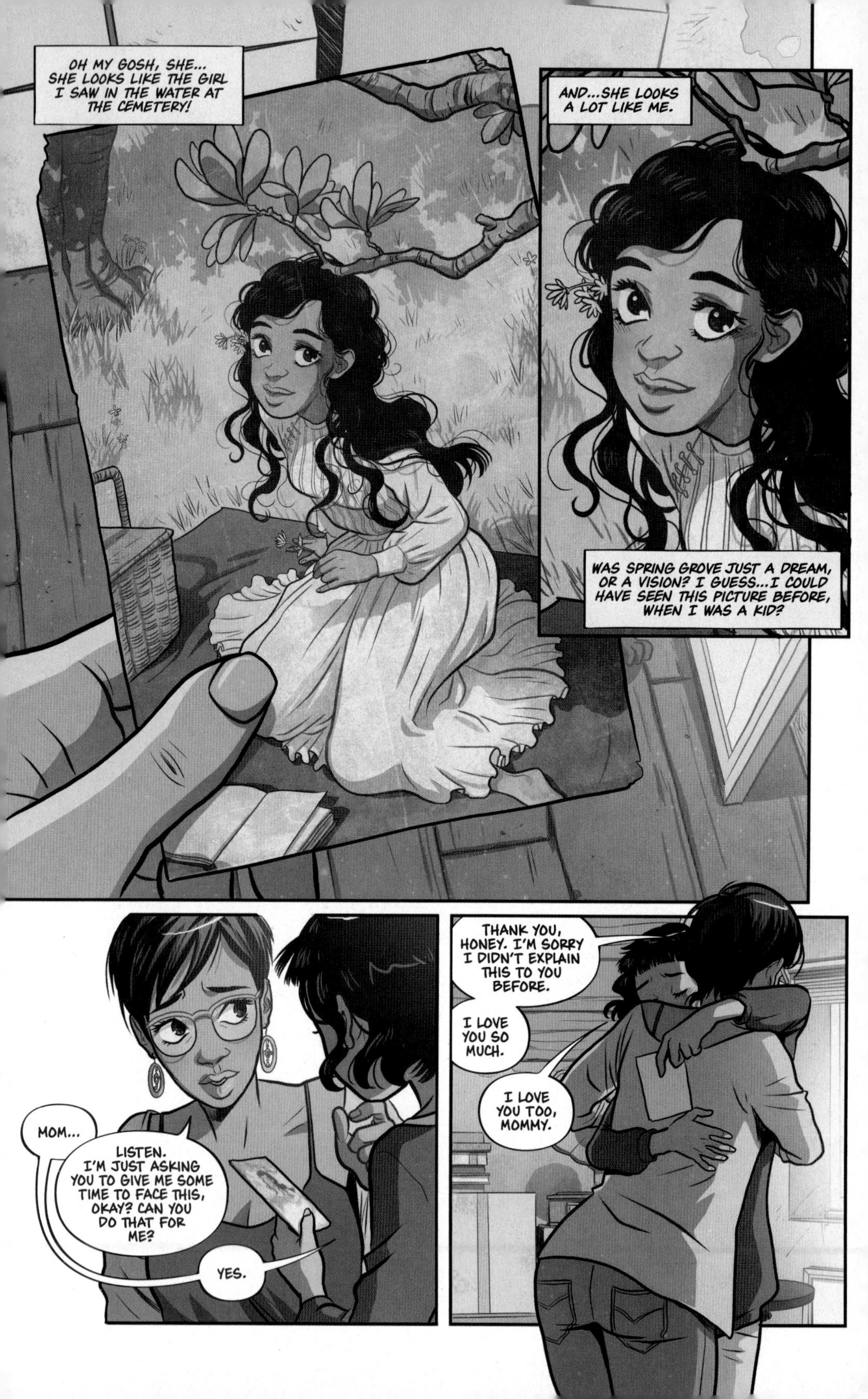
OH MY GOSH, SHE... SHE LOOKS LIKE THE GIRL I SAW IN THE WATER AT THE CEMETERY!
AND...SHE LOOKS A LOT LIKE ME.
WAS SPRING GROVE JUST A DREAM, OR A VISION? I GUESS...I COULD HAVE SEEN THIS PICTURE BEFORE, WHEN I WAS A KID?
MOM...
LISTEN. I'M JUST ASKING YOU TO GIVE ME SOME TIME TO FACE THIS, OKAY? CAN YOU DO THAT FOR ME?
YES.
THANK YOU, HONEY. I'M SORRY I DIDN'T EXPLAIN THIS TO YOU BEFORE.
I LOVE YOU SO MUCH.
I LOVE YOU TOO, MOMMY.

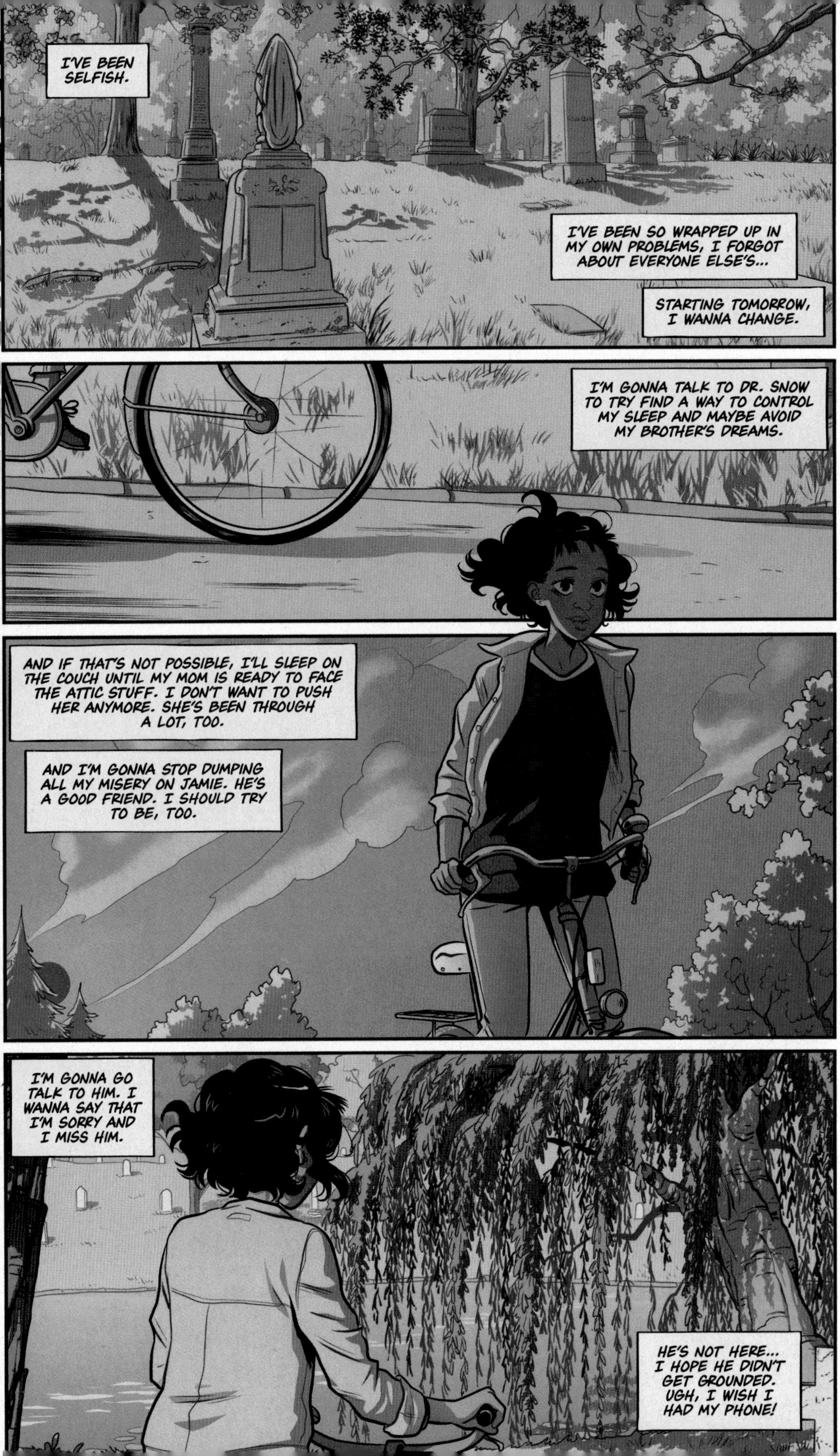
I'VE BEEN SELFISH.
I'VE BEEN SO WRAPPED UP IN MY OWN PROBLEMS, I FORGOT ABOUT EVERYONE ELSE'S...
STARTING TOMORROW, I WANNA CHANGE.
I'M GONNA TALK TO DR. SNOW TO TRY FIND A WAY TO CONTROL MY SLEEP AND MAYBE AVOID MY BROTHER'S DREAMS.
AND IF THAT'S NOT POSSIBLE, I'LL SLEEP ON THE COUCH UNTIL MY MOM IS READY TO FACE THE ATTIC STUFF. I DON'T WANT TO PUSH HER ANYMORE. SHE'S BEEN THROUGH A LOT, TOO.
AND I'M GONNA STOP DUMPING ALL MY MISERY ON JAMIE. HE'S A GOOD FRIEND. I SHOULD TRY TO BE, TOO.
I'M GONNA GO TALK TO HIM. I WANNA SAY THAT I'M SORRY AND I MISS HIM.
HE'S NOT HERE... I HOPE HE DIDN'T GET GROUNDED. UGH, I WISH I HAD MY PHONE!

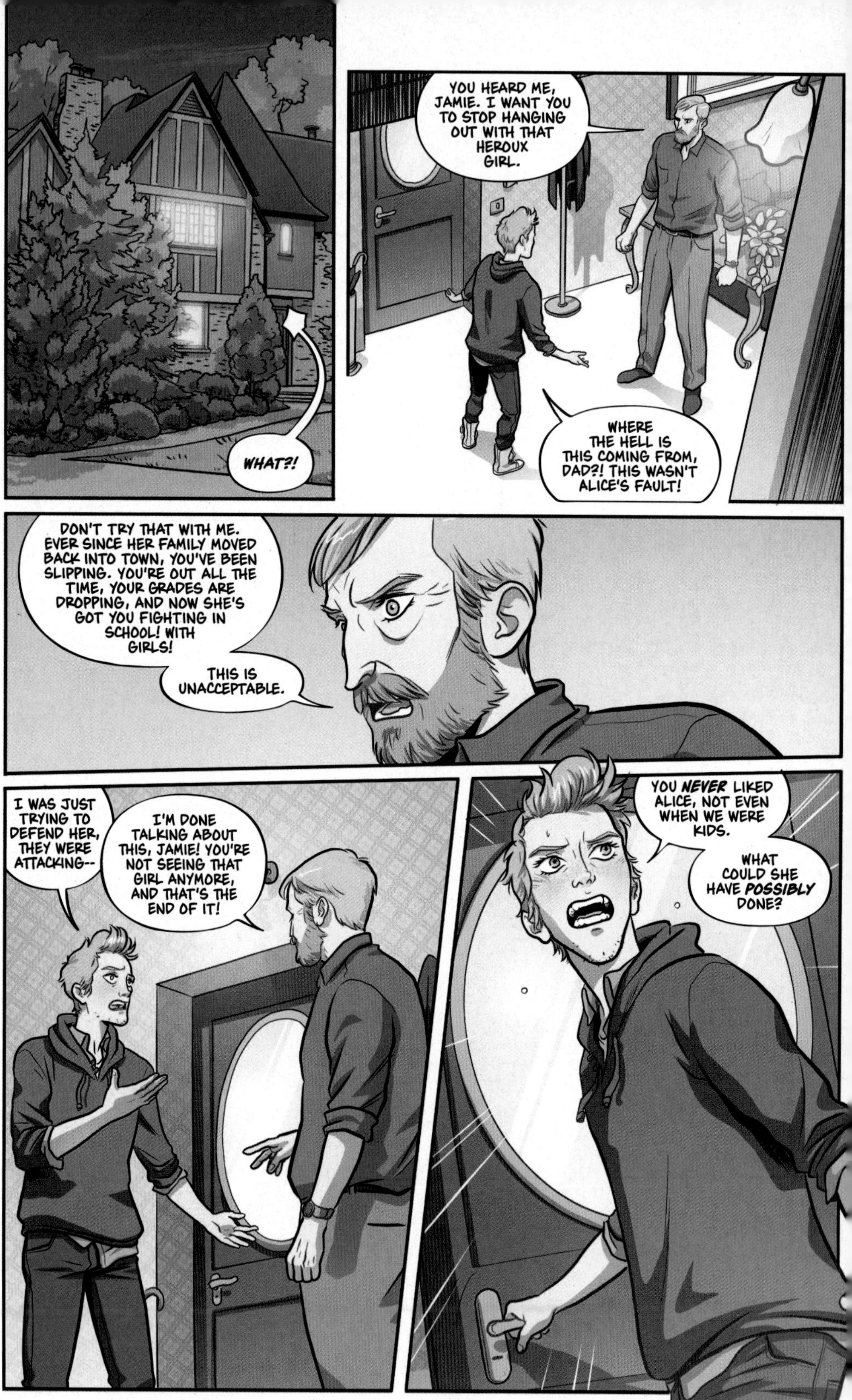
WHAT?!
YOU HEARD ME, JAMIE. I WANT YOU TO STOP HANGING OUT WITH THAT HEROUX GIRL.
WHERE THE HELL IS THIS COMING FROM, DAD?! THIS WASN'T ALICE'S FAULT!
DON'T TRY THAT WITH ME. EVER SINCE HER FAMILY MOVED BACK INTO TOWN, YOU'VE BEEN SLIPPING. YOU'RE OUT ALL THE TIME, YOUR GRADES ARE DROPPING, AND NOW SHE'S GOT YOU FIGHTING IN SCHOOL! WITH GIRLS!
THIS IS UNACCEPTABLE.
I WAS JUST TRYING TO DEFEND HER, THEY WERE ATTACKING--
I'M DONE TALKING ABOUT THIS, JAMIE! YOU'RE NOT SEEING THAT GIRL ANYMORE, AND THAT'S THE END OF IT!
YOU NEVER LIKED ALICE, NOT EVEN WHEN WE WERE KIDS.
WHAT COULD SHE HAVE POSSIBLY DONE?

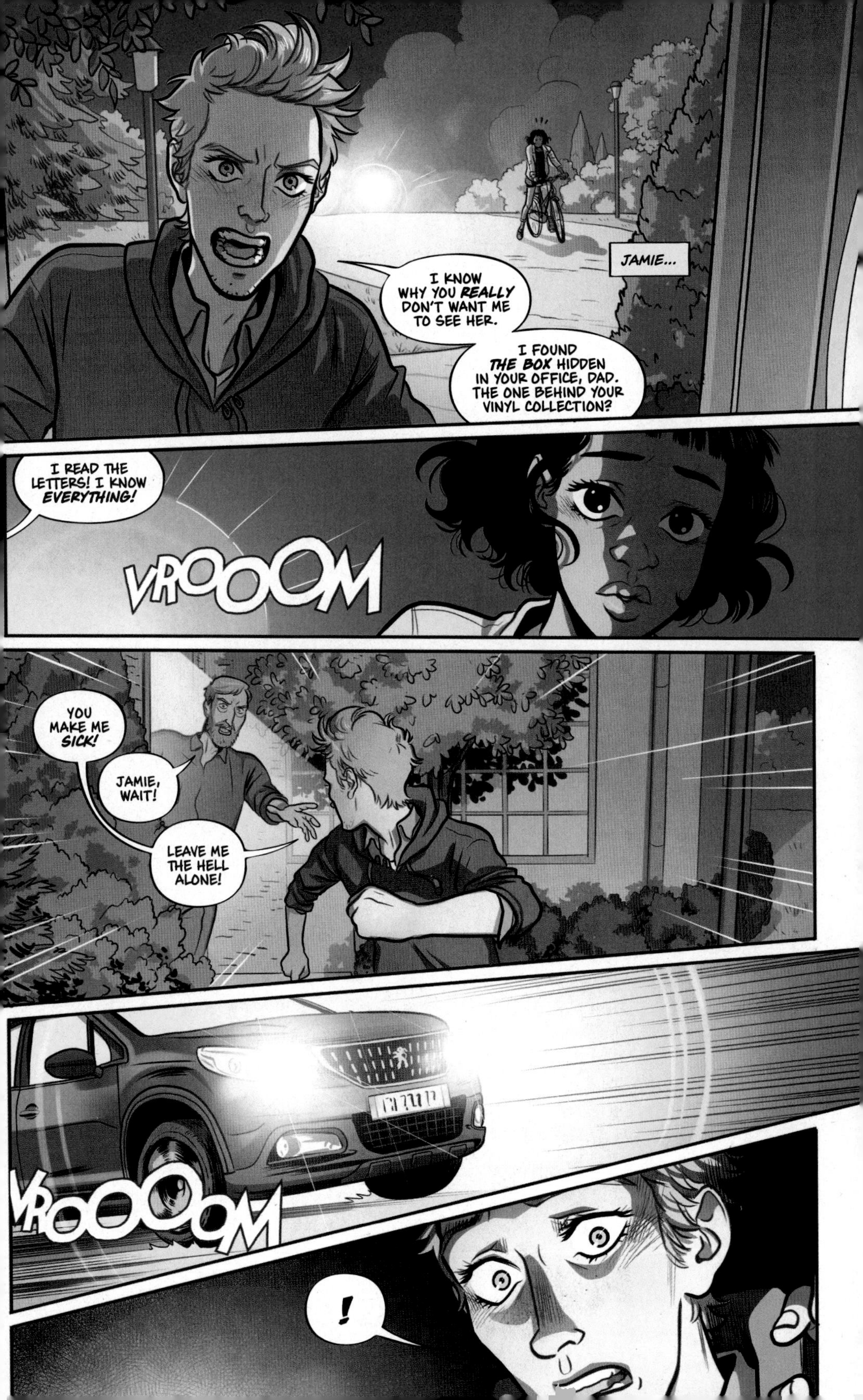
JAMIE...
I KNOW WHY YOU REALLY DON'T WANT ME TO SEE HER.
I FOUND THE BOX HIDDEN IN YOUR OFFICE, DAD. THE ONE BEHIND YOUR VINYL COLLECTION?
I READ THE LETTERS! I KNOW EVERYTHING!
VROOOM
YOU MAKE ME SICK!
JAMIE, WAIT!
LEAVE ME THE HELL ALONE!
VROOOOM
!

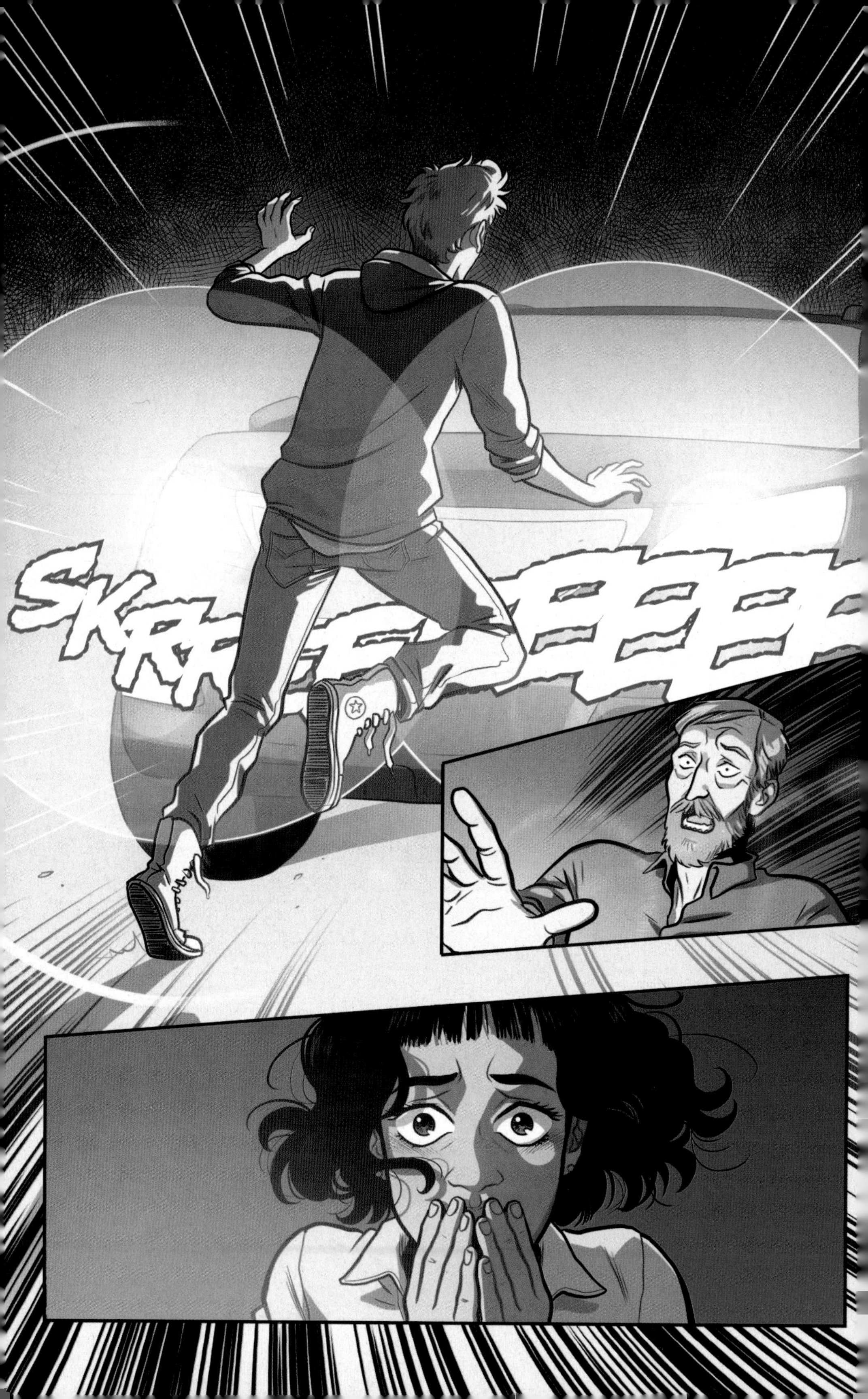
SKRREEEEEEE

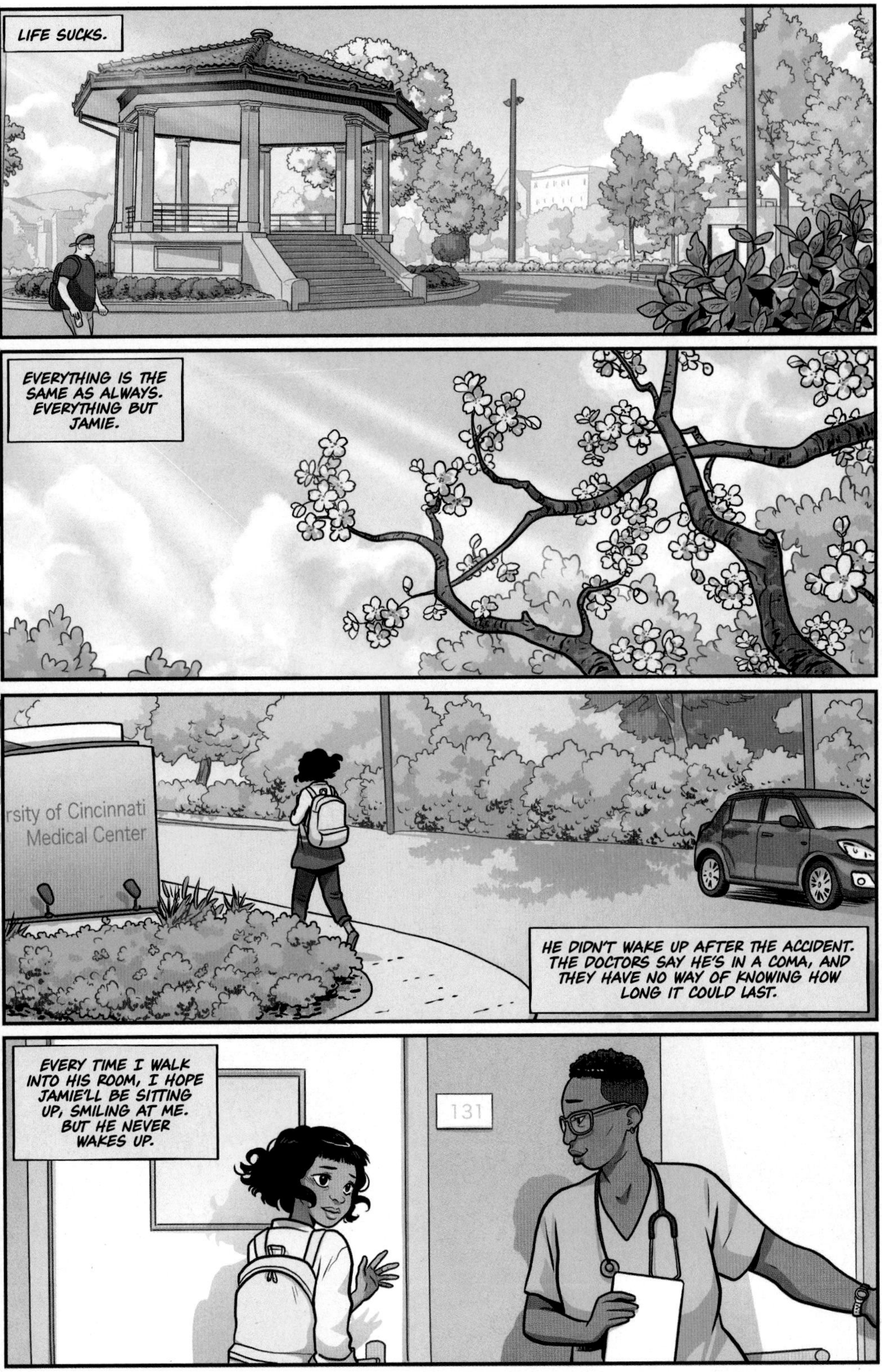
LIFE SUCKS.
EVERYTHING IS THE SAME AS ALWAYS. EVERYTHING BUT JAMIE.
rsity of Cincinnati
Medical Center
HE DIDN'T WAKE UP AFTER THE ACCIDENT. THE DOCTORS SAY HE'S IN A COMA, AND THEY HAVE NO WAY OF KNOWING HOW LONG IT COULD LAST.
EVERY TIME I WALK INTO HIS ROOM, I HOPE JAMIE'LL BE SITTING UP, SMILING AT ME. BUT HE NEVER WAKES UP.
131

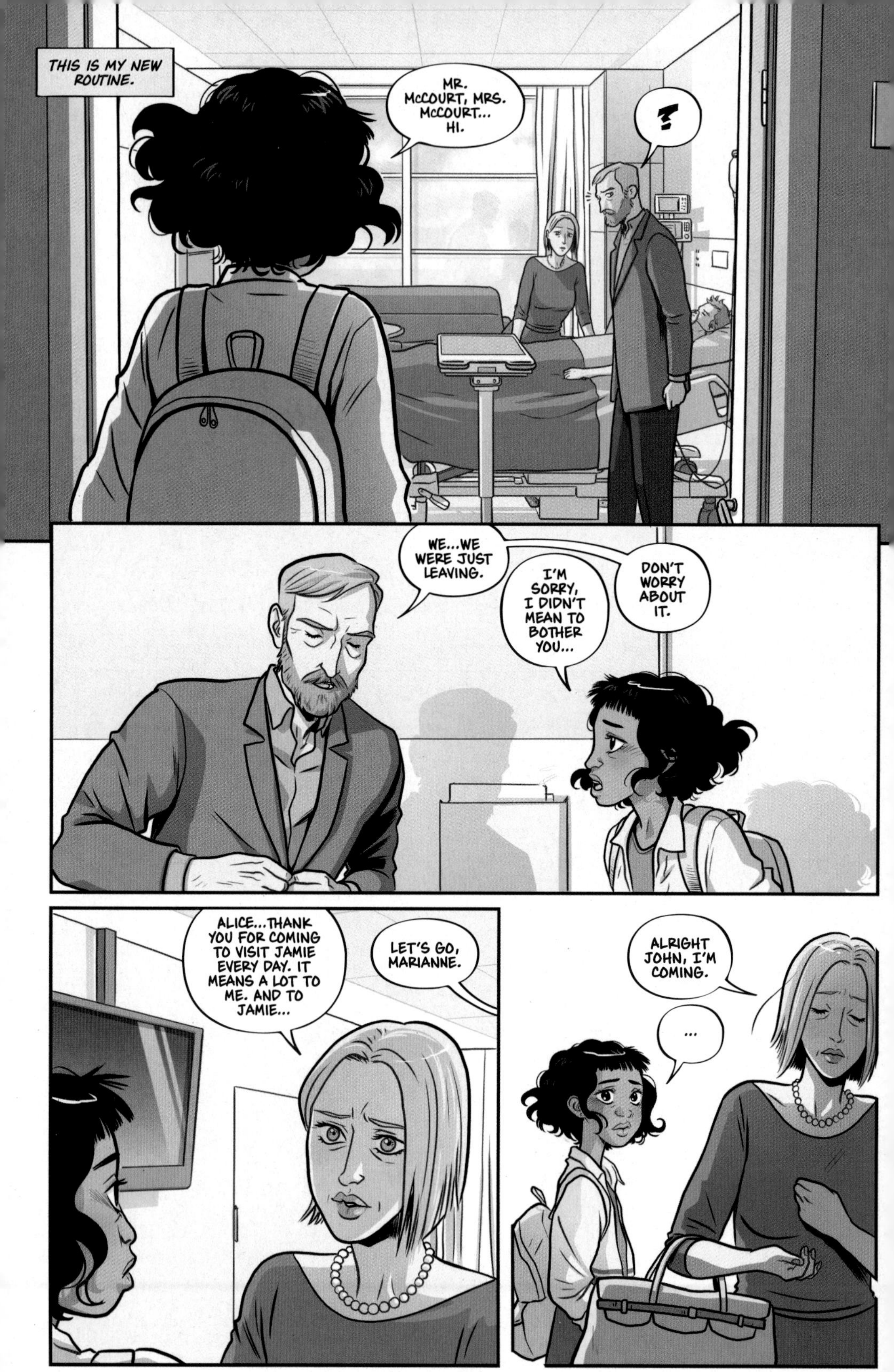
THIS IS MY NEW ROUTINE.
MR. McCOURT, MRS. McCOURT... HI.
?
WE...WE WERE JUST LEAVING.
I'M SORRY, I DIDN'T MEAN TO BOTHER YOU...
DON'T WORRY ABOUT IT.
ALICE...THANK YOU FOR COMING TO VISIT JAMIE EVERY DAY. IT MEANS A LOT TO ME. AND TO JAMIE...
LET'S GO, MARIANNE.
ALRIGHT JOHN, I'M COMING.
...

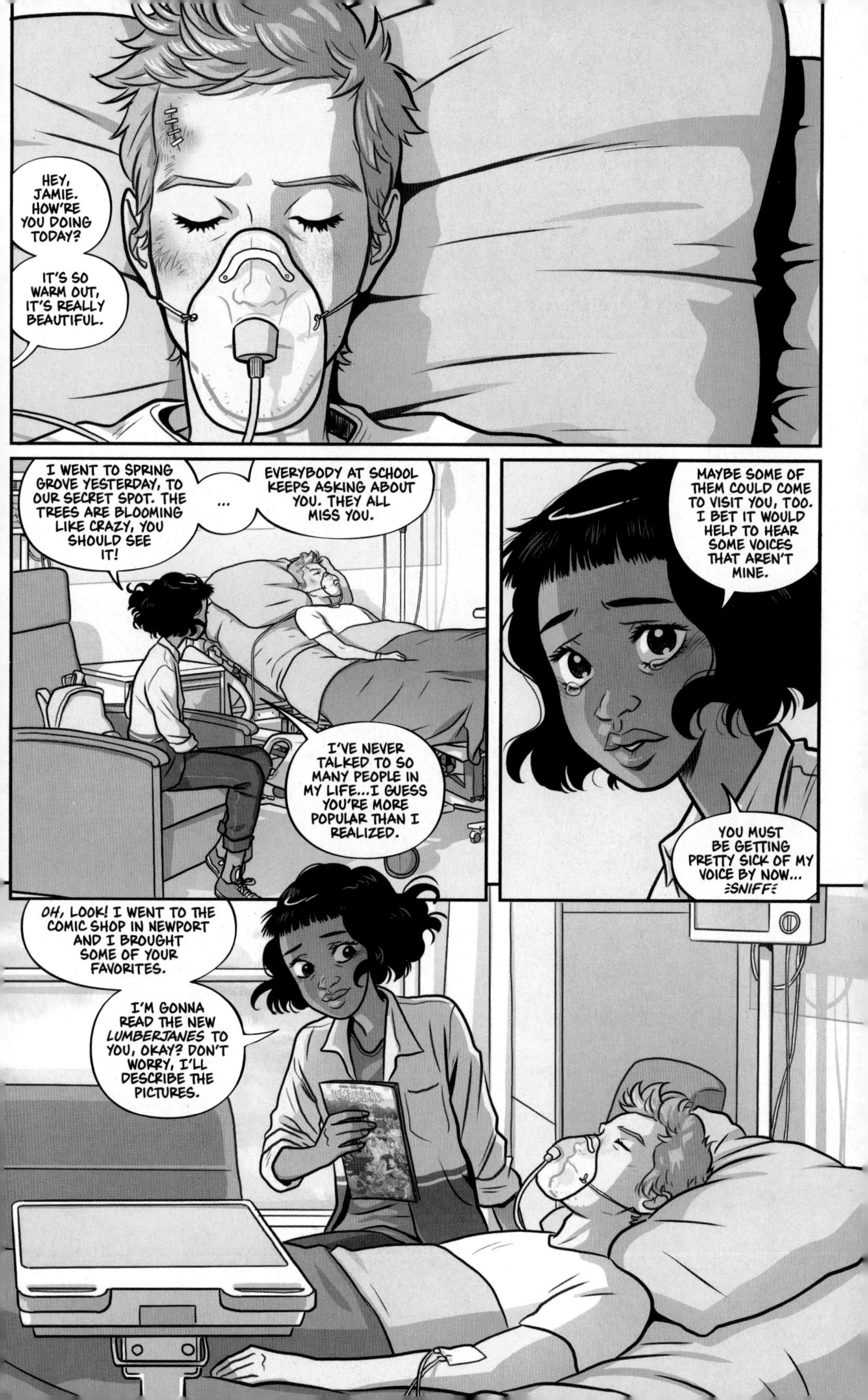
HEY, JAMIE. HOW'RE YOU DOING TODAY?
IT'S SO WARM OUT, IT'S REALLY BEAUTIFUL.
I WENT TO SPRING GROVE YESTERDAY, TO OUR SECRET SPOT. THE TREES ARE BLOOMING LIKE CRAZY, YOU SHOULD SEE IT!
...
EVERYBODY AT SCHOOL KEEPS ASKING ABOUT YOU. THEY ALL MISS YOU.
I'VE NEVER TALKED TO SO MANY PEOPLE IN MY LIFE...I GUESS YOU'RE MORE POPULAR THAN I REALIZED.
MAYBE SOME OF THEM COULD COME TO VISIT YOU, TOO. I BET IT WOULD HELP TO HEAR SOME VOICES THAT AREN'T MINE.
YOU MUST BE GETTING PRETTY SICK OF MY VOICE BY NOW... SNIFF
OH, LOOK! I WENT TO THE COMIC SHOP IN NEWPORT AND I BROUGHT SOME OF YOUR FAVORITES.
I'M GONNA READ THE NEW *LUMBERJANES* TO YOU, OKAY? DON'T WORRY, I'LL DESCRIBE THE PICTURES.

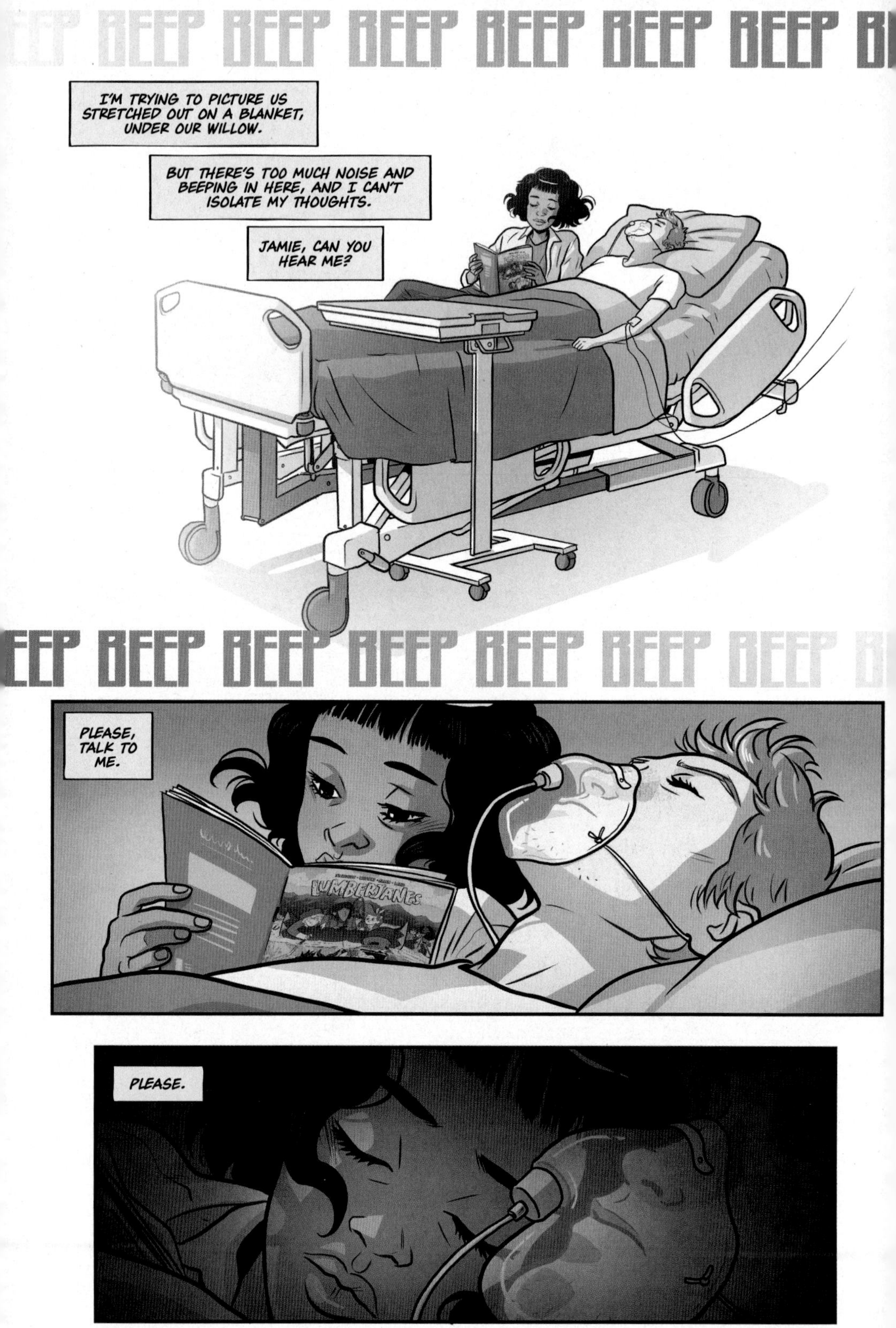
BEEP BEEP BEEP BEEP BEEP BEEP
I'M TRYING TO PICTURE US STRETCHED OUT ON A BLANKET, UNDER OUR WILLOW.
BUT THERE'S TOO MUCH NOISE AND BEEPING IN HERE, AND I CAN'T ISOLATE MY THOUGHTS.
JAMIE, CAN YOU HEAR ME?
BEEP BEEP BEEP BEEP BEEP BEEP
PLEASE, TALK TO ME.
LUMBERJANES
PLEASE.

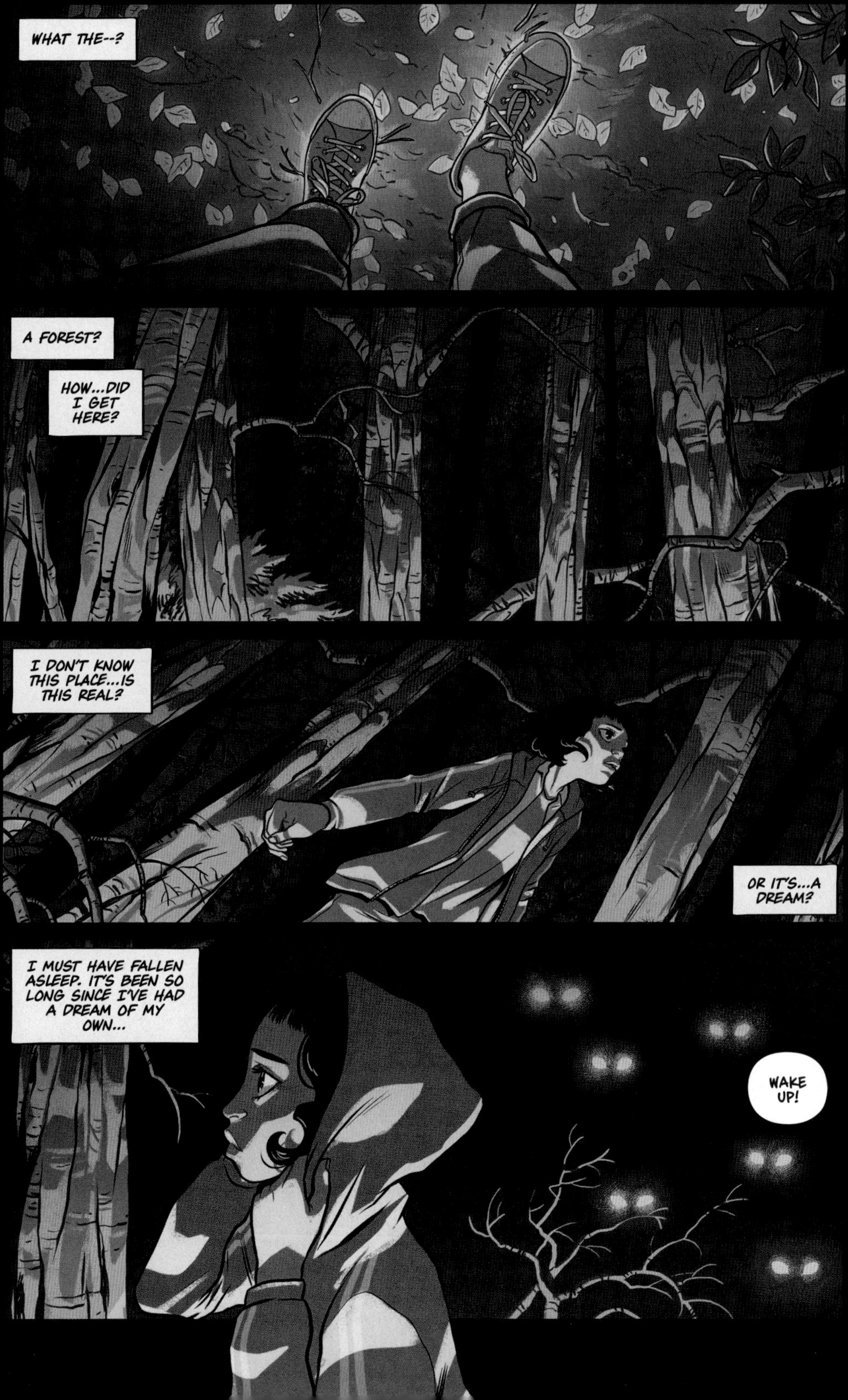
WHAT THE--?
A FOREST?
HOW...DID I GET HERE?
I DON'T KNOW THIS PLACE...IS THIS REAL?
OR IT'S...A DREAM?
I MUST HAVE FALLEN ASLEEP. IT'S BEEN SO LONG SINCE I'VE HAD A DREAM OF MY OWN...
WAKE UP!

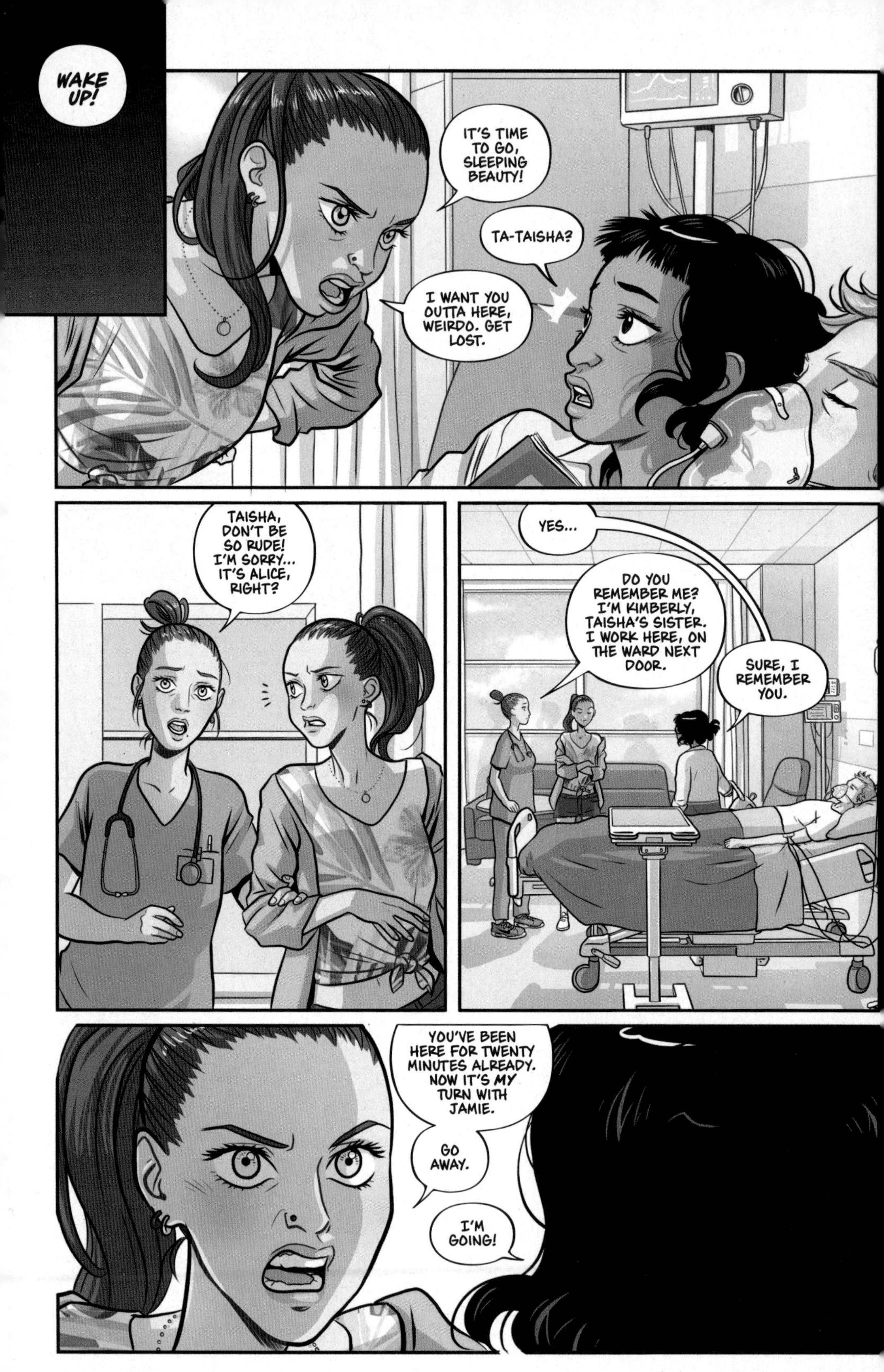
WAKE UP!
IT'S TIME TO GO, SLEEPING BEAUTY!
TA-TAISHA?
I WANT YOU OUTTA HERE, WEIRDO. GET LOST.
TAISHA, DON'T BE SO RUDE! I'M SORRY... IT'S ALICE, RIGHT?
YES...
DO YOU REMEMBER ME? I'M KIMBERLY, TAISHA'S SISTER. I WORK HERE, ON THE WARD NEXT DOOR.
SURE, I REMEMBER YOU.
YOU'VE BEEN HERE FOR TWENTY MINUTES ALREADY. NOW IT'S MY TURN WITH JAMIE.
GO AWAY.
I'M GOING!

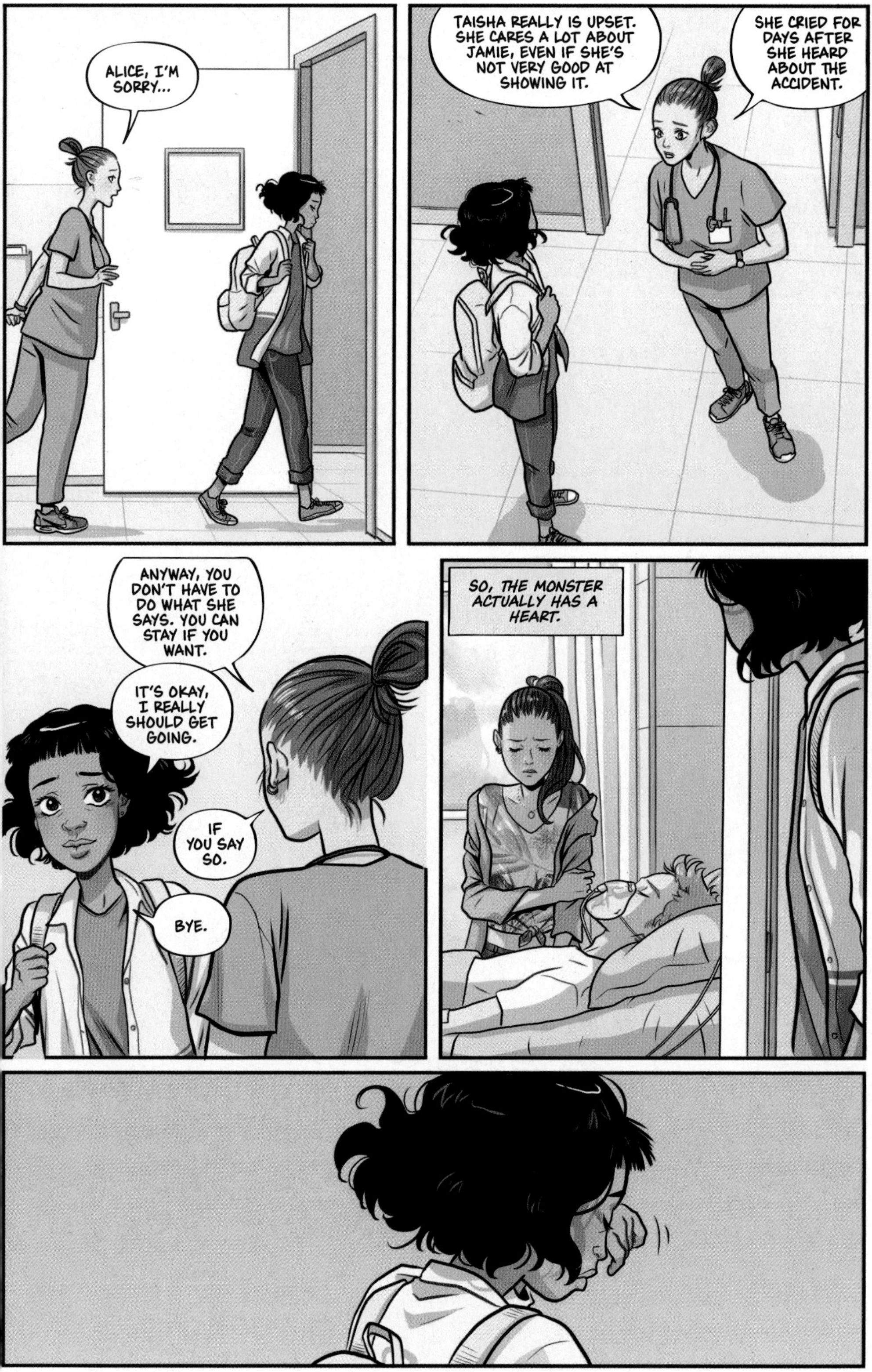
ALICE, I'M SORRY...
TAISHA REALLY IS UPSET. SHE CARES A LOT ABOUT JAMIE, EVEN IF SHE'S NOT VERY GOOD AT SHOWING IT.
SHE CRIED FOR DAYS AFTER SHE HEARD ABOUT THE ACCIDENT.
ANYWAY, YOU DON'T HAVE TO DO WHAT SHE SAYS. YOU CAN STAY IF YOU WANT.
IT'S OKAY, I REALLY SHOULD GET GOING.
IF YOU SAY SO.
BYE.
SO, THE MONSTER ACTUALLY HAS A HEART.

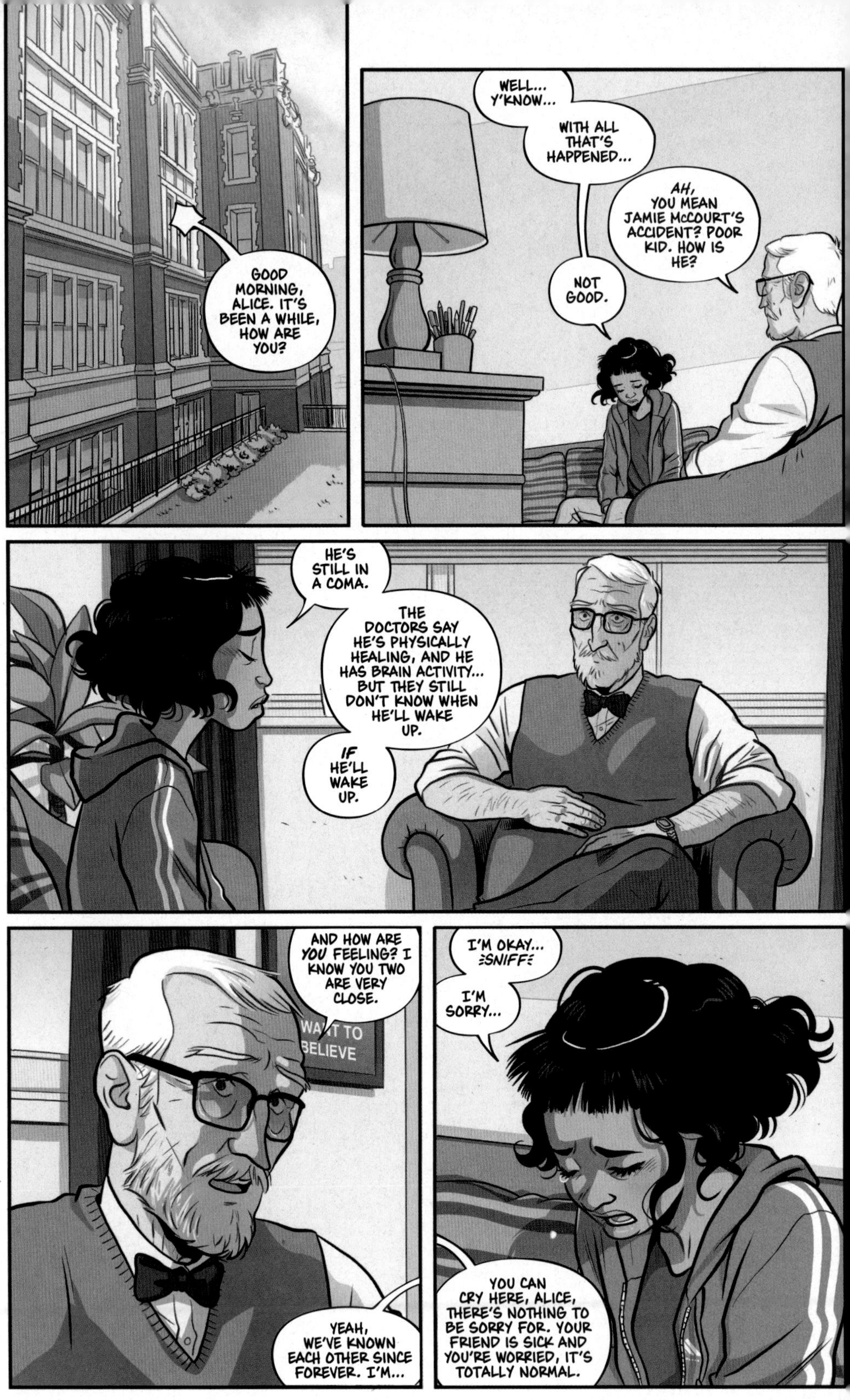
GOOD MORNING, ALICE. IT'S BEEN A WHILE, HOW ARE YOU?
WELL... Y'KNOW...
WITH ALL THAT'S HAPPENED...
AH, YOU MEAN JAMIE McCOURT'S ACCIDENT? POOR KID. HOW IS HE?
NOT GOOD.
HE'S STILL IN A COMA.
THE DOCTORS SAY HE'S PHYSICALLY HEALING, AND HE HAS BRAIN ACTIVITY... BUT THEY STILL DON'T KNOW WHEN HE'LL WAKE UP.
IF HE'LL WAKE UP.
AND HOW ARE YOU FEELING? I KNOW YOU TWO ARE VERY CLOSE.
WANT TO BELIEVE
YEAH, WE'VE KNOWN EACH OTHER SINCE FOREVER. I'M...
I'M OKAY... SNIFF
I'M SORRY...
YOU CAN CRY HERE, ALICE, THERE'S NOTHING TO BE SORRY FOR. YOUR FRIEND IS SICK AND YOU'RE WORRIED, IT'S TOTALLY NORMAL.

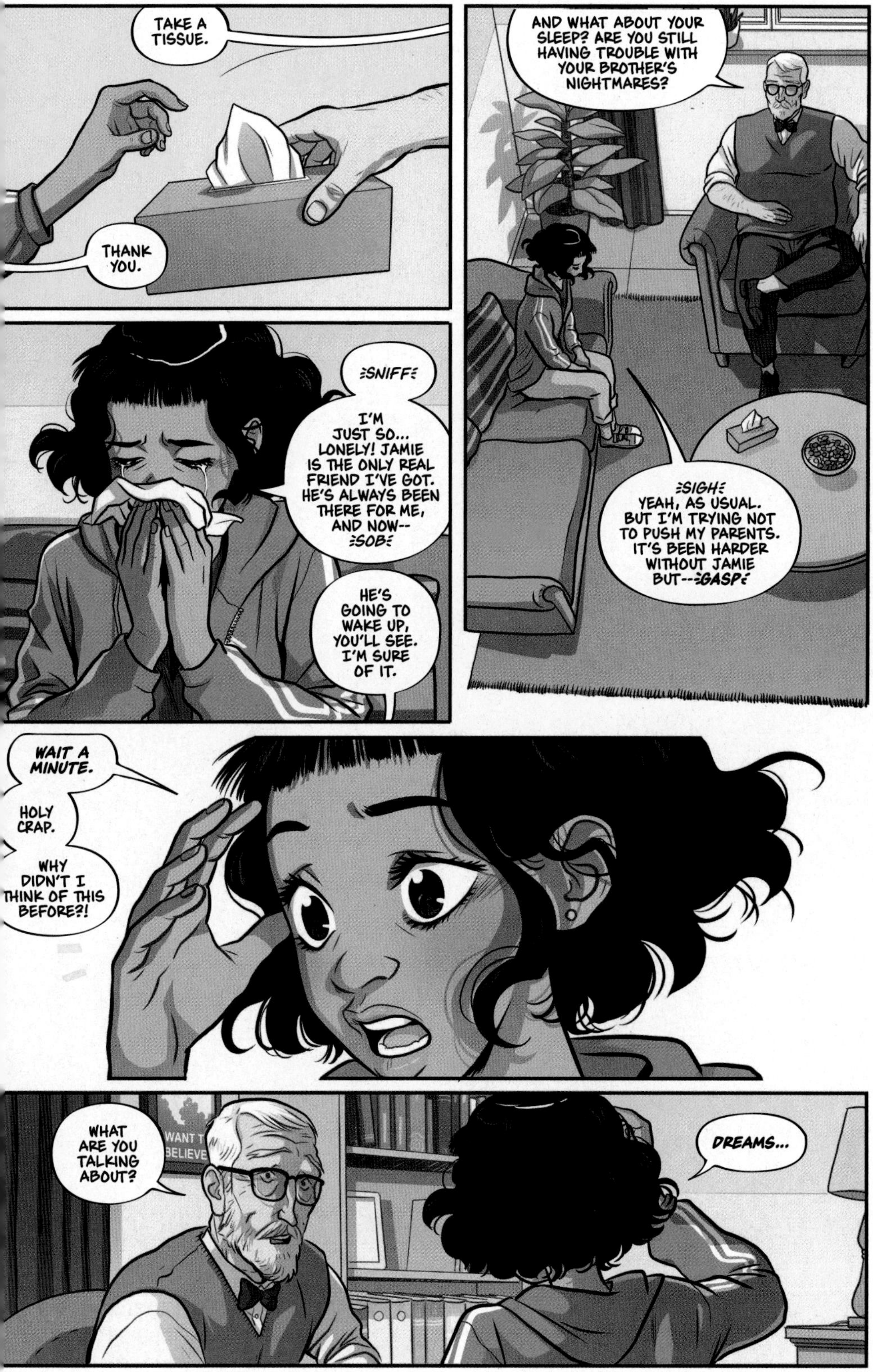
TAKE A TISSUE.
THANK YOU.
AND WHAT ABOUT YOUR SLEEP? ARE YOU STILL HAVING TROUBLE WITH YOUR BROTHER'S NIGHTMARES?
SNIFF
I'M JUST SO... LONELY! JAMIE IS THE ONLY REAL FRIEND I'VE GOT. HE'S ALWAYS BEEN THERE FOR ME, AND NOW-- SOB
HE'S GOING TO WAKE UP, YOU'LL SEE. I'M SURE OF IT.
SIGH YEAH, AS USUAL. BUT I'M TRYING NOT TO PUSH MY PARENTS. IT'S BEEN HARDER WITHOUT JAMIE BUT-- GASP
WAIT A MINUTE.
HOLY CRAP.
WHY DIDN'T I THINK OF THIS BEFORE?!
WHAT ARE YOU TALKING ABOUT?
DREAMS...

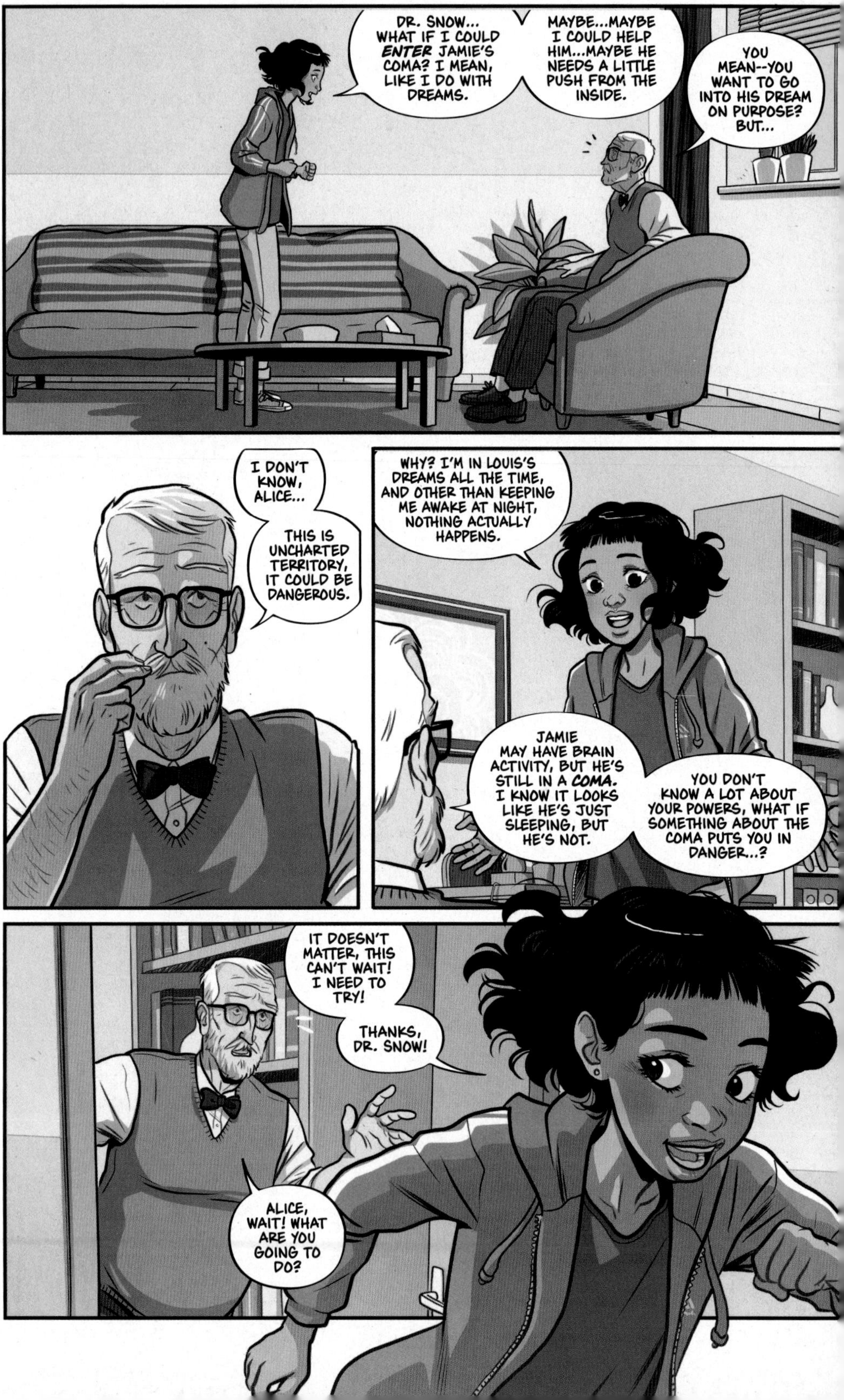
DR. SNOW... WHAT IF I COULD ENTER JAMIE'S COMA? I MEAN, LIKE I DO WITH DREAMS.
MAYBE...MAYBE I COULD HELP HIM...MAYBE HE NEEDS A LITTLE PUSH FROM THE INSIDE.
YOU MEAN--YOU WANT TO GO INTO HIS DREAM ON PURPOSE? BUT...
I DON'T KNOW, ALICE...
THIS IS UNCHARTED TERRITORY, IT COULD BE DANGEROUS.
WHY? I'M IN LOUIS'S DREAMS ALL THE TIME, AND OTHER THAN KEEPING ME AWAKE AT NIGHT, NOTHING ACTUALLY HAPPENS.
JAMIE MAY HAVE BRAIN ACTIVITY, BUT HE'S STILL IN A COMA. I KNOW IT LOOKS LIKE HE'S JUST SLEEPING, BUT HE'S NOT.
YOU DON'T KNOW A LOT ABOUT YOUR POWERS, WHAT IF SOMETHING ABOUT THE COMA PUTS YOU IN DANGER...?
IT DOESN'T MATTER, THIS CAN'T WAIT! I NEED TO TRY!
THANKS, DR. SNOW!
ALICE, WAIT! WHAT ARE YOU GOING TO DO?

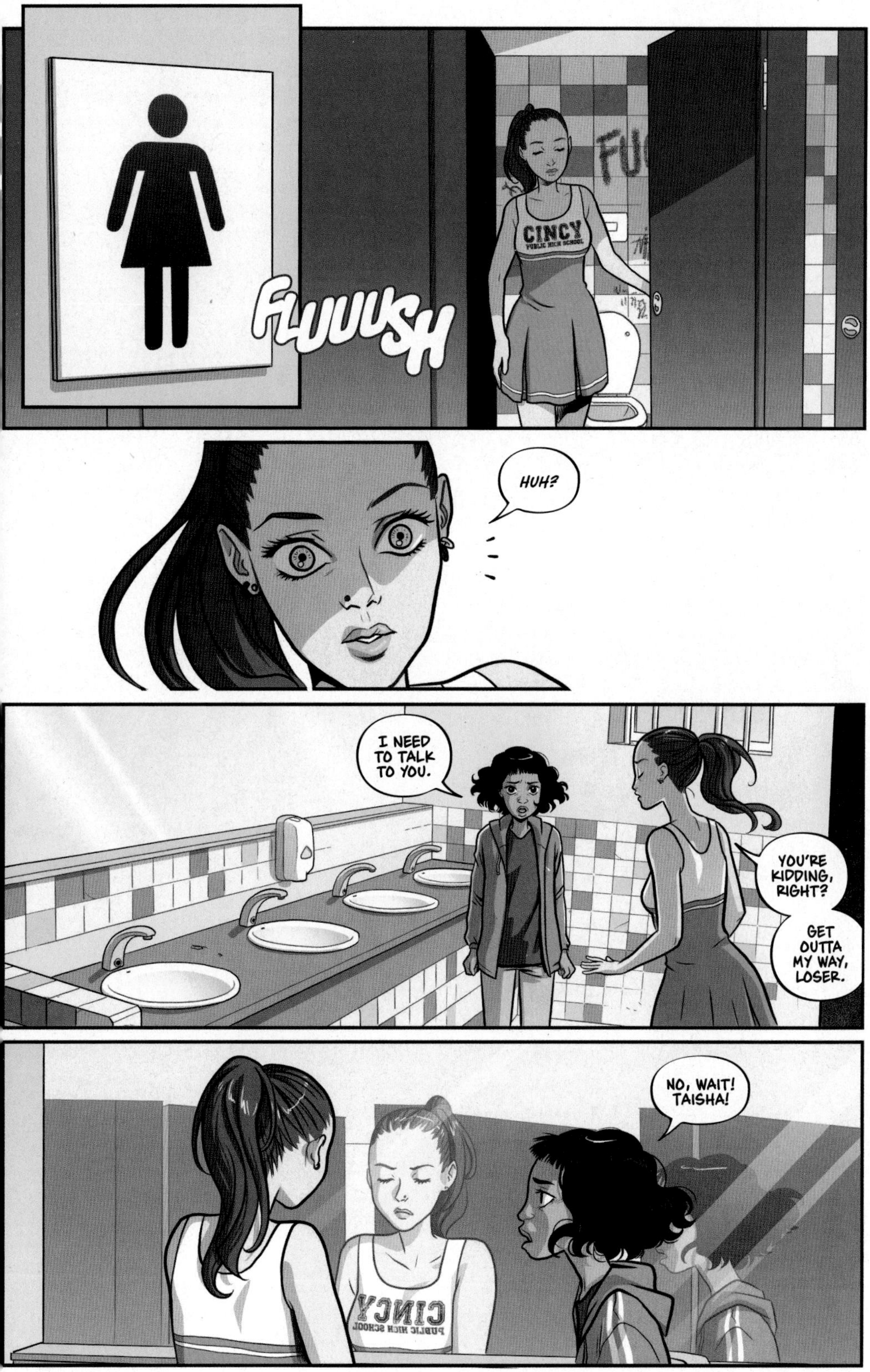
FLUUUSH
HUH?
I NEED TO TALK TO YOU.
YOU'RE KIDDING, RIGHT?
GET OUTTA MY WAY, LOSER.
NO, WAIT! TAISHA!

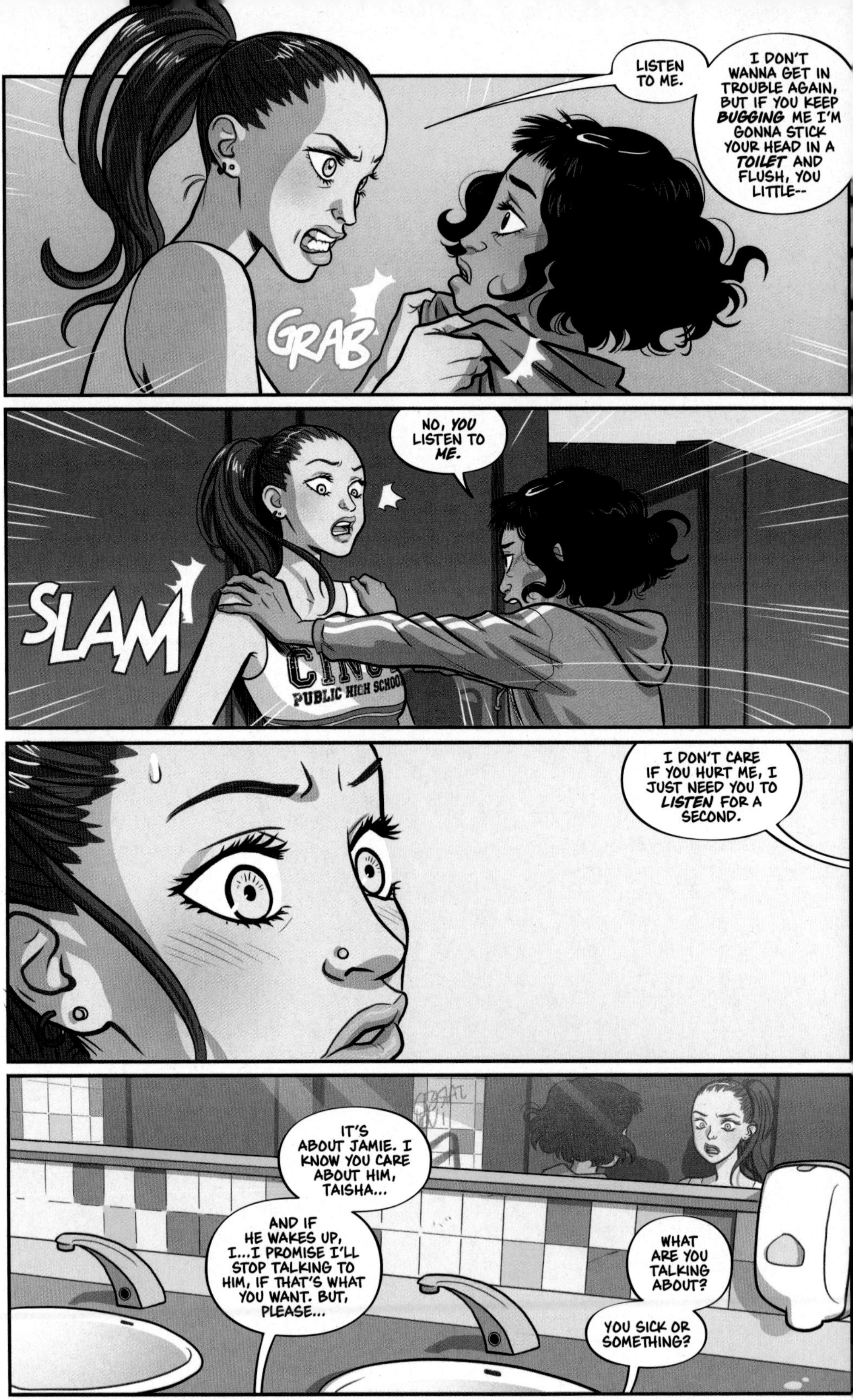
LISTEN TO ME.
I DON'T WANNA GET IN TROUBLE AGAIN, BUT IF YOU KEEP BUGGING ME I'M GONNA STICK YOUR HEAD IN A TOILET AND FLUSH, YOU LITTLE--
GRAB
NO, YOU LISTEN TO ME.
SLAM
CINC
PUBLIC HIGH SCHOO
I DON'T CARE IF YOU HURT ME, I JUST NEED YOU TO LISTEN FOR A SECOND.
IT'S ABOUT JAMIE. I KNOW YOU CARE ABOUT HIM, TAISHA...
AND IF HE WAKES UP, I...I PROMISE I'LL STOP TALKING TO HIM, IF THAT'S WHAT YOU WANT. BUT, PLEASE...
WHAT ARE YOU TALKING ABOUT?
YOU SICK OR SOMETHING?

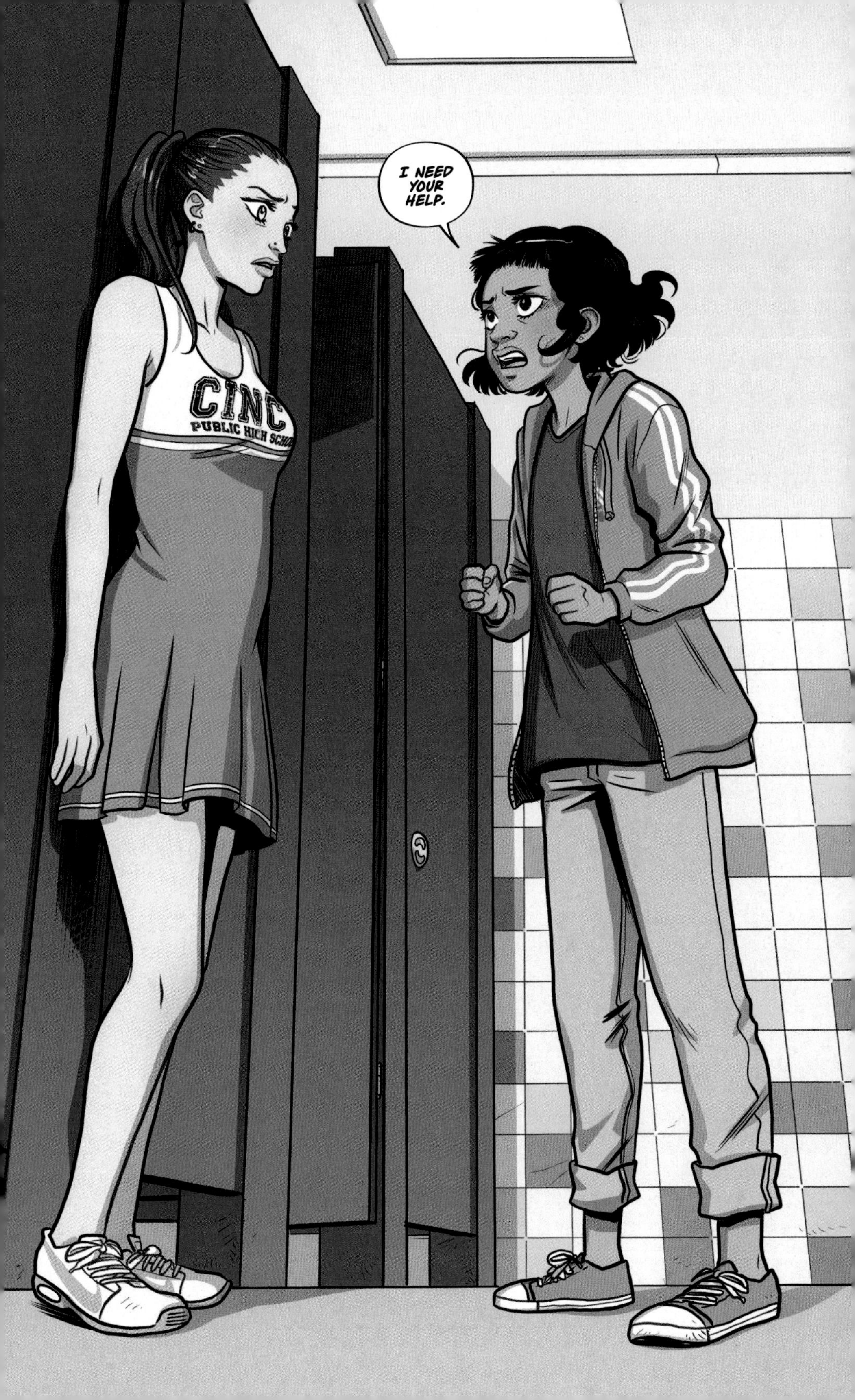
I NEED YOUR HELP.
CINC
PUBLIC HIGH SCHO

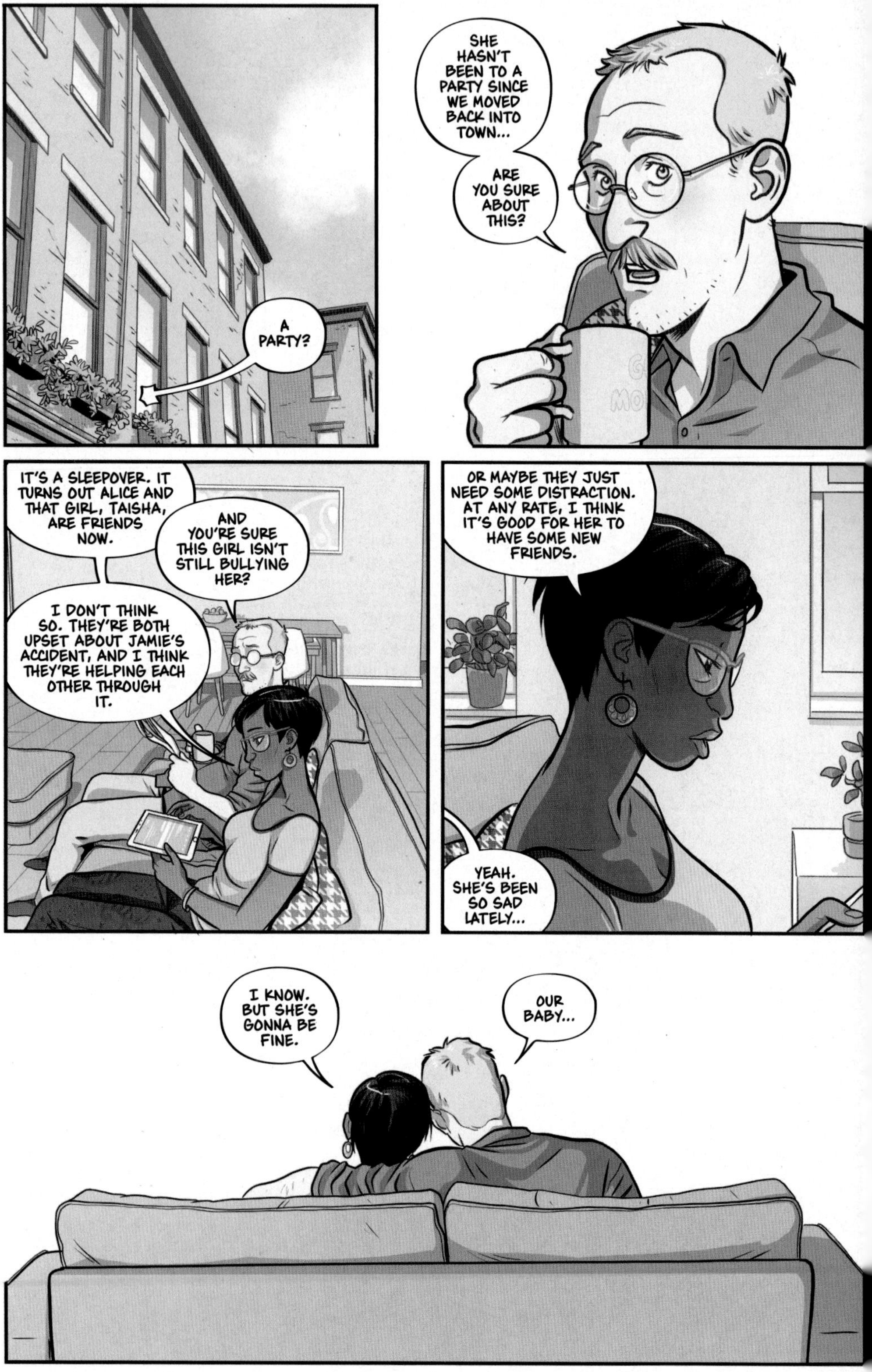
A PARTY?
SHE HASN'T BEEN TO A PARTY SINCE WE MOVED BACK INTO TOWN...
ARE YOU SURE ABOUT THIS?
IT'S A SLEEPOVER. IT TURNS OUT ALICE AND THAT GIRL, TAISHA, ARE FRIENDS NOW.
AND YOU'RE SURE THIS GIRL ISN'T STILL BULLYING HER?
I DON'T THINK SO. THEY'RE BOTH UPSET ABOUT JAMIE'S ACCIDENT, AND I THINK THEY'RE HELPING EACH OTHER THROUGH IT.
OR MAYBE THEY JUST NEED SOME DISTRACTION. AT ANY RATE, I THINK IT'S GOOD FOR HER TO HAVE SOME NEW FRIENDS.
YEAH. SHE'S BEEN SO SAD LATELY...
I KNOW. BUT SHE'S GONNA BE FINE.
OUR BABY...

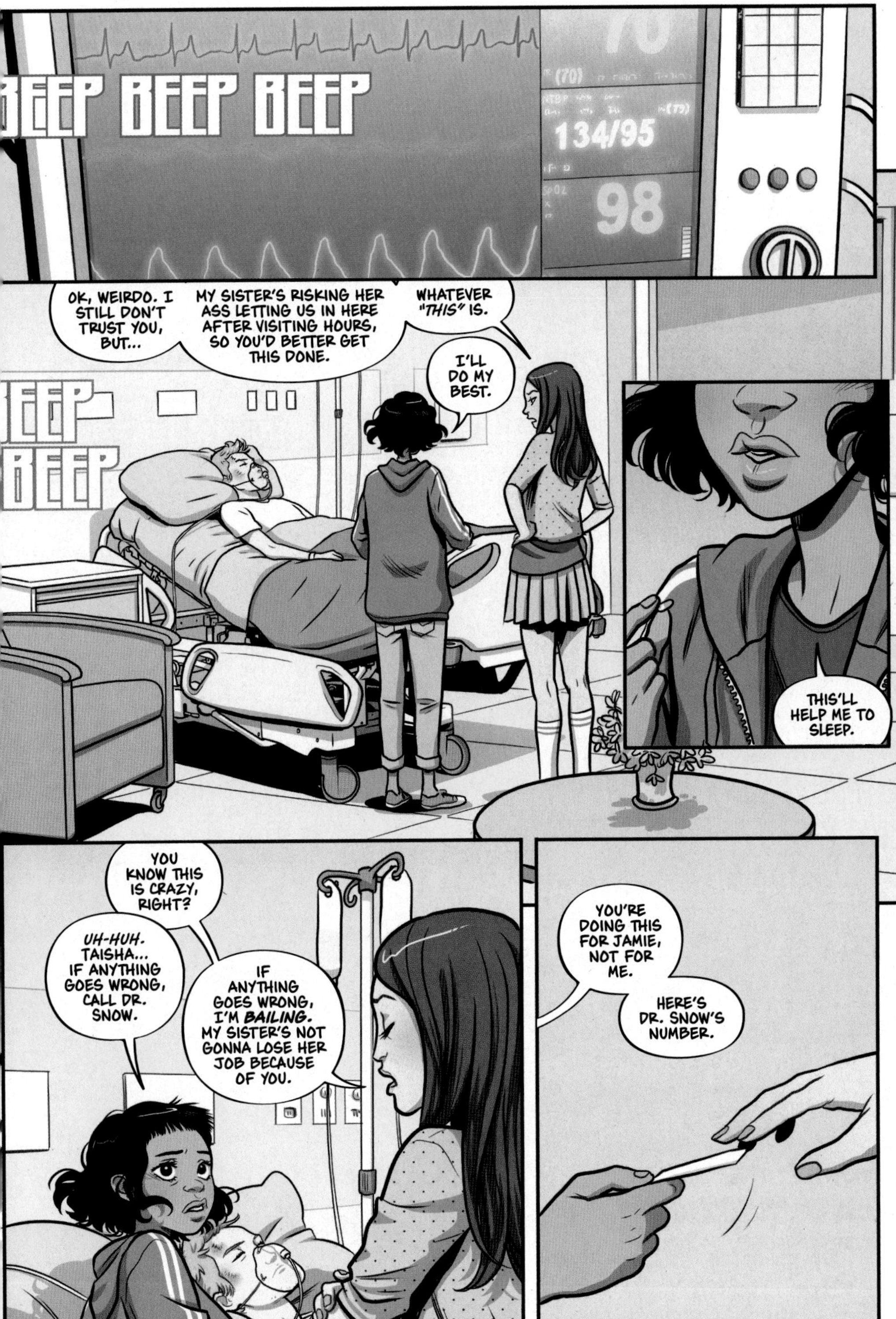

BEEP BEEP
134/95
98
OK, WEIRDO. I STILL DON'T TRUST YOU, BUT...
MY SISTER'S RISKING HER ASS LETTING US IN HERE AFTER VISITING HOURS, SO YOU'D BETTER GET THIS DONE.
WHATEVER *"THIS"* IS.
I'LL DO MY BEST.
BEEP
THIS'LL HELP ME TO SLEEP.
YOU KNOW THIS IS CRAZY, RIGHT?
*UH-HUH.* TAISHA... IF ANYTHING GOES WRONG, CALL DR. SNOW.
IF ANYTHING GOES WRONG, I'M *BAILING*. MY SISTER'S NOT GONNA LOSE HER JOB BECAUSE OF YOU.
YOU'RE DOING THIS FOR JAMIE, NOT FOR ME.
HERE'S DR. SNOW'S NUMBER.

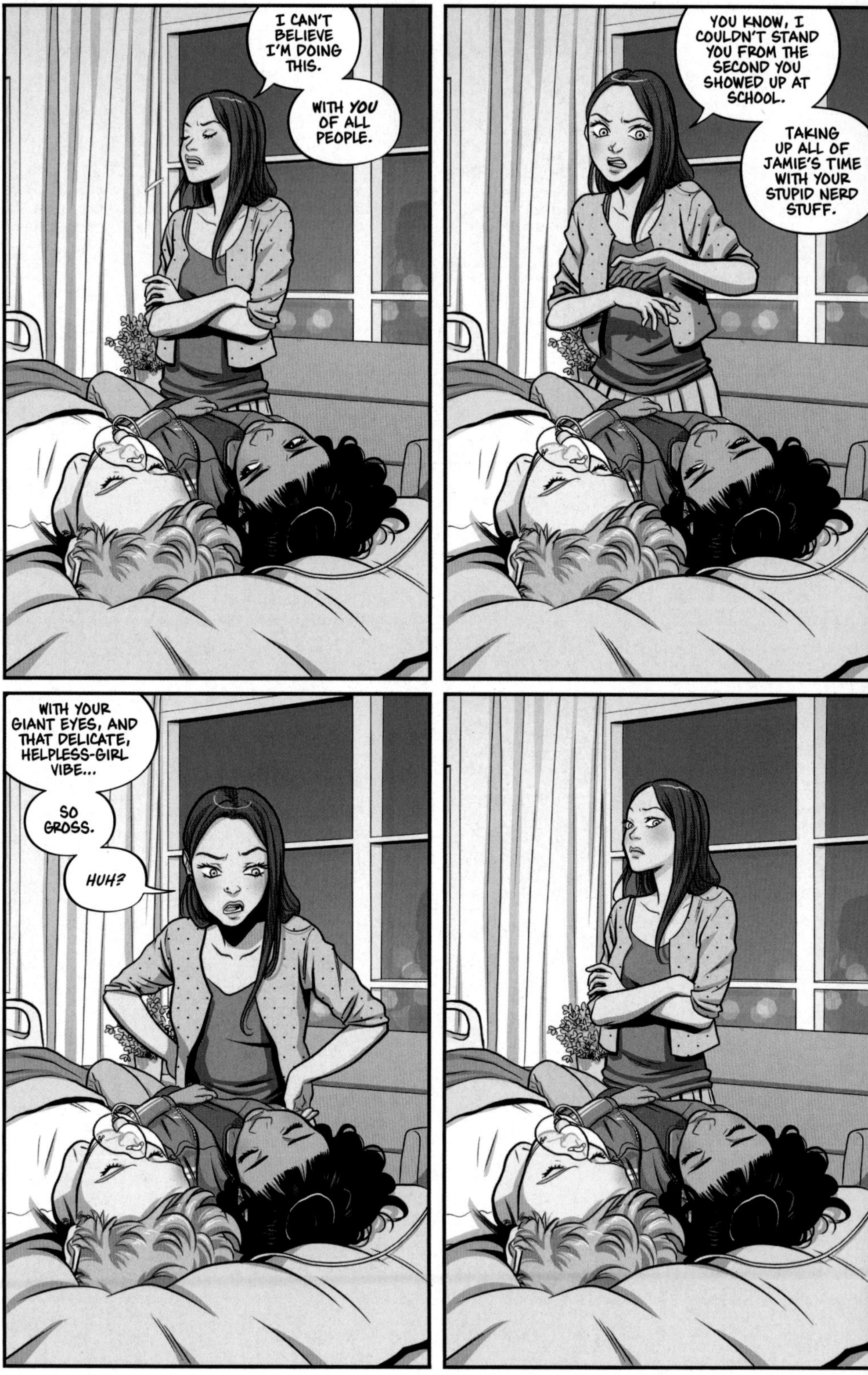
I CAN'T BELIEVE I'M DOING THIS.
WITH YOU OF ALL PEOPLE.
YOU KNOW, I COULDN'T STAND YOU FROM THE SECOND YOU SHOWED UP AT SCHOOL.
TAKING UP ALL OF JAMIE'S TIME WITH YOUR STUPID NERD STUFF.
WITH YOUR GIANT EYES, AND THAT DELICATE, HELPLESS-GIRL VIBE...
SO GROSS.
HUH?

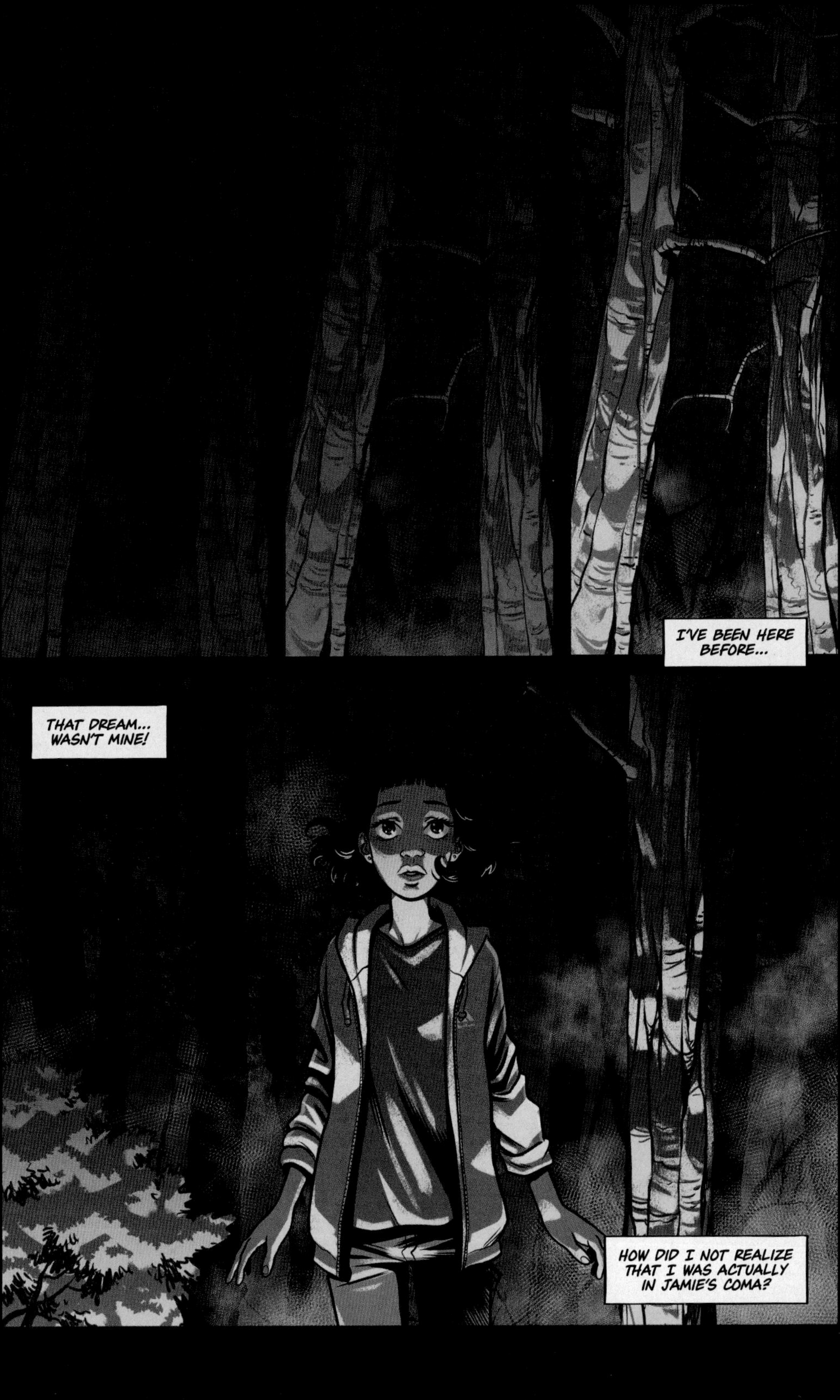
I'VE BEEN HERE BEFORE...
THAT DREAM... WASN'T MINE!
HOW DID I NOT REALIZE THAT I WAS ACTUALLY IN JAMIE'S COMA?

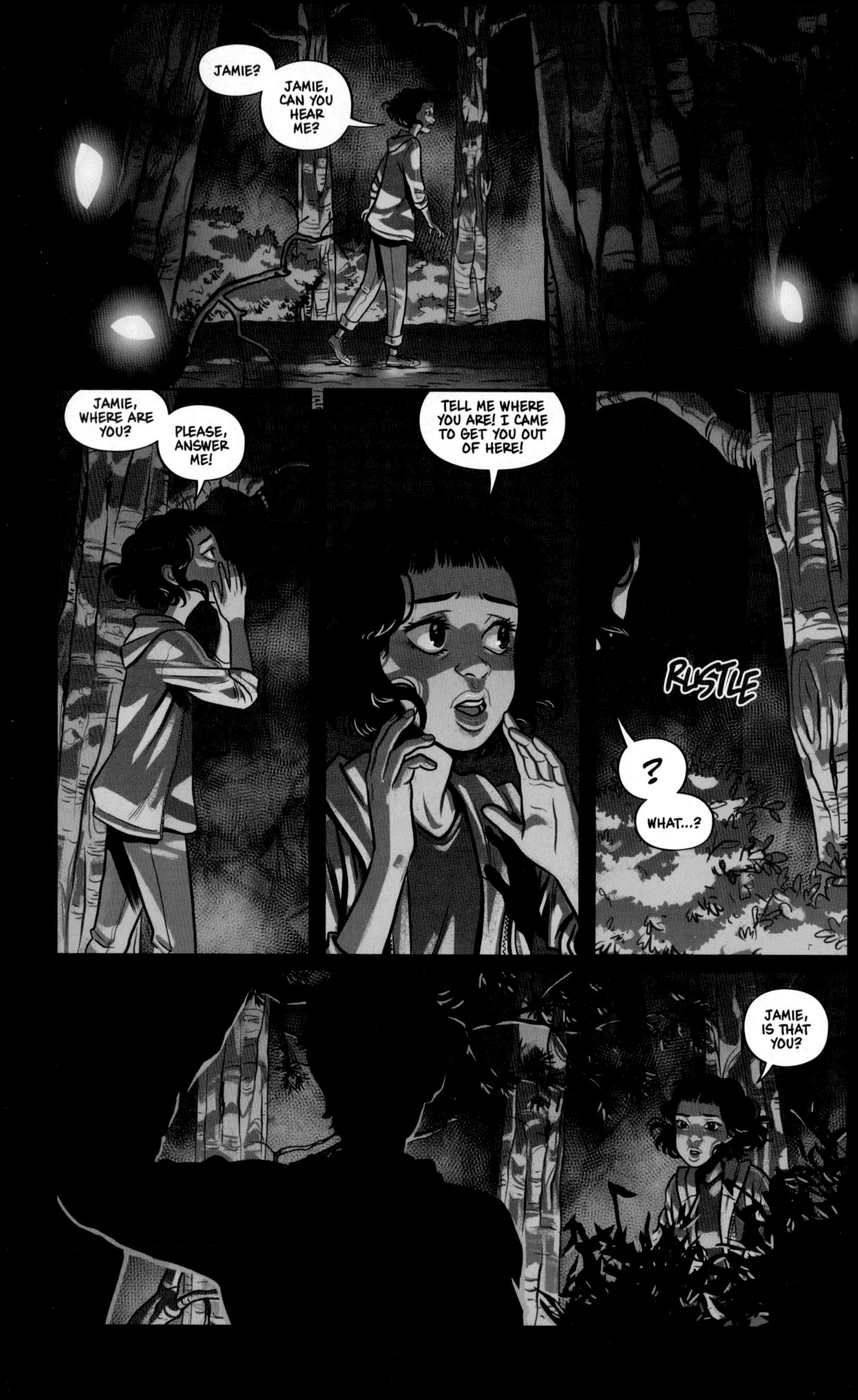
JAMIE?
JAMIE, CAN YOU HEAR ME?
JAMIE, WHERE ARE YOU?
PLEASE, ANSWER ME!
TELL ME WHERE YOU ARE! I CAME TO GET YOU OUT OF HERE!
RUSTLE
?
WHAT...?
JAMIE, IS THAT YOU?

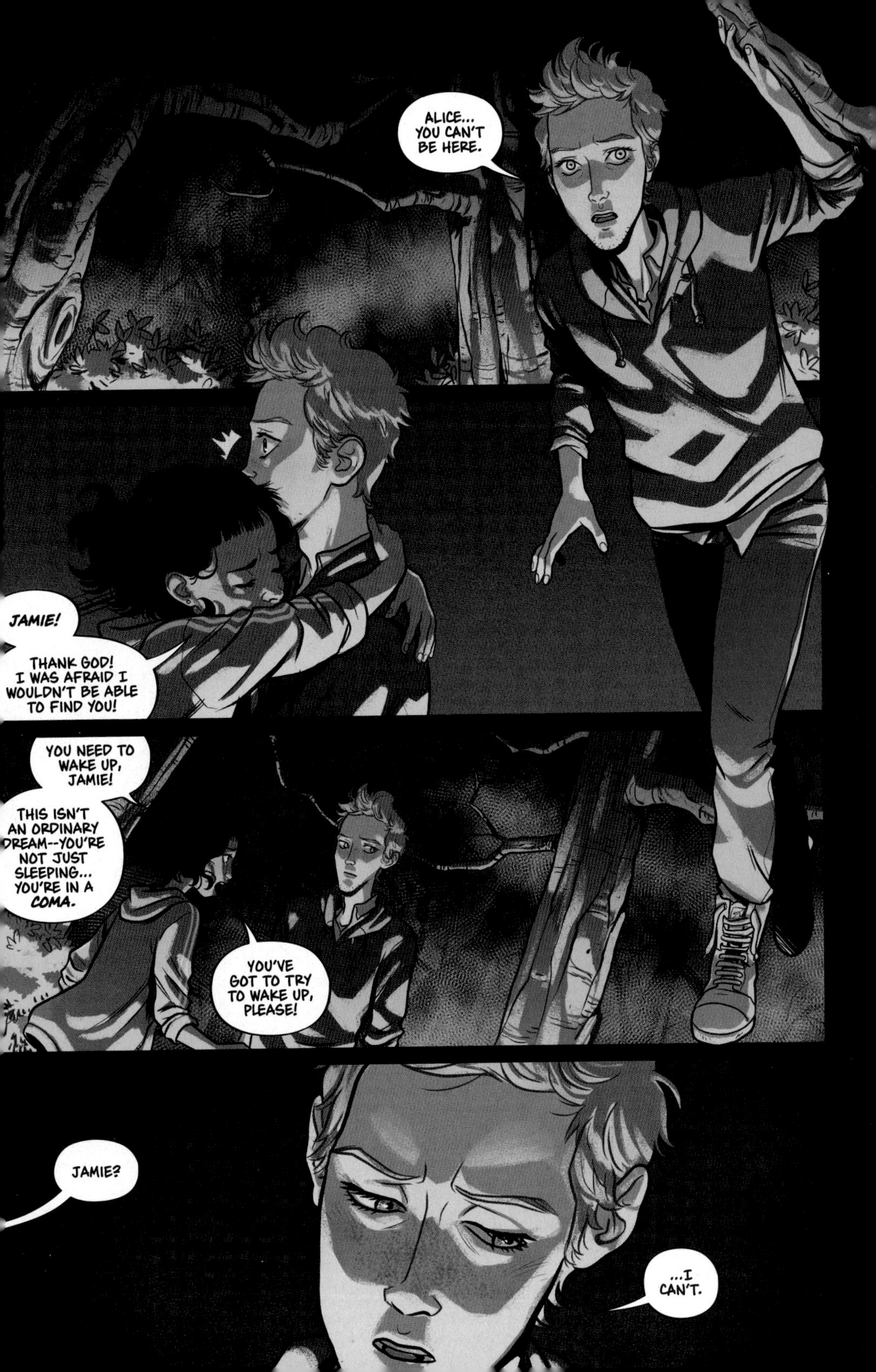
ALICE... YOU CAN'T BE HERE.
JAMIE!
THANK GOD! I WAS AFRAID I WOULDN'T BE ABLE TO FIND YOU!
YOU NEED TO WAKE UP, JAMIE!
THIS ISN'T AN ORDINARY DREAM--YOU'RE NOT JUST SLEEPING... YOU'RE IN A COMA.
YOU'VE GOT TO TRY TO WAKE UP, PLEASE!
JAMIE?
...I CAN'T.

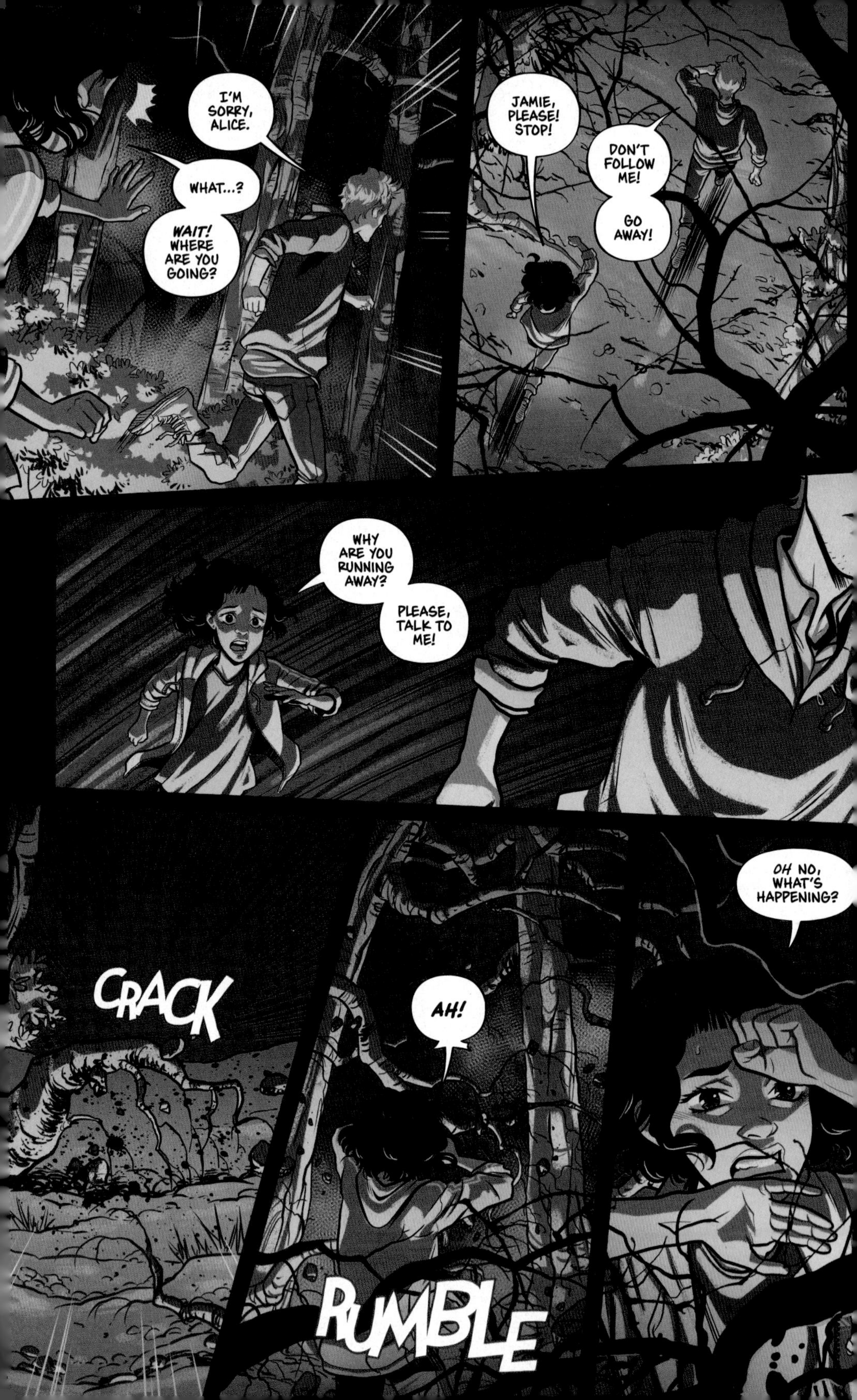
I'M SORRY, ALICE.
WHAT...?
WAIT! WHERE ARE YOU GOING?
JAMIE, PLEASE! STOP!
DON'T FOLLOW ME!
GO AWAY!
WHY ARE YOU RUNNING AWAY?
PLEASE, TALK TO ME!
CRACK
AH!
OH NO, WHAT'S HAPPENING?
RUMBLE

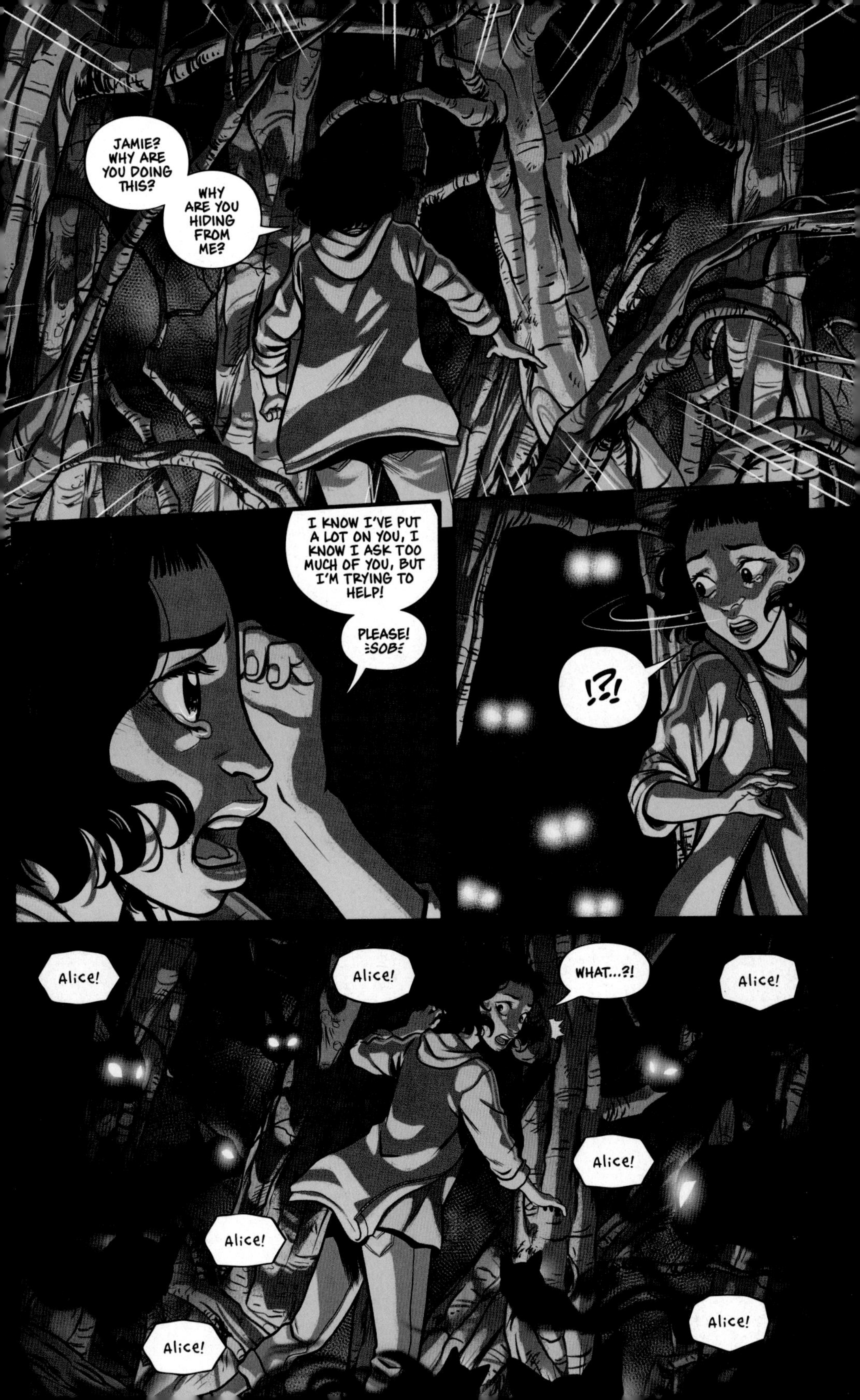
JAMIE? WHY ARE YOU DOING THIS?
WHY ARE YOU HIDING FROM ME?
I KNOW I'VE PUT A LOT ON YOU, I KNOW I ASK TOO MUCH OF YOU, BUT I'M TRYING TO HELP!
PLEASE! SOB
!?!
Alice!
Alice!
WHAT...?!
Alice!
Alice!
Alice!
Alice!
Alice!

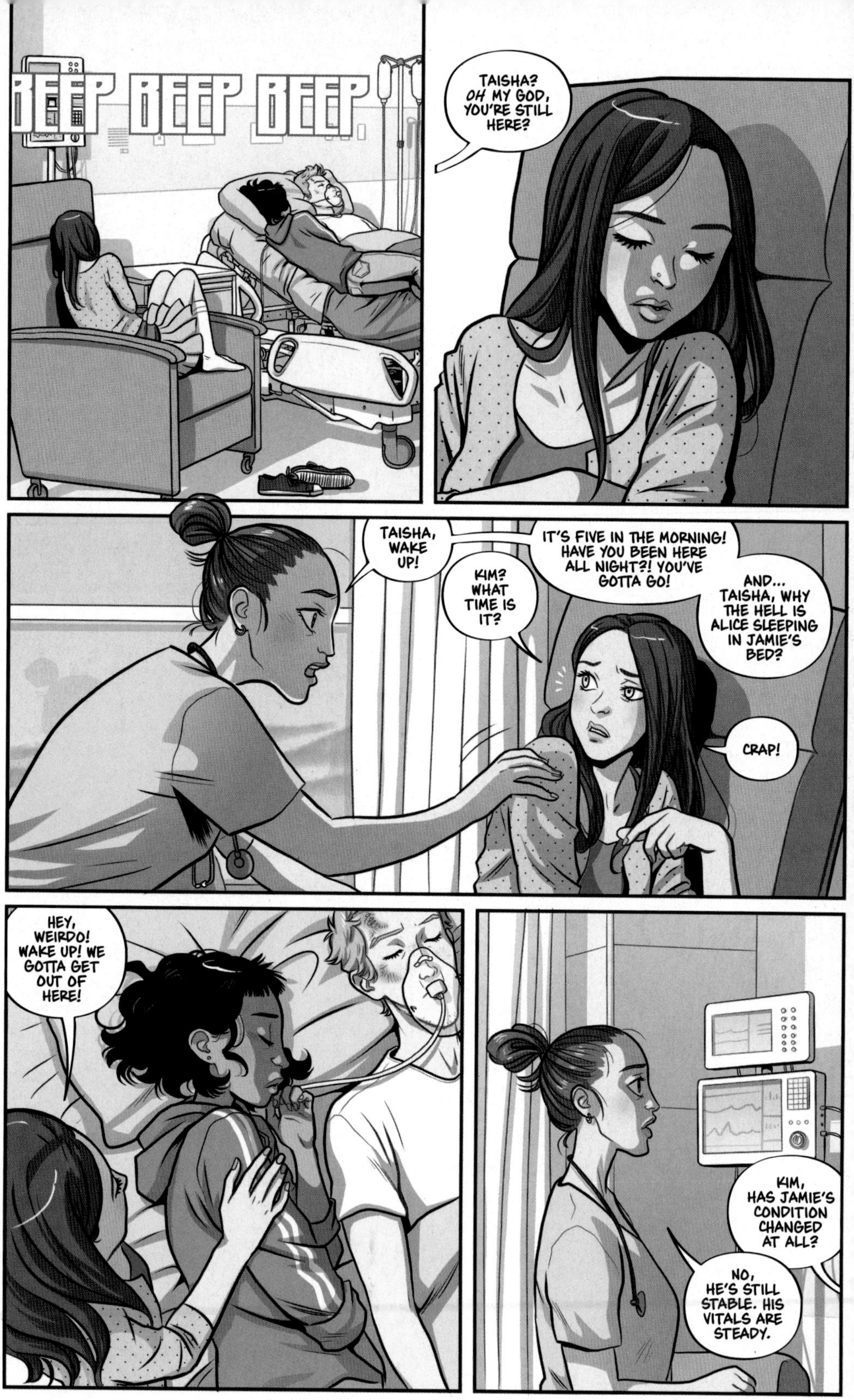
BEEP BEEP BEEP
TAISHA? OH MY GOD, YOU'RE STILL HERE?
TAISHA, WAKE UP!
IT'S FIVE IN THE MORNING! HAVE YOU BEEN HERE ALL NIGHT?! YOU'VE GOTTA GO!
KIM? WHAT TIME IS IT?
AND... TAISHA, WHY THE HELL IS ALICE SLEEPING IN JAMIE'S BED?
CRAP!
HEY, WEIRDO! WAKE UP! WE GOTTA GET OUT OF HERE!
KIM, HAS JAMIE'S CONDITION CHANGED AT ALL?
NO, HE'S STILL STABLE. HIS VITALS ARE STEADY.

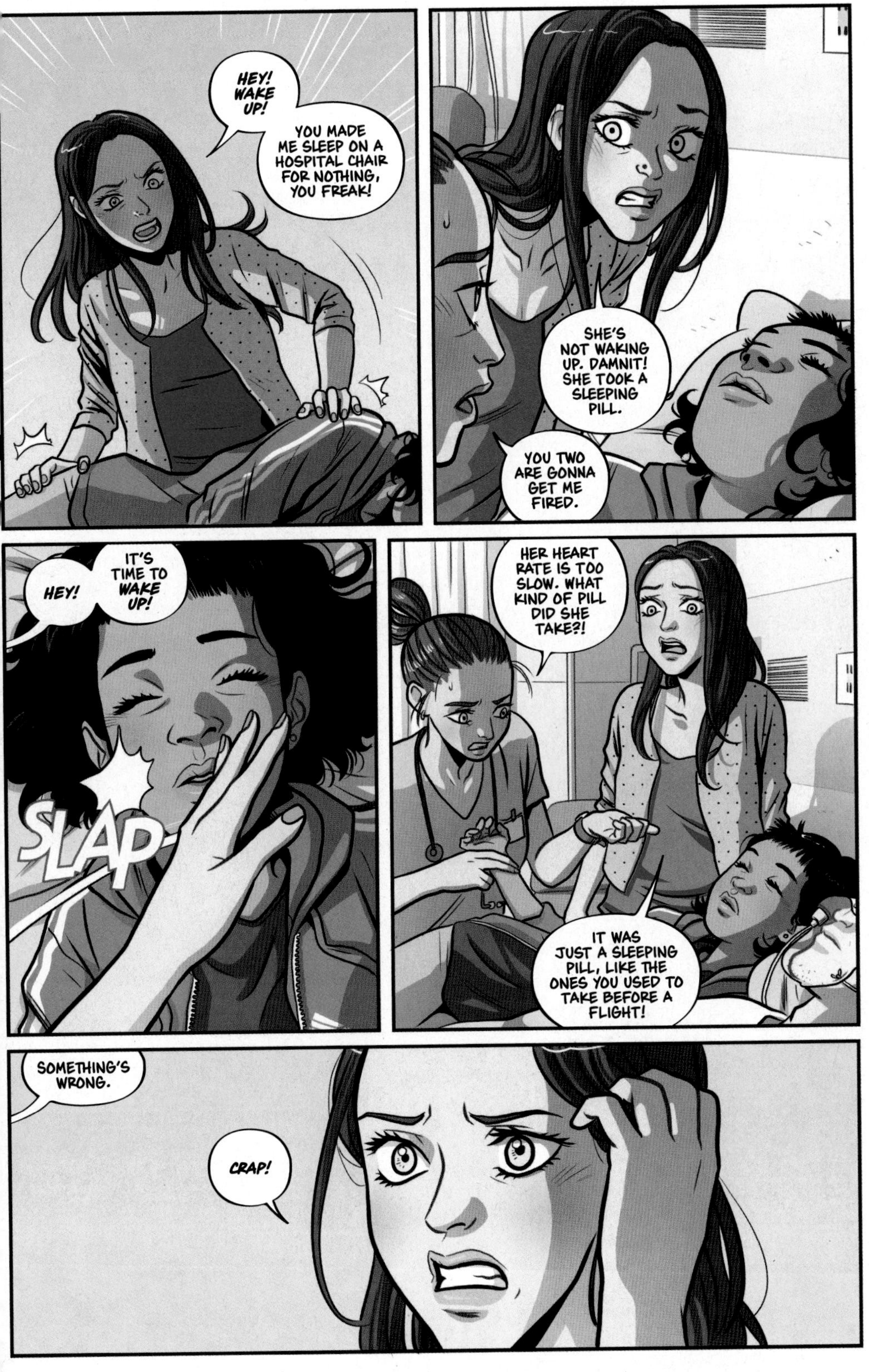
HEY! WAKE UP!
YOU MADE ME SLEEP ON A HOSPITAL CHAIR FOR NOTHING, YOU FREAK!
SHE'S NOT WAKING UP. DAMNIT! SHE TOOK A SLEEPING PILL.
YOU TWO ARE GONNA GET ME FIRED.
HEY!
IT'S TIME TO WAKE UP!
SLAP
HER HEART RATE IS TOO SLOW. WHAT KIND OF PILL DID SHE TAKE?!
IT WAS JUST A SLEEPING PILL, LIKE THE ONES YOU USED TO TAKE BEFORE A FLIGHT!
SOMETHING'S WRONG.
CRAP!

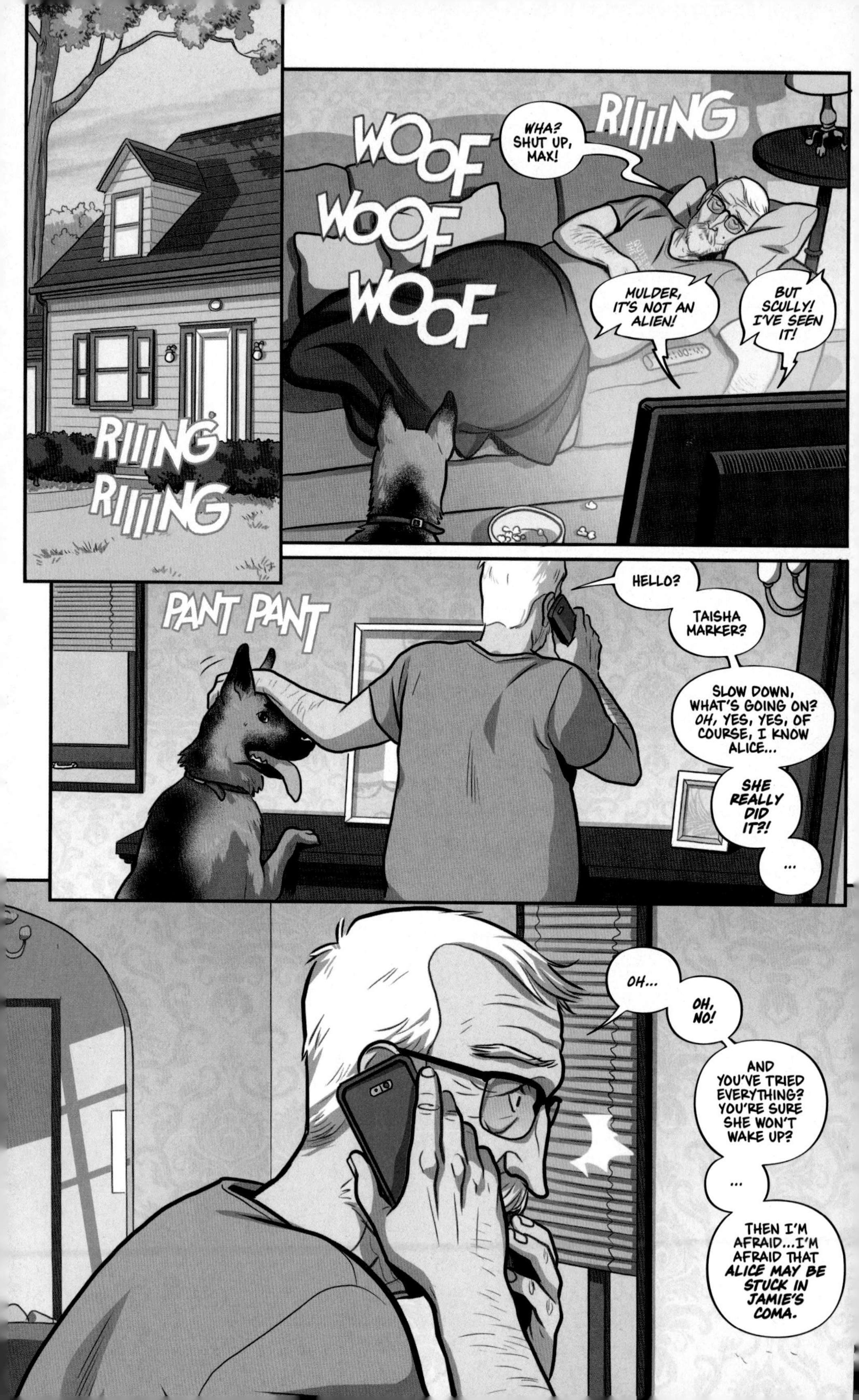
RIIING
RIIING
WOOF
WOOF
WOOF
WHA? SHUT UP, MAX!
RIIING
MULDER, IT'S NOT AN ALIEN!
BUT SCULLY! I'VE SEEN IT!
PANT PANT
HELLO?
TAISHA MARKER?
SLOW DOWN, WHAT'S GOING ON? OH, YES, YES, OF COURSE, I KNOW ALICE...
SHE REALLY DID IT?!
...
OH...
OH, NO!
AND YOU'VE TRIED EVERYTHING? YOU'RE SURE SHE WON'T WAKE UP?
...
THEN I'M AFRAID...I'M AFRAID THAT ALICE MAY BE STUCK IN JAMIE'S COMA.

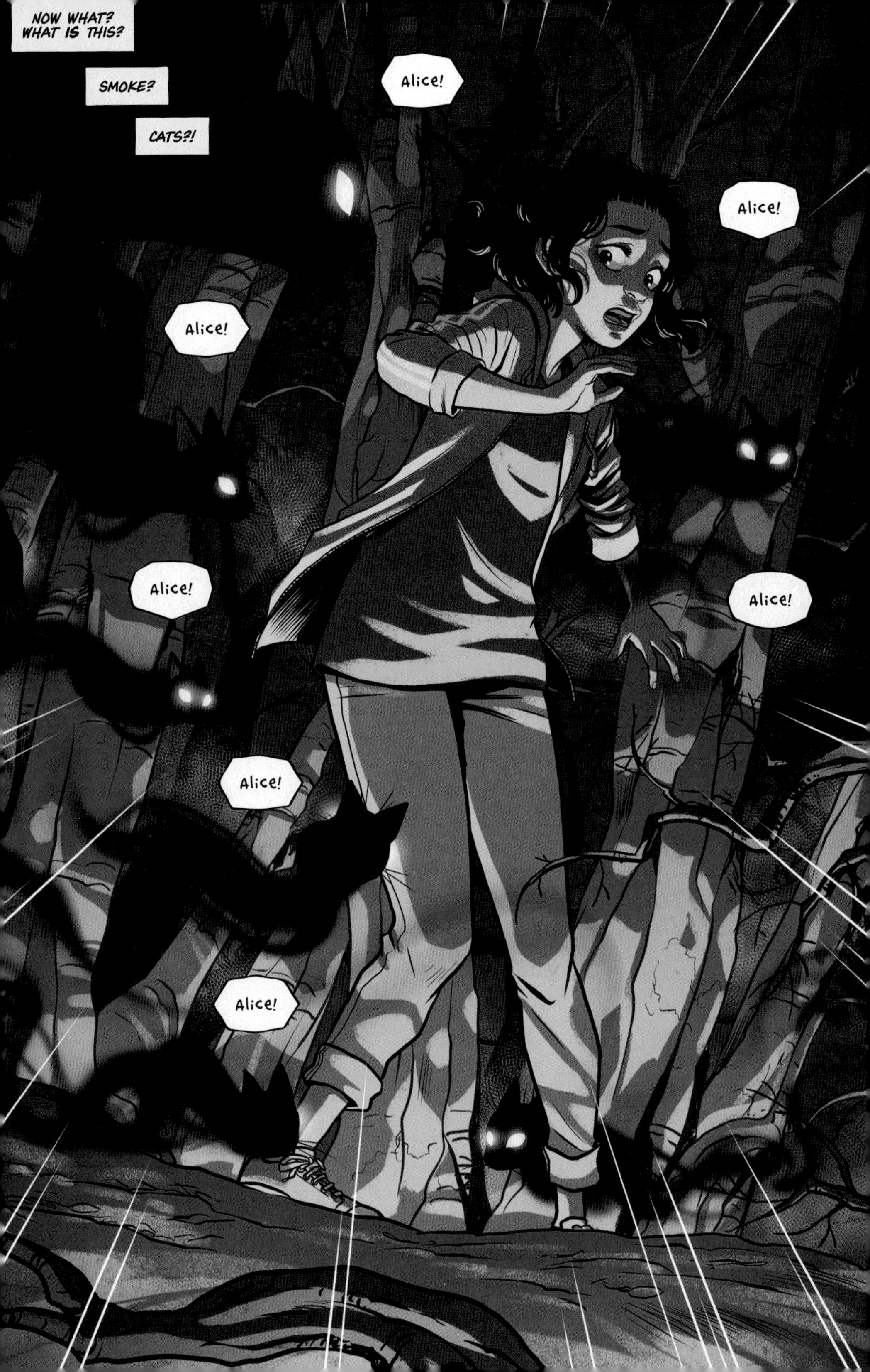
NOW WHAT? WHAT IS THIS?
SMOKE?
CATS?!
Alice!
Alice!
Alice!
Alice!
Alice!
Alice!
Alice!

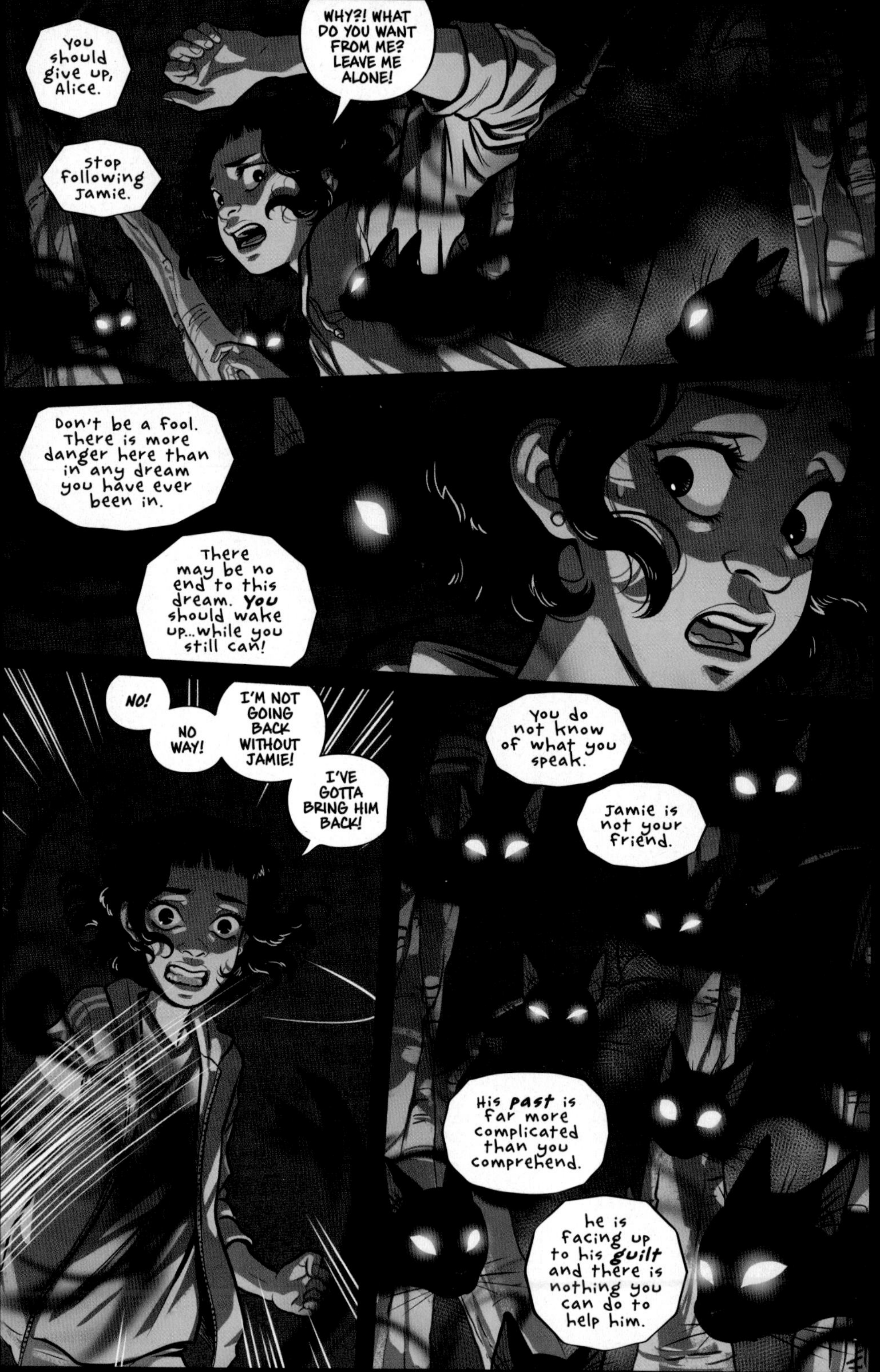
You should give up, Alice.
WHY?! WHAT DO YOU WANT FROM ME? LEAVE ME ALONE!
Stop following Jamie.
Don't be a fool. There is more danger here than in any dream you have ever been in.
There may be no end to this dream. *You* should wake up...while you still can!
*NO!*
NO WAY!
I'M NOT GOING BACK WITHOUT JAMIE!
I'VE GOTTA BRING HIM BACK!
You do not know of what you speak.
Jamie is not your friend.
His *past* is far more complicated than you comprehend.
He is facing up to his *guilt* and there is nothing you can do to help him.

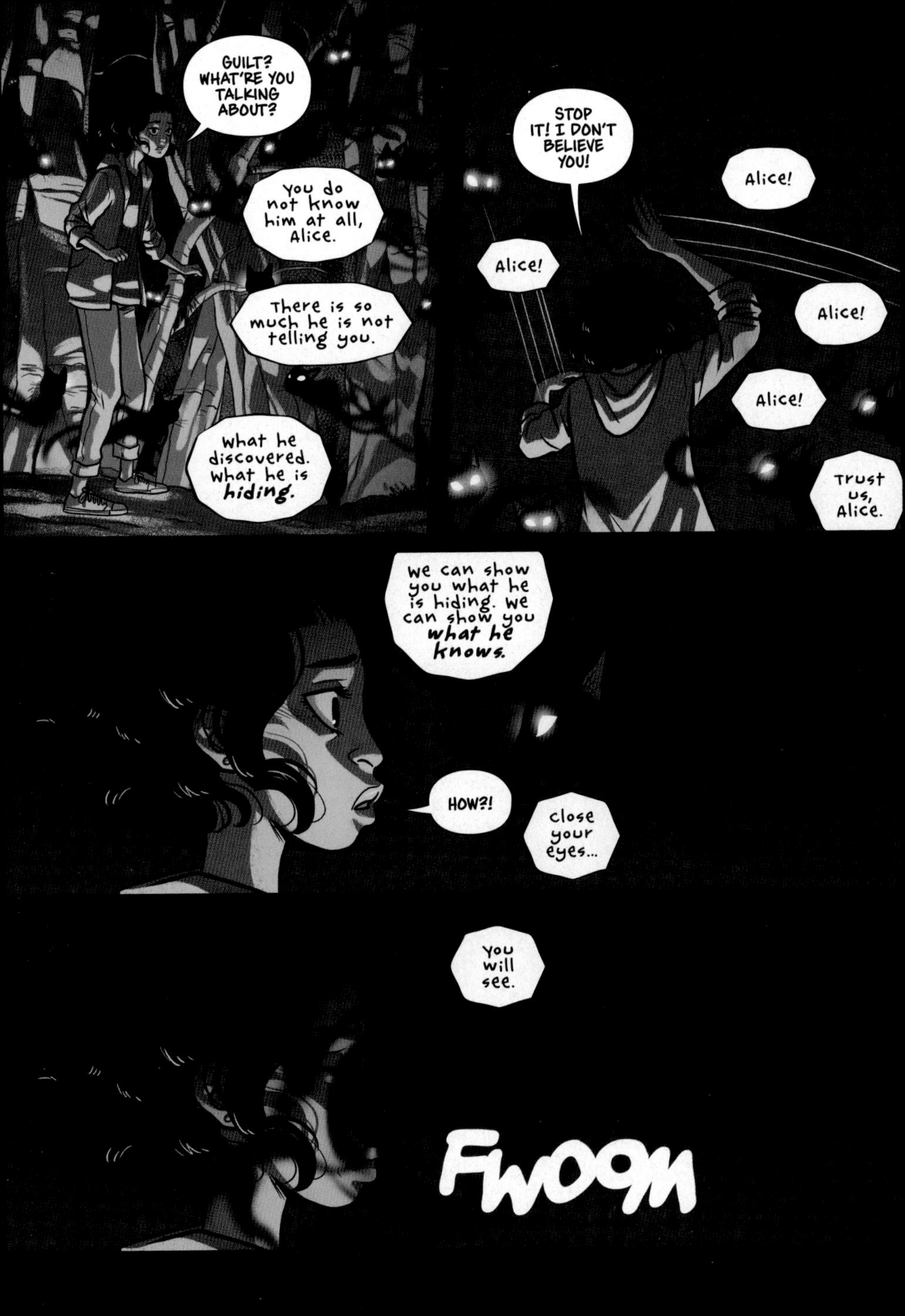
GUILT? WHAT'RE YOU TALKING ABOUT?
You do not know him at all, Alice.
There is so much he is not telling you.
What he discovered. What he is *hiding*.
STOP IT! I DON'T BELIEVE YOU!
Alice!
Alice!
Alice!
Alice!
Trust us, Alice.
We can show you what he is hiding. We can show you *what he knows*.
HOW?!
Close your eyes...
You will see.
FWOOM

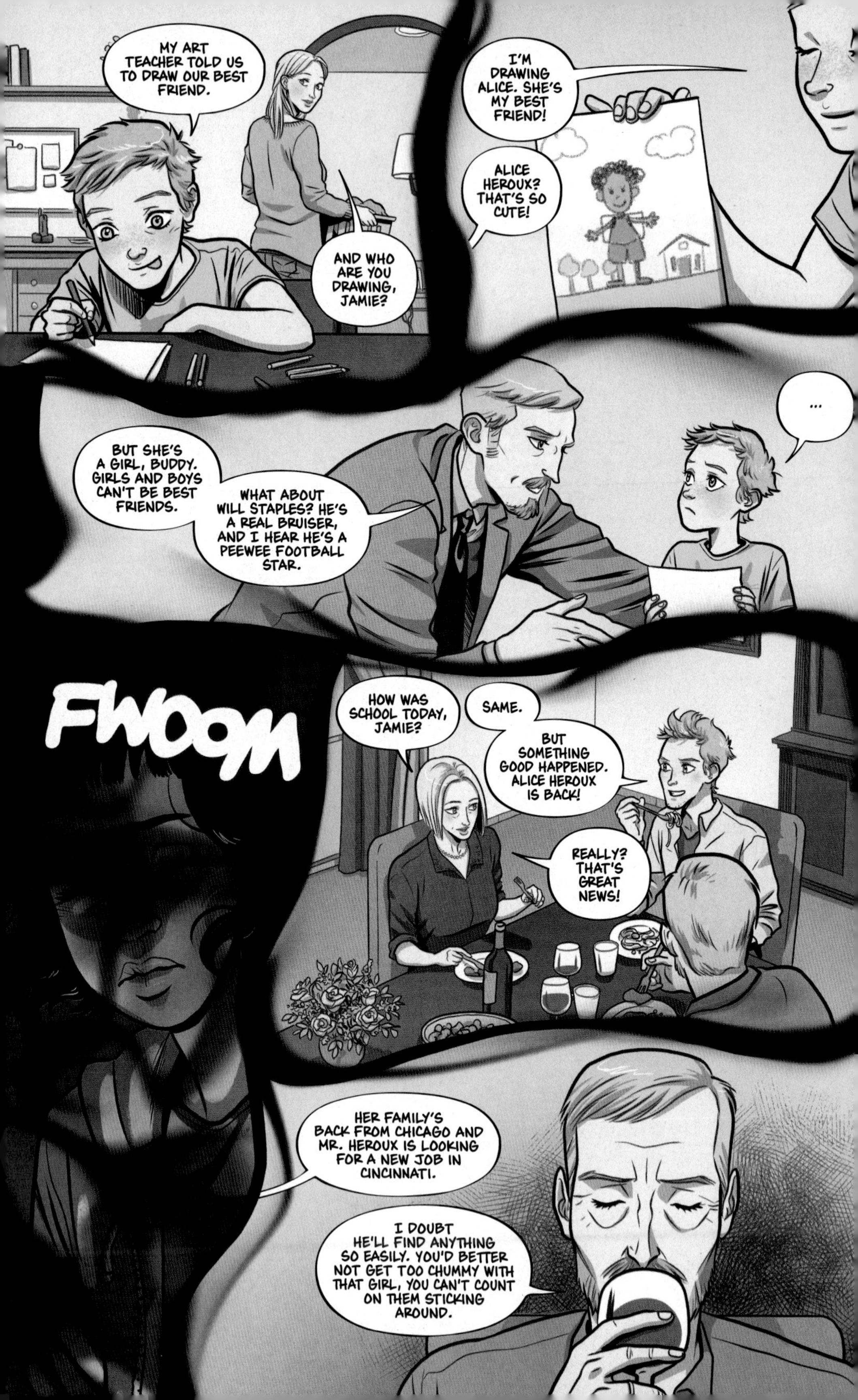
MY ART TEACHER TOLD US TO DRAW OUR BEST FRIEND.
AND WHO ARE YOU DRAWING, JAMIE?
I'M DRAWING ALICE. SHE'S MY BEST FRIEND!
ALICE HEROUX? THAT'S SO CUTE!
BUT SHE'S A GIRL, BUDDY. GIRLS AND BOYS CAN'T BE BEST FRIENDS.
WHAT ABOUT WILL STAPLES? HE'S A REAL BRUISER, AND I HEAR HE'S A PEEWEE FOOTBALL STAR.
...
FWOOM
HOW WAS SCHOOL TODAY, JAMIE?
SAME.
BUT SOMETHING GOOD HAPPENED. ALICE HEROUX IS BACK!
REALLY? THAT'S GREAT NEWS!
HER FAMILY'S BACK FROM CHICAGO AND MR. HEROUX IS LOOKING FOR A NEW JOB IN CINCINNATI.
I DOUBT HE'LL FIND ANYTHING SO EASILY. YOU'D BETTER NOT GET TOO CHUMMY WITH THAT GIRL, YOU CAN'T COUNT ON THEM STICKING AROUND.

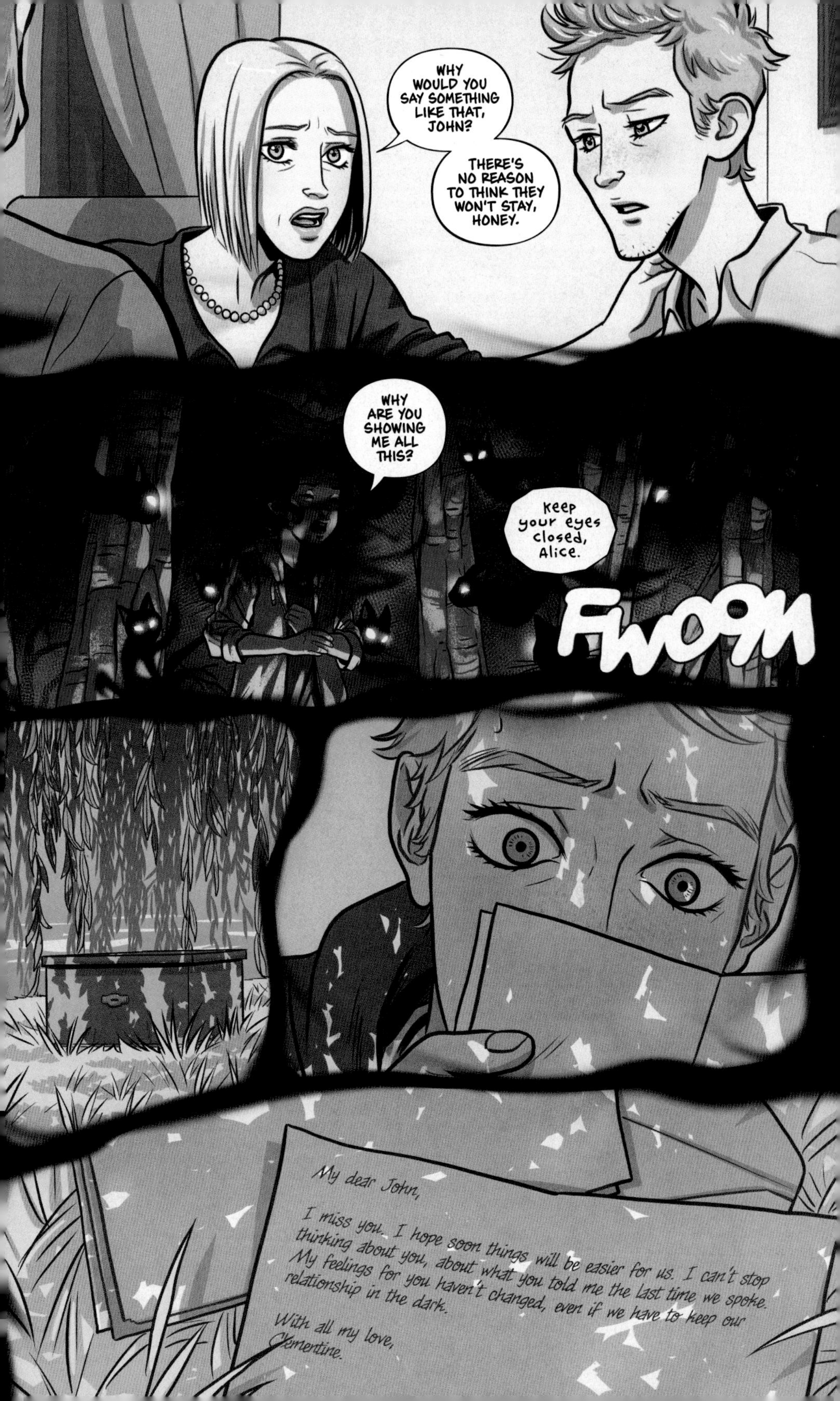
WHY WOULD YOU SAY SOMETHING LIKE THAT, JOHN?
THERE'S NO REASON TO THINK THEY WON'T STAY, HONEY.
WHY ARE YOU SHOWING ME ALL THIS?
Keep your eyes closed, Alice.
FWOOM
My dear John,
I miss you. I hope soon things will be easier for us. I can't stop thinking about you, about what you told me the last time we spoke. My feelings for you haven't changed, even if we have to keep our relationship in the dark.
With all my love,
Clementine.

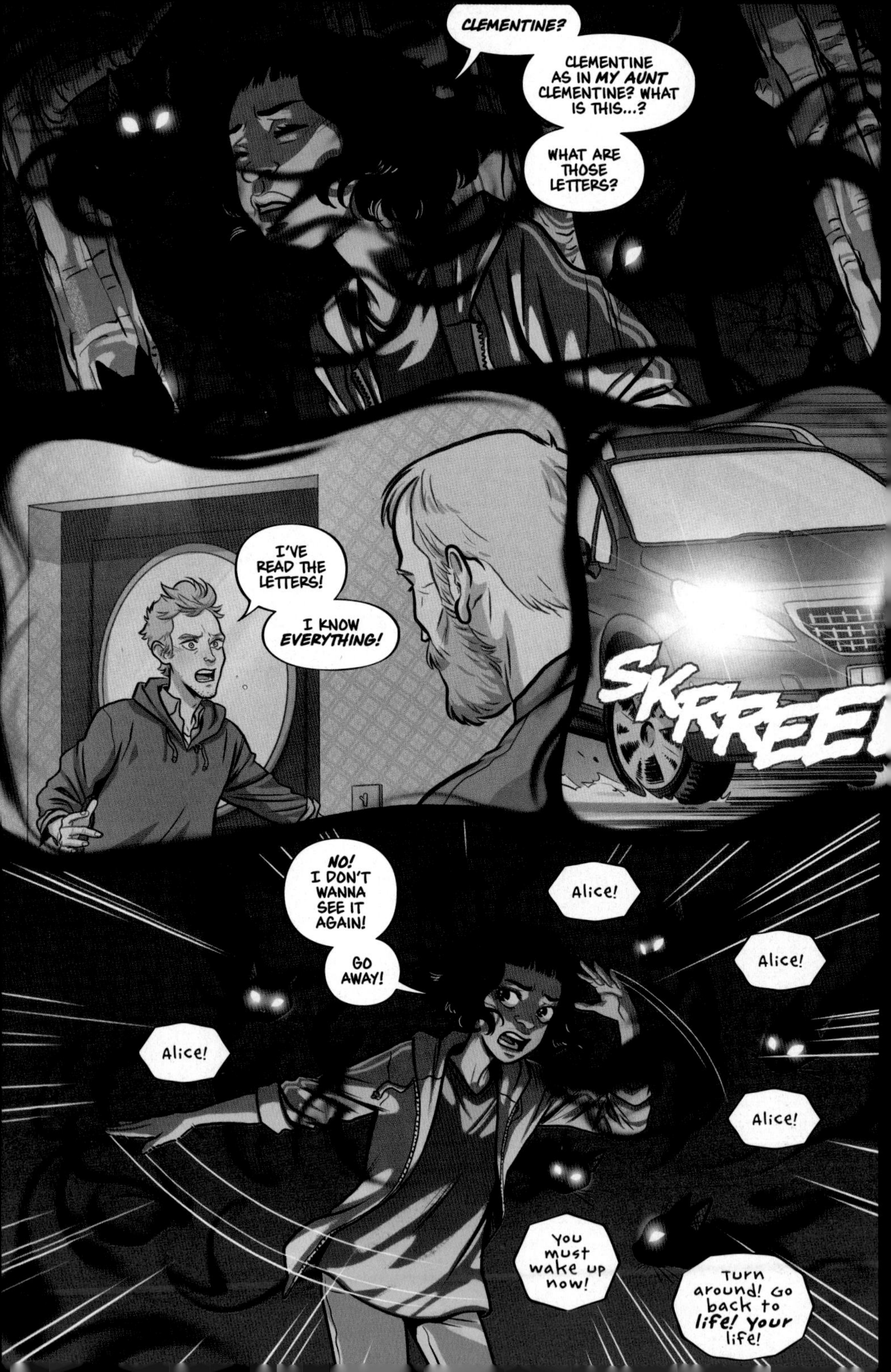
CLEMENTINE?
CLEMENTINE AS IN MY AUNT CLEMENTINE? WHAT IS THIS...?
WHAT ARE THOSE LETTERS?
I'VE READ THE LETTERS!
I KNOW EVERYTHING!
SKRREEE
NO! I DON'T WANNA SEE IT AGAIN!
GO AWAY!
Alice!
Alice!
Alice!
Alice!
You must wake up now!
Turn around! Go back to life! Your life!

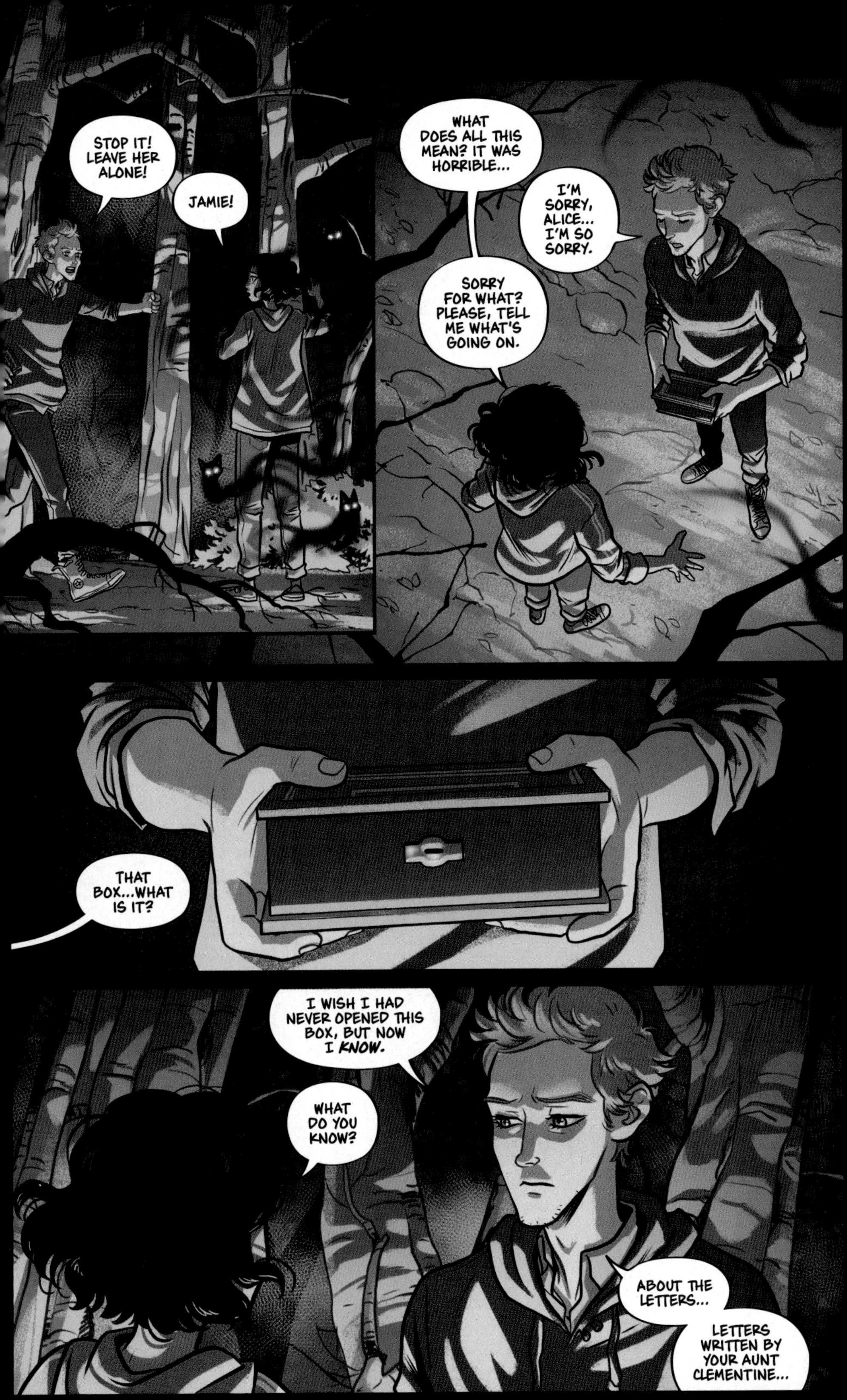
STOP IT! LEAVE HER ALONE!
JAMIE!
WHAT DOES ALL THIS MEAN? IT WAS HORRIBLE...
I'M SORRY, ALICE... I'M SO SORRY.
SORRY FOR WHAT? PLEASE, TELL ME WHAT'S GOING ON.
THAT BOX...WHAT IS IT?
I WISH I HAD NEVER OPENED THIS BOX, BUT NOW I KNOW.
WHAT DO YOU KNOW?
ABOUT THE LETTERS...
LETTERS WRITTEN BY YOUR AUNT CLEMENTINE...

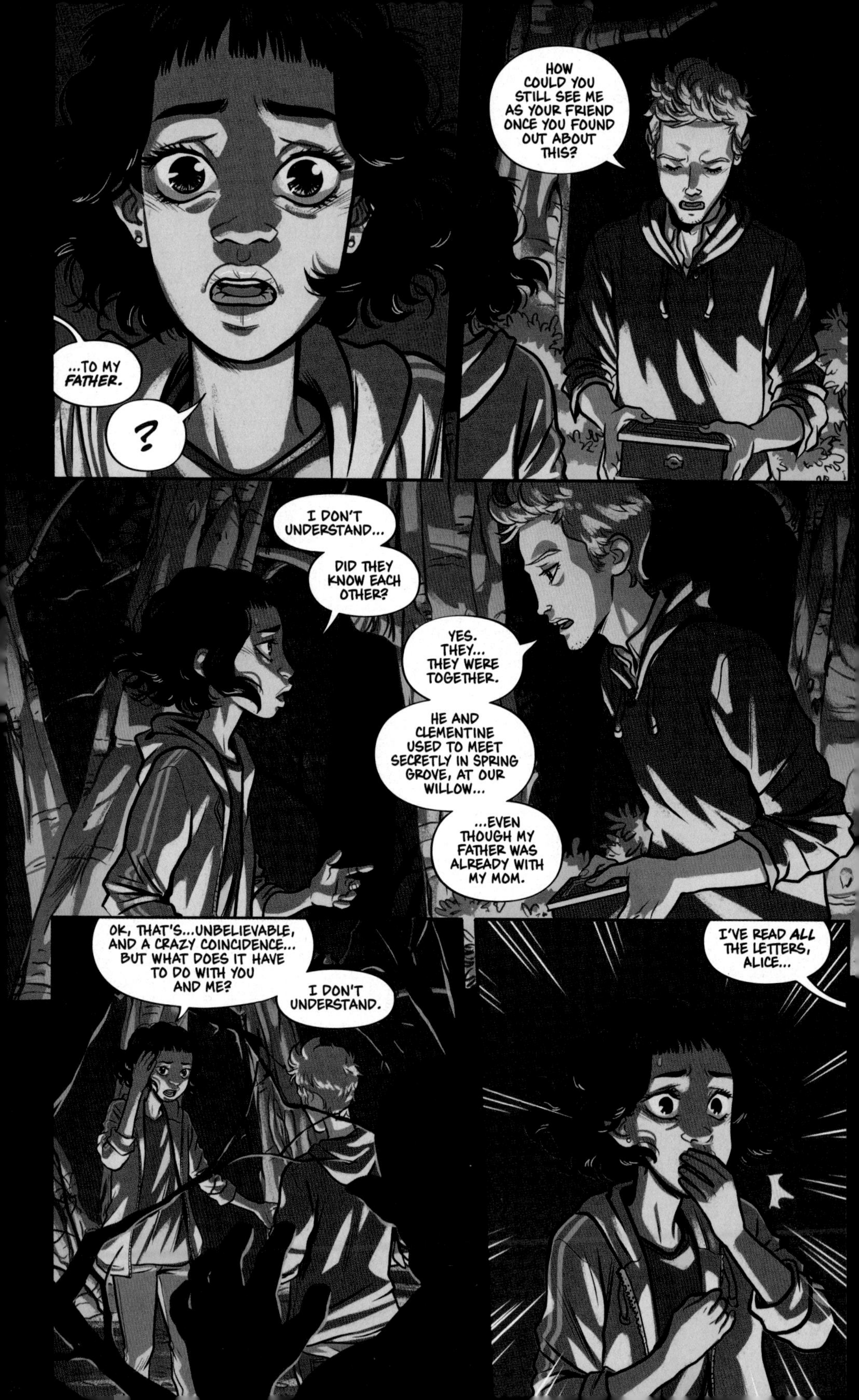
...TO MY *FATHER.*
?
HOW COULD YOU STILL SEE ME AS YOUR FRIEND ONCE YOU FOUND OUT ABOUT THIS?
I DON'T UNDERSTAND...
DID THEY KNOW EACH OTHER?
YES. THEY... THEY WERE TOGETHER.
HE AND CLEMENTINE USED TO MEET SECRETLY IN SPRING GROVE, AT OUR WILLOW...
...EVEN THOUGH MY FATHER WAS ALREADY WITH MY MOM.
OK, THAT'S...UNBELIEVABLE, AND A CRAZY COINCIDENCE... BUT WHAT DOES IT HAVE TO DO WITH YOU AND ME?
I DON'T UNDERSTAND.
I'VE READ *ALL* THE LETTERS, ALICE...

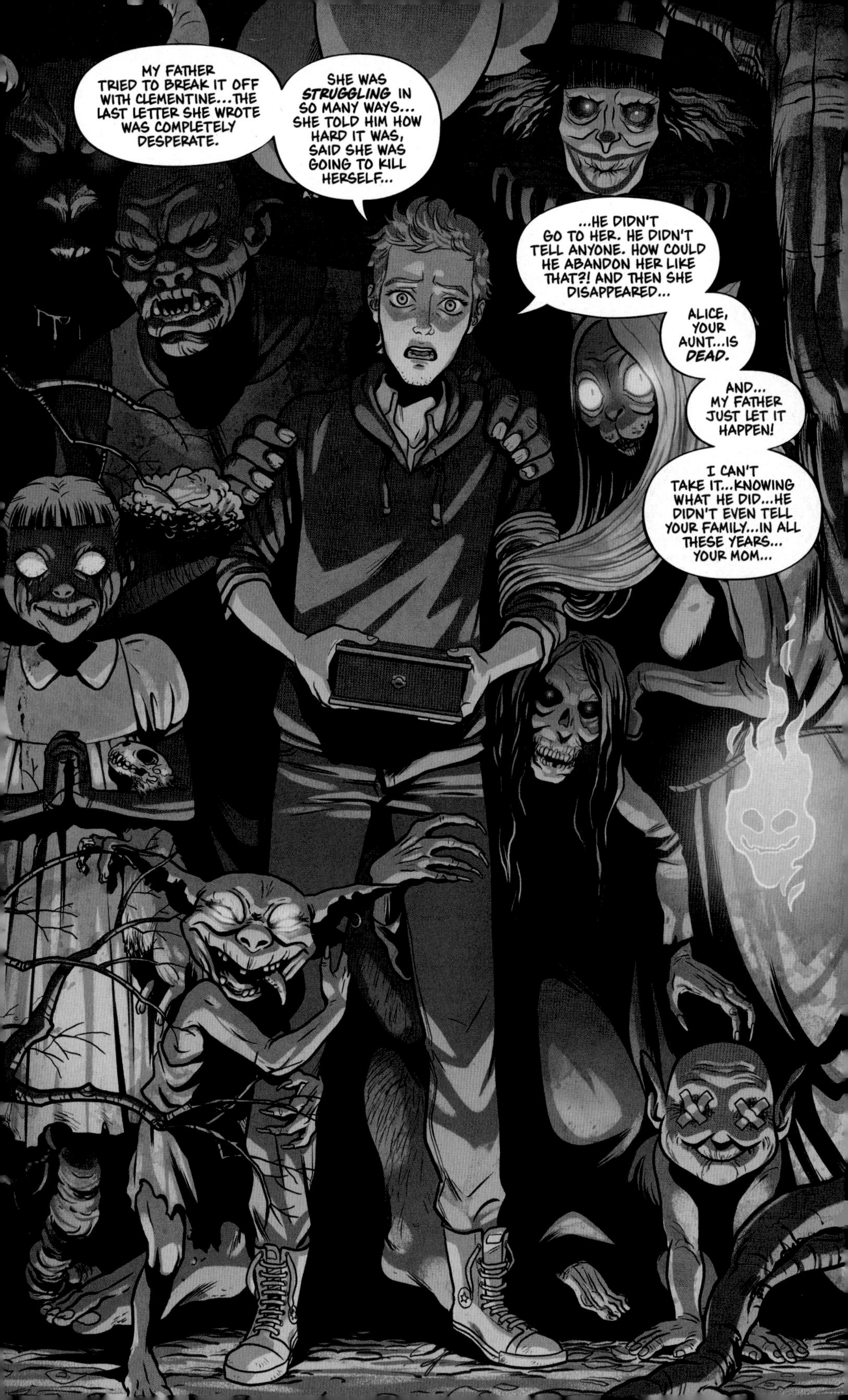
MY FATHER TRIED TO BREAK IT OFF WITH CLEMENTINE...THE LAST LETTER SHE WROTE WAS COMPLETELY DESPERATE.
SHE WAS *STRUGGLING* IN SO MANY WAYS... SHE TOLD HIM HOW HARD IT WAS, SAID SHE WAS GOING TO KILL HERSELF...
...HE DIDN'T GO TO HER. HE DIDN'T TELL ANYONE. HOW COULD HE ABANDON HER LIKE THAT?! AND THEN SHE DISAPPEARED...
ALICE, YOUR AUNT...IS *DEAD.*
AND... MY FATHER JUST LET IT HAPPEN!
I CAN'T TAKE IT...KNOWING WHAT HE DID...HE DIDN'T EVEN TELL YOUR FAMILY...IN ALL THESE YEARS... YOUR MOM...

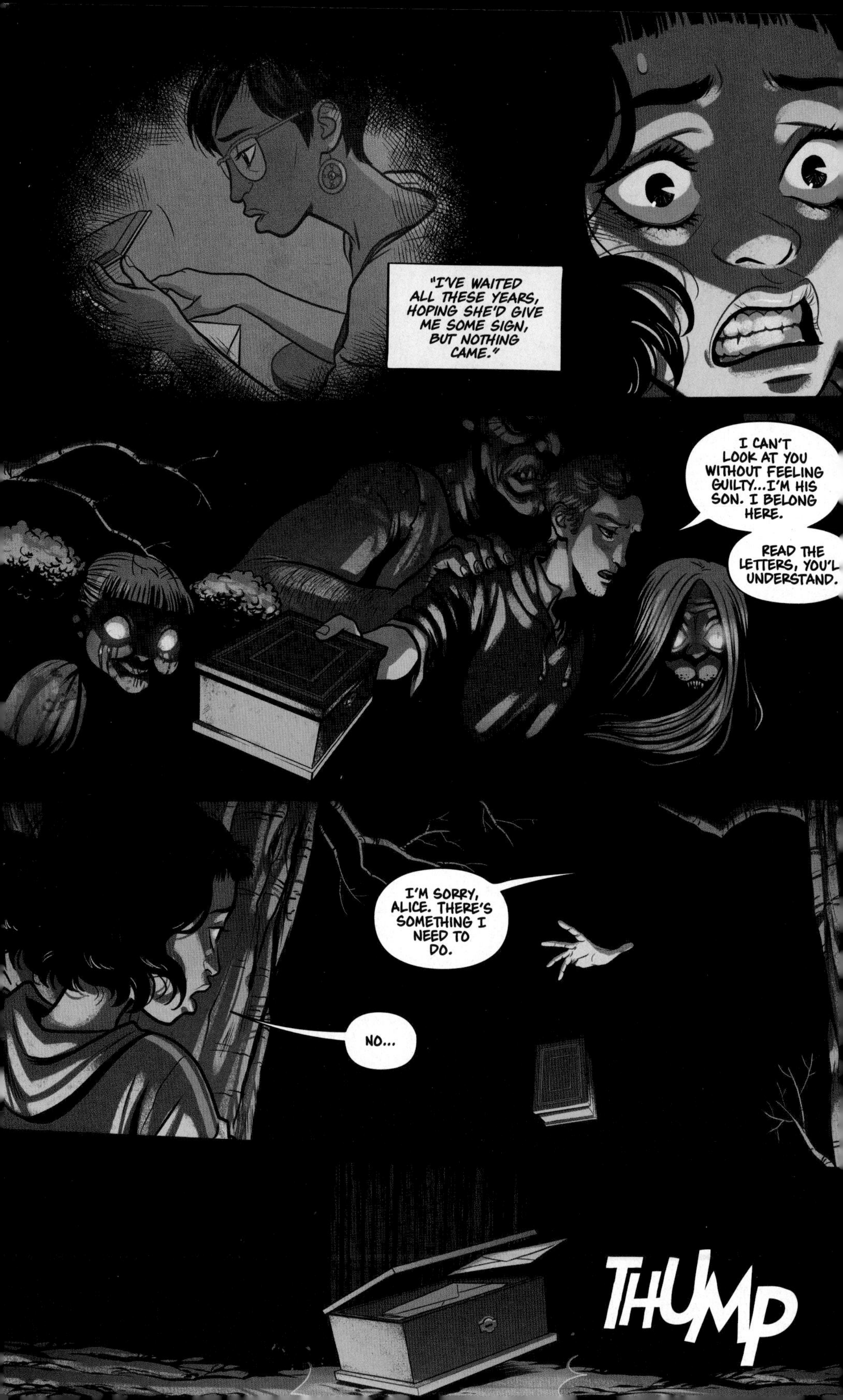
"I'VE WAITED ALL THESE YEARS, HOPING SHE'D GIVE ME SOME SIGN, BUT NOTHING CAME."
I CAN'T LOOK AT YOU WITHOUT FEELING GUILTY...I'M HIS SON. I BELONG HERE.
READ THE LETTERS, YOU'LL UNDERSTAND.
I'M SORRY, ALICE. THERE'S SOMETHING I NEED TO DO.
NO...
THUMP

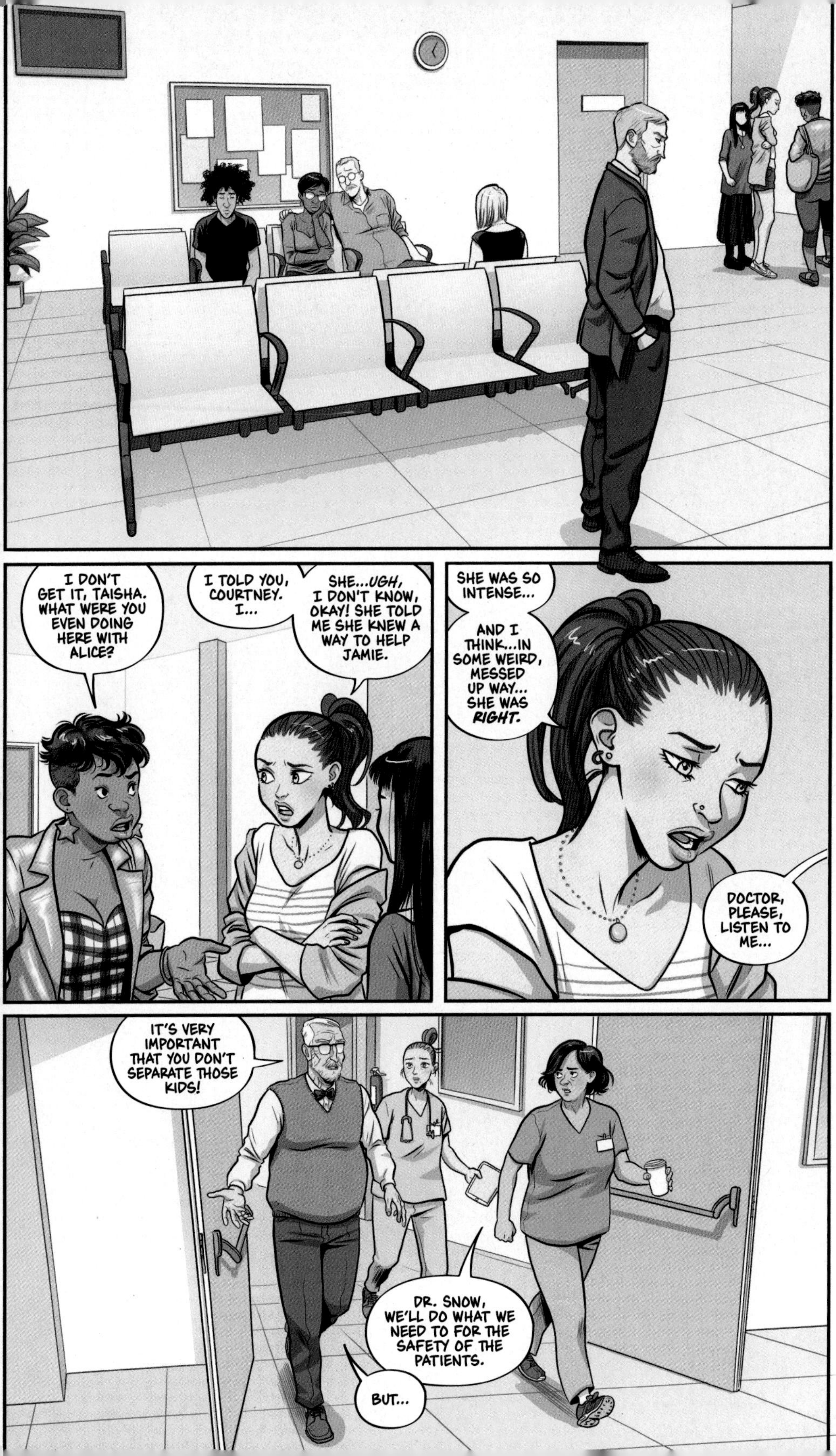
I DON'T GET IT, TAISHA. WHAT WERE YOU EVEN DOING HERE WITH ALICE?
I TOLD YOU, COURTNEY. I...
SHE...*UGH*, I DON'T KNOW, OKAY! SHE TOLD ME SHE KNEW A WAY TO HELP JAMIE.
SHE WAS SO INTENSE...
AND I THINK...IN SOME WEIRD, MESSED UP WAY... SHE WAS ***RIGHT.***
DOCTOR, PLEASE, LISTEN TO ME...
IT'S VERY IMPORTANT THAT YOU DON'T SEPARATE THOSE KIDS!
DR. SNOW, WE'LL DO WHAT WE NEED TO FOR THE SAFETY OF THE PATIENTS.
BUT...

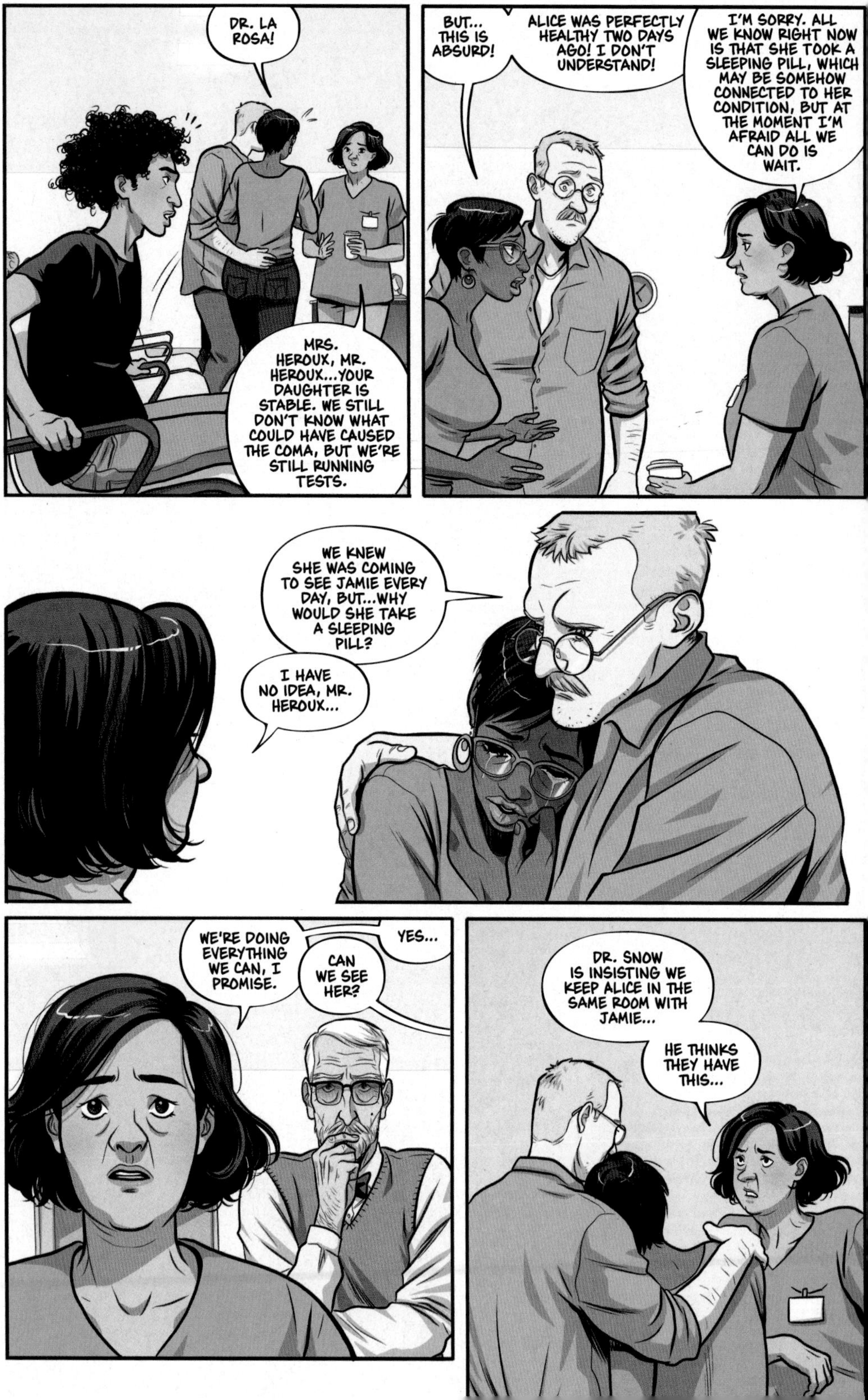
DR. LA ROSA!
MRS. HEROUX, MR. HEROUX...YOUR DAUGHTER IS STABLE. WE STILL DON'T KNOW WHAT COULD HAVE CAUSED THE COMA, BUT WE'RE STILL RUNNING TESTS.
BUT... THIS IS ABSURD!
ALICE WAS PERFECTLY HEALTHY TWO DAYS AGO! I DON'T UNDERSTAND!
I'M SORRY. ALL WE KNOW RIGHT NOW IS THAT SHE TOOK A SLEEPING PILL, WHICH MAY BE SOMEHOW CONNECTED TO HER CONDITION, BUT AT THE MOMENT I'M AFRAID ALL WE CAN DO IS WAIT.
WE KNEW SHE WAS COMING TO SEE JAMIE EVERY DAY, BUT...WHY WOULD SHE TAKE A SLEEPING PILL?
I HAVE NO IDEA, MR. HEROUX...
WE'RE DOING EVERYTHING WE CAN, I PROMISE.
CAN WE SEE HER?
YES...
DR. SNOW IS INSISTING WE KEEP ALICE IN THE SAME ROOM WITH JAMIE...
HE THINKS THEY HAVE THIS...

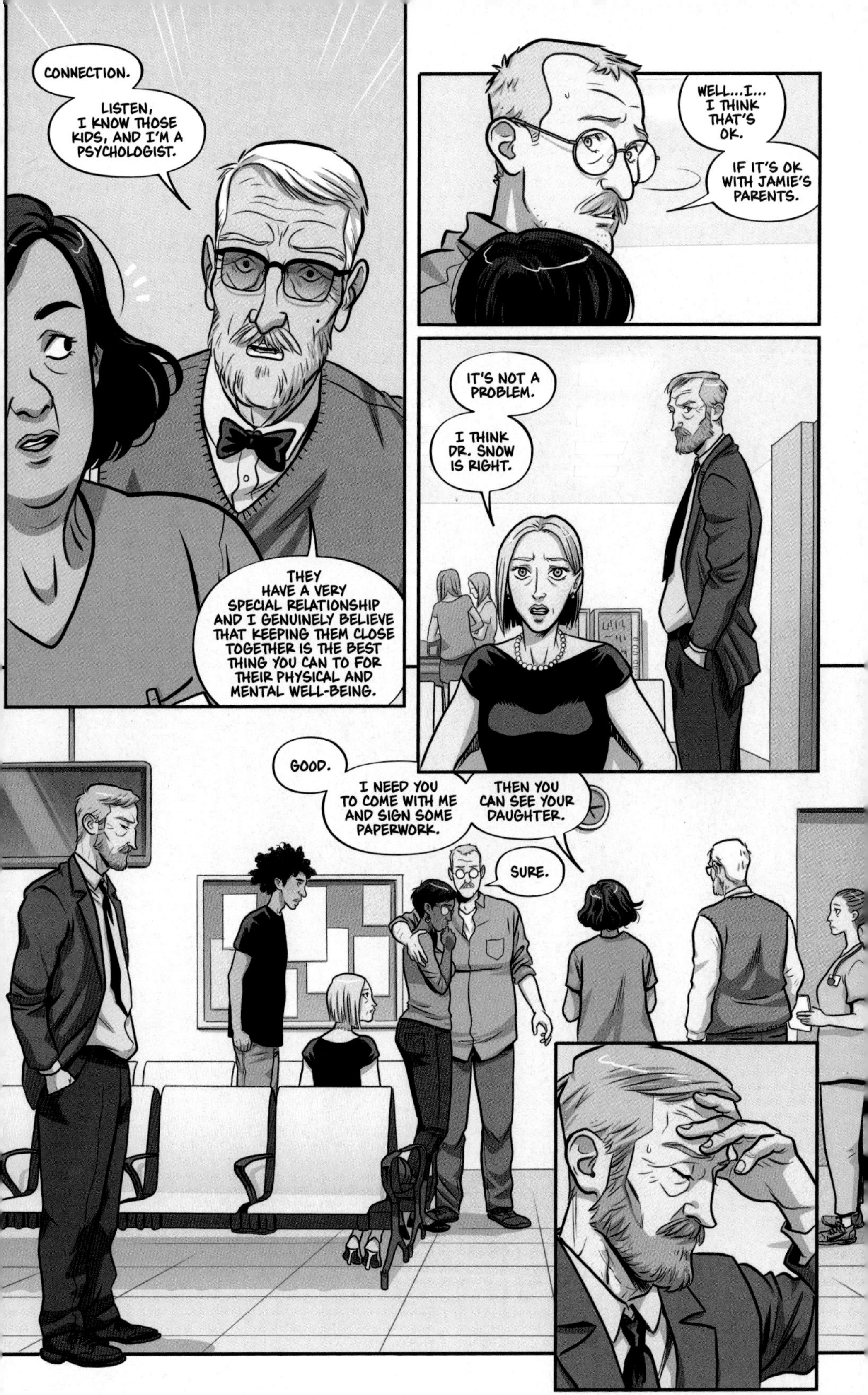
CONNECTION.
LISTEN, I KNOW THOSE KIDS, AND I'M A PSYCHOLOGIST.
THEY HAVE A VERY SPECIAL RELATIONSHIP AND I GENUINELY BELIEVE THAT KEEPING THEM CLOSE TOGETHER IS THE BEST THING YOU CAN TO FOR THEIR PHYSICAL AND MENTAL WELL-BEING.
WELL...I... I THINK THAT'S OK.
IF IT'S OK WITH JAMIE'S PARENTS.
IT'S NOT A PROBLEM.
I THINK DR. SNOW IS RIGHT.
GOOD.
I NEED YOU TO COME WITH ME AND SIGN SOME PAPERWORK.
THEN YOU CAN SEE YOUR DAUGHTER.
SURE.

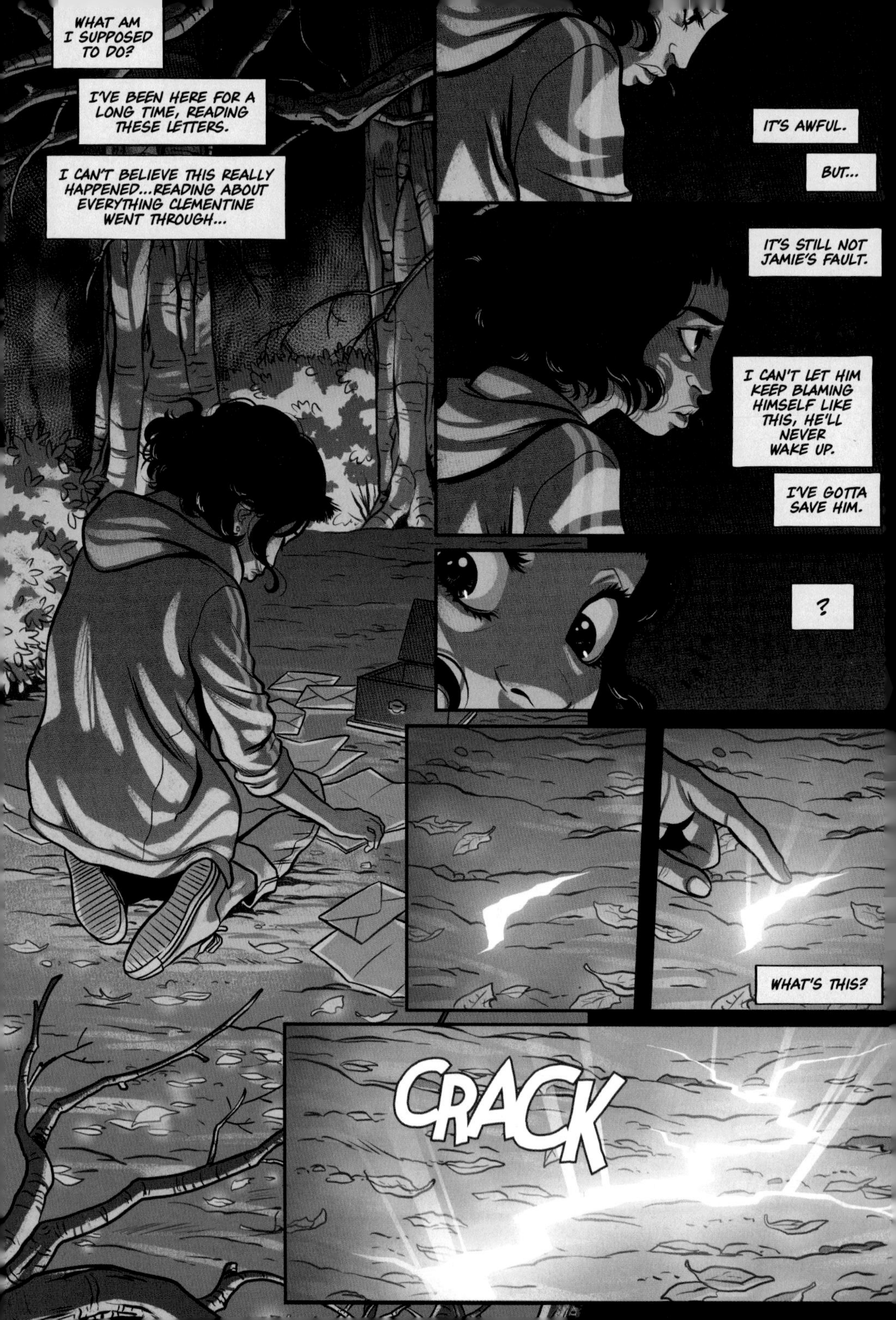
WHAT AM I SUPPOSED TO DO?
I'VE BEEN HERE FOR A LONG TIME, READING THESE LETTERS.
I CAN'T BELIEVE THIS REALLY HAPPENED...READING ABOUT EVERYTHING CLEMENTINE WENT THROUGH...
IT'S AWFUL.
BUT...
IT'S STILL NOT JAMIE'S FAULT.
I CAN'T LET HIM KEEP BLAMING HIMSELF LIKE THIS, HE'LL NEVER WAKE UP.
I'VE GOTTA SAVE HIM.
?
WHAT'S THIS?
CRACK

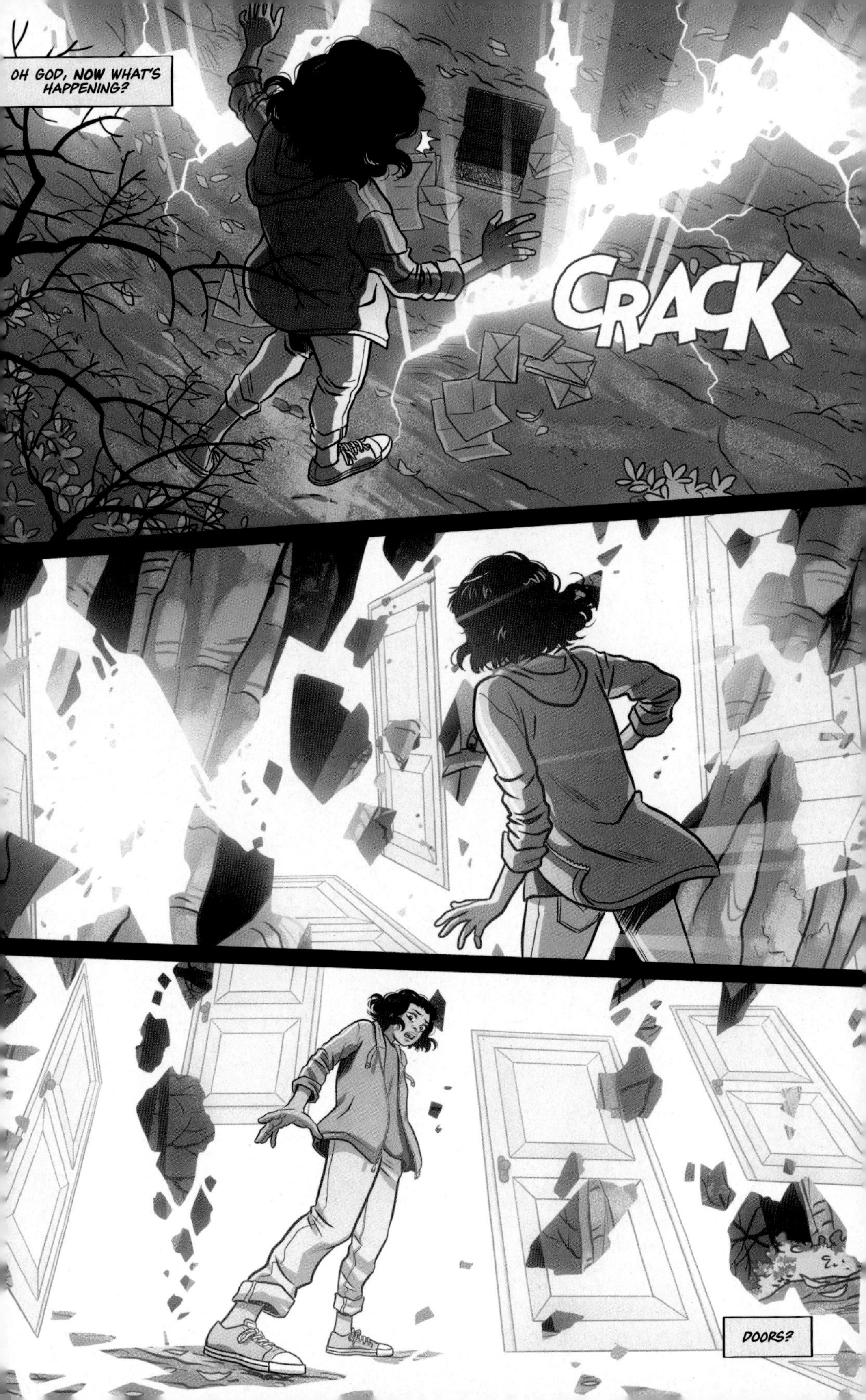
OH GOD, NOW WHAT'S HAPPENING?
CRACK
DOORS?

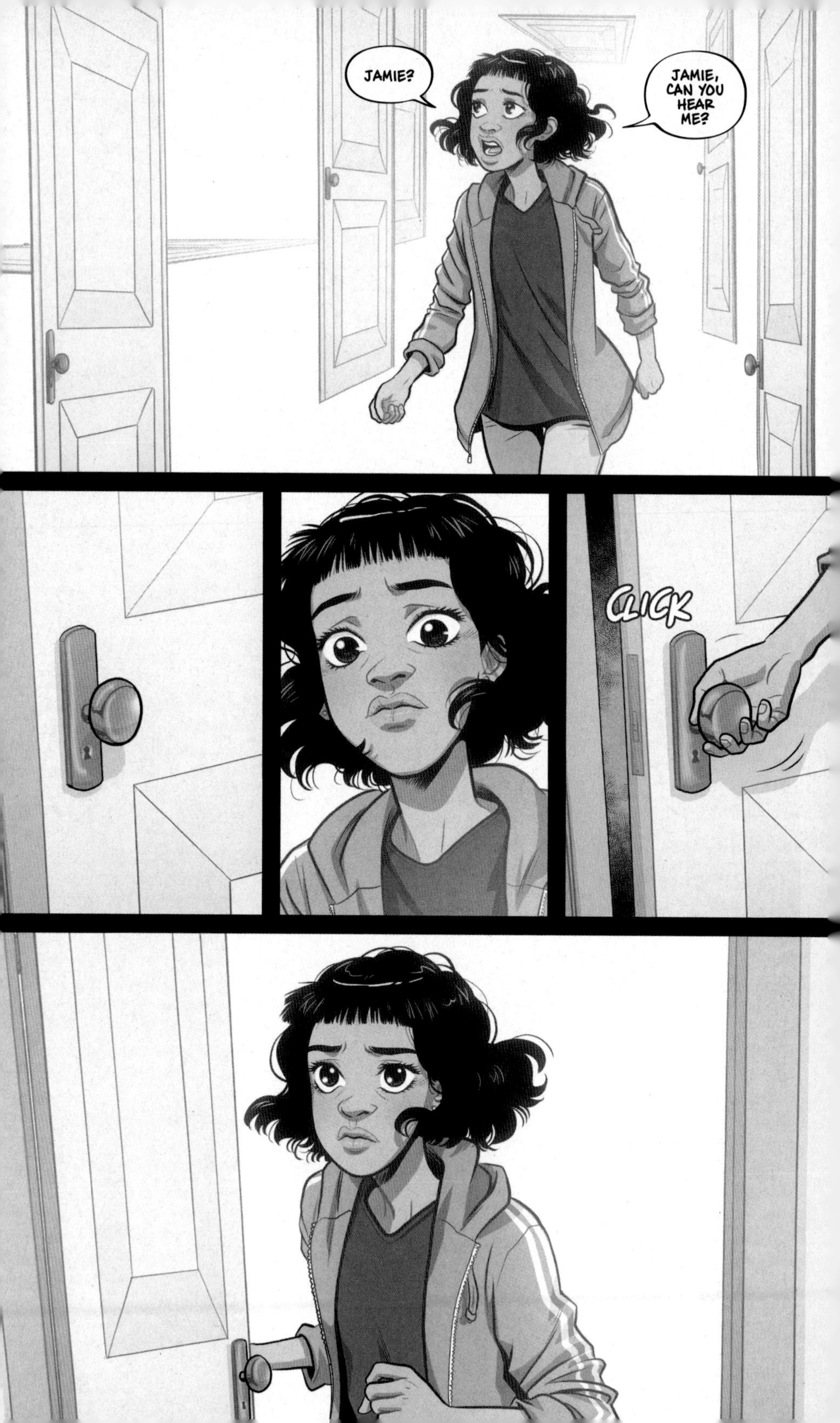
JAMIE?
JAMIE, CAN YOU HEAR ME?
CLICK

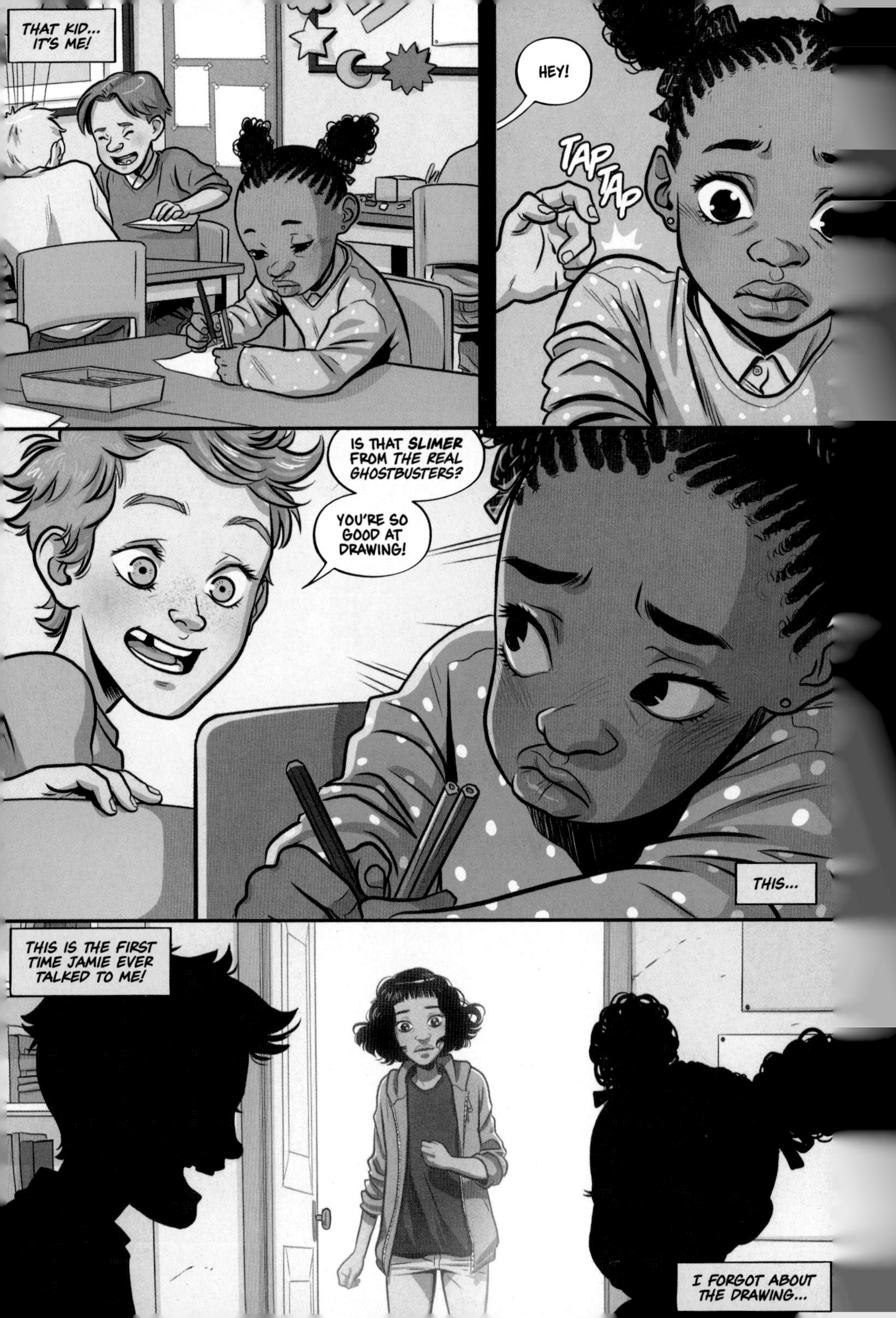
THAT KID... IT'S ME!
HEY!
TAP TAP
IS THAT SLIMER FROM THE REAL GHOSTBUSTERS?
YOU'RE SO GOOD AT DRAWING!
THIS...
THIS IS THE FIRST TIME JAMIE EVER TALKED TO ME!
I FORGOT ABOUT THE DRAWING...

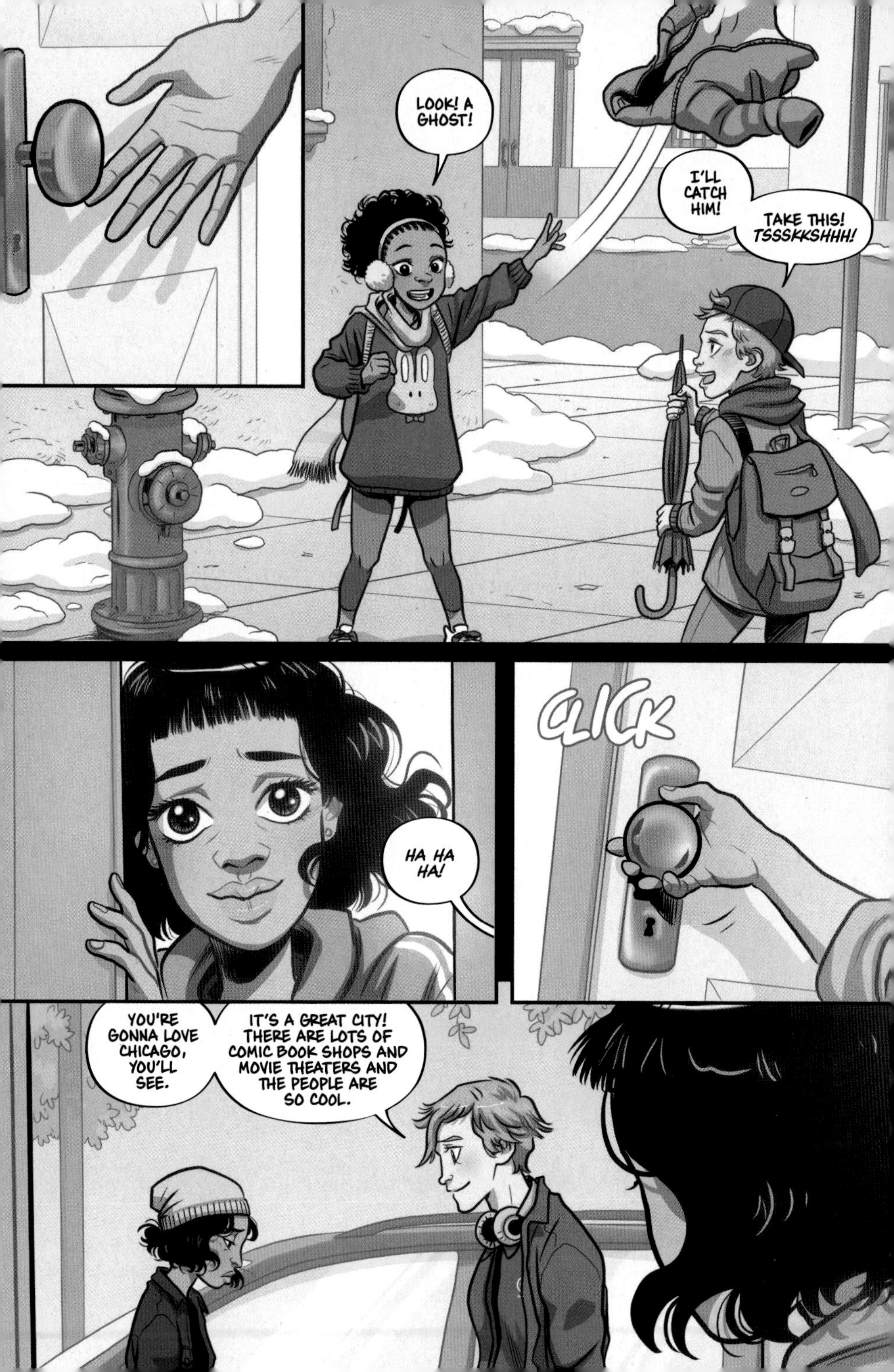
LOOK! A GHOST!
I'LL CATCH HIM!
TAKE THIS! TSSSKKSHHH!
CLICK
HA HA HA!
YOU'RE GONNA LOVE CHICAGO, YOU'LL SEE.
IT'S A GREAT CITY! THERE ARE LOTS OF COMIC BOOK SHOPS AND MOVIE THEATERS AND THE PEOPLE ARE SO COOL.

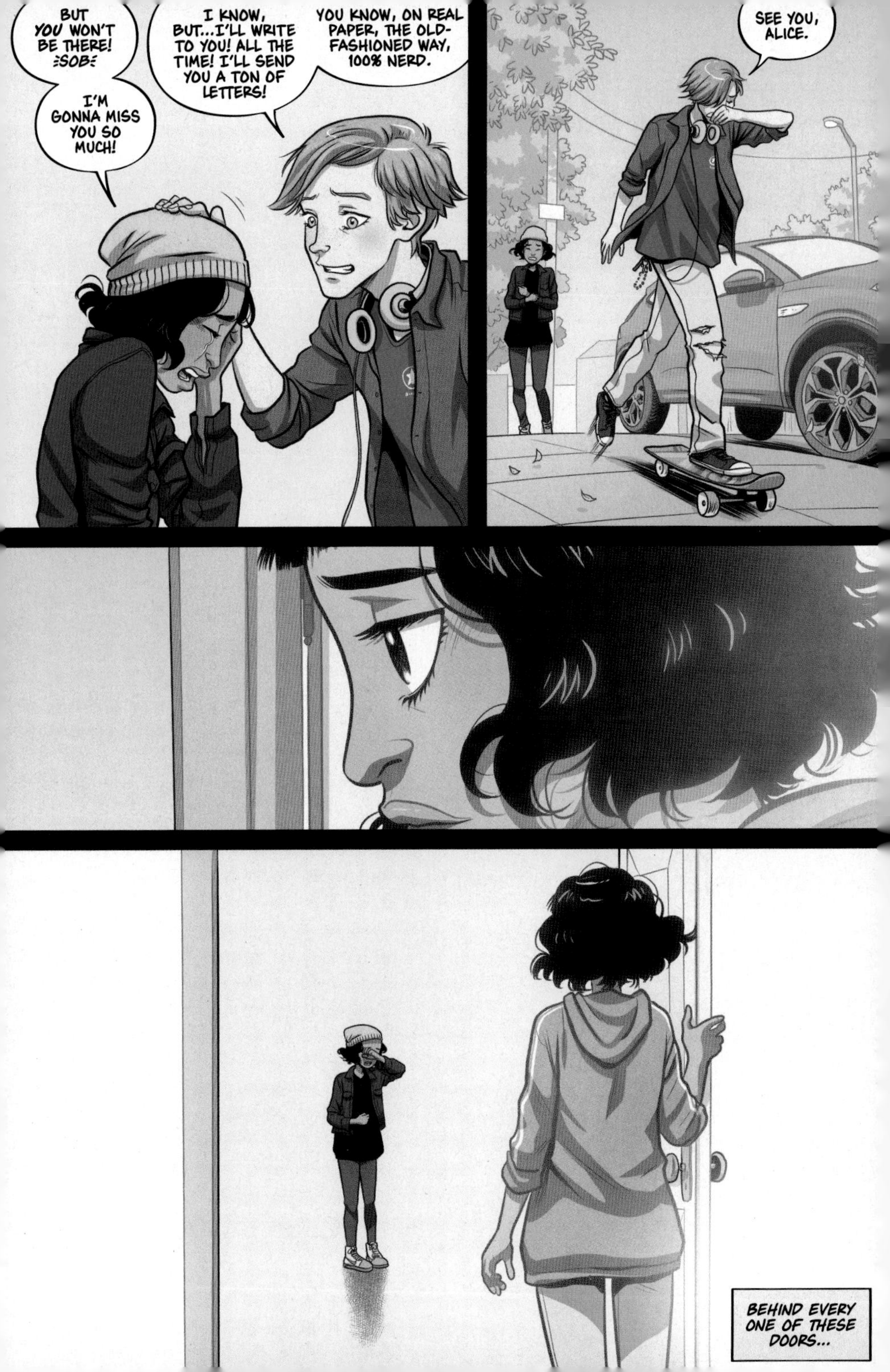
BUT YOU WON'T BE THERE! ≡SOB≡
I'M GONNA MISS YOU SO MUCH!
I KNOW, BUT...I'LL WRITE TO YOU! ALL THE TIME! I'LL SEND YOU A TON OF LETTERS!
YOU KNOW, ON REAL PAPER, THE OLD-FASHIONED WAY, 100% NERD.
SEE YOU, ALICE.
BEHIND EVERY ONE OF THESE DOORS...

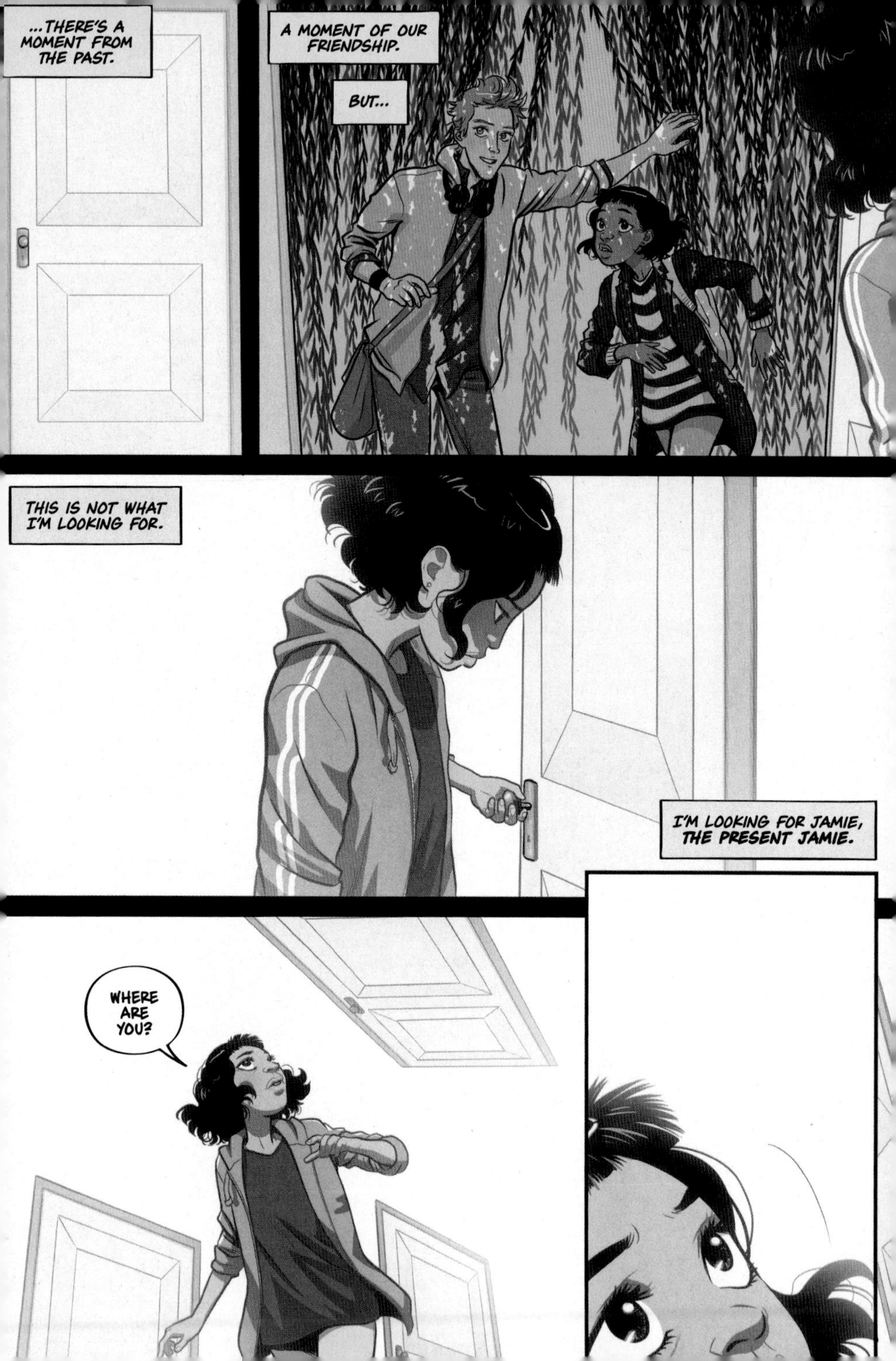
...THERE'S A MOMENT FROM THE PAST.
A MOMENT OF OUR FRIENDSHIP.
BUT...
THIS IS NOT WHAT I'M LOOKING FOR.
I'M LOOKING FOR JAMIE, THE PRESENT JAMIE.
WHERE ARE YOU?

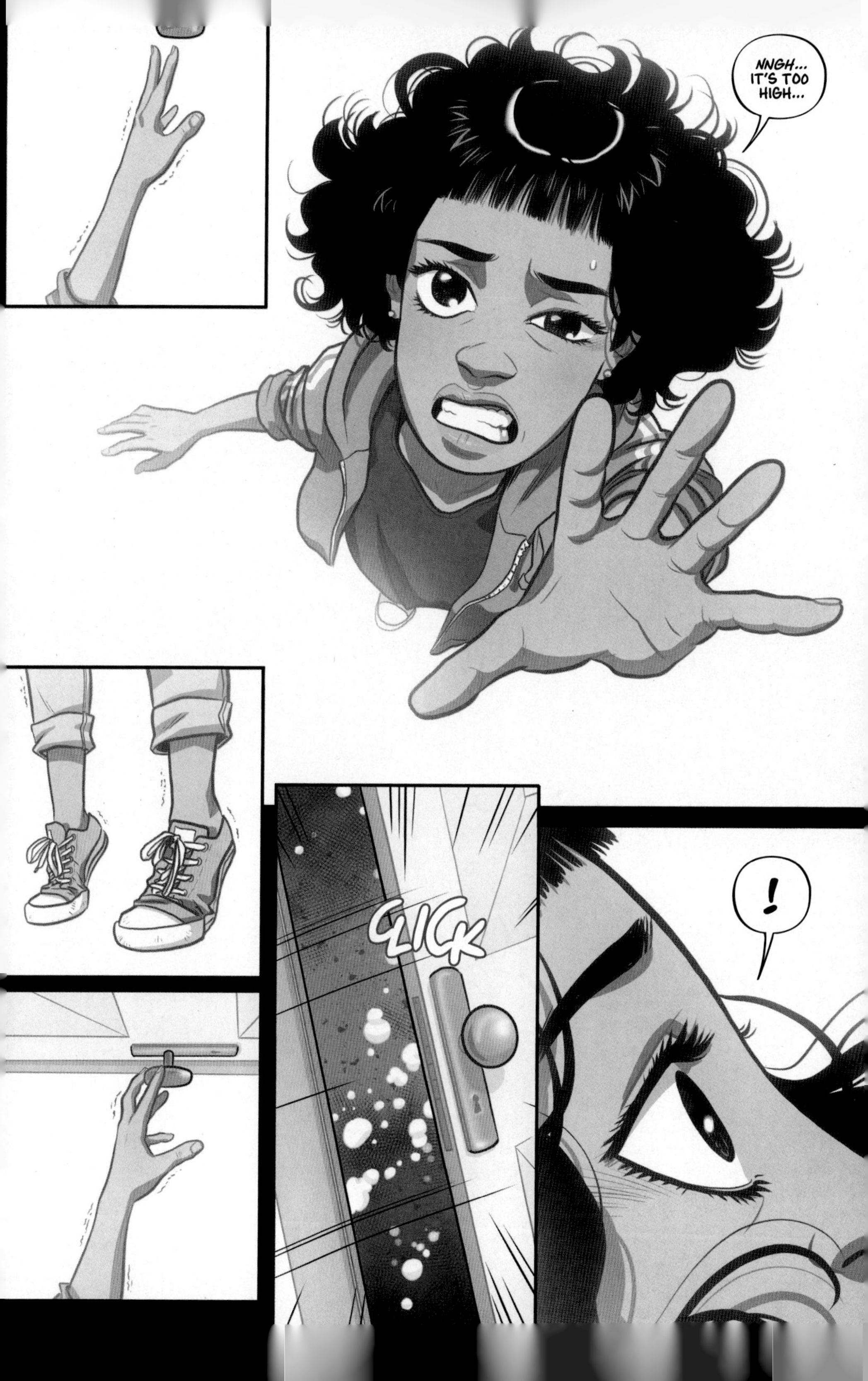
NNGH... IT'S TOO HIGH...
CLICK
!

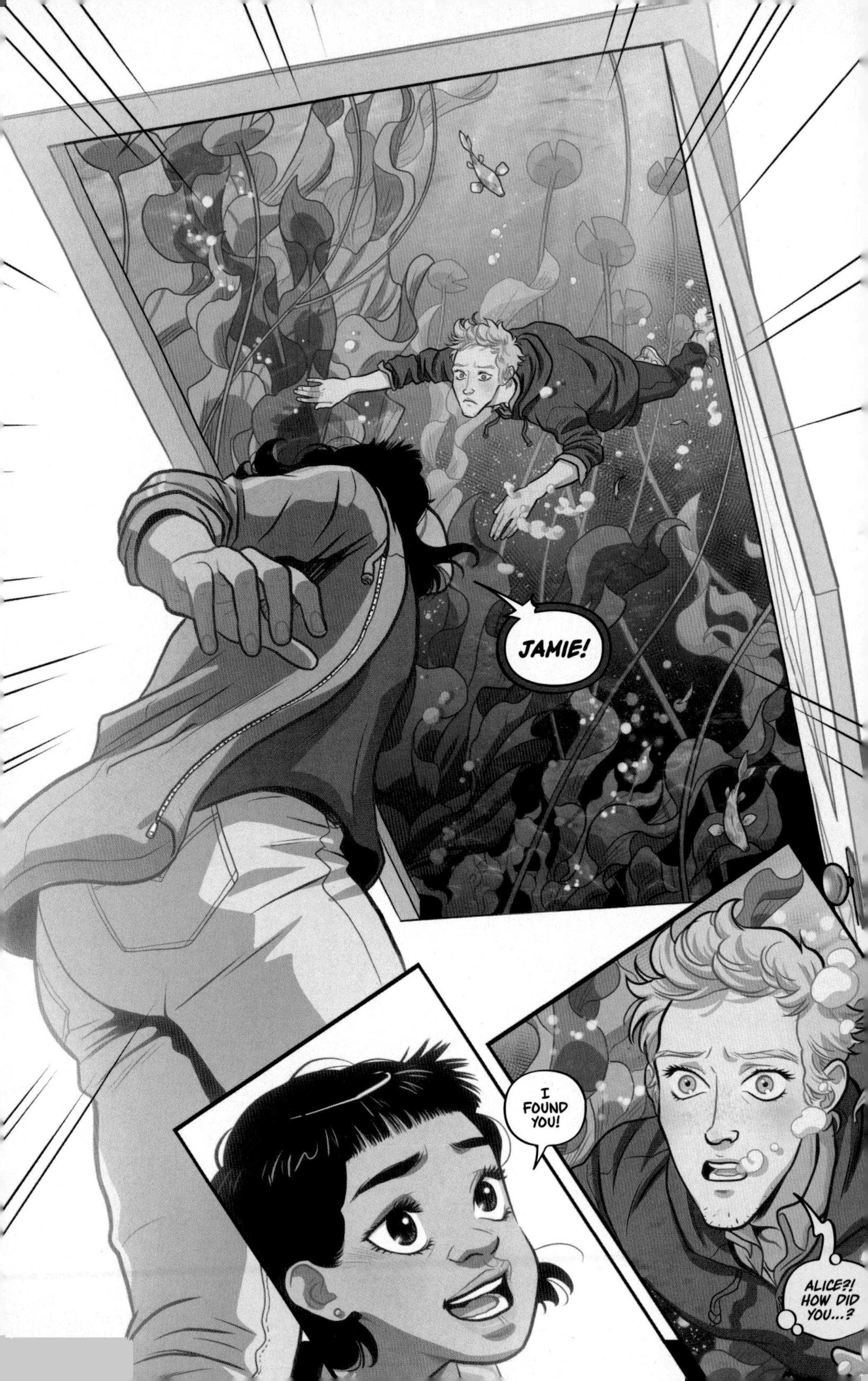
JAMIE!
I FOUND YOU!
ALICE?! HOW DID YOU...?

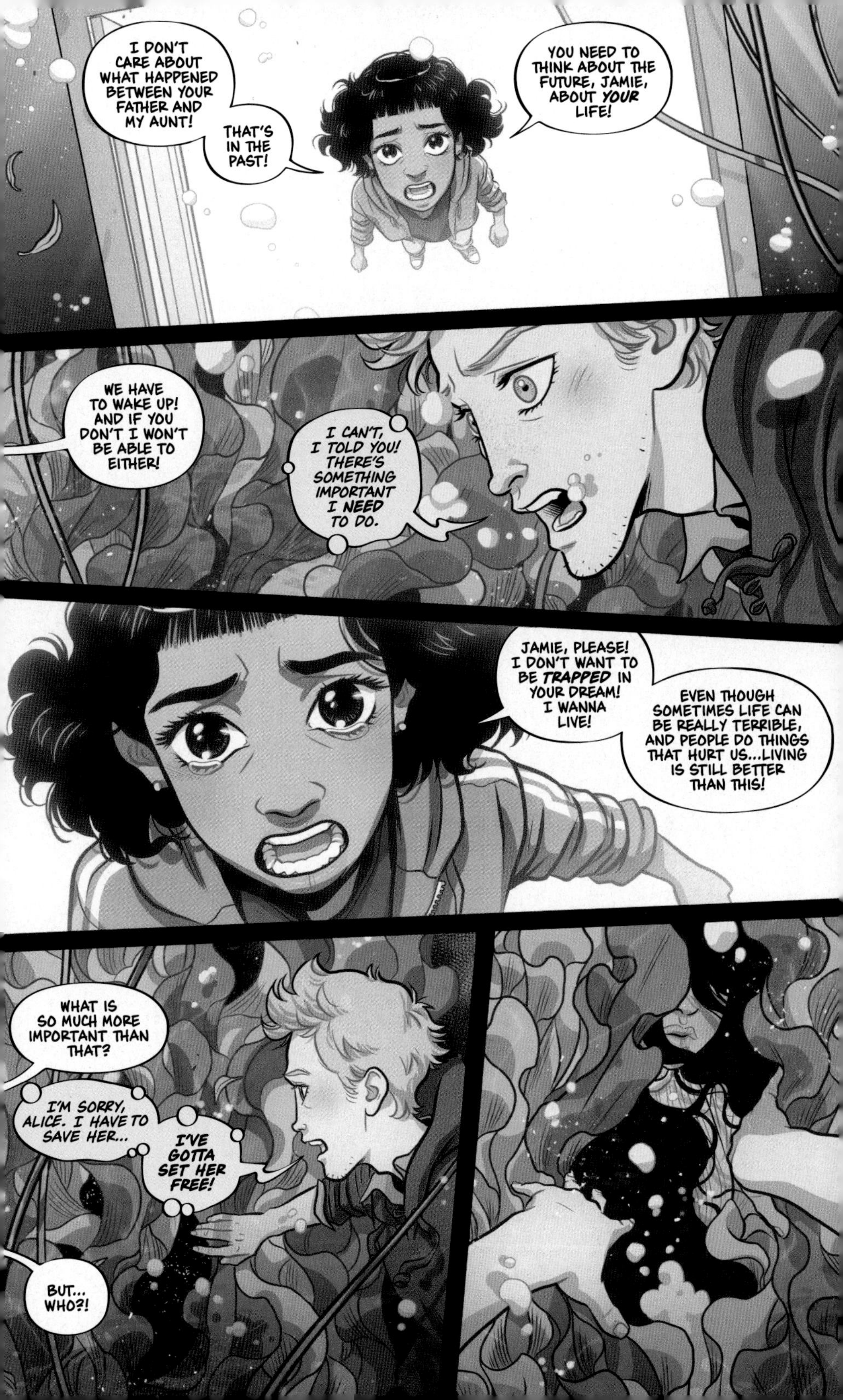

I DON'T CARE ABOUT WHAT HAPPENED BETWEEN YOUR FATHER AND MY AUNT!
THAT'S IN THE PAST!
YOU NEED TO THINK ABOUT THE FUTURE, JAMIE, ABOUT *YOUR* LIFE!
WE HAVE TO WAKE UP! AND IF YOU DON'T I WON'T BE ABLE TO EITHER!
I CAN'T, I TOLD YOU! THERE'S SOMETHING IMPORTANT I *NEED* TO DO.
JAMIE, PLEASE! I DON'T WANT TO BE *TRAPPED* IN YOUR DREAM! I WANNA LIVE!
EVEN THOUGH SOMETIMES LIFE CAN BE REALLY TERRIBLE, AND PEOPLE DO THINGS THAT HURT US...LIVING IS STILL BETTER THAN THIS!
WHAT IS SO MUCH MORE IMPORTANT THAN THAT?
I'M SORRY, ALICE. I HAVE TO SAVE HER...
I'VE GOTTA SET HER FREE!
BUT... WHO?!

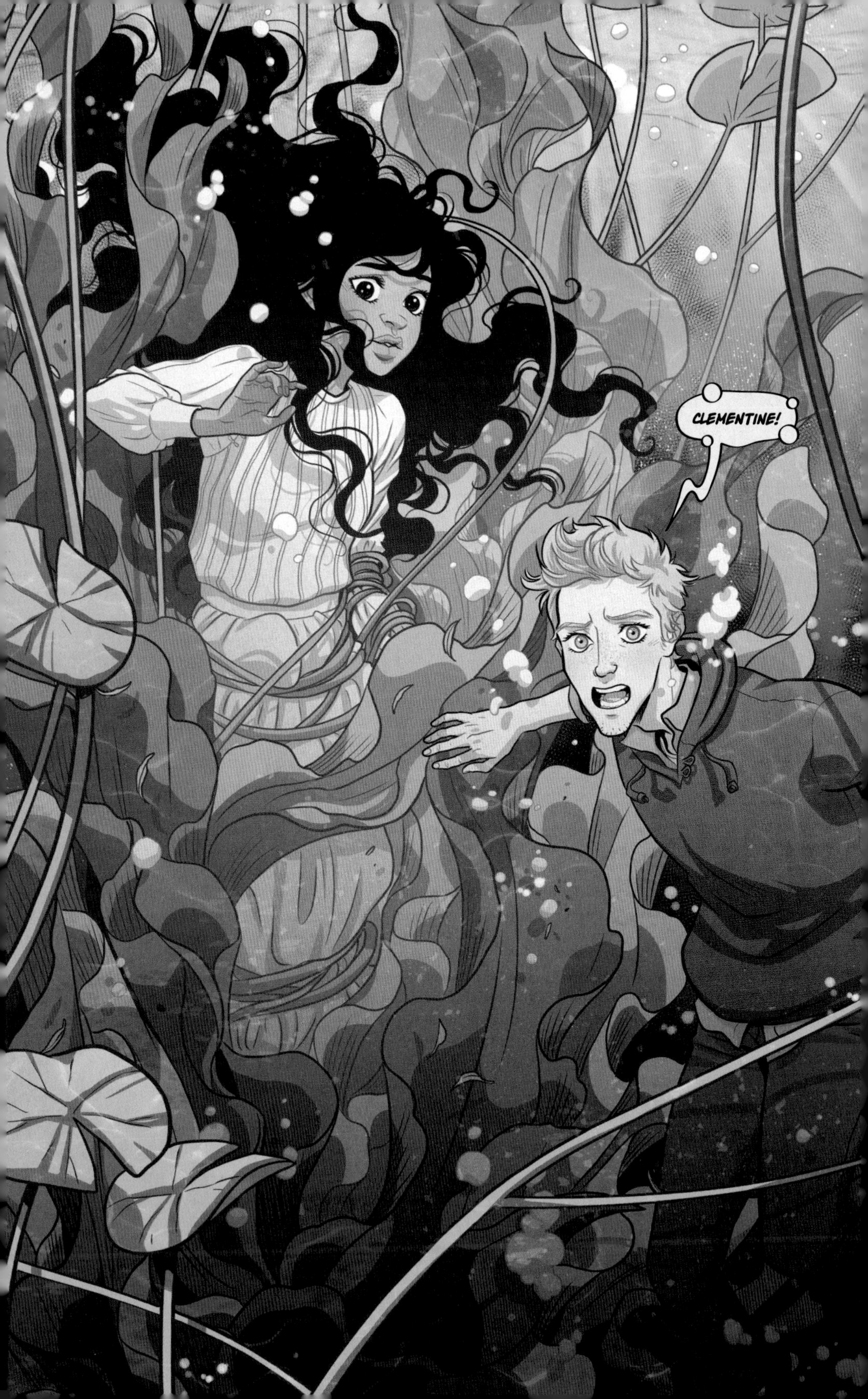
CLEMENTINE!

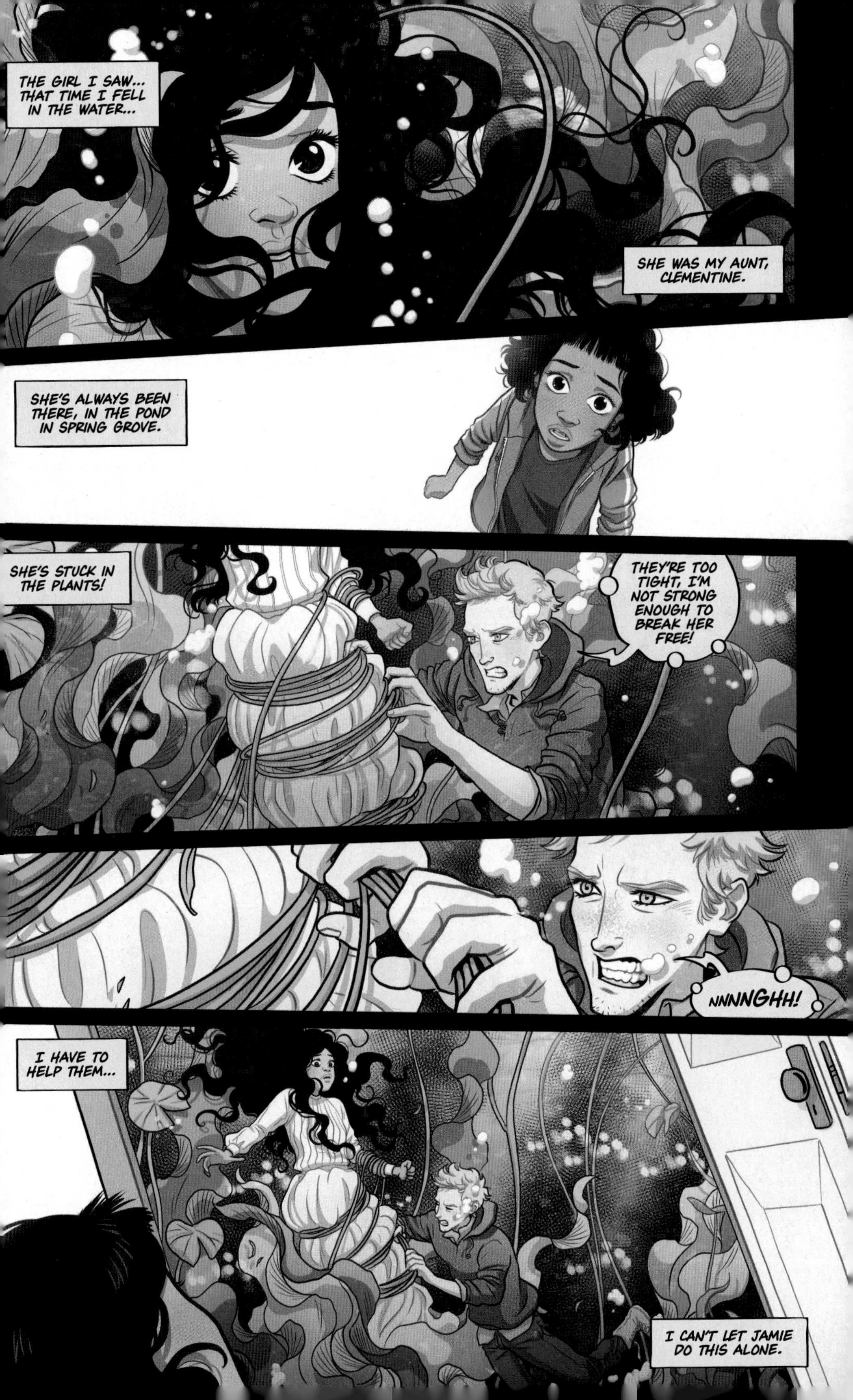
THE GIRL I SAW... THAT TIME I FELL IN THE WATER...
SHE WAS MY AUNT, CLEMENTINE.
SHE'S ALWAYS BEEN THERE, IN THE POND IN SPRING GROVE.
SHE'S STUCK IN THE PLANTS!
THEY'RE TOO TIGHT, I'M NOT STRONG ENOUGH TO BREAK HER FREE!
NNNNGHH!
I HAVE TO HELP THEM...
I CAN'T LET JAMIE DO THIS ALONE.

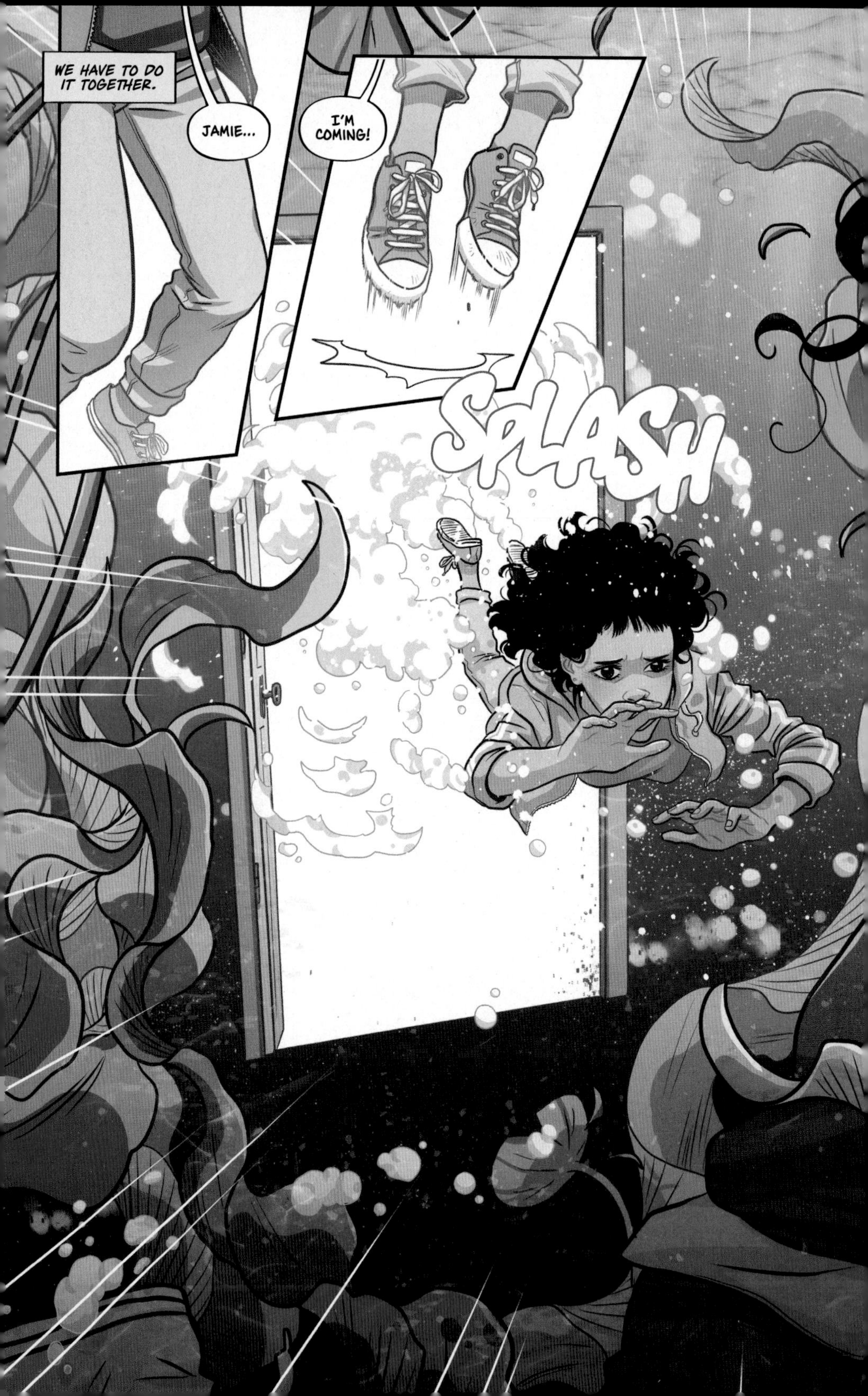
WE HAVE TO DO IT TOGETHER.
JAMIE...
I'M COMING!
SPLASH

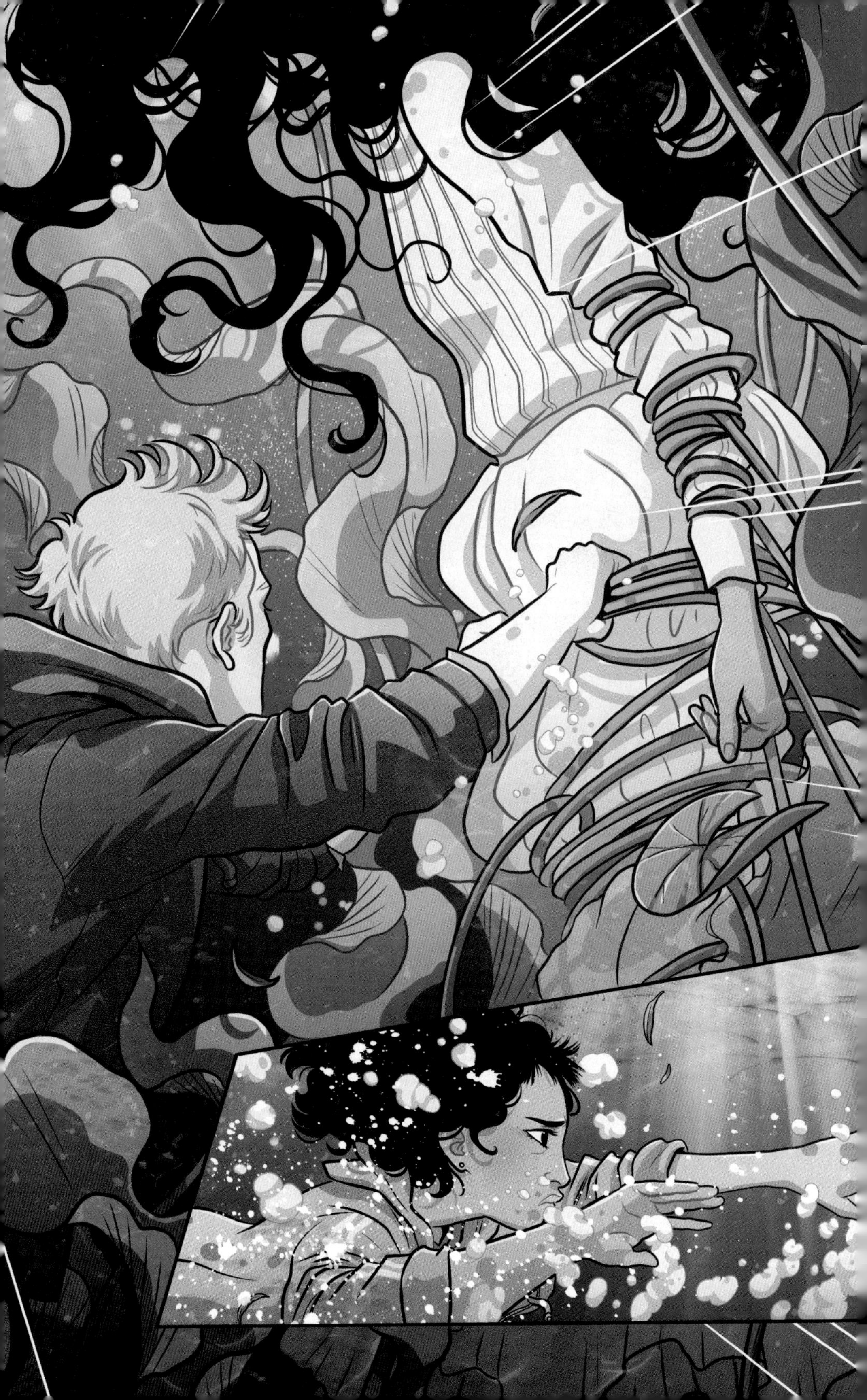

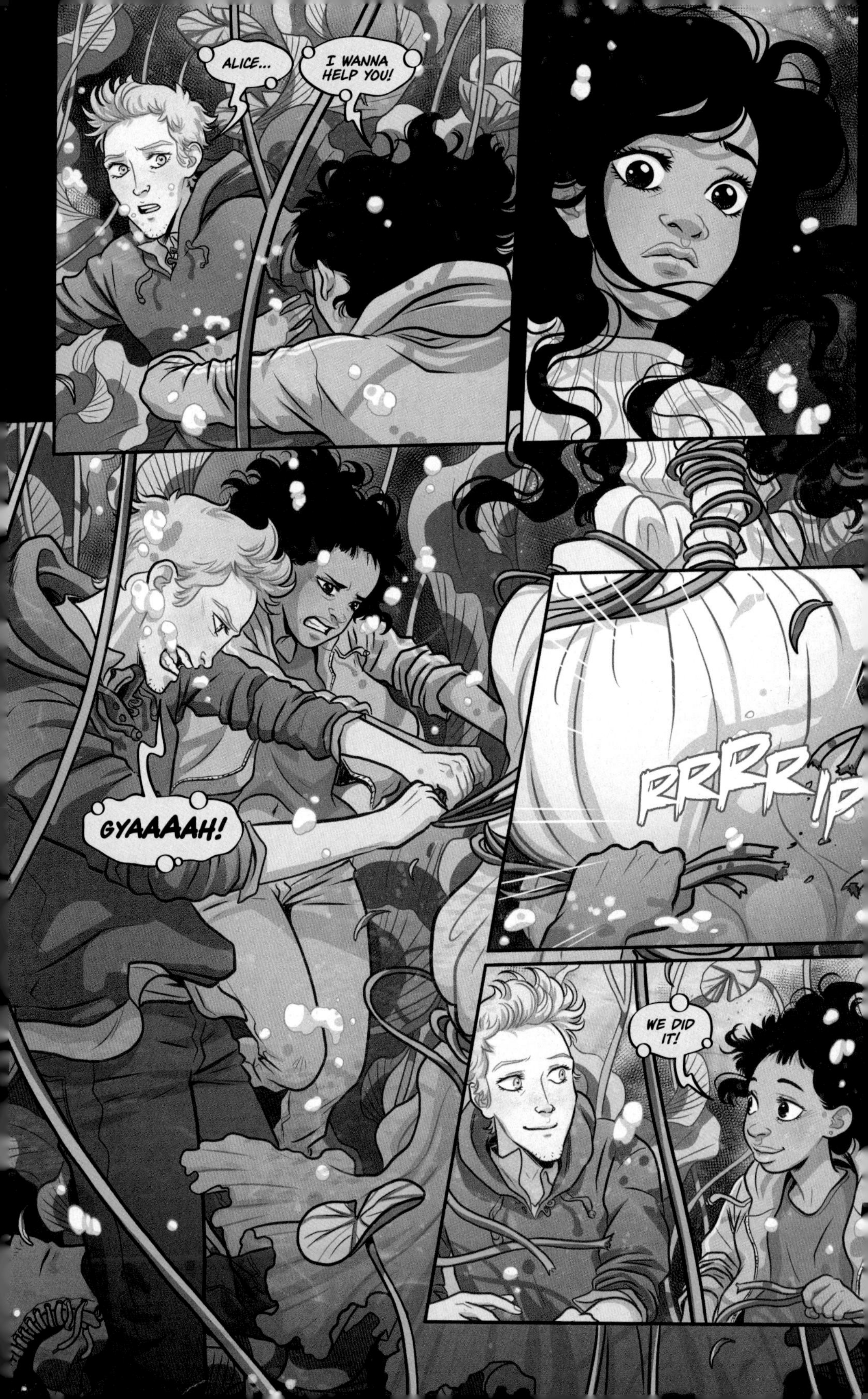
ALICE...
I WANNA HELP YOU!
GYAAAAH!
RRRRIP
WE DID IT!

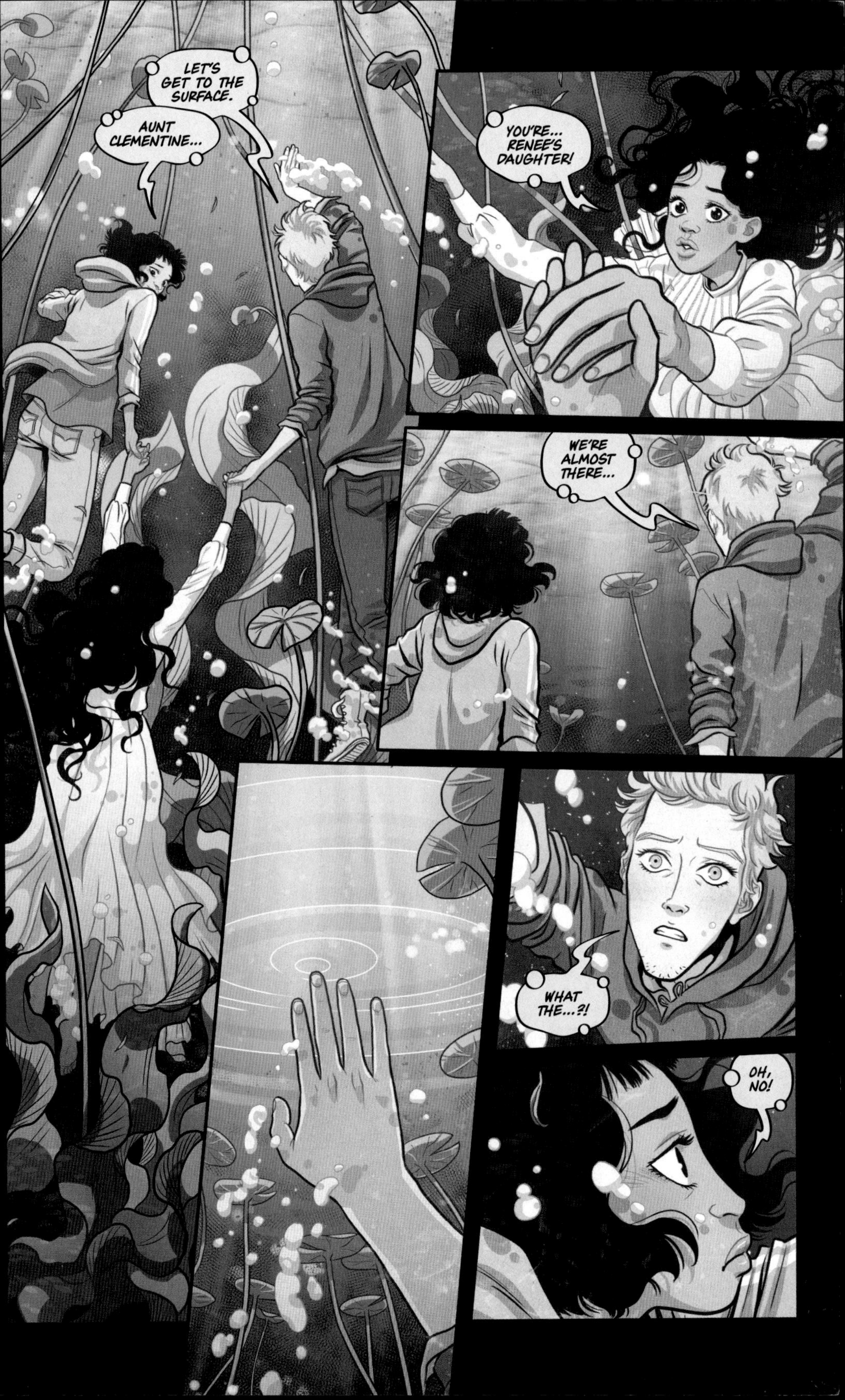
LET'S GET TO THE SURFACE.
AUNT CLEMENTINE...
YOU'RE... RENEE'S DAUGHTER!
WE'RE ALMOST THERE...
WHAT THE...?!
OH, NO!

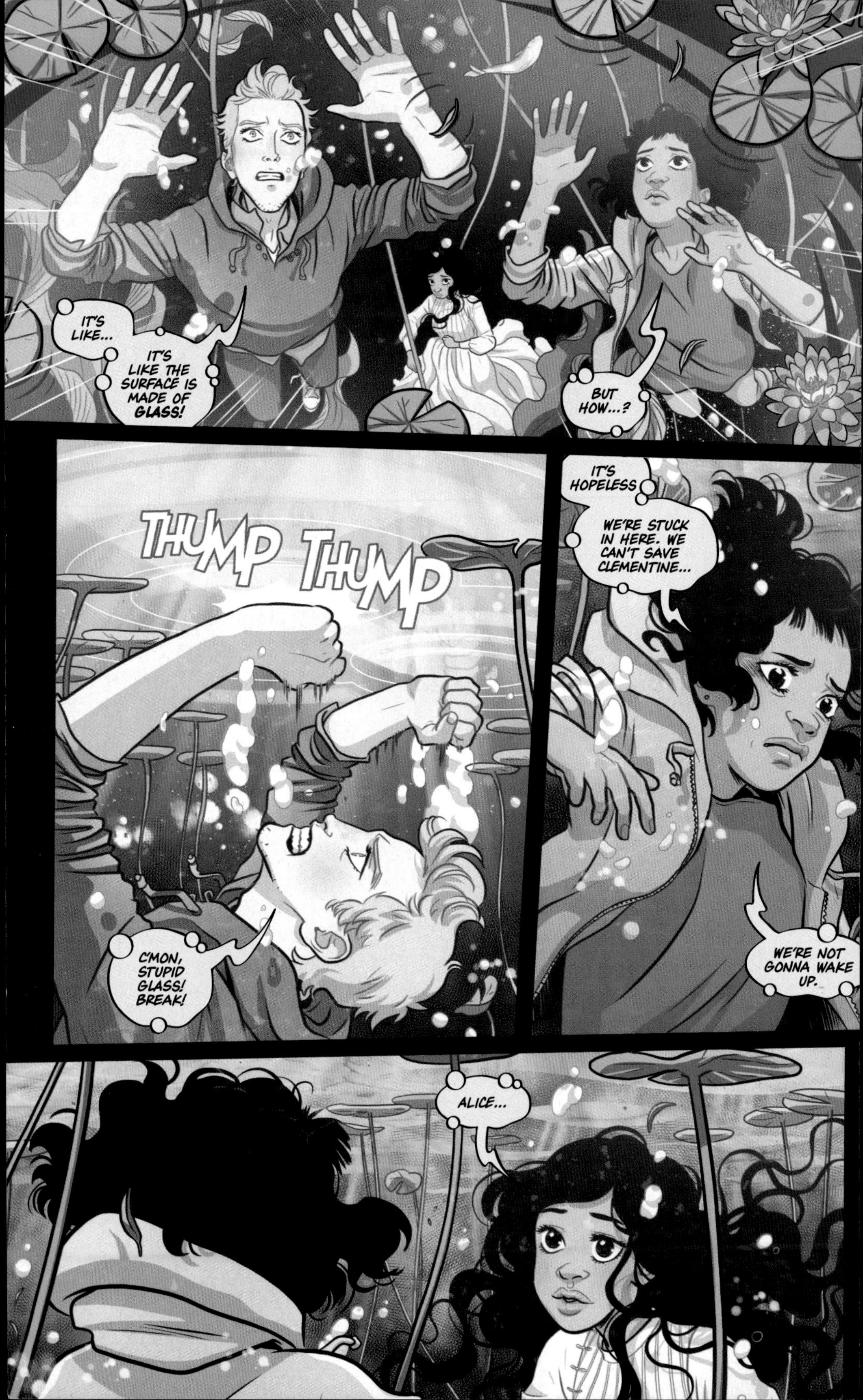
IT'S LIKE...
IT'S LIKE THE SURFACE IS MADE OF GLASS!
BUT HOW...?
THUMP THUMP
C'MON, STUPID GLASS! BREAK!
IT'S HOPELESS
WE'RE STUCK IN HERE. WE CAN'T SAVE CLEMENTINE...
WE'RE NOT GONNA WAKE UP.
ALICE...

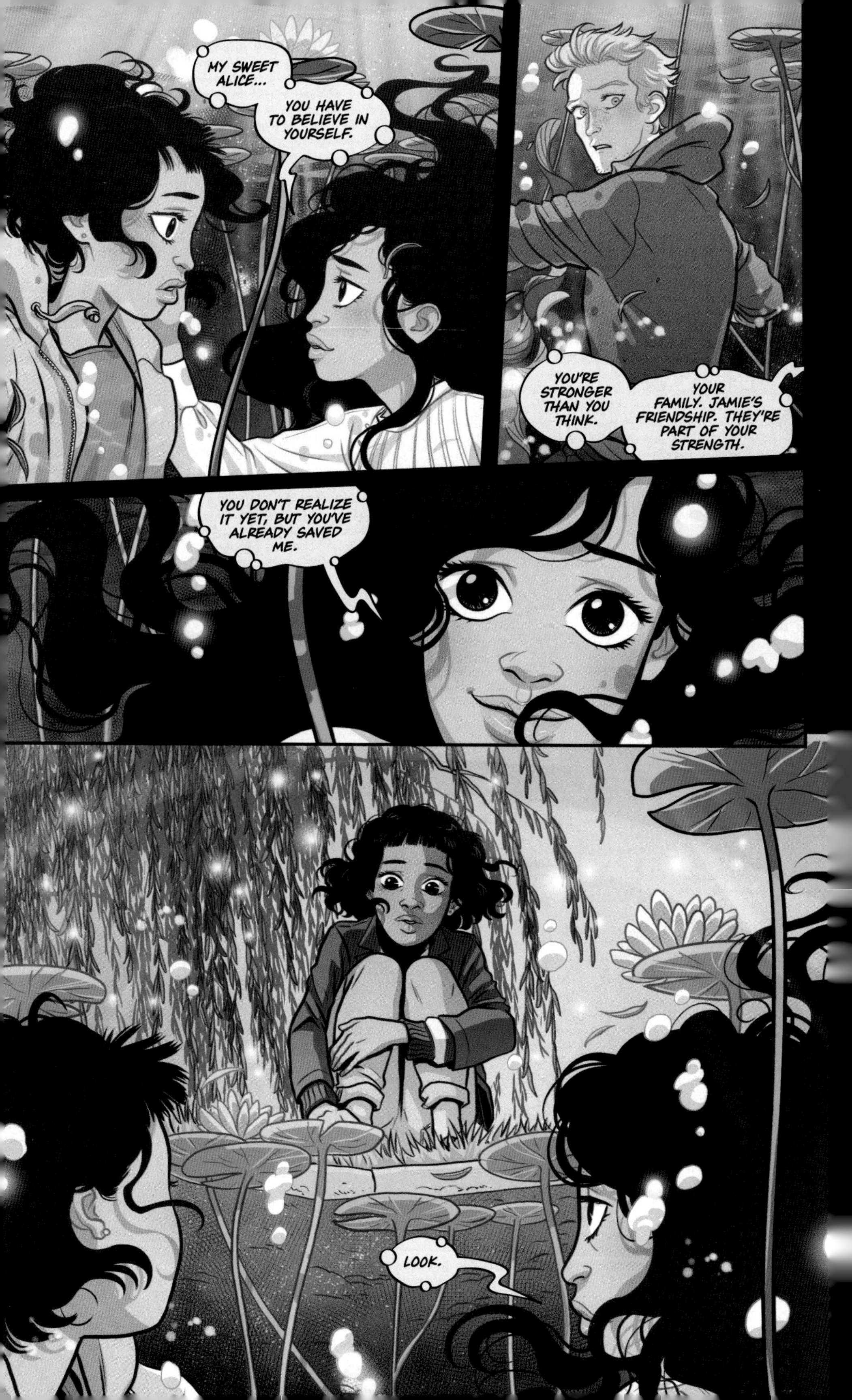
MY SWEET ALICE...
YOU HAVE TO BELIEVE IN YOURSELF.
YOU'RE STRONGER THAN YOU THINK.
YOUR FAMILY. JAMIE'S FRIENDSHIP. THEY'RE PART OF YOUR STRENGTH.
YOU DON'T REALIZE IT YET, BUT YOU'VE ALREADY SAVED ME.
LOOK.

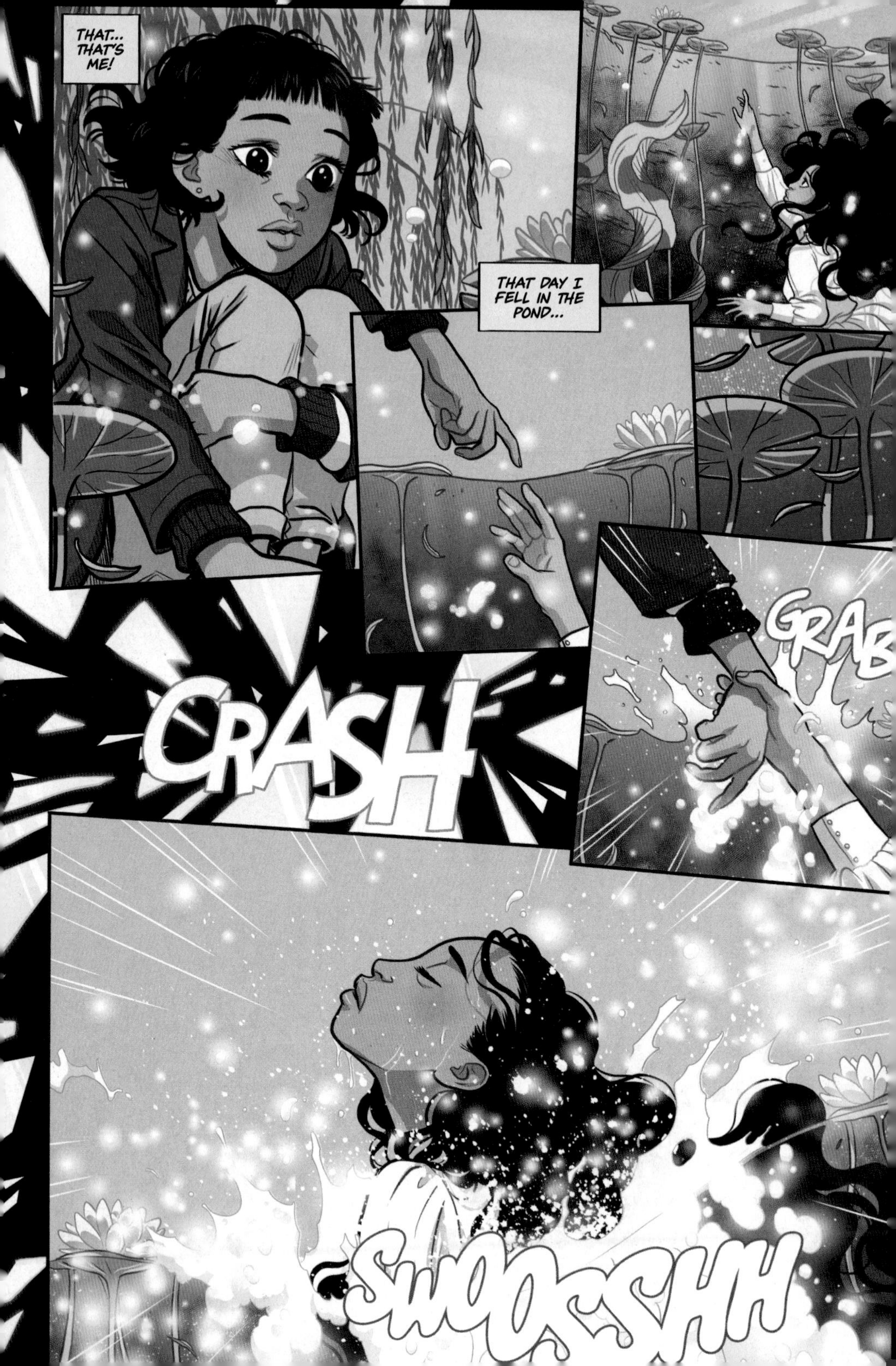
THAT... THAT'S ME!
THAT DAY I FELL IN THE POND...
CRASH
GRAB
SWOOSHH

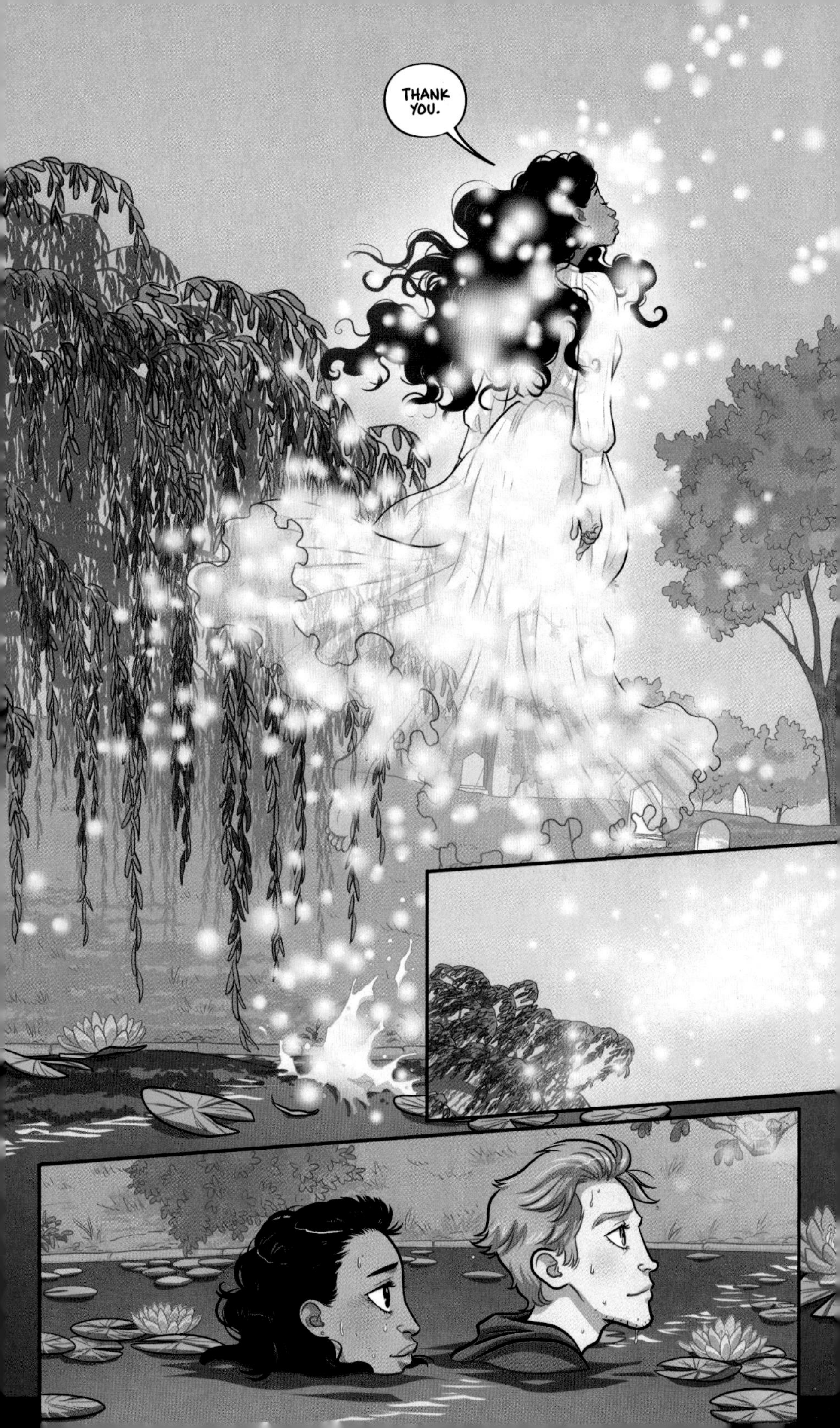
THANK YOU.

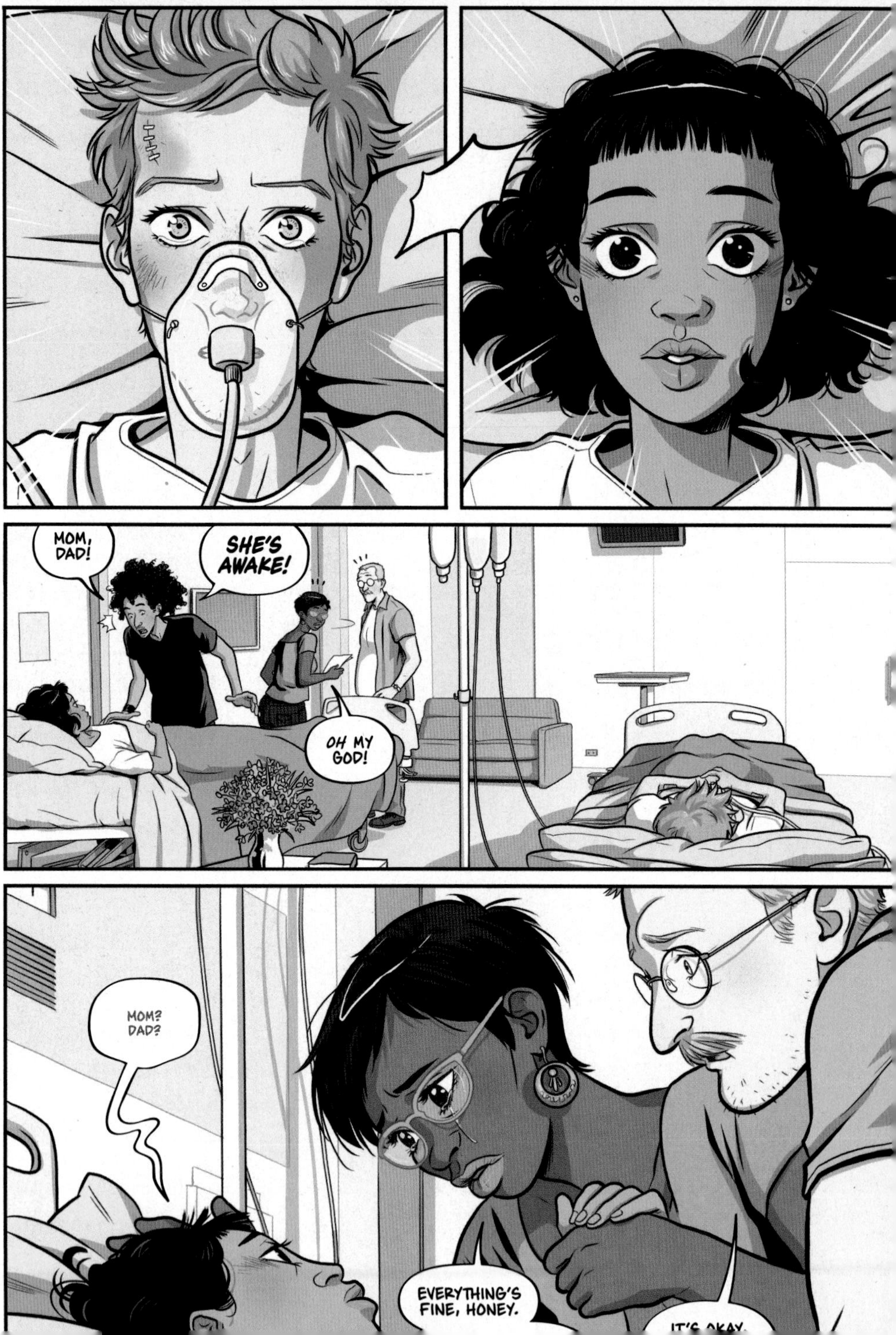
MOM, DAD!
SHE'S AWAKE!
OH MY GOD!
MOM? DAD?
EVERYTHING'S FINE, HONEY.

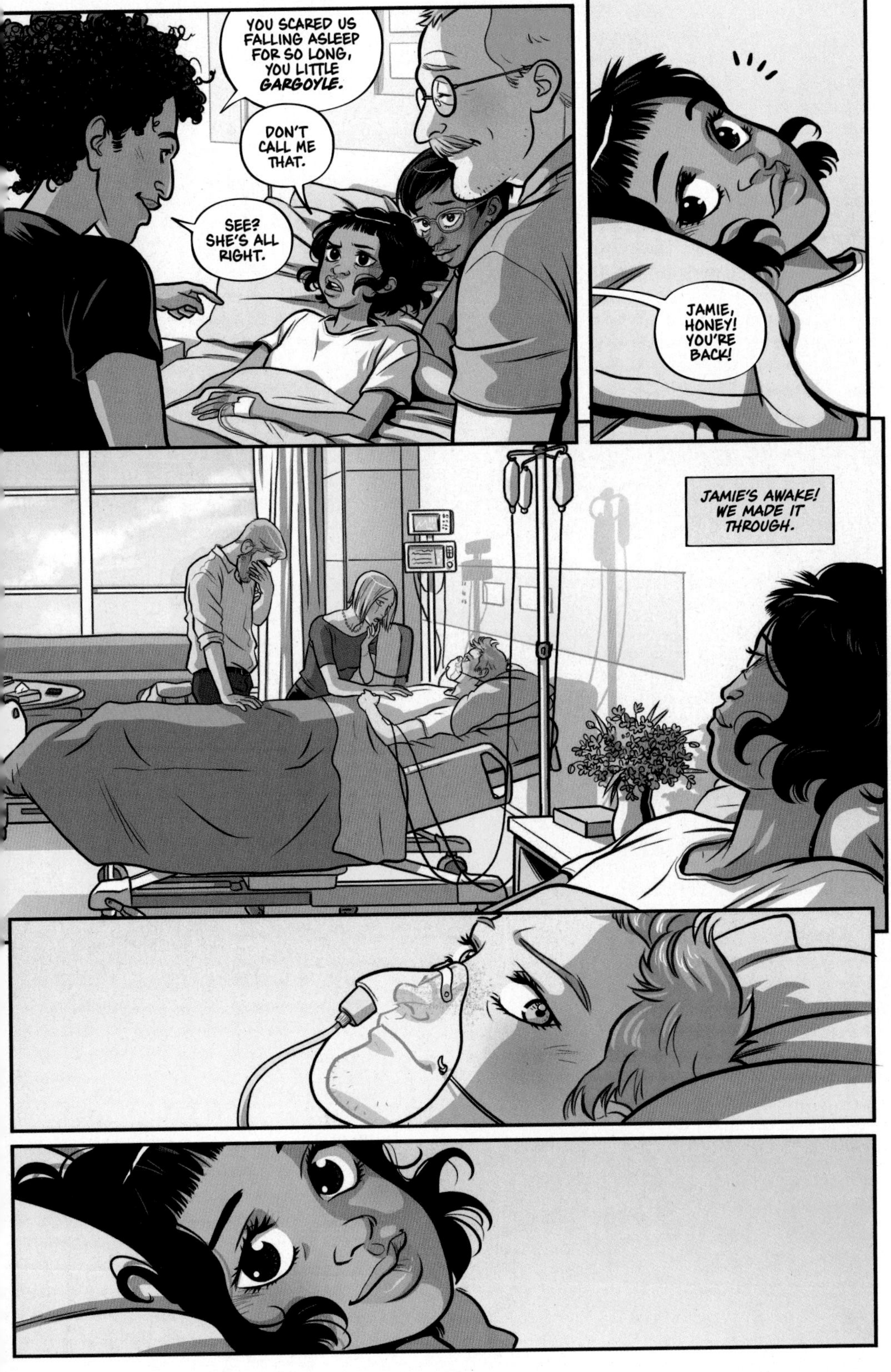
YOU SCARED US FALLING ASLEEP FOR SO LONG, YOU LITTLE GARGOYLE.
DON'T CALL ME THAT.
SEE? SHE'S ALL RIGHT.
JAMIE, HONEY! YOU'RE BACK!
JAMIE'S AWAKE! WE MADE IT THROUGH.

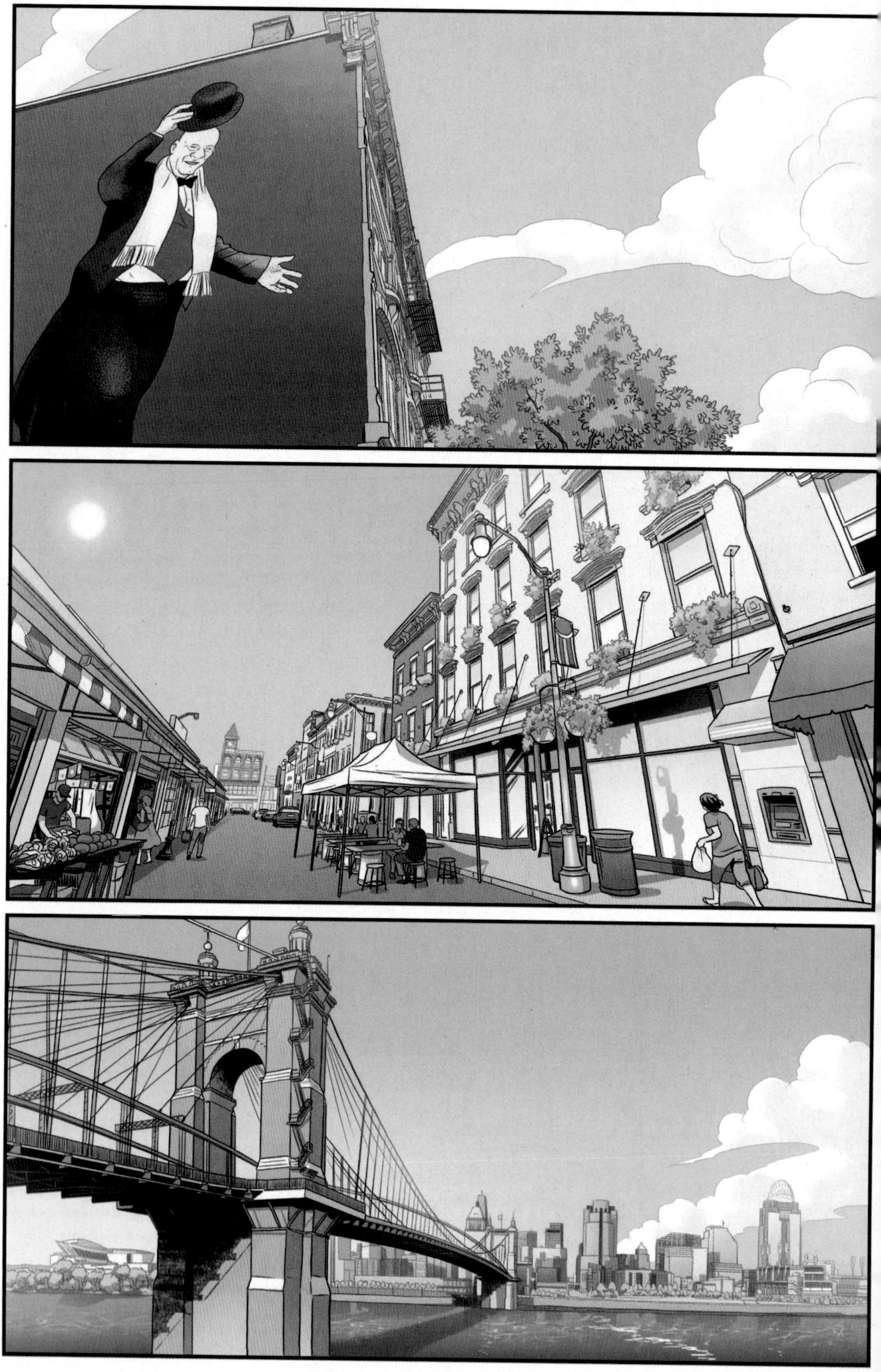

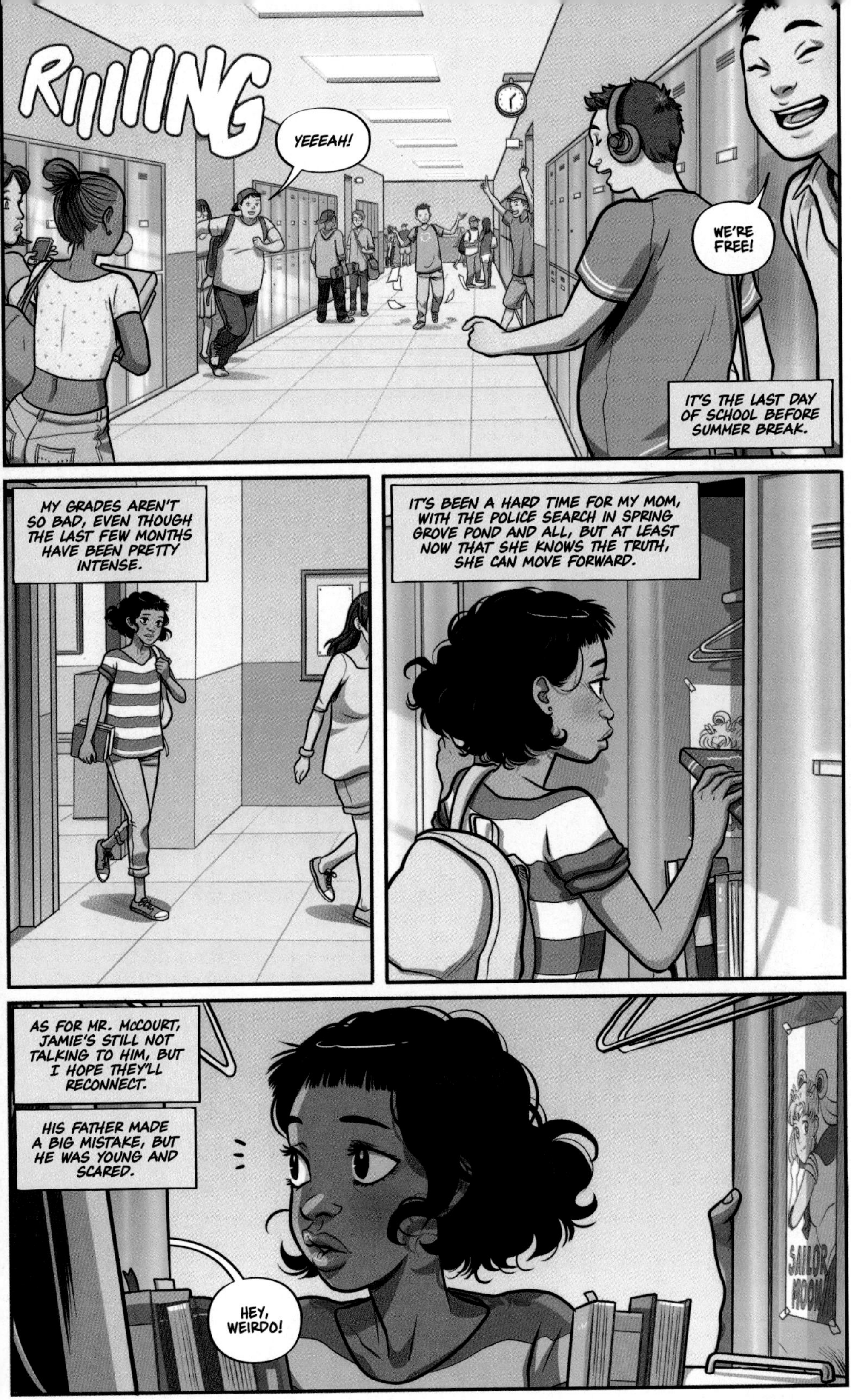
RIIIIING
YEEEAH!
WE'RE FREE!
IT'S THE LAST DAY OF SCHOOL BEFORE SUMMER BREAK.
MY GRADES AREN'T SO BAD, EVEN THOUGH THE LAST FEW MONTHS HAVE BEEN PRETTY INTENSE.
IT'S BEEN A HARD TIME FOR MY MOM, WITH THE POLICE SEARCH IN SPRING GROVE POND AND ALL, BUT AT LEAST NOW THAT SHE KNOWS THE TRUTH, SHE CAN MOVE FORWARD.
AS FOR MR. McCOURT, JAMIE'S STILL NOT TALKING TO HIM, BUT I HOPE THEY'LL RECONNECT.
HIS FATHER MADE A BIG MISTAKE, BUT HE WAS YOUNG AND SCARED.
SAILOR MOON
HEY, WEIRDO!

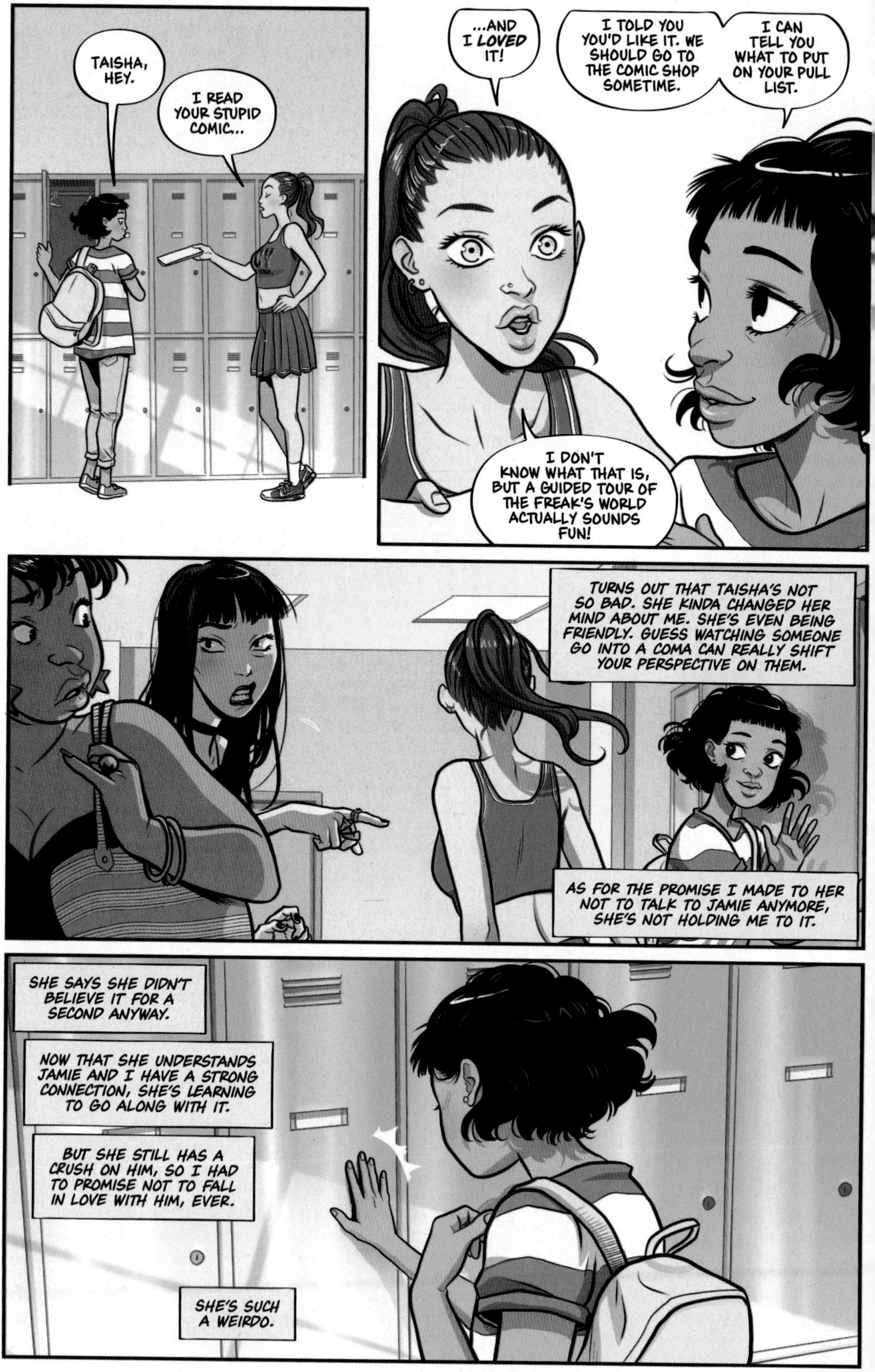
TAISHA, HEY.
I READ YOUR STUPID COMIC...
...AND I LOVED IT!
I TOLD YOU YOU'D LIKE IT. WE SHOULD GO TO THE COMIC SHOP SOMETIME.
I CAN TELL YOU WHAT TO PUT ON YOUR PULL LIST.
I DON'T KNOW WHAT THAT IS, BUT A GUIDED TOUR OF THE FREAK'S WORLD ACTUALLY SOUNDS FUN!
TURNS OUT THAT TAISHA'S NOT SO BAD. SHE KINDA CHANGED HER MIND ABOUT ME. SHE'S EVEN BEING FRIENDLY. GUESS WATCHING SOMEONE GO INTO A COMA CAN REALLY SHIFT YOUR PERSPECTIVE ON THEM.
AS FOR THE PROMISE I MADE TO HER NOT TO TALK TO JAMIE ANYMORE, SHE'S NOT HOLDING ME TO IT.
SHE SAYS SHE DIDN'T BELIEVE IT FOR A SECOND ANYWAY.
NOW THAT SHE UNDERSTANDS JAMIE AND I HAVE A STRONG CONNECTION, SHE'S LEARNING TO GO ALONG WITH IT.
BUT SHE STILL HAS A CRUSH ON HIM, SO I HAD TO PROMISE NOT TO FALL IN LOVE WITH HIM, EVER.
SHE'S SUCH A WEIRDO.

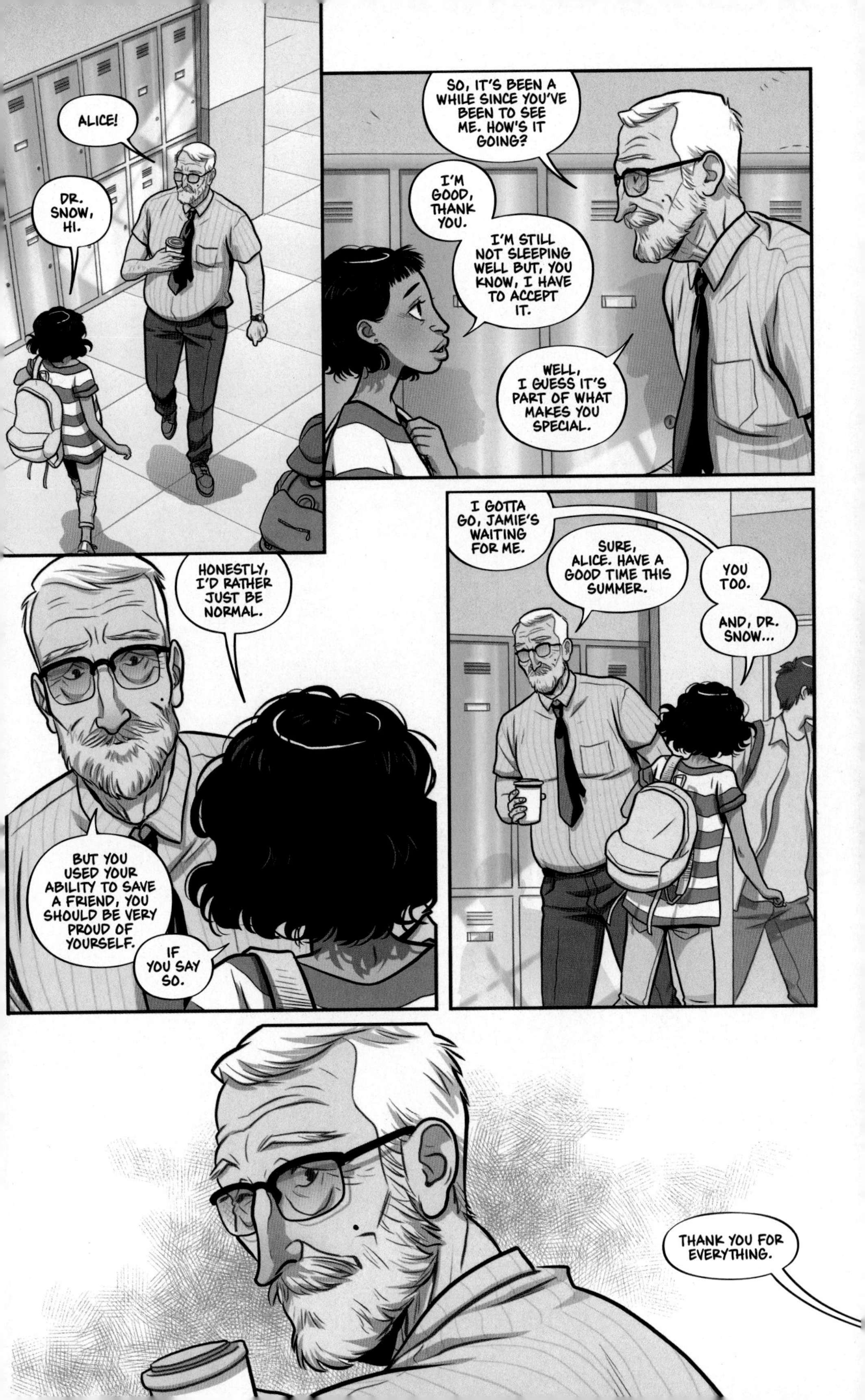
ALICE!
DR. SNOW, HI.
SO, IT'S BEEN A WHILE SINCE YOU'VE BEEN TO SEE ME. HOW'S IT GOING?
I'M GOOD, THANK YOU.
I'M STILL NOT SLEEPING WELL BUT, YOU KNOW, I HAVE TO ACCEPT IT.
WELL, I GUESS IT'S PART OF WHAT MAKES YOU SPECIAL.
HONESTLY, I'D RATHER JUST BE NORMAL.
BUT YOU USED YOUR ABILITY TO SAVE A FRIEND, YOU SHOULD BE VERY PROUD OF YOURSELF.
IF YOU SAY SO.
I GOTTA GO, JAMIE'S WAITING FOR ME.
SURE, ALICE. HAVE A GOOD TIME THIS SUMMER.
YOU TOO.
AND, DR. SNOW...
THANK YOU FOR EVERYTHING.

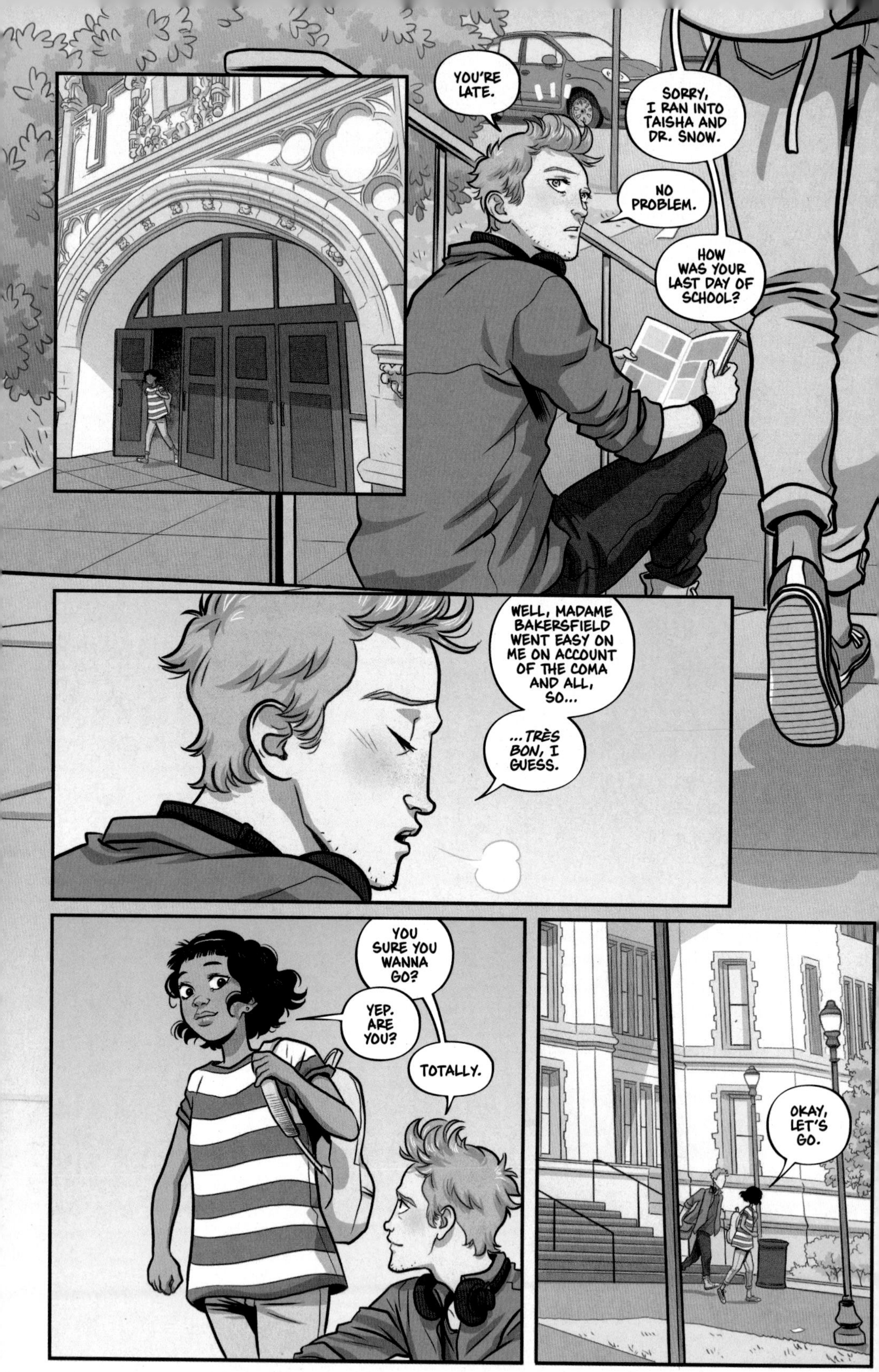
YOU'RE LATE.
SORRY, I RAN INTO TAISHA AND DR. SNOW.
NO PROBLEM.
HOW WAS YOUR LAST DAY OF SCHOOL?
WELL, MADAME BAKERSFIELD WENT EASY ON ME ON ACCOUNT OF THE COMA AND ALL, SO...
...TRÈS BON, I GUESS.
YOU SURE YOU WANNA GO?
YEP. ARE YOU?
TOTALLY.
OKAY, LET'S GO.

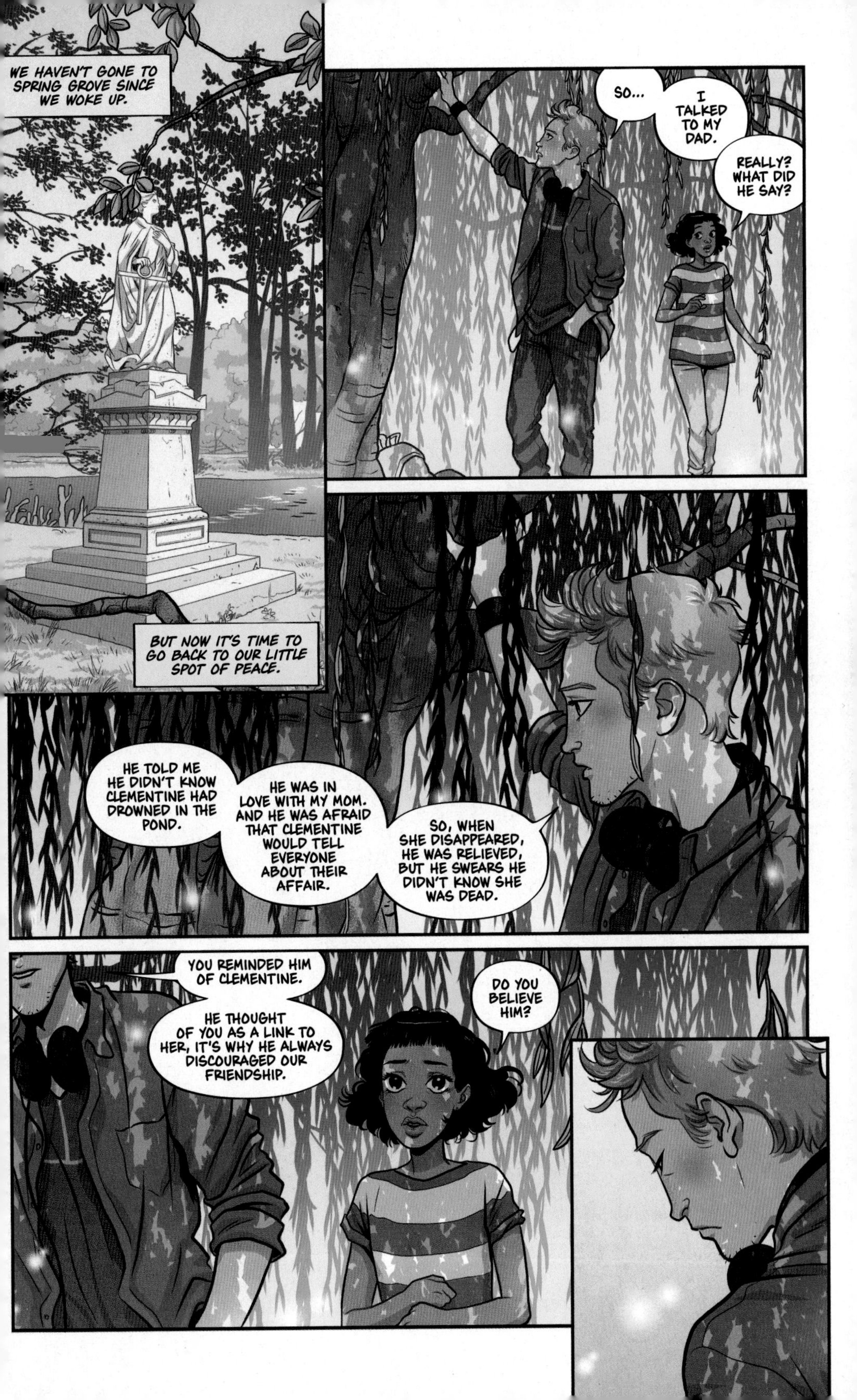
WE HAVEN'T GONE TO SPRING GROVE SINCE WE WOKE UP.
BUT NOW IT'S TIME TO GO BACK TO OUR LITTLE SPOT OF PEACE.
SO...
I TALKED TO MY DAD.
REALLY? WHAT DID HE SAY?
HE TOLD ME HE DIDN'T KNOW CLEMENTINE HAD DROWNED IN THE POND.
HE WAS IN LOVE WITH MY MOM. AND HE WAS AFRAID THAT CLEMENTINE WOULD TELL EVERYONE ABOUT THEIR AFFAIR.
SO, WHEN SHE DISAPPEARED, HE WAS RELIEVED, BUT HE SWEARS HE DIDN'T KNOW SHE WAS DEAD.
YOU REMINDED HIM OF CLEMENTINE.
HE THOUGHT OF YOU AS A LINK TO HER, IT'S WHY HE ALWAYS DISCOURAGED OUR FRIENDSHIP.
DO YOU BELIEVE HIM?

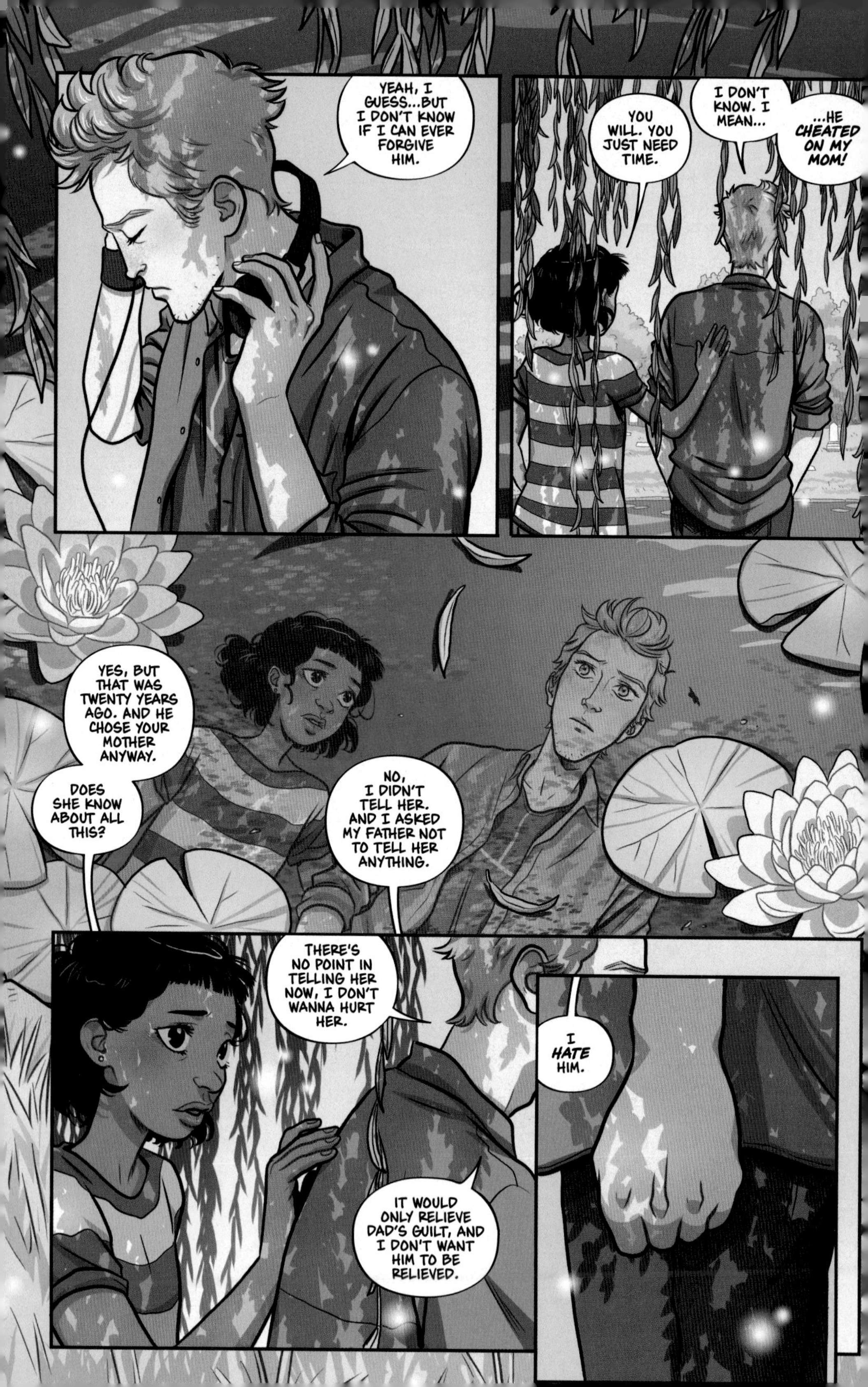
YEAH, I GUESS...BUT I DON'T KNOW IF I CAN EVER FORGIVE HIM.
YOU WILL. YOU JUST NEED TIME.
I DON'T KNOW. I MEAN...
...HE CHEATED ON MY MOM!
YES, BUT THAT WAS TWENTY YEARS AGO. AND HE CHOSE YOUR MOTHER ANYWAY.
DOES SHE KNOW ABOUT ALL THIS?
NO, I DIDN'T TELL HER. AND I ASKED MY FATHER NOT TO TELL HER ANYTHING.
THERE'S NO POINT IN TELLING HER NOW, I DON'T WANNA HURT HER.
I HATE HIM.
IT WOULD ONLY RELIEVE DAD'S GUILT, AND I DON'T WANT HIM TO BE RELIEVED.

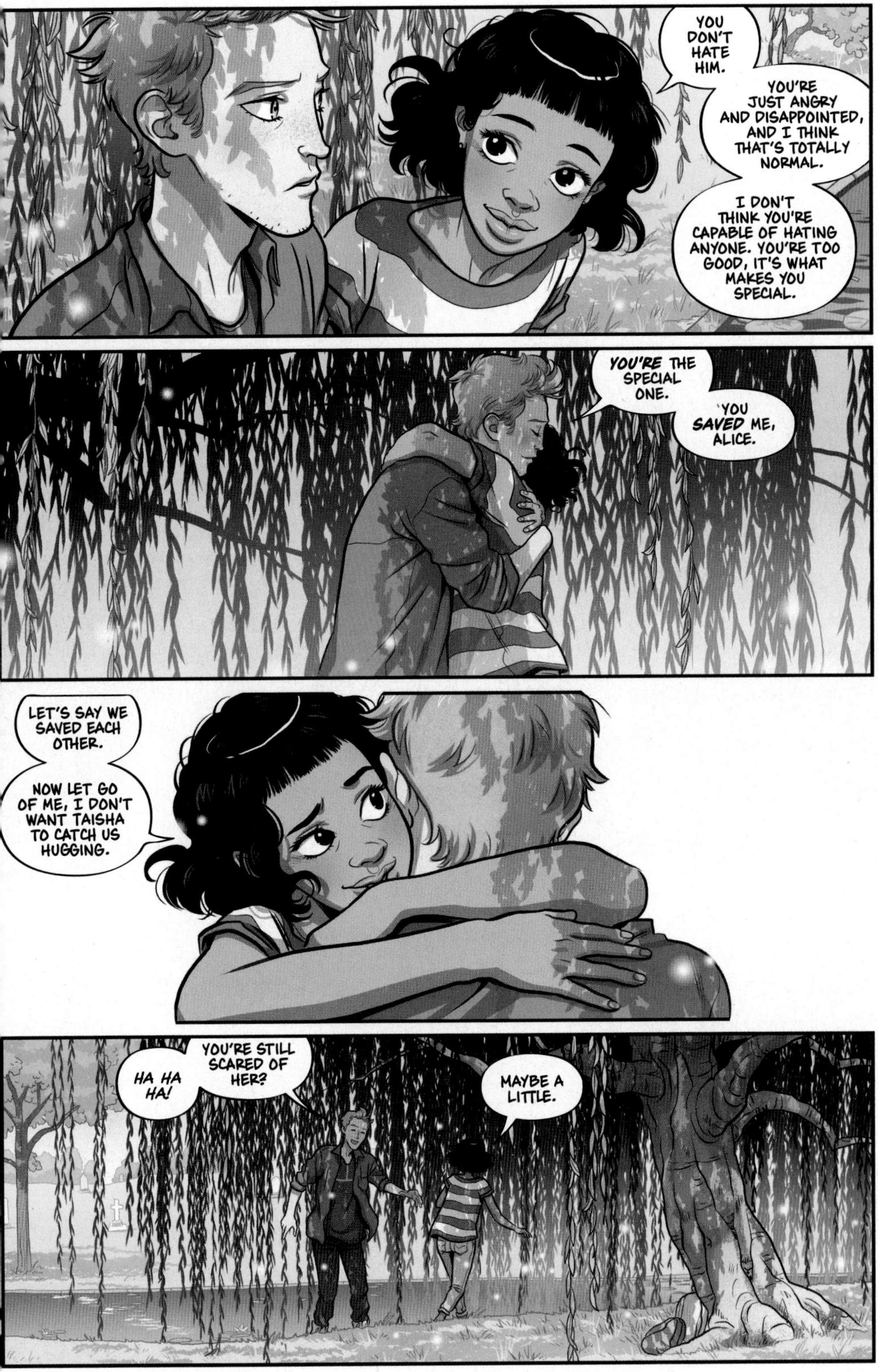
YOU DON'T HATE HIM.
YOU'RE JUST ANGRY AND DISAPPOINTED, AND I THINK THAT'S TOTALLY NORMAL.
I DON'T THINK YOU'RE CAPABLE OF HATING ANYONE. YOU'RE TOO GOOD, IT'S WHAT MAKES YOU SPECIAL.
*YOU'RE* THE SPECIAL ONE.
YOU *SAVED* ME, ALICE.
LET'S SAY WE SAVED EACH OTHER.
NOW LET GO OF ME, I DON'T WANT TAISHA TO CATCH US HUGGING.
*HA HA HA!*
YOU'RE STILL SCARED OF HER?
MAYBE A LITTLE.

I'M HOME!

HELLO? WHERE ARE YOU?

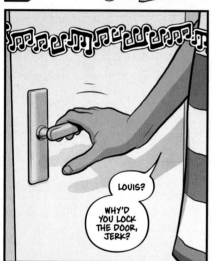

LOUIS? WHY'D YOU LOCK THE DOOR, JERK?

LOUIS?

GET OUT OF HERE! THIS ISN'T YOUR BEDROOM ANYMORE!

WHAT?! LET ME IN!

ALICE? WE'RE IN THE ATTIC. CAN YOU COME UP HERE, PLEASE?

IN THE ATTIC...?

WHAT ARE YOU DOING UP THERE?

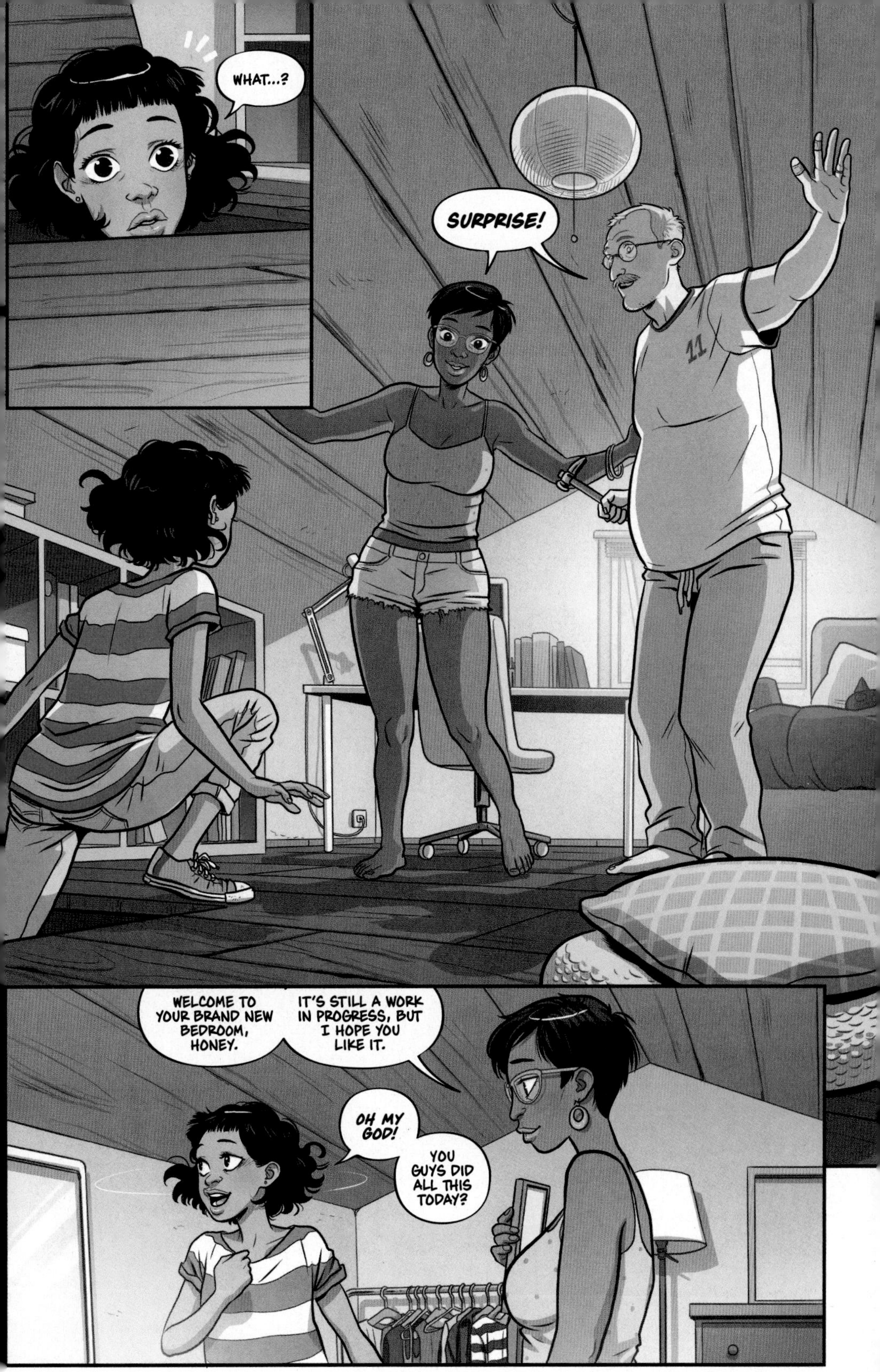
WHAT...?
SURPRISE!
WELCOME TO YOUR BRAND NEW BEDROOM, HONEY.
IT'S STILL A WORK IN PROGRESS, BUT I HOPE YOU LIKE IT.
OH MY GOD!
YOU GUYS DID ALL THIS TODAY?
11

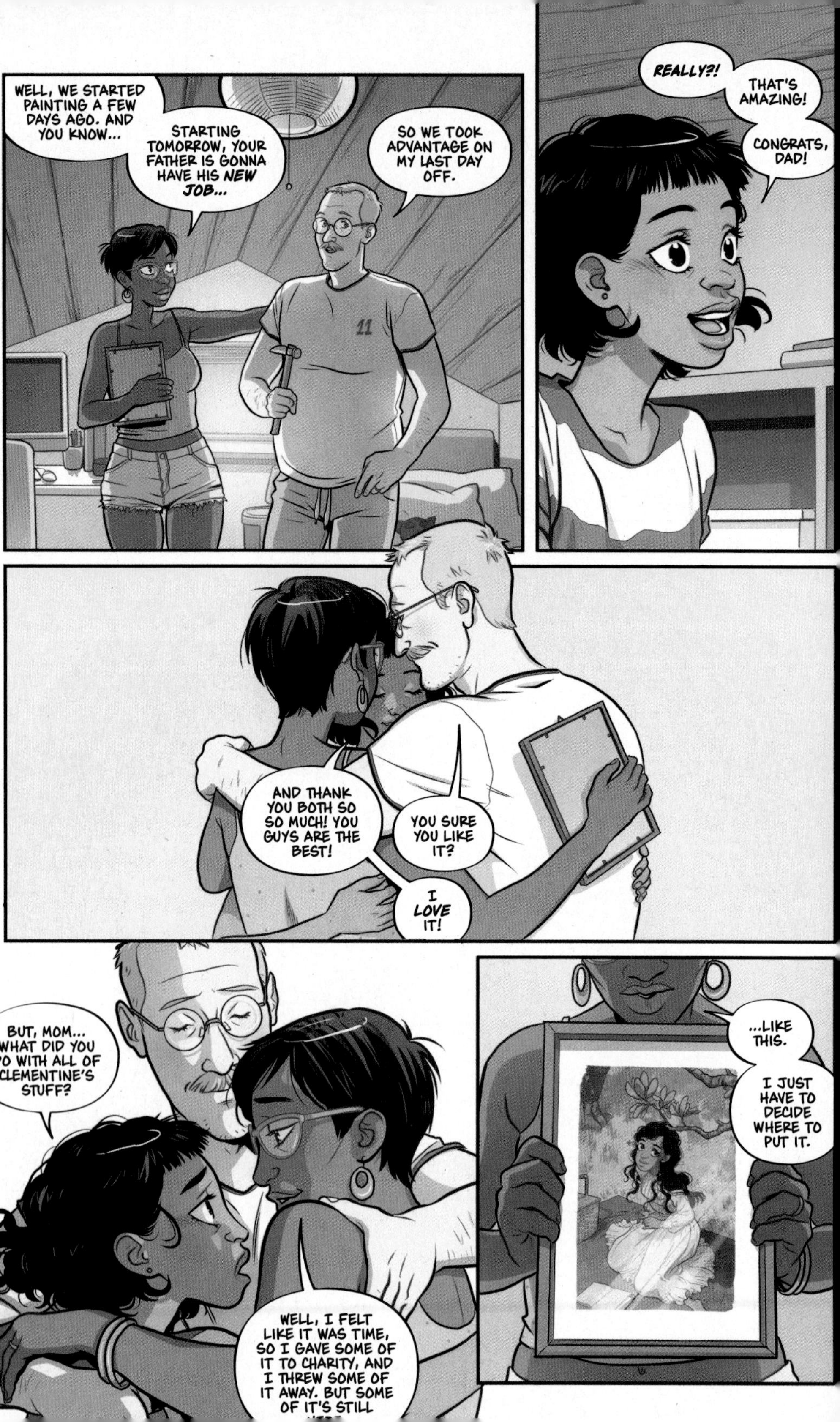
WELL, WE STARTED PAINTING A FEW DAYS AGO. AND YOU KNOW...
STARTING TOMORROW, YOUR FATHER IS GONNA HAVE HIS NEW JOB...
SO WE TOOK ADVANTAGE ON MY LAST DAY OFF.
REALLY?!
THAT'S AMAZING!
CONGRATS, DAD!
AND THANK YOU BOTH SO SO MUCH! YOU GUYS ARE THE BEST!
YOU SURE YOU LIKE IT?
I LOVE IT!
BUT, MOM... WHAT DID YOU DO WITH ALL OF CLEMENTINE'S STUFF?
WELL, I FELT LIKE IT WAS TIME, SO I GAVE SOME OF IT TO CHARITY, AND I THREW SOME OF IT AWAY. BUT SOME OF IT'S STILL
...LIKE THIS.
I JUST HAVE TO DECIDE WHERE TO PUT IT.

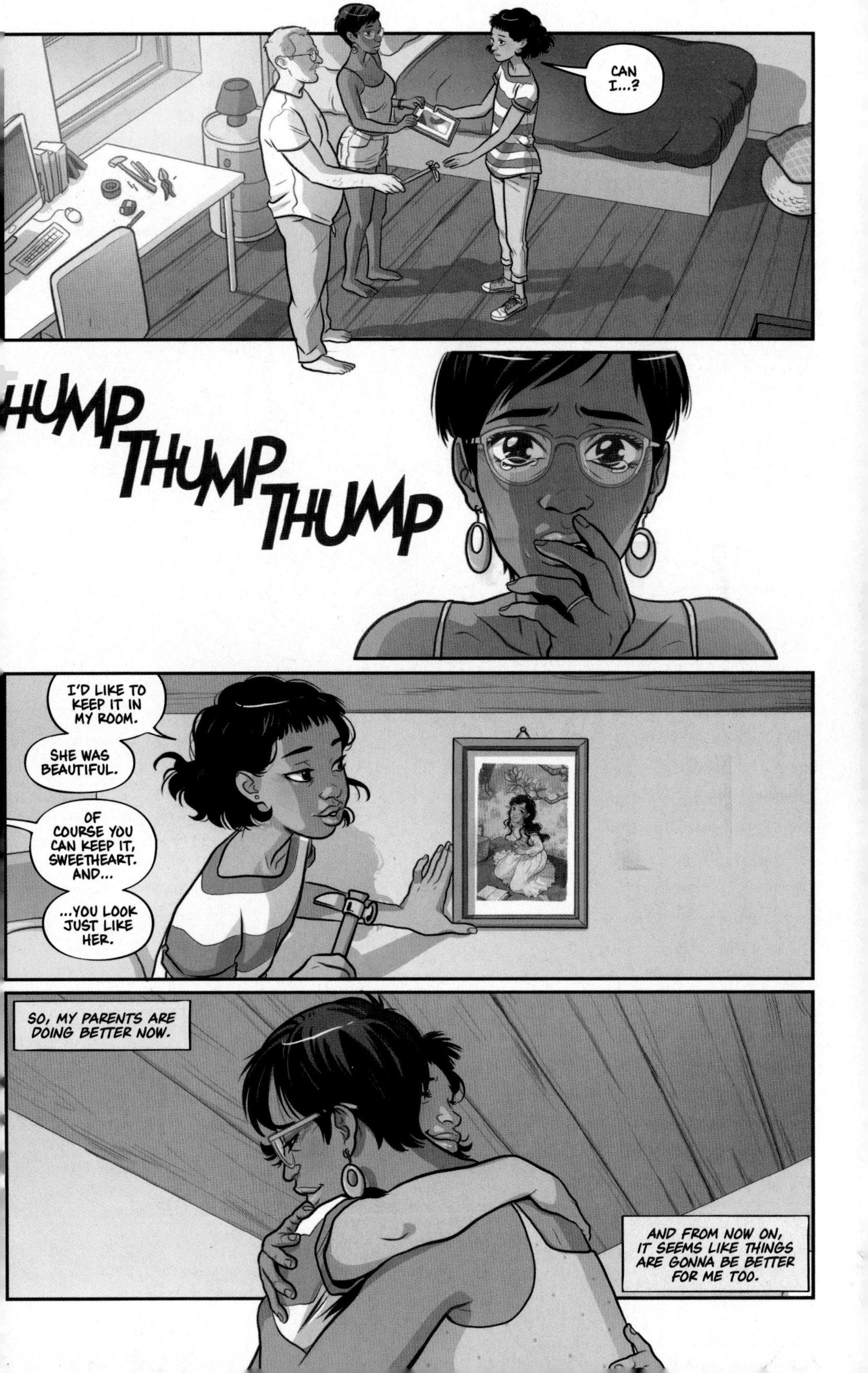
CAN I...?
HUMP THUMP THUMP
I'D LIKE TO KEEP IT IN MY ROOM.
SHE WAS BEAUTIFUL.
OF COURSE YOU CAN KEEP IT, SWEETHEART. AND...
...YOU LOOK JUST LIKE HER.
SO, MY PARENTS ARE DOING BETTER NOW.
AND FROM NOW ON, IT SEEMS LIKE THINGS ARE GONNA BE BETTER FOR ME TOO.

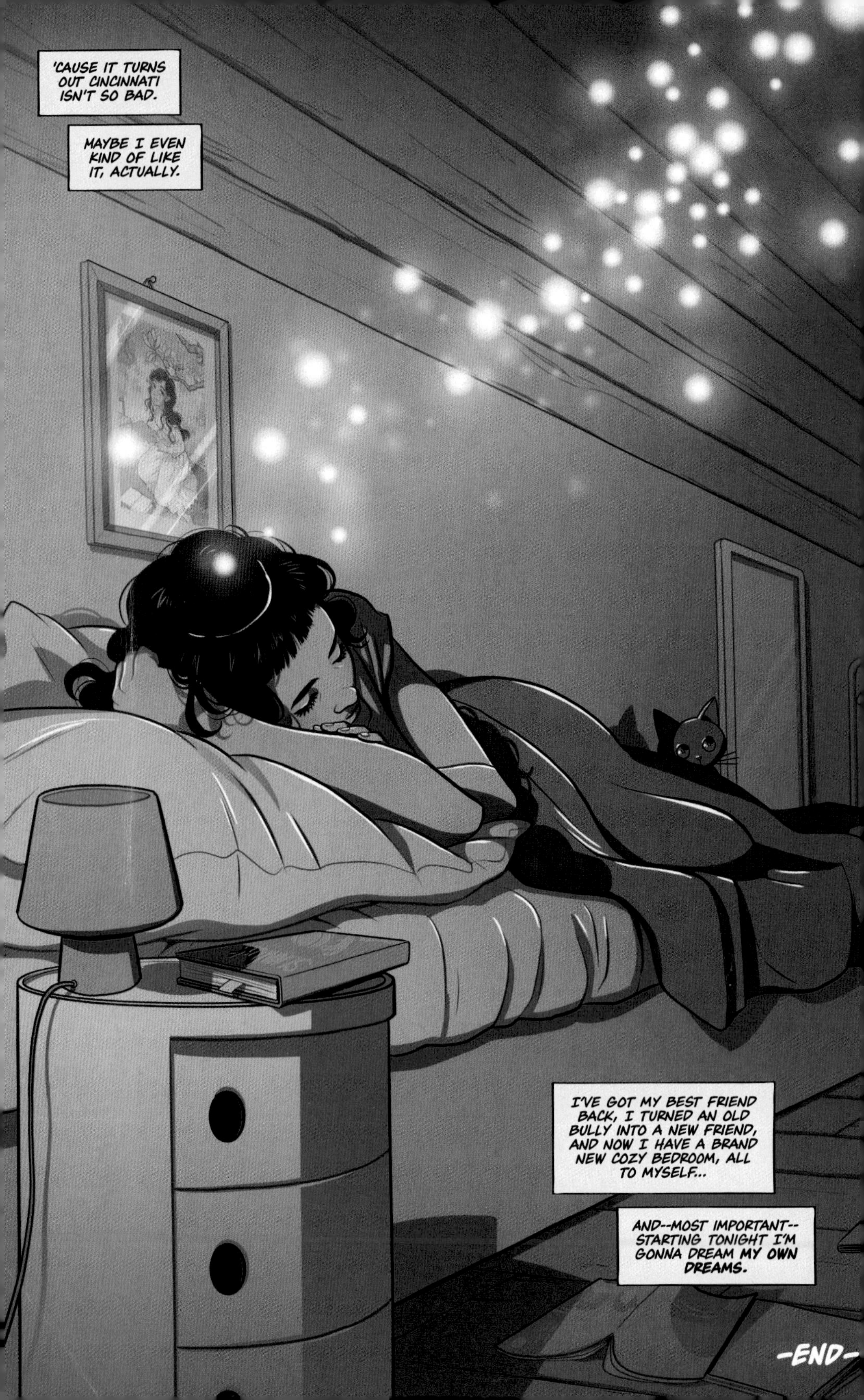
'CAUSE IT TURNS OUT CINCINNATI ISN'T SO BAD.
MAYBE I EVEN KIND OF LIKE IT, ACTUALLY.
I'VE GOT MY BEST FRIEND BACK, I TURNED AN OLD BULLY INTO A NEW FRIEND, AND NOW I HAVE A BRAND NEW COZY BEDROOM, ALL TO MYSELF...
AND--MOST IMPORTANT--STARTING TONIGHT I'M GONNA DREAM MY OWN DREAMS.
-END-

**GIULIO MACAIONE** IS A COMIC WRITER AND ARTIST LIVING IN BOLOGNA, ITALY. HIS MAIN GRAPHIC NOVELS INCLUDE *OFELIA* (PUBLISHED IN FRANCE BY EDITIONS PHYSALIS) *BASILICO* AND *STELLA DI MARE* (BOTH PUBLISHED IN ITALY BY BAO PUBLISHING). HE ALSO CREATED THE SELF-PUBLISHED COMICS *LA FINE DELL'ESTATE* AND *NEL BUIO TRA GLI ALBERI*. *ALICE: FROM DREAM TO DREAM* IS HIS FIRST GRAPHIC NOVEL FOR THE U.S.

**GIULIA ADRAGNA** WAS BORN AND LIVES IN ITALY. SHE WORKS AS A COMIC ARTIST AND ILLUSTRATOR FOR PANINI COMICS (*MIRACULOUS-TALES OF LADYBUG & CHAT NOIR, CIOE*). SHE ALSO TEACHES AT THE SAME COMICS ACADEMY WHERE SHE GRADUATED, "SCUOLA DEL FUMETTO" IN PALERMO. SHE WORKED AS A DIGITAL COLORIST FOR SERGIO BONELLI ED. (*MARTIN MYSTERE-LE NUOVE AVVENTURE A COLORI*) AND PANINI COMICS (*MAGICO VENTO DELUXE, MANARA MAESTRO DELL'EROS*). SINCE 2014, SHE MAKES SELF-PUBLISHED COMICS (*MISS HALL, SACRO BOSCO, AMNESIA, ASSOLO*).

THANK YOU,
TO MY FRIENDS RENIE AND MEGAN, FOR YOUR LOVE.
TO MOLLY, FOR YOU ENTHUSIASM AND YOUR SUPPORT.
TO THE CITY OF CINCINNATI. YOU ARE BEAUTIFUL.
TO GIULIA, WHO HAS EMBARKED ON THIS ADVENTURE WITH ME.

LAST BUT NOT LEAST, TO FEDERICO. FOR EVERYTHING.
                                        -GIULIO

THANK YOU TO GIULIO, FOR LETTING ME STEP INTO HIS DREAMS AND FOR HELPING ME DISCOVER THE POWER OF TEAMWORK.
                                        -GIULIA

ILLUSTRATION BY GIULIA ADRAGNA

DISCOVER
# ALL THE HITS

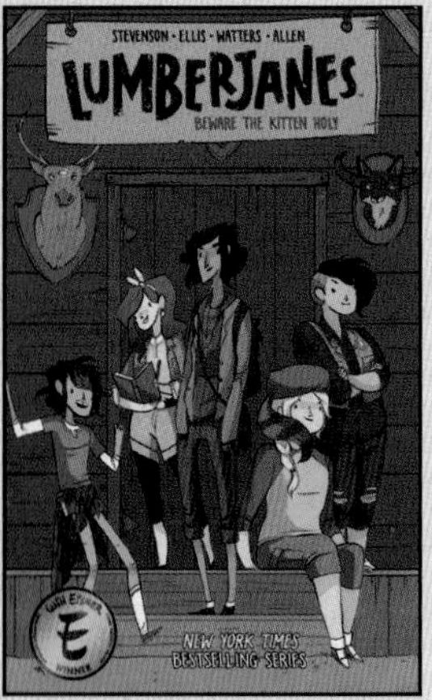
STEVENSON • ELLIS • WATTERS • ALLEN
LUMBERJANES
BEWARE THE KITTEN HOLY
NEW YORK TIMES BESTSELLING SERIES

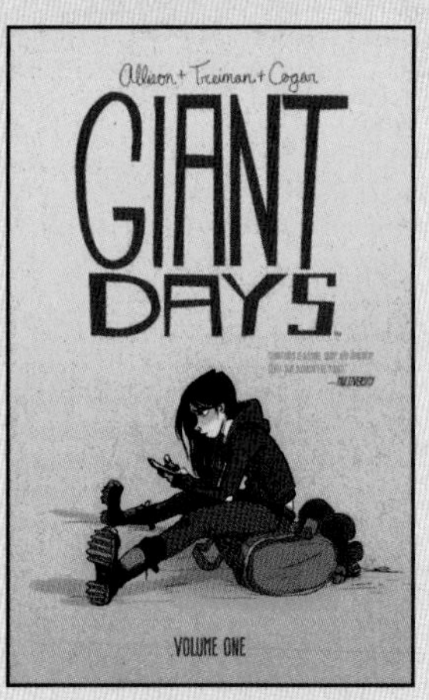
Allison + Treiman + Cogan
GIANT DAYS
VOLUME ONE

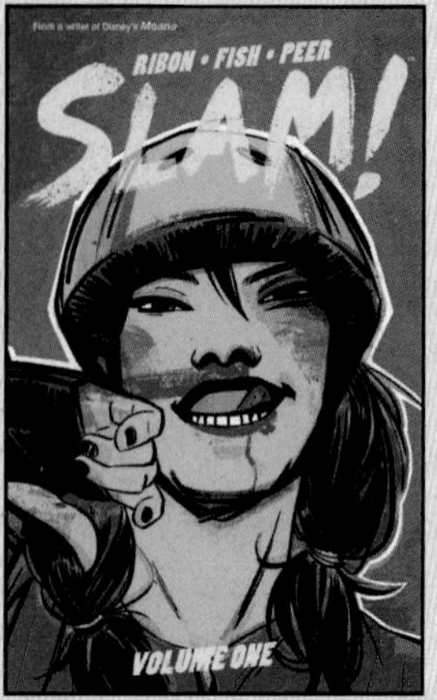
RIBON • FISH • PEER
SLAM!
VOLUME ONE

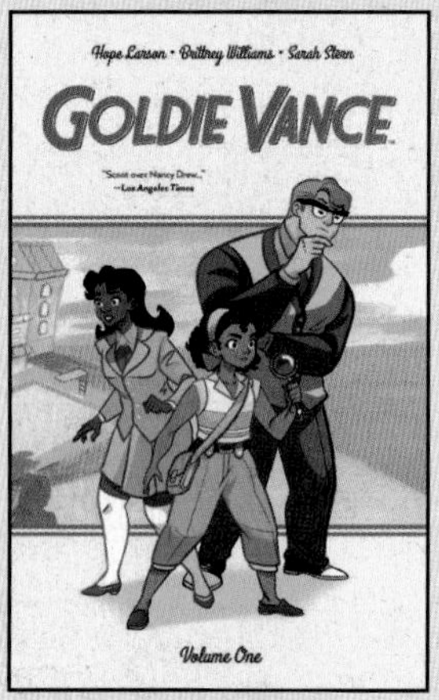
Hope Larson • Brittney Williams • Sarah Stern
GOLDIE VANCE
Volume One

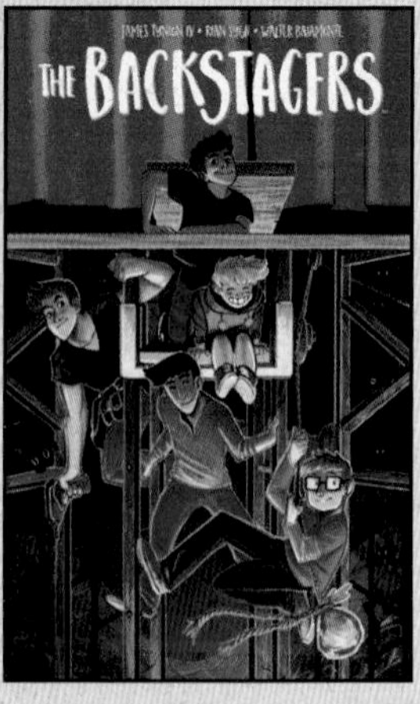
THE BACKSTAGERS

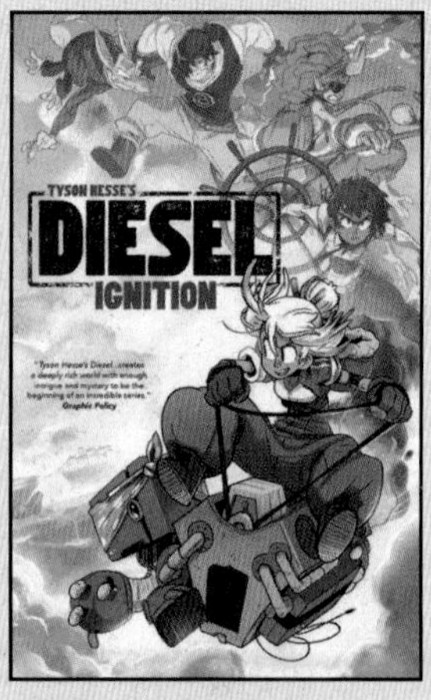
TYSON HESSE'S
DIESEL
IGNITION

BOOM! BOX

**AVAILABLE AT YOUR LOCAL COMICS SHOP AND BOOKSTORE**

To find a comics shop in your area, call 1-888-266-4226

WWW.**BOOM-STUDIOS**.COM



**Lumberjanes**
*Noelle Stevenson, Shannon Watters, Grace Ellis, Brooke Allen, and Others*
**Volume 1: Beware the Kitten Holy**
ISBN: 978-1-60886-687-8 | $14.99 US
**Volume 2: Friendship to the Max**
ISBN: 978-1-60886-737-0 | $14.99 US
**Volume 3: A Terrible Plan**
ISBN: 978-1-60886-803-2 | $14.99 US
**Volume 4: Out of Time**
ISBN: 978-1-60886-860-5 | $14.99 US
**Volume 5: Band Together**
ISBN: 978-1-60886-919-0 | $14.99 US

---

**Giant Days**
*John Allison, Lissa Treiman, Max Sarin*
**Volume 1**
ISBN: 978-1-60886-789-9 | $9.99 US
**Volume 2**
ISBN: 978-1-60886-804-9 | $14.99 US
**Volume 3**
ISBN: 978-1-60886-851-3 | $14.99 US

---

**Jonesy**
*Sam Humphries, Caitlin Rose Boyle*
**Volume 1**
ISBN: 978-1-60886-883-4 | $9.99 US
**Volume 2**
ISBN: 978-1-60886-999-2 | $14.99 US

---

**Slam!**
*Pamela Ribon, Veronica Fish, Brittany Peer*
**Volume 1**
ISBN: 978-1-68415-004-5 | $14.99 US

---

**Goldie Vance**
*Hope Larson, Brittney Williams*
**Volume 1**
ISBN: 978-1-60886-898-8 | $9.99 US
**Volume 2**
ISBN: 978-1-60886-974-9 | $14.99 US

---

**The Backstagers**
*James Tynion IV, Rian Sygh*
**Volume 1**
ISBN: 978-1-60886-993-0 | $14.99 US

---

**Tyson Hesse's Diesel: Ignition**
*Tyson Hesse*
ISBN: 978-1-60886-907-7 | $14.99 US

---

**Coady & The Creepies**
*Liz Prince, Amanda Kirk, Hannah Fisher*
ISBN: 978-1-68415-029-8 | $14.99 US